ALSO BY ZOSIA WAND

*Trust Me*

# the accusation

## zosia wand

HEAD
ℰ ZEUS

First published in 2018 by Head of Zeus Ltd

975312468

A catalogue record for this book is available from
the British Library.

ISBN (HB): 9781786692337
ISBN (XTPB ): 9781786692344
ISBN (E): 9781786692320

Typeset by Divaddict Publishing Solutions Ltd

Printed and bound in Great Britain by
CPI Group (UK) Ltd, Croydon CRO 4YY

Head of Zeus Ltd
First Floor East
5–8 Hardwick Street
London ECIR 4RG
WWW.HEADOFZEUS.COM

*For Judy Rouse, social worker, friend and Fairy Godmother, and to all those who work so hard, under pressure, to salvage families from turbulent lives. First in the firing line when things go wrong, yet seldom acknowledged for what they achieve; this book is dedicated to you.*
*Thank you.*

# Prologue

I know something about fear. I know it can be red and urgent, the roar of a dragon, flames in your face. We all recognise that. You will know it as something brief and fierce, leaving smoke and ashes, sometimes scalded flesh. This fear is different. My fear is not hot and fiery, but grey and quiet, lingering in the shadows. It's a chill breath on my neck, a whispered warning in my ear. I have no idea why it follows me. I have never experienced real danger, never suffered an act of extreme violence, but I live with a sense of something lurking. If I do the right thing, if I follow the rules and keep everyone happy, all will be well, but if I get it wrong, something terrible will pounce. I've learned to be one step ahead, becoming stealthy, slipping out of sight, dodging the icy drips and sidestepping the puddles. Always alert.

I sense it before the phone rings. Feel its cold grip on my hand as I try to accept the call. Neil's name on the screen. My fingers won't move. I have no reason to think this is anything other than the call I was expecting, to tell me that lunch is ready, that he and Milly are waiting for me. But I know before I tap the screen, before I hear the breathless panic in his voice, I know.

'Eve?'

'What's wrong?'

'It's Milly.'

A bitter cold pressing into my back, seeping through my flesh and between the bones beneath. Please, not this.

'She's gone.'

# Chapter 1

*Three Days Earlier*

The ferry, from Bowness-on-Windermere to Brockhole, is crowded with families, young lovers, older couples and dogs. A large party of sleek Japanese tourists look at the world through their iPhones, framing, snapping and sharing. They followed us around the Beatrix Potter museum, exclaiming over Jemima Puddleduck and Peter Rabbit with an infectious enthusiasm that intrigued Milly more than the exhibits themselves. 'But they're growed up,' she said, frowning. 'Peter Rabbit is for children.' We agreed it was a puzzle.

Milly is watchful, squinting in the late-August sunshine, head cocked to one side, taking it all in, her little hand in mine. The soft grip of her fingers is a new delight and I can't help stroking my thumb up and down her plump flesh. This precious little girl. Our daughter.

'Mummy?' She looks at me and I wait. She smiles. That's

all she wants to say. She is trying the word out for size. Claiming it.

Mummy. Daddy. Family. Words that were never mine are suddenly resting on my tongue, sweet and round as cherries. I say them out loud, one at a time, giving them space. 'Mummy.' Milly nods. I turn to Neil. His rusty hair and mottled jumper are the colour of the trees that line the lake shore. He has become substantial. Over the last weeks I've witnessed him expanding into fatherhood. I'm reminded of the day we married, glancing at him as he walked down the aisle beside me after the ceremony, how he seemed broader, more rooted in the world. He assumes these new roles with an enthusiasm that both exhilarates and daunts me. I don't have his confidence. I'm groping for it, hoping for it, but I haven't found it yet.

The water glints in the sunlight. The mountains beyond are mauve and moody. 'Daddy?' He grins, scooping her up, and as his arms fold around her, I whisper, 'Family,' to myself. Those arms that have held me while I wept. That solid chest I have leaned against, listening to the steady beat of his heart. That love we shared has grown to envelop this girl. Our daughter.

Milly has been with us since the beginning of June. Almost three months. I still can't quite believe they're letting us have this beautiful child. They trust us. We've been approved. In just over a month we'll be able to apply to the magistrates' court for an adoption hearing where it will all be ratified. After years of not being the lucky, the chosen, the blessed, after disappointment and bewilderment and the not knowing why, the brutal, not this time, not you, we're finally going to be given this opportunity. We're so close.

Will that be the moment when I believe?

Neil rests Milly on his hip, pointing out the boathouses that decorate the shoreline. The chair of my board lives in one of these grand old houses, but I have only approached the property from the road side and cannot get a sense of perspective from the lake. We have been invited for tea, once Milly's settled in, but for the time being it's just the three of us, getting to know one another, forming a world Milly can claim for herself. A safe place, as Shona explained, at the last review meeting. Milly needs time to establish her relationship with us before we can introduce anyone else.

Shona is more than a social worker. Hers is not the kind of job where you can tick the box and switch off the light at the end of the day. Her heart is invested in the families she creates. She is Milly's Fairy Godmother. Our Fairy Godmother, and I hope she'll remain part of our lives.

Adoption was always on the agenda, for us, whether we had our own children or not. Neil is adopted, his sisters aren't. We've seen a mixed family can work. While other couples might have kept hoping, investigated, turned to IVF, we simply sketched our dreams elsewhere and they exerted their own romantic pull. I've accepted that we may never have a child with Neil's eyes, or my smile, but with Milly we have something unique and equally precious in its own way; a little girl full of love and hope and her own personality waiting to be discovered. We have an adventure. I believe she was always waiting for us to find her, that some greater force out there was pulling us together. Romantic nonsense to some, but my story. My comfort.

Adopting Milly wasn't difficult or torturous. We looked forward to Shona's visits, the discussions that ensued. Our confidence grew. They wanted us as much as we wanted to be accepted by them. And there was Milly ready and waiting. Four years old with gold freckles and a neat fringe, frowning at the camera as if trying to work out a puzzle. A little girl brought up, for the most part, by her maternal grandparents, until Nana had a stroke and could no longer manage. Milly's mother has a heroin addiction and no one knows anything about her father. Shona phoned from the council offices in Kendal to deliver the news that we'd been approved, and followed her congratulations with, 'There's a little girl we think might be just right for you.' She came straight over with the photograph. It was that quick. It isn't always this way; sometimes it can take months before a match is made, but we were lucky. This was clearly meant to be.

'You OK?' Neil is watching me, searching my face.

I nod to reassure him. Milly points to a line of ducks making their steady way up the lake. I run my hand along her hair. I'm allowed to do this. Around me people will assume I've been doing it all her life. When we met Milly she was a stranger. I'd prepared myself to feel compassion, concern, possibly affection, but not love, not straight away. I expected that to be something that would grow, quietly, over time, for us and for her. But it's not like that for Milly. Her love is uninhibited, wild, provoking an instinctive affection that spills out of me. I find this a little overwhelming, almost frightening, because I haven't earned this love. It may not be real. It may simply be her enthusiastic response to this new world, a fantasy she's created, and our reality may yet disappoint. My fear fidgets in shadows. I feel it in the unexpected chill beneath the trees, a sharp reminder that this joy I'm feeling may yet be snatched away.

We're approaching the jetty. People are getting up, collecting their things. Neil lowers Milly to the deck and takes her hand, telling her how we came here at Easter, before she was part of our lives. That was less than five months ago, before we knew we'd be approved, before we knew anything about Milly. We'd brought a picnic, having no family obligations and no children to entertain. We'd sat in our matching camping chairs wrapped in hats and scarves and watched a vast family of three generations with a dozen grandchildren hunt for chocolate eggs. The kind of family I read about as a child, and longed for.

We alight at Brockhole, Milly swinging between us. As we clear the trees, she catches sight of the adventure playground and drops our hands with a shriek of excitement, charging forward, but after a few paces she hesitates, turning to look back, her face etched with that frown of uncertainty we've come to recognise.

'It's OK,' Neil calls after her. 'We're right behind you.'

She skips off with a grin, delight bursting out of her in little leaps and twitches. Neil raises the camera that's slung around his neck. We've taken so many photographs. If Milly had been born to us, would I be so aware of this joy? It's different with a baby, of course, but would I have been able to take it for granted? This chapter of our lives is unique and I'm so grateful for this gift. As Milly runs towards the wooden towers, tunnels and frames nestled beneath the green-gold trees, I'm silently filming that moment in my mind, to return to, years from now. Raising the camera to his eye, Neil captures it.

Milly is perfect. It's as if we'd conjured her. A little girl with chestnut hair and intelligent, curious eyes, looking for her Forever Family and seeing that possibility in us. And maybe sometimes it is like that. Maybe Neil's right, and after a lifetime of having to be patient, of swallowing my disappointment, dusting myself off and starting again, maybe this really is my time. But part of me is still afraid that it's all been a little too easy. Luck is something that happens to other people. I've always had to earn my joy and I've not yet earned this.

Neil slides his arm around me and I rest my head into the cradle of his shoulder as we walk along. 'Happy?'

I snuggle in closer by way of reply. 'It's all happened so quickly. I'm still trying to catch up.'

'The six months of assessment wasn't enough for you?'

I shrug. He wrinkles his nose in sympathy. He knows me. I'm a cautious person. Throwing myself at life is not my style. The adoption process began in a leisurely way and whilst I was impatient and wanted a family, I had adjusted to that rhythm. The weekly meetings, then waiting for Shona to complete our application, for it to go to the panel, another month for the panel to meet and approve us, but as soon as we got the approval, the snowball took off at breath-snatching speed. We were presented with Milly's paperwork that same day and within the month the match had been agreed and introductions begun. I've gone from being a potential adopter to being the mother of a four-year-old in a matter of weeks.

The sun is out. The lake is a glass pool reflecting smudged mountains. This is where we live, this place the tourists come to snatch in moments and photographs. This is our home and I'm here, with the man I love and our daughter, surrounded by families making the most of the last days of summer. I drink it up greedily, grateful for every precious moment. I'm enjoying Milly, this instant family we've created, this thoughtful girl with the serious gaze that's suddenly interrupted by the splash of a smile. I will not let the lurking fear in.

And then I see her. A grey-haired woman, sitting at a picnic bench, unwrapping a round of sandwiches. She's not my mother, but she could be. It's the sandwiches, the greaseproof paper and her grey hair, coarse waves brushed back from her face. It could be her, but it isn't.

She's with two children: a boy, younger than Milly, maybe two or only just three, and an older girl of about five with a thick ponytail. Two children, out with their grandmother. Milly talks about her Nana and Gramps constantly. They had a special bond, and, as far as possible, we hope to maintain this through supervised visits, but it will never be the same and we have been warned that Nana's health is deteriorating. We are a distraction for the time being, but the loss for Milly will be immense and we will never be an adequate replacement. Grandparents are important. As a child I remember longing for my own silver-haired supporters proudly attending school events, or waiting patiently for me in the playground with sweet treats and delighted smiles. My maternal grandparents died before I was born and I have no memory of my father or his family. The boy is kicking his legs backwards and forwards under the bench. His dark hair hangs low over his eyes in thick waves. His sister is slipping away, back to the climbing frames and slides. Her grandmother calls to her, but she is shaking her head, the ponytail bouncing. She doesn't want the sandwiches, she wants to play.

This is what happens. I'm happy for a moment and then suddenly something snatches it away. This is not my mother. My mother is not here.

Neil squeezes my hand. I glance up. He's seen what I'm looking at. He pulls me closer and I allow myself to be comforted. This is about us, I tell myself. We're here, Neil, Milly and I, and that's enough.

Milly has shoved open the gate and is barrelling across the playground to the tyre swings. There's one swing hanging empty and she's heading straight for it, but the little girl who has run away from the sandwiches sees Milly's target and she's closer. She decides to intercept and grabs the chain, pulling the tyre towards her as Milly approaches. I freeze. Milly jerks back and stops. There's a standoff. I want to run over and wrestle the swing from the older girl. She didn't want to swing until she saw that Milly did. This child is spiteful, she's cruel. I want to shove her aside and let Milly climb on, and as if he's read my mind, Neil pulls me back. I try to shake him off, but he's stronger than me. 'Don't,' he warns.

I wouldn't. This is a child. I'm not a monster. I'm surprised by the vehemence of my response. This isn't like me. 'It's not fair.'

'Why don't we see what Milly does?'

What Milly does is admirable. She asks the girl politely if she can have the swing. The girl shakes her head, but she doesn't get on the swing herself. She stands, holding it away from Milly.

I wait for Milly to turn to us for help, already rehearsing the scenario in my head. I will walk over, smiling. I will introduce myself and Milly to the girl and ask her name. I'll suggest they sit on the swing together.

But Milly doesn't turn around. What Milly does is to drop her head down and charge at the girl, knocking her backwards onto the loose wood chippings that form a protective layer over the tree roots and hard ground. Neil is the one to run forward, leaving me standing, gaping and useless. It's Neil who dusts the girl down and leads her, sobbing, back to her grandmother, with Milly dragging along beside him protesting. 'She maked me do it! She's nasty!' It's Neil who insists Milly apologise.

'Say sorry, Milly, or we will get straight back on the ferry and go home.' His voice is firm and carries on the breeze. And he insists she repeat her apology, sincerely, before it is accepted.

I watch all this in horror. I do not know how to do this.

What would my mother have done? I try to imagine her here. She would be confident. She wouldn't hesitate. She wouldn't stand here like a lemon unable to move.

I watch the grandmother reassure Neil that it isn't a problem. I watch her question her granddaughter. She's quite stern. Is she asking her why she stopped Milly having the swing? Is she suggesting Milly isn't the only one who needs to apologise? I can see she's addressing both girls and they seem to be listening. As I watch, the older girl holds out her hand and Milly takes it. They turn and skip back towards the playground together. For them it's all over. Neil says something to the grandmother and she laughs.

I stand in the playground, watching Milly on the swing with her new friend, and I feel utterly alone. The ache is sudden and fierce. A need to see my mother. To be with her. I need to talk to her about Milly, to tell her everything that's been going on, to share these feelings, these waves of emotion I hadn't anticipated: love, joy, gratitude, delight, but also my fear.

Loving someone, needing them so desperately, makes you vulnerable. You could lose them suddenly, brutally. When Neil's away I try not to imagine car crashes, random accidents. I'm not paranoid, I don't sit fretting the moment he's out of my sight, but sometimes the possibility that my happiness might end crashes in front of me. He feels it too; a call out of the blue, a need to hold tight for a moment.

It's the price of love, that fear.

But loss comes in different shapes. It isn't always solid and sudden; sometimes it trickles in. I've become a mother and now, more than ever, I need to talk to my own mother. And Milly needs her. Milly needs a grandmother. But I haven't seen my mother for more than two years. She no longer speaks to me.

Neil swings back through the gate. 'All sorted.'

'I didn't know what to do.'

He laughs, but stops when he sees I'm serious and takes my hand. 'Come on.' He points to a small coffee van parked just the other side of the low playground fence. 'He's got a proper espresso machine.' The van is within clear view. I follow him through the gate, glancing back to check on Milly. She waves from the swing as her new friend pushes her towards the sky.

As I warm my hands on the hot cup and sip the froth, watching Milly swing, I ask, 'What if I was here on my own with her?'

Neil pulls his head back, as if to say, Really? You need to ask? 'You would have rushed over to the girl and helped get her up. You would have told Milly to apologise and you would have gone and explained what happened to the grandmother.'

'That's what you did.'

He traces the line of my cheekbone with his thumb, his eyes on mine, that energy he has, that confidence, pouring into me. He believes in me, even if I don't. 'You would have been more apologetic.' I wouldn't have been as strict with Milly. I would have been too worried about upsetting her, but I can see Neil was right. She jumps down from the swing and takes her turn with the pushing. Neil adds, 'You would have assumed entire responsibility for what happened and set about trying to make peace.'

I look over towards the grandmother who is wiping the little boy's face with a tissue. 'She managed it really well,' I say.

'She's had years of experience.'

Was she like me once? Did she feel this incompetent? These are questions I'd like to ask my mother, but I can't. Is it like this for everyone or is it simply because Milly is a little girl already? If I'd adopted a baby, I'd have had time to build up to this, time to grow confident as she grew more independent, but we have been thrust into it. For all the assessment and preparation, there is no training you can do to become the immediate parent of a child who is about to turn five. 'I don't know if I can do this.'

Neil removes my coffee cup from my hand and places it on the ground alongside his. He takes me by the shoulders and looks right into my eyes. I love his face, the fine lines that creep out from the corners of his eyes, the ruddy flush to his cheeks, the coppery glint as the sun catches his hair. He is a good man. An attentive, kind and decent man and he loves me. Warts and all. I should have told him about the photograph. I should have talked it through with him before I wrote. Neil and I always talk. There are no secrets between us. I would like to talk to him now, but I don't want to spoil this moment. This is our time with Milly and I want to keep it for her. 'You,' he says, dropping a kiss on my nose, 'are going to be a wonderful mum.'

I try to believe him.

# Chapter 2

*Three Days Later*

'Gone?' There's a fist in my throat. I force my words past it.

'I can't find her. She was in the garden, on the trampoline. Is she with you?'

'No.' I'm in the park, looking towards my house, having gravitated out here to wait for their call. I manage this park – it's a community initiative – and I know most of the people who frequent it. I spin round, pulling my hair away from my eyes, searching for her. The young saplings that line the path bend in sympathy with the wind. Neil is head of sixth form at the high school and term doesn't start back for a few more days, so he was at home with Milly. I was going to meet them for lunch. I can see our house through the trees. Bay windows and sloping slate roof, a garden that rolls down to the park boundary. Perfect for a family. That's what I said. Perfect.

Please no. Don't let this be true. Let it be a mistake. Let it be all right. My fear has become flesh; a ghostly figure in a grey coat, hair damp-darkened and dripping, colourless lips whispering, 'You don't deserve her.'

Don't take her away. Please! Let us have this joy, let us keep this!

There's a family making their way through the gate. Two adults and a child. A girl. I run after them, wishing that the girl will be Milly, that, for some reason, I hadn't recognised her, but, of course, it isn't Milly. I apologise and look about frantically. I'm both part of what is unfolding and outside it, observing. I can see myself in the scene and hear what I'm saying, but I can't feel it. They haven't seen another little girl. They're distressed, I'm distressing them. They're saying something, trying to reach out to me, but there's nothing they can do. I pull away. I'm drifting somewhere outside all this; I'm not really here.

There are two of our volunteers working on the beds in front of the café: Kath and her daughter, India. I run over to them, but they've had their backs to the tarn and haven't seen anything. I run on, past the tarn towards our house. Why didn't I check the garden earlier? Was she there then or had she already gone? I scramble up the bank to the wall with its loose stones that we should have replaced. Neil is running towards me, his face stripped of colour. He's a big man, substantial. Seeing him, the bulk of him, should be a comfort, but the look on his face is as vulnerable as a child's. His huge hand reaches down and grabs mine and, in that moment, I am yanked back into the reality.

It's quieter here, the air stilled by the trees that divide us from the neighbouring gardens. A sudden and chilling quiet. 'I've looked everywhere. She was here. She was fine.'

There's a tray on the grass beside the trampoline. Three doorstep sandwiches on individual sheets of kitchen roll. Milly's is made with white bread and has the crusts cut off. Three plastic cups of juice. Green, pink and blue. The pink one has toppled over leaving a pool of orange across the surface of the tray.

'She wanted lunch on the trampoline.'

'How long was she out here?'

'I don't know. Five minutes? I don't know!' He runs his hand through his hair. 'She asked for a drink. I don't know!'

His mud-spattered mountain bike is propped against the garden shed, the two prongs of the tailgator, which attach it to a child's bike, project from the back like two fangs. Milly's gleaming purple bike has been detached and lies beside it in the grass. She has been insisting she can cycle without help and has resisted stabilisers. Did she fall off and lose her temper? Stamp off in a strop? Is she hiding somewhere, crying? 'Maybe she's headed up the street? She might have seen someone. One of the neighbour's kids?'

'I've been up and down. No one's seen her.'

'The Thomases?' They have a son a year or two older than Milly. She might have gone to play with him.

'They didn't answer.'

'She could be there. They leave the front door unlocked. She might have gone in and they didn't hear her?'

Kath calls to me from the other side of the wall. 'We'll keep searching the park.' I nod dumbly. Behind her, India's face is stricken; my own terror reflected back at me.

We start to walk along the access road that effectively divides our garden in two. There is the long, lower garden with the shed and trampoline that borders the park and, higher up, on the other side of the road, a smaller front garden that leads to our front door. These large Victorian houses were built in a crescent to overlook the park and tarn. Our street is a dead end, leading to a kissing gate, open fields and the fell beyond. Early leaves fill the street gutter. I'm dimly aware of the sharp bite of the wind that sweeps them into a soft bank against the garden walls. The Thomases live four doors up. I can't run. I don't want to run. I want to hang on to this possibility for as long as possible. Neil climbs the steps up to the front door ahead of me. Their garden is much neater than ours, with a clearly defined front path, tidy borders and a bay tree in a terracotta pot. The door is a shiny red with a gleaming brass knocker. Oliver Thomas goes to school in a neighbouring village, a school with an Outstanding Ofsted report, his mother drives him in and back every day, but today is not a school day. I haven't seen the Thomases for over a week. They're very likely to be on holiday. We wait and I know there'll be no answer, but still I cling to hope, as it slithers away from me. I don't want to turn away from this door and face what comes next.

'A cat? She might have seen a cat and followed it. Got distracted. Got lost.' I can imagine Milly leaning over to stroke a cat, watching it arch its back and walk away, calling after it, following it up the hill. *'It maked me follow it, Mummy!'* I walk back to the gate, expecting to see her standing there, waiting for us, but the road is empty. The Thomases' car isn't there.

Neil looks at me. His rusty hair stands up in tufts. His face sags. I don't want to see his fear. He says, 'I shouldn't have left her. Why did I leave her?' This isn't the Neil I know, but we're not the people we were. Milly has changed us. Being responsible for her, loving her, has made us vulnerable. He isn't saying it but I know what he's thinking. He's imagining Shona, the people on the adoption panel, social services. What will they say? We've been careless. We've proved ourselves inadequate. A row of stern faces glaring down at me. I prickle with shame. We've let them down. We've let Milly down.

This fear is both old and new. Red hot and angry, it breathes fire in my face. I can hear the roar of the flames, feel the singeing of my flesh, but there's more. This is vicious, a thing with claws. It reaches up inside me and tears at the underside of my skin. I take a deep breath, trying to steady myself. 'We need to calm down. This is Tarnside.' My breaths are short, my chest so tight, my skin burning. I can hear the wobble in my voice. 'She was in the garden. Children play in gardens. Parents don't have to stand guard over their children every moment of the day.' I'm trying to sound certain but I'm not certain. I don't know the rules. There are so many unwritten rules of parenting and I have no one to guide me. Have we made a mistake? Should Neil have taken Milly back into the house with him? 'There'll be an explanation.' I push on. I need to wrestle control of this. 'We need to think.'

'She might be hiding. She might think this is funny. All a game?'

I clutch this possibility for an instant, but I know that's not Milly. She'd have heard the anxiety in his voice. She'd have called out.

'Maybe she's trapped somewhere. A door swung shut?'

'How long has she been gone?'

He looks at his watch. Frowns. 'I was thinking it was getting late for her to eat. I was trying to get lunch ready for twelve. If we say just after twelve...'

It's nearly one o'clock.

We look at one another. There's nothing else we can do. He says it first. 'We have to call the police.'

# Chapter 3

I'm both relieved and terrified by the speed and energy of the police response. The police car pulled up outside in a matter of minutes. A young police officer now sits on the smaller sofa facing us with notebook and pen in her hand. PC McAdam. Police constable, not a detective inspector or a sergeant – she's too young for that. How old could she be? Late twenties? From the knowledge I've gained from countless television dramas, which I know isn't reliable, but will cling to now, things can't be so serious if it's a police constable. But outside I can hear the blades of the helicopter slicing the air as it circles the park, and through the bay window I can see uniformed officers struggling in the wind, with dogs on leads, snouts to the ground, searching for a scent.

The wind smacks against the bay window, rattling the frames, seeking cracks and weaknesses. PC McAdam is wearing a bulky black uniform which rustles when she moves. Her hair is pulled back in a rough ponytail at the nape of her neck. Her face is clear of make-up. She asked for an item of Milly's clothing. I brought down her pyjama top. In her bedroom, I hesitated for a moment and pressed it against my face, sucking in the memory of her, closing my eyes as I felt my way back down the stairs. Handing the thin turquoise T-shirt over was like giving up a part of myself. PC McAdam took it gently, as if she understood. 'She likes unicorns,' I said, though the picture on the front wasn't visible. We bought it the weekend Milly did her first sleepover with us. At Marks and Spencer in Kendal, where we stopped off to buy something for tea on the way home. She saw it on the hanger as we walked through to the food section and asked if she could have it. I knew she was testing me, pushing her luck, sensing that I would have bought her the world right then, and I should have been setting some boundaries, but I couldn't resist.

Above us I can hear the officers moving around, searching every cupboard and hidden corner of the bedrooms, though we all know she's not in the house. Other officers are searching the outbuildings and sheds up and down the street. Tarnside is on alert. People have joined the search party in the park and further afield. I don't want to think about the tarn. I'm sure they're thinking about it; they will consider that awful possibility too.

Neil is pacing the room. He is no longer substantial. He doesn't know how to play this role. PC McAdam asks how long Milly was left outside. Neil says about ten minutes or so. No more. 'I was making sandwiches. How long does it take to make a sandwich?'

I thought he came up to the house to get Milly a drink after he made the sandwiches. My stomach drops. I know how long Neil takes faffing about in the kitchen when he's preparing any kind of meal. He'll have been singing along to the radio. Did he unload and reload the dishwasher while he was there? Did he lose track of time? Why didn't he tell me he was making lunch while she was outside, alone?

He walks from the fireplace to the door and back to the fireplace over and over, like one of those wind-up toys, but he can't slow down. 'I have to do something.'

'We have a team out there looking for her.'

'I can't just sit here!' I follow him into the hall. He yanks his jacket from the hook. 'I have to help.'

I nod. I want him to stay here with me, but I want her found, and I want him to resume his role. To take control. He may be able to help.

As he slides his arms into his jacket he checks automatically for his phone. He feels the inside pocket, then the back pocket of his jeans, where he finds it, looks at the screen, then at me. 'Your phone? Have you checked your phone?'

I have checked it, repeatedly, but not since PC McAdam arrived. My phone is not a smartphone like Neil's, but an old Nokia. Smaller. More robust. I feel my back pocket. It isn't there.

'Where is it?' he asks, urgently. 'Where did you last have it?'

I try to picture where I was standing when I last checked. I had the phone with me. I put it in my pocket when I scrambled over the wall. Neil was the one to call the police, but I had my phone in my hand. We were in the kitchen. I turn and run the length of the hall. The cellar door is open and the door into the back yard, but the officers who've been searching have moved on. My phone is on the dresser. I grab it. There's a yellow envelope on the screen.

'What is it?'

'A message.'

My fingers slip on the keys. I can feel him next to me, willing me to get it right, ready to snatch the phone from my hand. I try again. Menu. Messages. A list of names appears down the left-hand side with a series of yellow envelopes opposite, one unopened envelope at the top. I read the name on the screen beside it, and freeze.

I step away from Neil.

'What?' He moves towards me, but I can't speak.

# Chapter 4

'Why, Eve? Why?' His wounded eyes search me. He has every right to be furious. I could cope with furious, but not this. I've betrayed him.

'I'm sorry.'

'Why didn't you tell me? Talk to me?'

'I miss her, Neil. I thought if she saw a photo—'

'She'd what? Phone you? Say everything is all right now? Let's play happy families?'

'This is why I didn't tell you! I can't talk to you about her.'

'And why is that, Eve? Is it *me*? Am *I* the one playing mind games?'

A police officer coughs, emerging from the top of the cellar steps before sliding out to the hall. Will he say something to social services? What will they do?

Neil's body is taut and trembling. I feel suddenly tired. I'd like to sink down onto the floor, close my eyes and sleep through whatever has to happen now and wake up when it's all over, but somehow I remain standing. In the back yard, the plastic lid of a recycling box has been blown against the stone wall. Bits of cardboard wrapping and newspaper flutter across the gravel. I'm desperate to reach out and touch his hand, but scared he'll pull away from me and I couldn't bear that.

He shatters the silence. 'Where the hell is she?'

I can hear footsteps in the hall, the rustle of PC McAdam's uniform as she approaches. 'Everything all right?'

'My mother,' I say, not knowing how to explain, where to begin. 'There's a text.' Her face is impassive. I'm grateful for that. I don't want to imagine what she thinks of us. 'She's with my mother,' I add, and then, 'Milly's safe,' reassuring myself as much as her.

'Shall we call your mother, to be sure?' The question sounds so reasonable. Maybe it isn't so bad after all. A misunderstanding, but then I think of all those officers, the waste of time and money. The local police force is stretched as it is.

Neil thrusts the phone at her. 'Be my guest.'

His anger isn't helping. While she's giving nothing away, I can see PC McAdam paying attention, storing all this for later. Will it go into a report? Will they make judgements? Express their concerns? Will they take Milly away?

She takes the phone and calls the number. We all wait for it to pick up. It goes to voicemail. 'Hello. This is PC McAdam speaking. We're trying to confirm the whereabouts of Milly…' She hesitates. We've told her Milly is in the process of being adopted, she won't have our surname yet. 'I'd be grateful if you could call back on this number immediately.' She hangs up and returns the phone. 'You believe she's safe?' The question is directed at me. I nod. She turns to Neil. He looks at me. He doesn't believe Milly is safe, but he knows my mother won't hurt her. 'Mr Wright?' she prompts, waiting for reassurance.

'I want her back.'

'I understand. But I need to establish there is no threat to Milly's safety right now.'

I answer for him. 'There isn't. My mother is a difficult woman, but she's not a threat to Milly. There will be an explanation.'

'We can call off the search?'

I nod. She waits for Neil to nod agreement before stepping into the hall with her radio. I hear her low voice issuing instructions while I close the back door against the wind. Neil seethes across the room. He can't bring himself to look at me. I'm responsible for all this: uniformed officers, a search team, dogs. What if there's been an accident out on the fells? What if a real tragedy has unfolded which could otherwise have been averted? I'll never forgive myself. The helicopter will be in the local paper tomorrow. A photograph of me, Director of Tarnside Community Park. Everyone will be talking about us, speculating, all this wasted police time. It will be reported to social services. I should have talked to Neil before I sent that photograph. I should have waited.

Through the window, I can see Shona's spiky white hair as she strides up the path to the front door. She looks coolly competent with designer jeans and smoke-grey T-shirt. A bulging bag is slung across her chest. Something inside me releases a little. She rushes in, touches Neil's arm as she passes, throwing him a look of support, and puts her arms around me, squeezing tight. I sink into her, feeling a fraud. I'm not the victim here; this is all my fault. She pushes me away a little so she can look at me properly. Intense brown eyes, that see right inside. 'Are you OK?'

'I'm sorry.'

'What are you sorry for?' She glances at Neil. He looks away. This is my mess.

'I sent her a photograph of Milly, telling her about the adoption.' Shona looks from Neil to me, nodding. 'I wanted her to, I hoped...' Neil shakes his head, but says nothing. I say, 'She'll have taken her for an ice cream. Got distracted. I'm sure she never intended...'

From outside, there's a low rumble as the helicopter rises and turns in the air above us.


Shona makes tea. The biscuit tin has a meagre offering of half a chocolate chip cookie and a stale digestive. I dig out a new packet which I tip onto a plate and carry through to the living room, as if this normal, domestic activity will somehow put everything right, but no one is in the mood for biscuits.

PC McAdam is making notes. 'You and your mother have been estranged for how long?'

Estranged? The word sounds hard, ugly. 'We're not estranged. We've not seen much of each other.' I hesitate. There are no words for this. I have no language to explain the loss of my mother. She didn't die, there was no trial separation or divorce, because divorce is not the language of mothers and daughters. There was no fight, no ultimatum, no show down, no speci

fic incident that resulted in this situation. But here we are.

Shona places a solid hand on my arm. I focus on her rings, a thick silver cuff and a hammered disc that reaches her knuckle. Everything about Shona is bold. Her clothes, her jewellery. She claims her place in the world. She offers ballast. 'Have a sip of tea. The officer just needs to know the facts. Where your mum lives, what her relationship is with you, at the moment, with Milly.' She looks at PC McAdam, whose face is pink. 'Am I right?'

The young policewoman nods and holds the tip of her pen against the open notepad, ready to record everything I say. I can imagine her going home tonight, to her parents' house where she still lives, sitting down to tea, telling them about this family she saw today, what a mess they were. Speculating on what kind of daughter I am, to have lost my mother in the way that I have, what kind of mother I can be, if I cannot maintain a relationship with my own. She begins. A new set of questions for this new situation. 'What is your mother's name?'

'Joan. Joan Leonard.'

'Where does she live?'

'Hitchin, in Hertfordshire.'

'You weren't aware she was intending to visit?' I shake my head, my face burning. 'When was the last time you spoke with your mother?'

I hesitate. The last time I phoned was about two years ago, but Mum didn't talk; I jabbered on as if nothing was wrong while she remained silent. I could hear her breathing on the end of the line, but she wouldn't say anything. Neil said she wouldn't be able to sustain it; she'd get bored and give in eventually. He said I had to be strong. I had to put us first. Our marriage. He was eager to get on with our life here. We took long walks, climbed fells, swam in lakes, ate in beautiful pubs in front of roaring fires. We sailed up Coniston on the restored gondola and pretended to be tourists, delighting in the fact that this was now our home. He kept me distracted, but all the time I was waiting. It was like a death, though it sounds terrible to say that when there are people who have genuinely lost someone they love through no fault of their own. I couldn't share my grief, because I knew he would see it as a betrayal of us. It was Neil and this life, or her; I had to make a choice.

I wrote her a long letter, explaining that it wasn't a rejection, that she was welcome to visit, that I'd love her to visit, to be able to show her my new life, but I needed to put my family first. She knew Neil and I had been trying to conceive for years. I hoped she'd understand.

We'd seen the GP and had some preliminary tests. There was no obvious problem. We could have continued but the tests became more and more invasive and we decided not to bother. Instead, we contacted social services to start the adoption process. Neil's parents went on to have two daughters of their own after adopting him. They're a wonderful family; warm, embracing, delightfully chaotic. It works. I don't think Neil and I will have any of our own now, but we'll adopt more. That's the plan.

If they let us. If they let us keep Milly after this.

PC McAdam is waiting patiently for an answer. 'I last spoke to my mother two years ago.' The word estranged doesn't seem so brutal any more. I look at Neil, remembering that immaculate hotel room, the rain-smeared view of the New York skyline. The Christmas surprise that blew up my life. *'When are you going to put us first, Eve?'*

'Mum was upset about us moving north. She found it hard to accept. I'm her only child. We are, were, are very close.' I glance at Shona who knows it all. 'Possibly too close. It's a bit intense. But she's no danger to Milly.'

'Where do you think she might have taken her?'

I try and think. 'I don't understand why she didn't come to the park. Unless she did, and we missed her.' But I know that's not possible. All those people searching. 'She may have taken her into town? To a café, possibly?'

Neil straightens up suddenly, straining his neck to look out. I stand and move towards the window. My mother is walking up the path, holding Milly's hand. Neil is on his feet. Mum is wearing her sensible shoes and a pale blue raincoat I haven't seen before. Her hair's shorter. She looks older, more fragile. Milly is skipping up the steps, clutching her grandmother's hand.

Neil is in the hall before I realise. I rush out after him as he throws open the door and snatches Milly up into his arms.

My mother's face drops. 'What's wrong?' Her voice is unsteady. 'Has something happened?'

# Chapter 5

Neil squeezes Milly to his chest. She looks at me a little anxiously over his shoulder and I give her a reassuring smile, leaning my face towards her, thanking the universe for her return. She smells of apple shampoo, her skin against my cheek is soft and plump.

When I open my eyes my mother is watching us, her forehead creased with worry. I usher her into the living room and remain in the hall, closing the door to give us a moment of privacy. Neil lowers Milly to the floor. Her eyes dart between us. He gives a low growl and presses his forehead against the wall. His fists are clenched.

'Are you cross, Daddy?'

He takes a long, deep breath and pulls himself upright. 'Not with you, sweetheart.'

I lean my cheek against his back, place my hands on his arms, melting into him, as if this will give him the resources he needs. My mother drives him to distraction. I don't want

PC McAdam to see him like this. I don't want Shona to, though she'd be more understanding.

'Why don't you go for a walk?' I say. 'Clear your head.' I can feel his rage throwing silent punches inside him. 'Go,' I insist. 'You're no good to us in this state.' He doesn't argue. He knows that a brisk walk will calm him. I lift Milly and press my face into the warm groove between her neck and shoulder, fusing myself to her as I return to the living room.

My mother is sitting on the sofa beside Shona, wringing her hands. 'I had no idea there'd be all this fuss.'

Lowering Milly to the floor, I demand to know, 'Where have you been?'

Milly answers. 'We seed a film! The lady buyed me popcorn and a big cup of lemonade!'

'Grandma,' my mother corrects.

'You didn't think to come in?' I snap. 'To let us know? To *ask*?'

'There was no one here.'

'Neil was here.'

My mother has a particular reaction to any mention of Neil. Her head shifts back a fraction, eyes narrowed to thin lines, and her mouth pinches, making each word a tight little tut of disapproval. 'I'm sorry, darling, but he wasn't here. Milly was on her own in the garden. We had a little chat. I was out there for quite some time with her and there was no sign of anyone.'

'Did you come up to the house?'

'I did.' She looks at Milly. 'Didn't I, dear?' Milly nods. 'I came to the front door and called through the letter box, but there was no answer, so I went around to the back of the house and knocked on that door, but there was no answer there either. I don't know where Neil was but he wasn't in the house.'

'Don't be ridiculous! Of course he was in the house. He was making lunch! He wouldn't leave Milly on her own and just go out!'

I glance at Shona. Mum gives a little frown then adds, brightly, 'It doesn't matter, does it?' smiling at Shona and the policewoman. 'I was here, and Milly is fine,' as if they'll be reassured by this.

PC McAdam turns to me. 'Where is your husband?'

'He's gone to get a bit of air.' The silence vibrates with questions.

'We will need to talk to him.'

'Of course.'

Milly tugs at my arm. 'The ice-cream man comed.'

Mum smiles. 'I bought the child an ice cream. The van was parked up on the next street. And then we thought we'd go for a little walk into town and we saw the advert for the film and Milly liked the look of it and it hadn't long started and I thought, why not? I sent one of those text message thingummies...'

'On your way back!'

She looks perplexed. 'No. I sent one before that.' She turns to Milly for reassurance. 'Didn't I, dear? I told you I was messaging Mummy so she wouldn't worry.'

Milly nods. I check, but there is only one text from my mother, the one sent as she was heading back. 'Give me your phone.'

Mum fumbles for the handbag at her feet and pulls out tissues, a box of ibuprofen, cough sweets, a small diary, the battered brown purse she's had for as long as I can remember, and, eventually, an iPhone. When did my mother graduate to an iPhone? I snatch it from her. 'What's your passcode?'

'One six oh three.'

Of course. My birthday. I check. There's nothing there, but there is a message in Drafts. *Don't worry, I'm with Milly. We're going to see a film. Having a lovely time! See you soon.*

'It was never sent.'

Her face falls. 'But I sent it.' She looks at Milly. 'Didn't I? I sat on the bench while you ate your ice cream.' Milly nods again.

'You saved it as a draft. You didn't send it.'

'Oh dear. I'm so sorry. I thought I... Oh no. You must have been... Oh, how awful! It's this new phone. I can't get to grips with it at all.'

'Mum, you've scared the living daylights out of everyone.'

'I'm so very sorry.'

'All these officers? The time, the money, the *worry*?'

'I'm sorry! I thought... Your letter... You have no idea...' Tears well in her eyes. Shona passes her a tissue. 'I came to see my granddaughter and when there was no one here I assumed you'd had to nip out and that you'd get my message. I was trying to be helpful.'

I crouch down to look Milly in the eyes. 'Are you all right, darling?'

'The lady maked Daddy cross.'

'He was frightened. We both were. We thought we'd lost you.'

'Where is Daddy?'

'He's gone for a walk. He'll be back soon.'

PC McAdam stands up. 'Well, it seems Milly's safe.' She looks at Shona. 'Could I have a word?'

Shona gets up and follows her into the hall. Low

murmuring, nothing I can make out, but I can guess. They're worried about Neil, about his reaction, about Mum's suggestion that he wasn't in the house. Did he leave Milly unattended? How long was she in the garden on her own? Where would he have gone?

Whatever Shona says seems to satisfy PC McAdam for the time being. I see her to the door and apologise again. She assures me that it's all in a day's work and not to worry, but I'm not convinced this is the last of it. I have a feeling she'll be discussing us with colleagues and professionals, people who have a say in our future, people who can make decisions about us, our life. What we are allowed.

And what we are not allowed.


'I'll have to report this,' Shona explains, as we wait for Neil to return. Her face is twisted with apology. She knows Neil's angry. During the assessment, we opened up to Shona. She didn't expect us to be perfect. She seemed to think that the very things we were anxious about sharing were the most interesting and relevant details. 'It's not about getting everything right,' she said once, 'but about a level of self-awareness, a desire to do it better.' She made us feel like we could be great parents. I feel safe with Shona, but even she will be challenged by what happened today. She places her hand on mine and gives it a squeeze. 'Don't worry. It sounds like it was all a misunderstanding. But if Neil did leave Milly in the garden and go out—'

'He wouldn't. He didn't.'

She nods. She wants to believe this. 'Well, I'll need to talk to him about that.'

Mum was adamant the front door was closed and there was no one in. 'It must have slammed shut in the wind,' I explain to Shona. 'Mum will have called through the letter box, but probably not very loudly. It's a big house. He didn't hear.'

We're tidying up after Shona's gone. We've agreed to meet on Monday. Milly is sitting at the kitchen table, busy colouring in a picture of a Disney princess in a comic Mum bought her. I put on a Van Morrison CD, the only thing I can find that Mum might tolerate, and let the music loosen the knots of panic and fury inside me. What matters is that Mum's here, finally. After all this time, she's got on a train and come to visit me. Us. I should be grateful for that and make the most of it. It's over. The horrible aching wound in my life can begin to heal. I need this to work. I couldn't bear for things to go back to how they were. I have become a mother and I need my Mum's support, now more than ever. When we've finished clearing up I'll drive her to the station to pick up her suitcase. It was too heavy for her to drag through town. 'Why didn't you call me from the station to say you were here?' More to the point, why didn't she call to say she was coming? But I don't want to start a row now.

'I wanted to surprise you.'

'Well, you certainly did that.'

'Is it really necessary to keep on about this? I've apologised. What else do you want me to do?'

I sigh. 'You're right. I'm sorry.' I give her a hug. She smells of roses. Hand cream, face cream, bath oil. Every birthday and Christmas. Now I find the smell too syrupy and pull away as soon as I can without offending her.

She's filling a bowl with soapy water, though most things have gone in the dishwasher and all that needs washing by hand is the coffee pot and milk frother. I'm emptying the coffee grouts into the compost bucket when she says, 'Is everything all right between you and Neil?'

'Neil and I are good,' I say, determinedly cheerful. 'We've always been good.' I glance across at Milly. Her head is down, but I can tell she's listening. 'It's been more than twenty years, doesn't that tell you something?'

Mum scrubs hard at the glass jug that's already perfectly clean. 'You were so young.' She hesitates. 'Has he ever talked to you about, you know?'

'What?' But I know what she's referring to. I should never have confided in her. 'Mum, this is none of your business. He was a teenager. If he doesn't want to talk about it, that's his prerogative.'

'It may not be my business, but surely it's yours?' Milly has looked up. I hand Mum the cafetière, giving her a warning look, and turn away to wipe the splashes and crumbs from the table. 'Why are you afraid to talk to him about?'

'I'm not afraid! It was a difficult time and, if he doesn't want to talk about it, I respect that.'

Footsteps approach up the gravel path to the back of the house as Mum says, 'I worry about you, Evangeline. This is a big commitment. A child is such a responsibility.'

I stare at her, winded. She's watching me, that eyebrow slightly raised. Unconvinced. She doesn't believe I can do this.

'Daddy!' Milly jumps down from the table and throws her arms around his legs.

'What's going on?' His nose twitches, sniffing her out.

Mum takes her soapy hands out of the washing up bowl

and wipes them on the tea towel. 'We're just having a little chat.'

'You OK, Eve?'

I nod, trying to steady my breath, aware of Milly watching us, her eyes moving from Mum to me. Neil carries her out of the kitchen.

My voice is tight. 'I know it's a big responsibility. And it's frightening. I don't need you to remind me of that.' I think of Shona, her quiet confidence, her assurances. Shona believes in us. Shona thinks we'll be good parents. 'We haven't entered into this lightly.' I feel a little stronger now. 'We've been through six months of assessment, talking about the kind of parents we hope to be, our family histories, how we were parented and what we learned from that—'

'What's that supposed to mean?'

'It means that I'm well aware of my inadequacies!'

'What inadequacies? There is nothing inadequate about you, Evangeline. I brought you up to believe in yourself. You were a confident young woman. You had such dreams. You were going to be a head teacher.'

'I didn't enjoy teaching. Most teachers would give their right arm to have the job I've got now, the creative freedom, the flexible hours, the quality of life—'

'You had the chance to go to London—'

'I didn't want to live in London.'

'You did before you met him.'

'How many times? Neil didn't stop me going to London!' I grip the table edge and take a long, steadying breath. I must not let her get to me. I need to be firm. 'I don't want Milly to hear you talking like this. We're supposed to be making her feel secure and the last thing she needs is to hear you bad-mouthing her daddy.'

I look up and see Neil in the doorway. I'm glad he's heard me. I want him to see I can stand up to her. 'Where's Milly?'

'She's playing a game on her tablet.'

'Is she OK?'

Mum interjects, 'She's fine. She wasn't listening to us and I didn't say anything that might upset her, I was simply asking questions. Important questions. You need to stop making such a fuss of that child, Evangeline. She has to understand she's not the centre of the universe.'

Neil voice whips the air. 'That's rich!'

'Excuse me?'

'No, no, I don't excuse you. Turning up, out of the blue, no warning, after years sulking—' His voice is getting louder. The telltale flush is rising up his neck.

'Neil.'

He turns on me. 'She kidnapped our fucking child, Eve! How far does she have to go?'

Mum gives a contemptuous puff. 'Don't be ridiculous!'

'Police? Sniffer dogs? Helicopter? You call that ridiculous? They'll have you for wasting police time!'

'I wasn't the one who left her unattended in the garden.'

'It was minutes!'

'So you say. Where were you?'

'I was making lunch!'

'Who with?'

He jerks back. 'What's that supposed to mean?'

'This is terribly inconvenient for you, isn't it? Me being here.'

'Inconvenient doesn't even begin to cover it.'

'Well, get used to it. You had your own way for a while, but that's over.'

'Mum, please!'

'Evangeline has a mother who loves her.'

'She has a husband!'

'You made her choose! What kind of man forces a woman to reject her own mother?'

Neil growls. 'Don't push me, Joan.'

'Is that a threat?' The silence gathers between them like fumes. I'm afraid to say anything that might send a spark and set the room alight. Her eyes become two thin lines and she lifts her nose a little. 'What is it you're afraid of, Neil?'

He watches her for a moment, then shakes his head and says, 'You.'

She gives a satisfied smile and Neil shoves his way out of the room.

I lower my forehead to the table. I want to close my eyes and pretend none of this has happened. The enormity of what I've got to get through to create peace again is too much to contemplate.

The front door slams.

# Chapter 6

I make up a bed on the first floor in the spare room next to Milly's. Neil and I sleep on the top floor in a large room under the eaves. He won't want Mum staying the night, but we can't expect her to get a train home today. A flight of stairs between them will have to do.

Neil has texted to ask what's on the shopping list, looking for excuses to stay away, and I'm in no hurry to bring him and Mum back together. I phone the office and Lizzie answers. She works alongside me, my right-hand woman and now job-share partner. 'Kath called me. Is Milly OK? India spoke to the policewoman. They said you found her?'

'She was with my mum.' I'm horribly embarrassed. India lives next door and will have seen the officers coming in and out of the house. She's a good neighbour, bringing us bits and pieces from her garden: dahlias, blackcurrants, apples. At Christmas, she delivered a home-made candle in a decorative jar. She will have been concerned, rather than nosy, seeking reassurance. We often exchange news over the garden wall and have given her regular updates about the adoption process. India was one of the first people to meet Milly when she skipped up the front path for her first visit, greeting her with a handful of wild strawberries from her garden, with her usual easy charm. Milly declared them fairy strawberries and that's what we've called them ever since.

I can see the park staff from my bedroom window, dealing with the aftermath of the search, the mess the helicopter has made of the grass. How do I explain what's happened here? What sort of family are people going to think we are? I won't be able to step out onto the street for days without someone approaching me to find out more. This wasn't how it was meant to be. I wanted Milly to be the centre of attention. I wanted these days to be about building relationships for our new daughter with our neighbours and friends, but now it's all about my mother inadvertently instigating a major police incident.

I say, 'It was good of you to come in to the office at such short notice.' Lizzie will have had to drop everything, organise childcare. 'What about Pearl?' Lizzie has a baby daughter of her own to consider.

'She's with India.'

Everyone has had to rally around. All this fuss. I itch with the shame of it.

My mother is disappointed that I gave up on teaching. I'd planned to do a degree in Theatre Studies when I left school, but she persuaded me to do History because it was more academic and I clearly had no intention of being an actress. With this job it didn't matter what degree I had, what was crucial was my experience. Mum was horrified when I left teaching and took a low paid job as a community arts worker, but it didn't take long for me to move into project management and fundraising, which provided me with an income to match what I had been earning, though it was freelance and precarious. Of course, she'd always hoped I'd be a head teacher, because this was the pinnacle of her profession, but I'm not that sort of person. I prefer to work in a more creative, flexible environment. I have a supportive board of trustees and a high-profile role within my local community. The park is a very special project, providing valuable training and support to vulnerable people through the volunteer scheme, a safe place for children and young people, a café that's popular with tourists and locals. I've earned the respect of my staff as an enabler rather than a manager and I'm proud of that. The kitchen garden project is flourishing and the outdoor pizza oven and cookery demonstrations have been a huge success. We regularly brainstorm ideas for new projects and raise money to implement them. My work is never repetitive or dull and the possibilities are limitless. Maybe, now she's here, Mum will see this for herself and appreciate it. Maybe, finally, she'll be proud of me.

I go into Milly's room to check today's events haven't disturbed her. She's sitting on her new white iron bed, playing on her tablet. I'd prefer her to be looking at a book, but the tablet came with her, a present from her mother, so it's not something that can be removed easily. The room is pink, her choice, surprisingly, for a girl who only wears black leggings and grey T-shirts. It's not a bright lipstick pink, but a more muted chalky shade which satisfied her and didn't grate on me too much. Next to her bed is a long shelving unit with books, games and soft toys and an entire shelf given over to her collection of plastic Moshi Monsters. At her age, I had a similar collection of china Whimsie figurines. My mother still has a few of them in among the ornaments on her window sill. Milly looks up and smiles at me through her hair as I perch on the edge of her bed.

'You OK?' She nods, but I get the impression this is to reassure me and not necessarily how she really feels. Her beloved Gerry is tucked beside her; a soft toy, in the shape of a cow with the colouring of a giraffe which, after much debate, we've agreed is a 'girrow'. She sleeps with him every night and if she's upset or anxious, she'll reach for him to comfort her. I wish I knew his history, but her grandparents couldn't remember where he came from or why he became significant. 'I'm sorry we got cross earlier.'

''S'OK.'

How did this happen? Only a matter of weeks in and we've already hurt this little girl we promised to protect. 'Grown-ups can get it wrong sometimes too.'

'That's what Nana says.' Nana. Not my mother, nor Neil's, but Milly's maternal grandmother. The woman who's been caring for her since she was born.

'She does?'

'Mummy was cross. She broked the glass in the back door.' While Milly's grandparents have done their best to provide her with a stable and loving home, her troubled birth mother, Claire, has been a sporadic, at times difficult, visitor. 'I had to wear my wellies even after Gramps swept it up.'

We were supposed to be taking her away from all that. 'Sometimes people get angry because they're afraid. Daddy was afraid we'd lost you.'

'The lady maked him cross.'

I nod. There's no disputing that. 'Grandma should not have taken you without checking with Daddy.' I hesitate. 'And you should not have gone with someone who was a stranger to you.'

Milly is thoughtful and for a moment I think she's going to say something, but before she can speak my mother calls from next door. 'Evangeline?'

Milly looks puzzled. I explain that Evangeline is my name. I lean in and whisper, 'But I prefer Eve.'

That thoughtful look again. I remember my best friend, Naz, telling me that her son, Max, has wise eyes. 'He's been here before,' she said, cradling him, something new and tender blossoming in her as I watched. I think I understand what she meant now, looking at Milly; there's a lot going on behind those eyes.

'Evangeline!'

'You have to go.' Milly turns her attention back to her screen.

I feel absurdly dismissed and simultaneously irritated by my mother's summons. I don't want to go; I want to stay here with Milly and find out what she's really thinking, but I get up and call out, 'Coming,' before my mother can shout again.

Mum has her suitcase open on the floor and a number of blouses laid out on the bed. The wardrobe door is open. 'Do you have any more hangers?'

'I'll have a look upstairs.'

She unfolds another blouse. How long is she planning to stay? 'Are there no curtains in this room?'

'There's a blackout blind.'

From this window she has a perfect view of the park. We were going to use this as a bedroom for Milly, but she preferred the smaller room that looks out over the back.

We've lived in this house for two years, but this is the first time my mother has visited. When we first moved up, I'd travel down to see her regularly, every other weekend. Neil would catch up with his parents and siblings in Stevenage, while I hung out with Mum in Hitchin. It was my way of making up for leaving her, giving her my undivided attention for two days. She was still stinging after the New York fallout, but once Neil was out of the way, she couldn't have been more attentive. We developed a routine and there was something comforting and rather lovely about that. We'd mooch around the shops, sometimes lunch in a café, then head back home and watch an old black and white film with Ingrid Bergman or Bette Davis. I'd make something simple for the two of us for dinner, letting her relax and be looked after for a change, and we'd eat it from a tray on our knees, watching Saturday night family TV with a glass of sherry for Mum and wine for me. It would be Neil's idea of hell, but with just the two of us, it was fine. I quite enjoyed these little forays back into my childhood for a limited period, and it made Mum happy.

After a few months, Neil stopped travelling down so often, preferring to stay in Cumbria and go cycling or sailing on Sundays with Guy, India's husband. Guy also teaches at the school, and has a friend with a sailing dinghy. While I kept returning to Hitchin that summer, Neil was out on the lake and in the forest, enjoying his new life. His parents and siblings would take it in turns to visit, but Mum refused to come. She expected me to go to her. *This will always be your home, Evangeline.* Every time I tried to suggest a change to the routine, she'd have a reason to keep things as they were. There were the cats to consider. One has a heart problem of some sort, apparently, and can't be left at a cattery. When I suggested someone cat-sit, she told me she didn't like the idea of a stranger in her house while she was away, and the journey north was too much for a woman of her age, her knee was playing up, she had a cold. 'Face it,' Neil said, 'she isn't prepared to come.'

'Who's taking care of the cats?'

'There's only one cat now. Sheba died last year and Woody was hit by a car.'

'No!' Woody was a Siamese with a creamy coat and blue eyes. He liked to sleep on my bed. 'Why didn't you tell me?'

'I didn't think you'd be interested.' I bite my tongue. 'I have someone popping in to check on Inky.'

I wonder who the someone is, but she clearly wants to keep that information to herself for now. 'So, what do you think of my home?' I ask, changing the subject.

'Your home, Evangeline, will always be Hitchin.'

The park volunteers are migrating towards the café. Lizzie will be offering them tea and scones to thank them for their efforts supporting the police search. I stand beside Mum, looking out over the tarn and the town nestled beneath the fell. 'It's beautiful, isn't it?'

She makes a little sound that could be agreement, or not, it's difficult to tell. 'It must get terribly cold in winter, exposed like this.'

What would it cost her to say something nice? How can she look out at that view and not be moved? 'There's heating.'

She looks down at the bare floorboards Neil sanded over a half-term break. He appeared in the kitchen like a ghost of himself, covered in a fine, pale dust and chased me up the stairs into the bathroom. I remember thinking, am I fertile right now? Could this be it? My mother's house has wall-to-wall carpet and the heating is always on, the windows sealed.

'The money he spent on that trip to New York could have paid for some double glazing.'

It will be three years this Christmas, and she's still smarting. But all that's in the past. What matters is that she's come, finally. I am not going to let anything spoil that. Milly, currently singing along to a Disney song in the room next door, is an opportunity for things to shift into a different gear. I've become a mother and I want my mother to delight in that with me.

I think of the grandmother sitting at the picnic bench outside the adventure playground at Brockhole. I imagine her looking out of this window, admiring the view, telling me how happy she is for me. 'So,' I prompt, 'how was it with Milly?'

She frowns. 'Milly,' she says, eventually. 'What kind of name is that?'

I glance to the hallway. 'Mum! Ssssh!' and pull the door to, just in case. 'It's a lovely name.'

Mum wrinkles her nose. 'It's something you'd call a cat or a small dog, not a child. What's it short for?'

'It's not short for anything.'

'What does it say on her birth certificate?'

'Milly.'

'Not Millicent?'

'Millicent?'

Mum concedes with a smile. 'It is a bit dated. Camilla? Camellia?'

'Camellia? That's a plant!'

'It's a very beautiful flower. My favourite.'

'It's not a name.' Before she can say it could be, I add, 'More to the point, it's not *her* name.'

'Amelia? Amelia. Now that's lovely.'

'But it's not her name.'

She gives a little shrug and turns back to her suitcase. 'It doesn't matter. I'm sure you'll be able to change it when you get the new birth certificate.'

'We're not changing her name. Social services won't let us.'

'Won't *let* you? Who's adopting this child? What business is it of theirs what you call her? I'm going to call her Amelia.'

'Mum, stop.'

'You're doing them a favour, remember.'

Again, my mind leaps back to the grandmother at Brockhole, but I shove her aside. I don't know her. She won't be perfect either. I nod to the bed. 'Sit down. I need to talk to you about this.'

'Oh, for goodness' sake, it's not important. Call her what you want.' She continues to unpack, pulling out underwear, large, waist-high cotton pants. As she shakes them out onto the bed, one pair on top of the other, I wonder at what age I will move into big pants. When did my mother become a grandmother? It was long before Milly. She used to be slim, dark-haired, young, but I can't remember when that was and when it stopped. She says, primly, 'You're the parents, not social services—'

'Listen to me!' Her eyes narrow. 'No one is doing anyone any favours. We want to be a family. Milly needs a family. And, as a matter of fact, we are not yet her parents; we're still in a trial period. Until the adoption hearing, social services are Milly's legal guardians and we need to respect that. I'd like you to respect that.'

She turns back to her suitcase. 'Well, I'm sorry if you found me disrespectful.'

I've hurt her feelings. She doesn't appreciate being pulled up by her daughter and she'll do her injured thing now until she feels she's made her point. I let it go. Milly is in her bedroom and I'd much rather be with her. I leave my mother to her unpacking.

\*

Neil arrives home with two large bags of shopping from Booths and dumps them on the table. 'Has she gone?'

'Of course not.'

'I'll drive her to the station.'

'Don't be daft. Have you seen the time?'

'Well, she's not staying here.' I knew he was angry, I expected him to moan, but not this. 'That woman is not staying in my house!'

'*Your* house?'

'Don't do this, Eve.'

'This is my mother! I'm not kicking her out. She's travelled for hours to get to us today. She can't go back tonight.'

'Eve, she's trouble and we don't need trouble right now.'

He's afraid of her. He did make me choose and that's not fair. Why should I have to choose? I've missed my mum. I chose him, I put my marriage and our need to create a family first, but that can't go on for ever. We have Milly now and I want my mum back in my life. I love her. I want Milly to love her.

But Mum will keep poking at him until she gets the reaction she wants, anything to undermine him, and we can't risk that right now. I can't throw her out tonight. We have the weekend before Shona returns. 'Look, it's Milly's birthday on Sunday, the Play in the Park tomorrow. I want her to be here. Can you just put up with her for a couple of days? For me? I've missed her.'

'Whose fault's that?'

'She was hurt. I'm her only child.'

'You moved to a different town!'

'To the opposite end of the country!'

'No one was stopping her coming here.'

'Well, maybe she doesn't feel welcome!'

He takes a step back. 'Oh, come on! She's not welcome *now*! Not after this, but before...'

'You welcomed her? Really?' He says nothing, but I've wounded him. 'I need her, Neil.' He shakes his head. 'Give me this chance? Please?'

I glance up and see Milly hovering in the doorway, watching us, Gerry dangling from her hand. Her face is impassive, reading the scene, storing it up. 'Coming in for a cuddle?' I ask, not knowing what to say to put this right, needing to feel her little body close to mine.

Neil turns and crouches down to her level. She drops Gerry and runs to him with arms outstretched. How easy it is with children. No grudge, no lingering unresolved issues. He lifts her up and I wrap my arms around them both, creating a circle with her in the centre. Our girl. My family.

She soon starts to wriggle. 'Let me down! Too hot! Too hot!' and Neil lowers her to the floor, laughing.

'Where is your mum?' he asks.

'Upstairs.'

'Good,' says Milly firmly. Neil laughs.

I slap his arm. 'Don't.' If I'm honest, I don't really want her here, any more than he does right now, but I want her to be part of my life, Milly's life, our life. This is difficult. She's struggling to adjust. I was her world and then Neil took me away and now Milly has come along. Mum needs time to get used to this, and I can set some boundaries. 'If we send her home now I might not get another opportunity.' He gives a long, resigned sigh. 'We'll make it work. I'll make it work. We'll do things together. She'll get to know Milly.' I drop a kiss on his mouth and whisper, 'Be nice.'

# Chapter 7

The next morning, I lie fretting while the rest of the household sleep. Mum causing all that fuss with the police has put us in a seriously precarious position. Cold fingers of fear scratch at me. Shona phoned as she left the office yesterday to tell us that Milly's social worker has scheduled an emergency review meeting for Monday morning. Shona did her best to reassure me, but we are vulnerable. Quick, short breaths. Milly is not our child yet, not in the eyes of the law. We could lose her. My body is alert in the half dark. Milly, who fills this house, whose giggle echoes in every corner, who has claimed her space in our world, could be gone in a moment. The prospect of this is as real as if she'd been snatched already and I have to slip out of bed and creep downstairs into her room to prove to myself that she's still there.

The slow, steady rise and fall of her chest. The deep sleep of contentment, unaware that this may all end abruptly. I stand, drinking in her warm, honeyed smell, filling myself up, as if this might be enough to keep her here.

Mum said that Neil was not in the house when she arrived, which is nonsense, but he did leave her unsupervised in the garden, and that's serious. They may decide, on reflection, that we're unable to provide a stable enough environment. They could take Milly back.

I close my eyes. Keep breathing her in. Try to steady the clackety-clack of my heart behind my ribs. I remind myself that Shona seems to think it will be OK. If we're honest and reasonable on Monday, we'll keep them onside. Helen, Milly's social worker, likes us. She is as keen as we are for this to go ahead and, above all else, Milly is happy.

I know there's no chance of getting back to sleep. The sun will be up within half an hour. I pull on a pair of leggings and a T-shirt. I'm reaching for my hoodie when Neil stirs. 'Just going for a run.' He sits up, rubbing his face with the flat of his hand, and blinking. If he gets up now, I'll be leaving him and Mum alone together. 'Milly's still fast asleep. Why don't you have a lie in until I get back and then you can take your bike out for a bit? I'll be back before she wakes up.'

A silent conversation passes between us which ends with a nod from him, and I creep downstairs to get my trainers.

I started running when we got back from New York. I needed something to distract me. I'd seen women jogging through Central Park, independently and in groups, and thought how powerful they looked, how at ease with their bodies. They weren't all stick thin and athletic, but energised and taking control. I was nervous, didn't know if I'd be able to do it. Neil downloaded some practical advice from the internet and I started with sixty-second bursts interspersed with plenty of walking. Now I try to run every day for half an hour. Nothing too demanding or ambitious. I'm not particularly fast, not fast at all, really, but I can do this and the feeling is magnificent. I run up Fell Rise, a long hill lined with irregular, brightly painted houses. Some are still the traditional grey or off-white, but more and more are being revived in claret, indigo blue, moss green. Three-storey Victorian terraces nudge up against squat, low-beamed cottages. Some have pillars and steps up to the front door, others traditional shuttered windows and delicate gables. The steady rhythm of my trainers, beating against the pavement, echoes in my chest. This first stretch as I climb out of town is hard, that pull on muscles that really want to give up, but I know once I reach the crest of the hill and the road flattens out it will get easier, and when I'm off the road and onto grass, then open countryside, I'll be in my stride. It's invigorating, empowering. I feel in control. Just me, this body, and the landscape. I am claiming my place in the world in this moment. I'm owning it.

I have headphones on, music propelling me forward and drowning out the sound of my panting. It also means no other early birds can attract my attention to ask about Milly. Everyone will be eager to hear, first-hand, the story behind the police search. The remainder of the weekend rolls out in front of me like a minefield. We're hosting the annual Play in the Park this afternoon, which should be a distraction for everyone. I will dismiss yesterday's events with an embarrassed laugh. I'll turn it into an anecdote. Something and nothing. History. Other people have difficult parents and manage to laugh it off. I need to learn to do the same. My problem is I take it all too seriously.

Though I'll be working today, I'll have plenty of time with Milly. The show is a touring outdoor adaptation of Enid Blyton's *Magic Faraway Tree*, with songs. A family event with picnic blankets, macaroons and lashings of ginger beer provided. Think positive! The sun is out, the clouds are plump and white and my family are coming to see the show. Three generations. I lengthen my stride, kicking the road out behind me. I'm strong. I'm free. I am invincible.

It's a relief to be on speaking terms again with Mum. Milly will help us forge a new relationship, though that will take time. Milly's not stupid; she can sense the tension and she made it quite clear over dinner last night that she doesn't want to be called Amelia. 'Tell the lady, my name is *Milly*.' This was met with a sharp, 'Tell the child my name is Grandma!' which didn't help.

Neil is prepping his bike in the garden with Milly, when I get back. We wave him off and head up to the house.

Mum intercepts me in the hall. 'Good God! Look at the colour of you! You'll give yourself a heart attack!' I bend down to undo my laces. 'Evangeline, this is ridiculous. You're forty years old and you need to take care of your joints. You'll be a cripple like me if you carry on like this.'

'I'm off for a shower.' I turn to Milly. I was about to suggest she stay downstairs with Mum, but something about her expression stops me. Before I can say anything, Mum suggests the TV and Milly rushes into the living room while Mum makes her way to the kitchen. Her gait has become more lopsided. Her knee is clearly troubling her.

I follow. 'Couldn't you read to her or play a game with her?'

'She'd rather watch her programme.'

'What's *her* programme?'

'I don't know. Something she used to watch with her nana.' Mum leans against the kitchen counter for support, looking at me helplessly and I shift from irritation to guilt in an instant.

'Was Milly rude to you?' I know she can be terribly stubborn when she wants to be and if she's taken a dislike to Mum after yesterday's drama, she won't hide it. Milly may be young, but she is intuitive. The conflict between Mum and Neil is palpable; she will sense it, and it's only natural that her allegiance would be to Neil. Of course, the rational part of my brain tells me this is Mum's own fault, but that doesn't stop me feeling her hurt. And I want this to work. We have an opportunity here. Milly needs a grandmother and my mother needs to loosen her grip on me. If she shifts the focus of her attention onto her granddaughter, this could be the beginning of a new chapter for us. I need my mother in my life, but we have to find a more adult, less claustrophobic way for us to be. 'Did something happen this morning?'

A little shrug. 'I offered her some breakfast, but she said she didn't want any.' She hesitates. 'She went upstairs to fetch Neil. They had breakfast together and went straight out.'

'You didn't have breakfast with them?'

'It's fine. I had some tea and toast.'

There's more to this. Milly said or did something. Mum is going to have to work a bit here to earn back Milly's trust. She was an infant school teacher, this should be her forte, but right now she looks vulnerable.

'The child hasn't taken to me.'

'No! No! Don't take it personally. She's probably worried that you're trying to replace her nana. She'll be missing her.' Mum doesn't look convinced, but she managed to charm Milly easily enough when she first arrived, persuading her away from the house with offers of ice cream and treats. She was a popular teacher in her time, though of the old-school 'firm but fair' variety. She didn't have the luxury of time, being a busy working mum and a single parent. I had to wait in the school library until she finished work and my memories are of always having to hurry to keep up as we rushed to and from school. The best times were weekends, when we'd snuggle up on the sofa together and watch films. *Bedknobs and Broomsticks* with Angela Lansbury was our favourite. She didn't have a lot of time back then, but she does now. This is an opportunity for her too.

'I'll have a word with Milly.'

'No, don't. Don't make an issue of it.' She pauses. A change in tone. 'I'm afraid I have no idea where Neil is.'

'He's gone out on his bike. He's probably cycled up to Grizedale. He'll be at least a couple of hours.'

She raises an eyebrow. 'You aren't sure where he's going?'

'What's that supposed to mean?'

'Nothing.' I wait. She gives that little shrug. 'What if you need him here? Or he has an accident?' But that wasn't the point she was making.

'He has his phone.'

'Does he disappear on his own like this a lot?'

'He hasn't disappeared!'

She watches me. 'Has he told you where he was when I arrived?'

'He was in the house.' The eyebrow again. 'I don't have to check up on him, Mum. I trust Neil.'

She says nothing. My mother is the queen of loaded silences, but this is serious now. I take her by the arm and steer her down the hall, away from the living room and out of Milly's earshot. Once we're inside the kitchen I close the door and turn to face her. She looks small and rather tired. 'Mum, you have to stop this. Do you understand? We've got another review meeting on Monday because of what happened, with the police search. The adoption isn't secured yet. We need them to believe in us. That Milly's safe with us. We need to make sure that she isn't upset, because if they think she's distressed in any way, they...' I struggle to swallow, the words blocking my throat.

Mum nods. She takes both my hands in hers and I feel her courage, as I have done so many times when I've been anxious: before my first school trip, the morning of my maths O level, the day of my interview for uni. She's strong, my mother. My protector. 'It will be fine, Evangeline. If you like, I'll explain. I'll say I was mistaken about the front door being shut.'

'No. No, don't do that. Don't lie, but don't, don't...' She looks at me, doing that thing she does; creating a story where there isn't one. 'Just try and... try and be nice? Try and get along with Neil. I know it's difficult, but if you could just... be nice? Please?'

'Of course.' She wraps her arms around me and I'm forced to bend down to her, like a clumsy, overgrown child. 'Now don't you worry. The meeting will be fine.' She pushes me away to look me in the eyes. 'You are a wonderful mother, Evangeline. That child is lucky to have you and anyone with an ounce of sense can see that.'


Reassured, I go to check on Milly. She's engrossed in the TV. It's not a children's programme but an episode of *The Simpsons*. I don't know how appropriate that is for a child of Milly's age. 'Did Nana watch this with you, darling?' She shakes her head, her eyes not leaving the screen.

'Matty and Frankie.' The two teenage sons at the foster parents' bustling farm outside Carlisle where Milly lived after her nana's stroke. Cheeky boys with a playful affection for Milly. If they take her away from us, that's where she'd go, until another couple are identified for her.

But that isn't going to happen. I can feel Mum's strength. What felt awful and inevitable in the early hours of this morning seems a little hysterical now. There was a misunderstanding. Milly was safe enough. She's settled. I can imagine Ruth, the foster mother, a no-nonsense farmer's wife, hands on her broad hips, batting away my worries with a wave of her floury hand: *'Now why would you be fretting about stuff that's never going to happen?'*

Milly lived with the foster family for almost a year, while the wheels of bureaucracy ground slowly on. She missed her grandparents, but there were regular visits to look forward to, and her new life had so much to distract her. Ruth's house was full of life and warmth. Dogs, cats and rabbits wandering in and out of the yard, a poorly lamb curled up in a box in the airing cupboard. Milly loved it. And there was a Forever Family to get to know. I had to pick Neil up from work every day and drive up the M6, where we'd join Milly for tea, along with her foster brothers, Ruth, her jolly husband and various farm labourers. We'd put Milly to bed, read her a story, and gradually built a relationship of trust. In the second week, we stayed over, in a tent, on the small campsite run by the family. (I was hoping we'd be able to sleep in the delightful Shepherd's Hut, but it was high season and booked up.) Staying over allowed us to be at the house when Milly woke and familiarise ourselves with her breakfast and morning routine. The plan was for her to visit us in Tarnside for a day and eventually an overnight in the third week, before moving in, but it soon became clear that things were going to move a lot quicker than that.

This is something I should be sharing with my mother. She knows nothing of this story: how Milly blocked the door to her bedroom as we went to leave that first evening and demanded to know when she could come to our house. How a Tarnside sleepover for Milly was agreed in the middle of the second week and she moved in for good, a week ahead of schedule. 'No different to the lambs we wean,' Ruth said, taking it all in her stride. Everyone agreed; her social worker, the foster family, Shona. Things couldn't have been better.

Mum was not part of that. She doesn't understand. Because I chose to do it without her. My choice. I created that wound in my life and now I have to do what I can to heal it.

I pick up the remote and press the play button to see how much is left of this episode. Five minutes. 'Would you like to play a game with me and Grandma when I've come out of the shower?' I turn around, expecting my mother to have followed me, but from the kitchen I hear the click of the kettle. Milly takes the remote from my hand and switches off the screen. 'Why don't you go and ask Grandma if she wants to play a game of Happy Families? I bet you can beat her.'

But Milly slips off the sofa and stands in front of me. 'I want to come with you.'

'For a shower?' I hesitate. Is this OK? I'm painfully aware of the training we've had from social services, the things we need to be cautious about. Is it appropriate for Milly to see me in the shower? Why don't I know? A mother would know. If Milly had been with us since birth, something would have developed naturally between us, but I don't have that history and I don't know what to say. I don't want to make an issue of this, but I don't want to get it wrong. I can hear Mum moving about in the kitchen, but she won't understand the subtleties of this. Why is she in the kitchen drinking tea on

59

her own while her granddaughter's here with nothing to do? Why doesn't she understand how important it is to create a bond with Milly?

I bend down to Milly's eye level and smile into her big, trusting eyes. 'I think Grandma might like to spend a bit of time with you. She's not here for long.'

She puts her hands over her ears and shouts, 'No! No! No!'

'Milly, stop. Stop. It's fine.' I pull her close. 'You don't have to if you don't want to.' There's silence from the kitchen. I wonder if Mum has heard this exchange and the pain I imagine her feeling is as raw and acute as if it had happened to me. What if Milly reacts like this at the review meeting? What if she says she doesn't like Mum?

Leading Milly upstairs to her bedroom, I leave her with a colouring book and a Roald Dahl story CD. This seems to satisfy her. She does wander into the bathroom after a while, but by then the glass door has safely steamed up. She asks me to make a peephole, which I do at knee level, so she has to crouch down to peek in. As the water streams down the glass I try to be positive. I tell myself that Shona and the panel are reasonable people. I rehearse speeches. The key is to be honest. We've always been honest. If Milly doesn't like Mum, it's not the end of the world. She's a child. She is bound to resent another presence in the house, particularly this soon. She's jealous, it's only natural; she wants me for herself. I'll persuade them. But, as the water pours over me I still feel a deep ache inside me, like I've lost something that was never mine in the first place.

# Chapter 8

Neil came back red and sweaty and caked in mud. It was all I could do not to look at Mum and say, 'See?' but that wouldn't help the situation and I didn't need to. She made her excuses and went upstairs, apparently to rest her knee and probably sneak a nap. Neil offered to make the picnic once he'd showered, so I took Milly and came ahead to the park, to make sure everything's ready for the theatre company this afternoon.

Milly's fizzing with excitement, skipping along. She's wearing her trademark leggings and T-shirt. Clothes are an issue with Milly. She has four pairs of identical leggings, a series of plain T-shirts in grey, blue or white, and two plain cotton hoodies. She refuses to wear anything else. Her unicorn pyjamas were a major step forward but daytime clothes are still carefully managed. As a child, she has two areas of control in her life: what she eats and what she wears. Her world's been turned upside down; I'm not going to force things with her. As long as she's clean, warm and nourished, we can work with her eccentricities. The forecast is for the weather to remain dry, though the clouds have thickened and it's not as warm as it was. I send Neil a text to suggest he packs a hoodie for Milly and warn Mum. She feels the cold and I don't want her complaining and spoiling the afternoon.

The stewards collect their hi-vis jackets from the office. Lizzie greets Milly with a high five. Her daughter, Pearl, is strapped into a high chair that's been dragged into the office to contain her. Lizzie used to be the festivals coordinator while I managed the park on a more strategic level. Now she and I share a combination of my job and hers, each of us working three days a week, employing an administrator to cover the day-to-day financial work and fundraising. It's the perfect set-up, allowing both of us to focus on the things we enjoy most about the community park and festivals and have half the week for our children.

Children. Family. Mothering. Words that were unavailable to me for years. Words for the privileged, the chosen, the more fortunate. Now they belong to me too.

Pearl thumps her plastic cup on the wooden tray of the high chair. Unimpressed at being ignored she flings it at the filing cabinet. Lizzie, without looking up, passes her a box of tissues while continuing to talk to me. Pearl plucks out a tissue and tears it into strips. Milly slips free from my hand and picks up the cup. She puts the strips of tissue inside it. Pearl pulls them out, Milly puts them back. A game ensues.

'Eve? Are you listening?'

I grin and shake my head. 'Sorry.' I just want to watch them, to drink it in. I still can't believe that I'm allowed to have this, but with Lizzie and Pearl that drip-drip-drip of worry subsides a little. This is happening, this family I dreamed of, this life I longed for, is unfolding in front of me. My mother is tricky, but she's always been difficult. At least she's here. We're speaking again. That's progress.

Milly. My daughter. Grinning at Pearl. 'Say Milly? Milly?'

Pearl frowns, purses her lips, makes an M sound.

'Good girl.'

Pearl has grown to fit her name, a round ball of a baby, with a shine to her hair and a glow to her skin. I'd assumed she'd been named after a grandmother or an elderly godparent, but when I told Lizzie this she snorted with laughter. 'Elkie Brooks,' she explained. '"Pearl's A Singer". Always loved it. And pearls come from grit. I like that; something beautiful growing out of something difficult.' Lizzie's life hasn't been easy, but she makes it work. She and Jonty split before Pearl was born and he's old enough to be her grandfather, but he lives around the corner and is actively involved in her day to day life. His teenage children are Pearl's siblings.

'My mum wants to call Milly Amelia.'

Lizzie frowns. 'Is that her name?'

Milly says, 'No,' without looking up.

I shake my head. 'Milly on her birth certificate.' She's been Milly for five years.

'Isn't it your birthday, tomorrow?' Lizzie asks, as if she doesn't know. Milly looks up, eyes bright with anticipation. Third of September. I had thought about throwing a big party: a cake with five candles, the house draped in bunting and filled with squealing children, but the reality, when I came to plan it, was quite daunting. Milly doesn't have any friends here yet. I could have invited people with children the right age, but it felt forced. I need to let things develop naturally.

Milly says, 'Can Pearl come for my birthday?'

'Are you having a party?' Lizzie had a lovely first birthday party for Pearl a couple of weeks ago, in her little cottage, where we squeezed in alongside her wonderfully complicated family and eccentric neighbours, but we don't have that network locally and it feels a bit too soon to have Neil's extended clan visit.

Milly shakes her head, but she doesn't seem disappointed. 'Mummy is making a cake.'

'Oh, well then, we'll have to come,' says Lizzie. 'Am I allowed to come?'

Milly gives a grave nod. 'I should think so,' much to Lizzie's delight.

We've talked through the birthday plan with Shona, who phoned Helen, Milly's social worker, to find out what sort of celebrations Milly has had in the past. There were no parties, just a cake and a special tea at her grandparents' house. Mum, Claire, would be invited and sometimes came, sometimes didn't, so it was played down not to raise Milly's expectations. We've decided to keep it low-key this year, but Lizzie and Pearl will be a lovely addition. 'You don't have to do it all at once,' Shona reminded me. 'You have the rest of your lives.'

The rest of our lives.

'Next year, when you've made more friends, you can have a proper party.' Milly will be starting school this year. She will be one of the oldest in the year. Had she been born a few days earlier we would have had another year with her at home. That feeling I had in the shower swamps me again. Like arriving at the station to see your train pulling out, or opening your diary to discover the party you were looking forward to is not tonight, as you'd thought, but yesterday. Gone. Nothing to be done. But there will be other trains, other parties, other milestones in Milly's life for us to enjoy together.

Schools start back from Wednesday, though Neil will be going in straight after Monday's review meeting to prepare. The reception class at the infant school doesn't start until the following week, once the older children have settled back in. And the school's policy is for the reception class to be split, with all children attending part-time for two weeks after that. Milly has been allocated mornings for the first week, which will give us the rest of the day. Lizzie and I have planned our hours to accommodate this. I will have to make the most of this extra time; a taste of what might have been.

When Milly slips off to the toilet, Lizzie says, 'You can't change her name. It would be too weird for her, with the move, and all the other changes going on, to have her name taken from her. She'd lose all sense of who she is.' It's a relief to hear it put it so unequivocally. Mum made it seem much less certain. 'Amelia's a nice name, but it's not her name. You don't want to make it sound like there's something wrong with the name Milly; she'll think there's something wrong with her. Tell your mum she's Milly. End of.'

I laugh, imagining my mother's face if I spoke to her like that. What would Mum think of Lizzie with her blunt London accent and her no-nonsense approach? Lizzie's right, I need to make it clear, my daughter's name is Milly and it's staying Milly. Mum is old-school, a teacher through and through, and she'll never accept me as an equal. To her I will always, fundamentally, remain her child, but I can manage that. Isn't that what women do all the time? All those PAs who manage their bosses, the nurses who quietly prompt the consultants, I've had to do it myself with board members, time and again. I can manage my mother.

*

The car park is full and the crowd gather around the performance area like a colourful garland tossed across the grass. The minimal set is in place, beneath the ancient oak that will serve as the Faraway Tree for this afternoon's production. Moonface and Silky the Fairy, with their outsized, papier-mâché heads, are laying out props, engaging with the children and young families in the audience, and the general chatter is beginning to subside as people prepare for the show to begin. There's still no sign of Neil and Mum. We're too late to get a place near the front, but Lizzie laid out a large blanket for her and Pearl earlier and said we're welcome to join them. She waves and I send Milly to pick her way through the crowd, promising I won't be far behind. Kath and India are also there, with India's husband, Neil's cycling buddy, Guy. It will be fun to sit and watch the show with them. I'm about to call Neil to find out what the hold-up is when I see our grey Golf coming up the drive. There's nowhere left for him to park. He winds down the window as Mum climbs out of the passenger seat, groaning.

'Why did you drive?' It's a five-minute walk along the footpath from our house, but in the car, he'll have had to navigate his way right around the park perimeter, and now he'll have to drive back out onto the street. There's no way he'll find a space anywhere near here.

He rolls his eyes. 'Your mum's knee's playing up.'

My mother gives another groan, hobbling around the back of the car towards me. She looks at the gathered crowd. 'Is there no seating?'

'I told you it was a picnic.'

'I thought there'd be benches.'

I grit my teeth. 'Picnic blankets. We've got a place down at the front.'

Neil interrupts. 'I'll take the car to the house and nip back. Where's Milly?'

I point to Lizzie who's waving one arm above her head. Milly is standing next to her, frowning at us.

As Neil pulls away, Mum says, 'I'll need a chair. I can't sit on the ground.'

There are people with camping chairs, but they're sitting at the periphery so as not to obscure the view for those behind them. Lizzie's blanket is in the centre at the front. I won't be able to put a chair there. 'How about a cushion?'

'A cushion? On the ground? I'll never be able to get up again!'

I hold up my hand to Milly and Lizzy, indicating that I'll be five minutes, and run to the office to get a chair. By the time I've carried it back, Neil has dropped off the car and climbed over the garden wall to join us. 'What are you doing?'

'Mum needs a chair. You go and sit with Milly. Guy's there with India.' I don't look at him, but take the chair to the edge of the crowd, as close as I can get to where my family will be sitting, and beckon for my mother to follow. She lowers herself in with a grunt, while I stand beside her. Milly calls out to me, 'Mummy! Come *on*!' I wave, waiting for Mum to reassure me she'll be fine, to tell me to go and join my daughter, but she says nothing. She knows no one here, I can hardly leave her alone. Neil holds up his palms in a question. I mouth *sorry*, watch him shake his head and sit down, taking Milly onto his knee. She looks at me over his shoulder, but what can I do?

\*

I watch the production through a resentful rage. I can feel it crackle the air around me. If my mother so much as speaks I feel I will, quite literally, bite her, but she doesn't. Behind me she chuckles at something silly Moonface has said to entertain the children and I am sorely tempted to turn around and tip her out of her chair. I'm just wondering how I can join my family without creating a disturbance when Milly comes to my rescue, standing up and picking her way through the crowd. Neil, crouched over, follows, issuing apologies, until they are both beside me. I sit down on the grass with my back to Mum and Milly climbs into my lap while Neil wriggles into position and slides his arm around me. Behind us Mum mumbles something about the grass being too damp to sit on, but we pretend we can't hear her. I try not to picture the expression on her face and focus on Saucepan Man's noisy arrival down the tree.

Milly appears to be more impressed with the ice cream Kath's bought her than the production, but I don't mind. It's enough to have her here, sharing my world, whatever she chooses to take from it. I've agreed to stay until the park is cleared and check the litter has been collected. Neil goes to help the company manager load the van while I sit with Milly on the grass by Mum's feet making daisy chains. As I drape the flowers over Milly's head, she asks, 'When are we going to see Nana?'

I scan her face for signs of distress. 'Are you missing Nana and Gramps?'

She nods, but she doesn't seem tearful or anxious. 'Can they come?'

'Here?'

She grins and I feel a surge of joy that she wants to share this new life with them, that it's something she feels good about and wants to show off, but it isn't that simple. Contact must be carefully managed, with supervised visits in neutral places, most likely an anonymous room in a social services family centre in another part of the county. Milly must be kept safe. Not from her grandparents, but from her mother, Claire, whose drug problem causes her to behave unpredictably. Milly's grandparents have accepted that it's better they don't know the details of Milly's new life. They have the bald facts: professional couple, early forties, with a large house in a rural area, though not necessarily Cumbria, and no other children yet. They haven't been told our names or seen what we look like. We have chosen to remain anonymous, given the high profile nature of my job. My photograph appears regularly in the local press when I'm promoting festivals and park projects and if Milly's birth family were to recognise me this would jeopardise her anonymity. It wouldn't necessarily be a problem with her grandparents, but could put Milly at risk with respect to her mother. I'd love to reveal more with Milly's grandparents, to share photographs and short films we've recorded, invite them here to share Milly's new world, but it's not an option and I can understand the reasons for that. I'm quietly relieved, if I'm honest. Without those rules I'd find it difficult to set my own boundaries. I'd probably end up adopting the entire family.

'They can't come here, sweetie.' My mother gives a cluck that suggests, I should think not, but I don't want this to be the message Milly receives. 'Nana is poorly. It would be difficult for her to travel all this way, but we can go and see them. Would you like that?'

She grins again, nodding. I don't mention not going back to the house where Milly spent the first three years of her life, until her nana's stroke put an end to that chapter, or the fact that it would probably be Helen and not me or Neil who would accompany her for that visit. 'We'll talk to Shona and see what she can do. OK?' But reassured and no longer interested, Milly has run off after India's little border terrier, before I've finished the sentence. I laugh.

Mum gives another cluck. 'You aren't seriously going to take her back there?'

'We've agreed to regular contact.'

'Why?'

Everything is so simple for my mother. Black and white. But there's nothing black or white about our relationship with Milly; this is every shade of grey. 'They are her family.'

'You're her family now.'

'They don't stop existing.'

'They stop having rights.'

'They're good people.'

'Which is why they're giving the child up for adoption?'

I breathe. Count to five. Milly is running circles with the dog yapping at her heels. 'She's their granddaughter. And they were taking good care of her, but Margaret's had a stroke. She's lost the use of her right side and Reg can't cope.'

'And what about the mother?'

'Claire isn't in a position to take care of Milly.'

'For goodness' sake. Say it like it is, Evangeline. I assume the woman's a druggie?'

'Please don't use that word.'

'If the cap fits.'

Claire has lived with Milly and her parents, on and off, for brief periods of Milly's life, but hasn't been able to sustain a drug-free existence, repeatedly retreating to that world, stealing from her parents, lying and breaking their hearts, but I'm not going to tell my mother this. 'Contact with Claire hasn't been agreed. But the grandparents are a different issue.'

'If they were any sort of parents their daughter wouldn't be a drug addict with a baby she can't take care of.'

'Keep your voice down,' I hiss, scanning the crowd, but most people have packed up and started to leave and there's no one close enough to have heard. 'It isn't easy when you're a single parent. You of all people should know that.'

'I do.' She has, at least, lowered her voice. 'I do know that. And social services have never had to step in to help me out!'

'Well, lucky you.'

We sit in fizzing silence.

India has given Milly a ball and she's preparing to throw it, while the dog sits, trembling with anticipation. I get up to join them, wiping grass from my jeans. Tomorrow is Milly's birthday and Lizzie is coming with Pearl. I'll invite India to pop in. That should provide enough of a distraction. The review is the following day and Mum will be heading home then. Think positive. We're nearly there.

# Chapter 9

Neil cooks tea when we get home. It's late and Milly needs to eat quickly so it's pasta shells with a simple tomato sauce. Milly wolfs it down and asks for seconds. Mum makes a barbed comment about the insubstantial meal. 'A child needs vegetables.'

Neil tells her, 'There are peppers and mushrooms in the sauce.'

Mum picks at the pasta with her fork. 'Really?' He's chopped them small, so Milly will eat them. She raises an eyebrow at my empty bowl. 'Is this all you're having?'

'That's plenty for me.'

'You're looking terribly thin.' She looks at Neil. 'You need to feed her up.'

Neil spoons more pasta into Milly's bowl. 'Eve's an adult. She can decide for herself how much she needs to eat. Would you like some more, Joan?' He pauses, serving spoon hovering over the pan.

'Not at the moment, thank you.' Her tone is prim. I'm

dreading her saying anything else to prickle him, but instead she changes the subject and addresses Milly. 'I have a surprise for you upstairs.'

'What is it?'

'Well, it won't be a surprise if I tell you, will it?'

Milly looks at me. I give her a smile of encouragement. She finishes her pasta slowly and slips down from the table. My mother stops her. 'What do we say?'

I feel Neil shift in his seat. Milly looks from him to me. 'Thank you?'

'No.'

Neil says, 'Thank you is fine, Milly.'

My mother says, 'It's polite to ask if you may leave the table.'

Neil clears his throat. 'That's enough, Joan.'

Mum glares at him. I intercept. 'Milly has lovely manners.' Giving Milly's hand a supportive squeeze, I add, 'Asking permission to leave the table is a bit old-fashioned these days,' and before my mother can retaliate, I lead Milly out.


We're in Milly's bedroom when Mum makes her laborious way up the stairs. Milly is giving me the story of each of her Moshlings, taking them down from the shelf to introduce them, one at a time. Mum hovers in the doorway waiting for us to notice. I wish she'd either come in and join us or go to her room, but she does neither. Finally, I look up. 'What is it?'

'Nothing. I don't want to disturb the two of you.'

This is my cue to ask her what's wrong, but I resist and return my attention to the wide-eyed Moshling Milly is handing me.

My mother coughs. 'So, Milly. Do you want to see what I've got for you?'

'Not at the moment, thank you.'

Milly has mimicked Mum's voice perfectly. I bow my head to hide my smile. Mum turns away and gives a little yelp of pain, rubbing her knee. 'Are you all right?'

'It just takes me unaware sometimes.' She limps into her room.

Her room. Neil told me off for calling it that last night. 'She's not bloody moving in, Eve!' He's assuming she's leaving on Monday morning. He doesn't want her here for the review. Nor do I, if I'm honest. What if she says something tactless? Or upsets Milly? But I haven't had the courage to talk to her about when she's going home and I can see she's got no plan to leave anytime soon. If the worst comes to the worst, I'll have to think of an excuse to get her out of the house while the social workers are here. Maybe Kath will keep her entertained with a tour of the park and a cup of tea in the café.

We have about three minutes of reprieve before she calls me, 'Evangeline? Do you have a moment?'

Milly looks at me. She takes the Moshling from the palm of my hand. 'You have to go.'

'Sure you don't want to come with me?'

Milly shakes her head firmly and flashes a wicked smile. 'Not at the moment, thank you.'


Mum pulls out a tissue-wrapped item from her suitcase. She places it on the bed. 'Look what I found!'

I watch with an increasing sense of foreboding as she unwraps the tissue carefully and pulls out a small garment.

The dated Liberty print is vaguely familiar. Shaking it out, she holds it between thumbs and forefingers. Dangling before me is a dress. My dress.

I remember her making this dress for me. Standing on a stool, pins held between her teeth, hissing at me to keep still while she worked her way around the hem. It's yellow with tiny white and green daisies, a fitted bodice, full skirt, lace collar. I try to swallow but my throat has closed.

She made this dress for my fifth birthday party. Everyone else was wearing jeans and fancy T-shirts with glittery motifs. I had to wear this. I instinctively rub my neck, remembering the itch of the lace. I have a photograph of me standing in the front room of our house, my hair scraped back into two hideously high bunches with slippery yellow ribbons. I was too hot when she took the photograph, my skin prickled, my cheeks were crimson and there was sweat around my hairline. I can feel the heat rising in my cheeks now. My smile is stiff. I hate this dress.

'I thought it would be just right for the birthday girl.'

How do I contain my horror? How could she think, for a moment, that Milly would want to wear this?

'Shall I call her?'

'No!'

'What's wrong?' Her voice wobbles. I know she spent hours making that dress. I know every stitch is filled with love. I know that bringing the dress is saying something significant. I understand that, for my mother, offering this dress to Milly is an act of love and I don't want to reject that, but Milly isn't going to understand this.

Before I can stop her, my mother calls, 'Amelia!'

'Mum, not now.' I hear Milly get up, her footsteps across the wooden boards, onto the hall carpet. Her head appears around the door. A comma across her forehead as she frowns. She looks directly at Mum and says, 'My name is *Milly*.' I hold my breath, delighted in her courage, ashamed at my own fear. I could learn a thing or two from this daughter of mine.

Mum is still holding out the dress. She waits, but Milly doesn't understand, of course she doesn't. All she sees is an ugly dress.

I'm desperately trying to think of a way to intercept this without hurting Mum's feelings when she prompts, 'What do you think?', a lamb to the slaughter.

Milly wrinkles up her nose. 'Yuck!'

Mum's face falls. She drops her arms. I try to intervene. 'Milly, love, do you know that Grandma made that dress for me when I was the same age as you? She brought it to show you.'

And we might have got away with it, but Mum, keen for her gesture to be appreciated, takes a step towards Milly. 'Would you like to try it on?'

'No!' Milly snatches the dress from Mum's hands and tosses it to the floor.

'Milly! That's naughty!'

Milly bursts into tears and runs out, down the stairs. Mum sinks back onto the bed, visibly shaken. I step onto the landing and lean over the banisters to see Neil lifting a sobbing Milly into his arms, looking up. 'What's going on?' Behind me my mother gives a hiccupy sob. I shake my head, leave Neil to comfort Milly and go to take care of my mother.


I drive Mum to the station for the train on Monday morning. Lizzie and Pearl were a delightful distraction for Milly on her special day. India popped in carrying a fat, wobbly cake and, with the help of Lizzie's present (a CD of children's favourites) we managed to put on a reasonable show, but the underlying atmosphere was horrible. This was not the way I'd imagined Milly's first birthday with us. Mum spent most of the day in her room, complaining of a migraine, which was marginally better than her being among us, parading her injured feelings, but they still radiated down through the ceiling while we sang 'Happy Birthday' and did our best to pretend everything was fine. Lizzie and India, to their credit, pretended they hadn't noticed a thing, and I was grateful for that; had either of them expressed any sympathy I'd have gone to pieces.

I thought Neil would be angry with Mum, but he sounded more weary when he came upstairs after comforting Milly. He stood looking at us from the doorway of the bedroom. 'This isn't working, Joan.'

Mum sniffed and touched her nose with her tissue. I picked up the dress and smoothed out the wrinkles. 'It was a really nice thought.'

'It's too soon.' He was using his teacher voice. His head-of-sixth-form voice, outranking Mum. 'This is meant to be our bonding time with Milly and having another person here is confusing her.'

'You want me to go.' To hear it said, so simply, was devastating. My immediate reaction was to reassure her and say, no, but Neil got there first and, if I'm honest, I was relieved.

'I'm telling you to go.'

I knew what he was saying made sense, but he sounded so cold. I knew we should be putting Milly first, and I'd had enough of Mum myself, but I felt awful. It wasn't necessary for him to be so hard. And Mum, being Mum, retaliated, because that's what she does with Neil. It's war between the two of them, and she is not about to surrender.

'I know about you.'

He flinched. I saw it. Had I been facing her in that moment, I'd have missed it, but I wasn't. I'd looked at him, to try and signal to him to go easy, and I saw. He flinched. And then in an instant he'd composed himself again. 'What is it you think you know, Joan?' But she'd scored her point. She shook her head, that satisfied smile stretching her mouth, giving nothing away.

But her moment of glory has passed. If she had anything to say she would have told me by now. She was bluffing. I can see in the harsh sunlight that streams down onto the station platform that Mum barely slept last night. Her eyes are swollen from crying. She's broken. I don't know if she really had a migraine yesterday or if she was simply staying out of our way. I can't bear to think we made her feel unwelcome. This was meant to be such a special time. It could have been, should have been, so different. I don't know how to fix this right now. But Neil is right, she can't stay; we need to be alone together. Mum can come back or we can go there once Milly's settled in. It's not unreasonable, but I still feel wretched about the way it's happened.

We're watching the train approach when Mum puts her hand on my arm. 'Could you do something for me?'

'Of course.'

'The adoption hearing. Is there any possibility you could postpone it for a bit?'

Neil's planning to submit the application as soon as we get the go-ahead. Milly has marked the date of the final review on the calendar with a red flower in felt-tip pen. Monday

2 October. One month to go. All being well, this will mark the end of the trial period and we should get permission to apply for the adoption order. Shona says sometimes it can be just a couple of months for everything to go through. We could be a proper family by Christmas. 'Why do you want to postpone it?'

She shakes her head. 'Don't worry. If it's a problem. I shouldn't have said.' But something's worrying her.

'What is it?'

She hesitates. The train draws closer. 'It's just that I'm waiting for a date for my knee operation. I've been waiting so long and I'm in so much pain, but if it clashes with the adoption date, then...'

She wants to come and celebrate with us. She wants to be part of it. Everything – all the irritation and hurt is dissolved by this simple fact. My mother wants this as much as I do. We can be a family.

'It won't clash.'

'But it will take me a while to recover. And travelling up here... It's such a special day...' She smiles at me. Beseeching. She does understand, after all. It matters to her. She's planning to travel up. She's prepared to make that concession, finally. 'The day you become a family.' I will have my mother with me the day I become a mother. There are tears in her eyes. I pull her towards me. She's so much smaller in my embrace than I remember. More fragile. She shudders and I feel terrible. 'I don't want to miss it,' she sobs into my shoulder as the train comes to a halt in front of us.

'Don't worry,' I say, rubbing her back. 'You won't miss it. We'll work something out.'

# Chapter 10

Shona and Helen have come to discuss the 'incident'. Mum taking Milly and the resulting police search must be formally discussed and documented. Shona has reassured me there's nothing to worry about, but there is Mum's claim that Neil wasn't in the house to deal with and I'm still sick with nerves.

The trial period was going so well, but nothing is confirmed yet. On 2 October, if nothing goes wrong, we can apply for an adoption hearing at which, hopefully, we'll be approved as adopters and Milly will become our child in law. Only then will we be a Forever Family. We are not there yet.

There have been many visits over the last three months. Shona and Helen came once a week to check on Milly from the day she was placed in June, until the first formal review meeting at the beginning of July. That was a milestone for us. All those women lined up on the sofa: Shona, representing us, Helen, not much more than a girl herself, and the reviewing officer, a large woman with a flushed complexion and breathing difficulties. I can't remember her name, I was too busy worrying that she might have a heart attack at any moment. They'd come to talk, but most importantly to observe. This trio of women, clearly overworked and under-resourced, struggling to create some semblance of order for children escaping chaos, were gathered in our home to decide whether Milly should stay with us. They were relieved, I think, to see her settled. I told myself that, given the difficult situations they all deal with on a day-to-day basis, we were probably a bit of a treat, an unusually happy scenario and a job well done, but this niggling little voice in my head kept whispering: What if they don't trust what they see? What if they dig a little deeper?

That voice is bellowing at me now: What if they think our family is too much of a mess? What if this business with Mum tips the balance? I'm terrified that Milly might say something to suggest she's unhappy. Shona, Helen and the reviewing officer left the last review meeting full of praise for how well Milly was doing, what a great home we were providing, what good coffee and delicious cake. We didn't expect to see any of them again until October. But that was before Mum got involved. Before I sent that bloody photo and jeopardised everything. I should have talked to Neil. I should have talked to Mum. Sending the photo without any other communication was cowardly. It was irresponsible and this is the consequence. It's only 5 September and they're back. They're digging deeper.

Shona removes her files from a dove-grey handbag. The reviewing officer shakes our hands and collapses onto the sofa with a huff. I realise that she's introduced herself and once again I wasn't listening. Lisa? Linda? There's something about her demeanour that reminds me of my O-level Physics teacher, who'd bark instructions that I could never retain. This woman is watching us both carefully, her gaze sliding from Neil to me, to Milly. I can see her assessing, sifting, making her judgement.

Shona writes notes in longhand on sheets of lined A4 paper. What has she added to that file since Friday? Her bag is leather. Expensive. Knowing Shona, it's a sale item. She's a shrewd shopper with an eye for quality, happy to disclose the bargains she's discovered: a new discount outlet in Barrow, a sale rail, a clever find in the indoor market. She may have changed her mind about us as a family and be wondering if she's made a mistake. Does she believe Neil left Milly unattended?

'*I know about you.*' What did Mum mean? Why did he flinch?

Helen sifts through her paperwork, leans over and says something to the reviewing officer in a low voice. Shona straightens her spine, wriggling her shoulders into place. I've seen her slicing her way up and down the pool during the early morning lanes. I prefer the more leisurely lunchtime sessions. Shona thought we deserved to be parents. She thought we'd make good parents. Does she still think that?

Neil places three cups of coffee on the table in front of the three women. Strong, black for Shona, white and milky for the other two. The reviewing officer asks for sugar and Neil hurries out to get it, returning to sit down beside me. We're facing the bay window and the view across the tarn. Shona sits to the left of the window on the smaller sofa, knees drawn together, file on her lap. The reviewing officer and Helen sit on the longer sofa beneath the window. Shona smiles. That's a good sign. She has a generous smile. One of the things that's always impressed me about Shona is how she listens. She doesn't think she has all the answers and she doesn't make assumptions. I cling to this.

She asks, 'Is your mother still here?'

'She left this morning.' I glance at Neil. When I look back all three women are watching us.

Helen asks, 'Is everything all right?'

Neil answers, 'It wasn't a good time. It was confusing for Milly. I thought it was best if she gave us a bit of space.'

Shona nods, looking at me. 'What about you, Eve?'

I don't want to be disloyal to Neil, but I can't lie. 'It's difficult for me. She's my mum. I don't want to exclude her.'

Shona nods. 'But this is your time with Milly and that's important, Eve. More important than your mother's feelings.'

I can feel Neil's relief beside me. They're right. But that doesn't make it easier. 'I should have explained it to her. I should have talked to her before she came.'

Neil places a reassuring hand over mine. 'She should have talked to us,' he says calmly, 'instead of just turning up.' Is it me, or does he sound a little smug now she's gone?

Shona leans in closer to Neil. 'Can you tell me what happened on Friday? What was your experience in the run-up to Milly's disappearance?'

'I went in to get the drinks. Milly was fine in the garden.'

The reviewing officer asks, 'How long were you gone?'

He shakes his head. 'Not long. I don't know. The radio was on.' He frowns. 'Some sort of comedy? I was half listening to the story. I made the sandwiches and when I went back out she was gone.'

Had he made the sandwiches before he did the drinks? If he had, then he would only have been gone for a few minutes. How long does it take to pour orange juice? But if he had to make sandwiches, then that would have taken longer. What was he listening to? One of those thirty-minute comedy things that are on mid-morning on Radio 4. The reviewing officer is making notes, so is Shona. Helen is watching us both. They aren't asking these questions. Why am I asking these questions?

Shona asks, 'The front door was closed?'

'I didn't close it. I wouldn't. Why would I?'

I interrupt. 'The wind must have blown it shut.'

Shona remains focused on Neil. 'You didn't hear your mother-in-law knock?'

'She didn't knock.'

Helen and the reviewing officer exchange a look. Shona says, 'She says she came around to the back of the house.'

He sighs, and then he says, 'She's a liar.'

The words land in the room like a brick through the window. How could he say that? In front of these people? I look down at my feet, unable to watch the reaction he's caused. I'm trembling. This is not Neil. Neil is diplomatic. Neil knows what's at stake here. I want to speak, to tiptoe over this, but the broken shards of this word litter the floor and I'm frightened to put a foot wrong.

He's called my mother a liar, but has he been entirely honest? How long was Milly on her own? Is he angry because Mum's caught him out? I appeal to Shona. 'Will this mess things up for us? It was a mistake. It wasn't intentional. I don't know about the door. She might have got the wrong gate when she came around the back – they're all very similar, you need to count your way up. She thought no one was in. She didn't mean any harm. And Milly was safe.'

Shona looks at me for a moment. 'Have you explained the situation to your mother? How the adoption process works?

Milly is still the responsibility of the local authority. There are procedures that need to be followed.'

'I'm sorry. She didn't realise. I've explained to her now.'

Shona nods and turns to Neil. 'So you can confirm you were in the house all the time, preparing the lunch?'

'Yes.' One word. Solid. Heavy. Fact.

*I know about you.* What does she think she knows?

We wait as Shona writes something down that I can't read from where I'm sitting. Outside, a delivery truck is reversing, the insistent beep of the sensor piercing the silence. Eventually Shona places the papers back in her file and looks across at the reviewing officer and Helen. A silent communication between them. They discussed this before they came. Shona will have made our case to the best of her ability. Is it enough? Have we proved ourselves?

The reviewing officer gives a nod. Shona turns back to us. 'It seems this was all an unfortunate misunderstanding. What's important is Milly's well-being. I would be a little more careful about leaving her unattended, particularly in that lower garden on the other side of the street. I know it's a private access road, but vehicles do still move up and down it. And the wall between your garden and park needs some attention.' A smile. She's on our side. A reprieve. I hadn't realised how tightly I'd been clenched until this moment. I feel the blood returning to my muscles. 'I think it would be a good idea for you to have a chat with your mum, Eve, and try to establish some boundaries. It's important that you bond with Milly before you start introducing her to extended family.'

Neil exhales and his body relaxes. Is his relief simply to do with Milly, or is it more than that? He says, 'Thank you,' as if he's been vindicated, but the word 'liar' still reverberates in my ears. Why is he so keen to keep Mum at a distance? He told her he was afraid of her. Why is he afraid of her?

There are places I feel I cannot go with Neil. Bruised places. I am not going to press on those bruises. We all have our wounds.

I know that Neil went through a dark period when he turned eighteen. His family joked about it, saying they were relieved when he met me and snapped out of it. He always dismissed it, 'I was a bit of an arse to everyone,' clearly embarrassed, 'said and did some stupid things,' but never entered into any detail and I hadn't pushed. At first I assumed he'd just been a bit moody and hormonal, but then at one of our early sessions with Shona, he told her he'd made contact with his birth mother just after his eighteenth birthday. I was stunned by this. He'd never said a word to me about it. We'd been discussing adoption for months. Why didn't he confide in me? When I asked him, later, after Shona had gone, he told me he hadn't meant to say anything. That it just came out. He hadn't mentioned it to me because he didn't want to remember. It was a very upsetting experience and he just wanted to put it behind him. That explains his dark period. Whatever happened with his birth mother disturbed him. He told Shona he met her once. It was 'disappointing' for them both. He didn't want to say any more. Shona accepted that and, eventually, so did I.

The reviewing officer smiles. Helen smiles. Everyone is relieved. Everyone wants this to work. The reviewing officer says, brightly, 'So, not long now before you can apply for the adoption order.'

Shona looks at us expectantly and I should be delighted, but all I want to do right now is cry.

Helen says, 'Shona mentioned something about you having a welcoming ceremony of some kind for Milly? That's a nice idea. There is the celebration hearing at the magistrates' court, but it can be a bit dry. It's a special day. Nice to make an occasion of it.'

I take a deep breath. 'About the hearing.' Neil stills beside me. 'I was wondering, is it a problem if we postpone?'

Shona looks at Neil. I can't. He's stiff, but says nothing, waiting. 'Mum would like to be there. I'd like her to be there.' I place my hand on Neil's thigh, willing him to keep his cool. 'Like you say, it's a special occasion.' I'm looking at Shona, appealing to her, but it's Neil I'm addressing. He's called my mother a liar. He's implied that she deliberately set out to create trouble for us, for me, but that's not true. She meddles and she's insensitive, but she isn't malicious. He's sore because she's suspicious of him, but she'll always be suspicious. My mother was betrayed by the man she loved and she'll never trust a man again. Neil knows this. He should be more understanding. I'm her only child. She's only looking out for me in the same way I'd look out for Milly. If he was a little less hostile towards her, if he could try and be a bit more patient and not make it so obvious how much she irritates him, she might back off a bit. I want my mother in my life. It might make it easier for him if she wasn't but that's too bad. I say to Shona, 'It's the day we become a family, that I become a mother, and I'd like my mum to be here.' Neil's thigh is rock hard beneath my palm.

Shona is nodding understanding. 'Of course.'

'The thing is, she's waiting for a knee operation and she's worried that it might clash.'

Neil shakes his head. His voice is low. 'No, Eve. No.'

'Neil, listen!'

'She can change the date of her operation, if she has to.'

'But it's a long waiting list. And there's the recovery period. She won't be able to travel for a while.'

'That could take weeks.'

I look at Shona. 'Is it a problem if we wait? What does it mean?'

'Well,' Shona adjusts the file on her knee, 'you need to do this when you're ready. It's a big step.'

'We are ready!' There's a slash of anxiety through Neil's voice. 'We've got one month to go. Milly's marked it on the calendar.' He turns to me. 'What message is it giving her if we stall?'

I know what he's saying makes sense, but it's not that simple. I can see Mum's swollen eyes, feel her juddering body inside my arms. She wants to be part of this. I want her to be part of this.

Neil is watching me, his face puckered. '*Milly*, Eve. This is about *Milly*.' I know, I know, but Mum wants to be here. I want her here. His eyes are fixed on mine like two pins. 'You want us to tell Milly to wait?'

The room is silent. Neil's right. I can't do this to Milly. How could I even consider it? What kind of mother am I if I fail to put my child first? I shake my head. 'No, no.' But how am I going to explain this to Mum? If she takes offence and refuses to speak to me or come and visit, she will miss out on such an important period in Milly's life and our opportunity to create a different, more healthy relationship will be lost.

Shona says, 'This needn't be a problem.' A reassuring smile. She appreciates that it's possible to be infuriated by someone's behaviour but forgive it. She understands how difficult it was for me to be estranged from my mother. The loss. The grief I felt. It's worse than death. If your mother dies you are sympathised with, supported. This is a situation society understands; there is a language for it, a recognised protocol. But to exclude your mother from your life is something else entirely. It is, quite simply, unacceptable. People assume there must be something wrong with you, that you are somehow lacking in compassion or the generosity that is expected of an adult daughter. The mother-daughter bond is revered. Daughters do not cut off from their mothers and mothers do not give up on their daughters. It's unforgiveable.

I don't want this shame within my family, because that was how it felt for those two years while we had no contact; shameful. I avoided the subject of mothers in conversations with people locally. I remember Kath touching on the subject so gently, assuming my mother was dead. I almost let her continue believing that, but I had to come clean, and I found myself stammering, trying to explain, sounding as if I was justifying myself or hiding something. I don't want Milly to be part of that, to witness me struggling with it, or to feel it herself. She deserves better. Other people manage to make it work and so will we. Shona confided in me once that her own mother was a demanding woman, unable to see things from anyone else's point of view, but she still has a relationship with her. I'm sure it takes a monumental amount of patience and resilience but she has pulled it off and I will too.

She explains, 'It's not the adoption hearing that adopters attend. I go to that on your behalf. You're confusing it with the celebration hearing. That's what Helen was referring to. That takes place at the magistrates' court about four to six weeks after the adoption order has been agreed by the judge.'

Neil says, 'You mean she won't be legally adopted for another two or three months?'

'No, no.' Shona shakes her head. 'The celebration hearing is automatic. Milly will be legally adopted the moment the adoption order is agreed, and I'll phone to let you know that decision as soon as I leave the court, but the celebratory hearing will be some time after that and it may be possible to rearrange that date if your mother is recuperating.'

The reviewing officer clears her throat. 'We may be jumping the gun a bit here.' Cold creeping up my spine. I hold my breath. 'I'm sure Shona will have mentioned this, but just to be clear: Claire may still contest the adoption.'

'But she's had no contact with Milly for almost a year.'

Helen answers. 'It can happen. If Claire has managed to turn things around and persuades the judge that she deserves another chance, the adoption order may not be given.'

Neil's voice is small and thin as a thread. 'She could take her back?'

I'm momentarily paralysed. I think Shona did explain this. I know, somehow, that this is not new information, but when we were presented with this possibility, months ago, we were confident, certain that we were offering Milly a much healthier, more stable environment. It was almost preposterous to consider a better option for Milly might be to stay with Claire. But the last few days have shaken that confidence. We've seen Milly worried, at times distressed. She's witnessed arguments and hostility. We have not been the perfect family we hoped to be. It is no longer preposterous to consider she may be better off elsewhere.

It's only now the gravity of it hits me. Because while I was afraid that Mum's accusation, the police search, that whole ugly episode might delay things, I always believed we'd pull through. There was a possibility Milly might be returned to her foster family, but Ruth was on our side that Milly was better off with us. This is different. This is Milly's mother. Her claim is greater than mine.

Helen is talking. I try to focus. 'If Claire appealed, I'd have to ask for more time. I'd explain to the judge that there had been a development with the birth family that required assessment.'

I need to stop her. 'But it's not likely. She's had so many chances. Why would it be different now?'

The reviewing officer says, 'Birth parents do sometimes attend the adoption hearing.'

Neil snaps back, '*They* can and we can't?'

I wince. There is no room in this scenario for Neil's outrage. There is no room for us to be anything other than a perfect option right now because Milly needs to be safe. The purpose of this adoption is to improve her circumstances, not exchange one dysfunctional family for another. The reviewing officer continues in her flat, horrid voice. I hate her. I want her and Helen to leave. I want Shona to reassure us, to remind us how unlikely this scenario is, but she keeps talking. 'It's their last opportunity to contest the adoption. If the judge feels they have a case, the adoption order can be postponed while matters are investigated further. We'd need to schedule more visits to reassess the mother's circumstances.'

'Claire may give it one last shot,' Shona adds, before the reviewing officer catches her breath, 'but there is no indication, at this stage, that her circumstances have changed. Let's not dwell on this now. What's important is that you continue with your plans and assume the best. Postponing the celebration for your mother is neither here nor there in terms of the legal process.'

It's as if my heart has stopped beating. I'm not Milly's mother. She may call me Mummy, but the truth is, I'm not.

Claire may come back for Milly. She may clean up, get somewhere to live and want her child back. And if she does that for Milly, who am I to stop her? If she can provide a safe, loving environment for her daughter, with the support of two doting grandparents, then she can offer more than I can right now.

A flash of memory: Milly running towards the adventure playground at Brockhole, hesitating, looking to us for reassurance. And Milly grabbing at Neil's legs as he walks through the door, waiting to be scooped up into his arms. Milly's little hand reaching up to grasp mine. Milly turning the pages of the life-story book we created to introduce her to our world. I bought an enormous A2 artist's pad and filled it with photographs of me and Neil, the places we've been on our travels, the world tour, Australia, the year teaching in an English language school in Greece, our wedding day, the delayed honeymoon to Rome (Mum had a fall and we had to postpone until she could manage on her own). I've decorated the pages of the book with coloured pencil drawings, little maps, handwritten annotations and glittery stickers. Milly likes to look at that book before she goes to sleep, drinking us up. She's happy with us. She wants to be here. We have to do our best for her. We have to prove ourselves.

Shona stands up. 'I'll leave the two of you to talk it through.'

I stand, trembling. I've been so stupid, worrying about Mum and Neil and their petty little spats, when I should have been thinking about Milly. This is all about Milly. She needs us.

Neil's on his feet, shifting his weight from one foot to the other, trying to contain his frustration. I want them to go.

Shona adjusts the strap of her bag on her shoulder and looks at me. She places her hand on my arm. 'Be confident. Milly's happy. This is the right place for her to be.'

'I know.' And I do. I must make sure, to the best of my ability, that we remain, at the very least, a viable option.

Neil follows us into the hall and calls out goodbye as Shona makes her way down the front path. She waves. Helen is already closing the passenger door of a silver Ford. The reviewing officer is at the wheel. She twists in her seat to throw her bag into the back. They're talking. What will they be saying about us now? I wait until Shona's out of earshot and turn to face Neil.

'How could you say that about Mum in front of them?' He frowns. 'What is Shona going to think?'

'You think she doesn't know already?' He shakes his head and turns away from me. 'Why Eve? Why do you let her do this to us?'

'You're scared of her.'

'Yes! Yes, I'm scared of her. She's toxic! Can't you see how dangerous this is? We could lose Milly! We could lose everything!'

We could lose Milly. He's right, and I'm responsible. I sent the photograph. I let her stay. I let her plant little worms of doubt into my head about Neil, about us, about my ability to be a mother. I was about to postpone the adoption hearing. But it's Milly I need to be thinking about. We need to press ahead. We must focus on 2 October and get this adoption approved. And if that means keeping Mum away from here for the time being, that's what we'll do.

# Chapter 11

The new school term started on Wednesday and Neil has been back at work. Things are scratchy between us right now. It's like it used to be when we were living in Hitchin and Mum was just around the corner. She does this to us. That's why we moved away. Neil's right. I need to to establish some firmer boundaries. I'm a mother now, with a daughter of my own, and I don't want this to affect Milly. I want my relationship with my daughter to be different. None of that claustrophobia and neediness. I want Milly to be free of all that. If I lead by example, my mother might follow.

Milly doesn't start school until next week, which has given us day after day to enjoy just hanging out, the two of us, before I go back to work. Lizzie has covered my days at the park. We've been to Coniston on the bus (Milly's request) and fed the ducks at the lake edge in the grey gloom. It was a bit wild and windy so we sheltered behind the glass veranda of the Bluebird Café and had plump curls of Cumberland sausage for lunch. Yesterday we drove further into the lakes and took the Ratty Railway, from Eskdale to Ravenglass and back, in the drizzle. Milly loved the tiny open carriages and made friends with another little girl and her lively sheepdog which kept jumping on us with its muddy paws. Milly's been begging for a dog since she arrived and Neil's keen, having grown up with dogs himself, but I'm not so sure. I've never had a dog and, with work and Milly, it might be too big a commitment.

It's Sunday. Neil has gone out for a few hours on his bike and we've decided to have a lazy day at home and bake a cake together. Milly is assembling the ingredients on the table. She's done a lot of baking with her nana and wants to show me how it's done. The doorbell is an interruption neither of us is too pleased about. Leaving Milly to continue her preparations, I go to see who it is.

Dawn, our squeaky-clean neighbour from a few doors up, is waiting on the doorstep. Perfectly straightened amber and honey highlights, ironed jeans and a crisp white shirt. Even the soles of her trainers gleam. She's holding a plastic doll's house and a bulging cotton shopping bag.

'Oh, hello, Eve,' she says, breathlessly, as if I've surprised her by opening the door. Milly wanders into the hall behind me and Dawn leans forward, as if drawn by a magnet, her face creasing into an even smile exposing straight, white teeth. There's something slightly manic about her expression. 'Is this Milly?' Her voice has risen in pitch, that irritating thing some people do when they talk to children. 'Hello, Milly! I'm Dawn. I live in the blue house up the street. It's so lovely to meet you. I've brought you some toys.'

I'm touched. Dawn has never really had much to say to me, though she's always polite and cheerful, waving as she glides past in her white Mini. She never appears to walk anywhere. A woman with things to do, people to meet, places to be. She's waiting to be invited in. I hesitate. Dawn's house is immaculate. She has regular parties for the neighbours: 'Drinks and Nibbles' to celebrate her latest extension or make-over. The Plaster and Paint van is permanently parked outside the house. I open the door and usher her in to the living room, not wanting her to see the mess in the kitchen. I love this room, with its comfy sofas, the view over the tarn, the way the light falls. At night, with the fire glowing in the hearth and candles burning on the marble mantelpiece, it's inviting, but I'm painfully aware of how shabby it all looks in the sunlight. There are cobwebs above the bay window, the rug is tattered around the edges and grubby from coal dust and the sofas have seen better days. Dawn has designer chairs in funky modern upholstery, Farrow and Ball walls and full-length Orla Kiely print curtains. If I'd had any warning I would have rushed through with the hoover and dusted the shelves, but it would have made no difference and I console myself that I've spared myself the effort. I suspect that when Dawn leaves here she'll phone her polished friends and bitch about what a state my house is in. Do I care? I look at Milly, eyeing the doll's house. No, I don't.

I'd like to connect with other mums. Not Dawn, her children are older and we have very little in common, but other mums with children Milly's age. Lizzie's great, but she's quite a bit younger than me. India has been helpful, but her son is a teenager. Milly needs friends. If I was back in Hitchin there would be friends from school I could hook up with now. Naz has twin boys and we keep in touch by email and Facebook, but we haven't met up since I stopped going down to Mum's, and she hasn't been here because one of her twins,

Cameron, has severe disabilities, mental and physical, and going anywhere with him is an enormous upheaval. They do get respite care, but it's sporadic and they need to prioritise that time for Max, the other twin, to redress the balance. Naz is stoic and blunt about the situation. This is the hand she's been dealt and she makes the best of it.

We were asked if we'd be prepared to adopt a child with a disability. I remember looking down the crude tick box list on the form, horrified. Would we be prepared to accept a child with a visual impairment? A hearing impairment? A physical disability? Asperger's? Autism? Down's? How do you answer a question like that? We wanted a family. I was happy to accept whatever they offered us. How could I say, 'No thank you, I don't want something that's less than perfect'? I thought of Naz. When the teachers asked Naz what she wanted to do when she left school she didn't hesitate: 'Foreign Correspondent.' She was going to be the next Kate Adie. She never wanted children. She was working for a tabloid in London, getting some experience on a national paper and doing freelance features for local radio, but she was hungry to get into television with an interview lined up to take part in a scheme for working-class Asian women to get them into broadcasting. I'd persuaded her to go for it. She'd been reluctant, wanting to achieve on her own merit, needing to prove to herself that she could do it regardless of the colour of her skin, but that route would have taken so much longer. It was all about to happen for her when she discovered she was pregnant. There was never a doubt in her mind that she'd go through with the pregnancy. She saw it as a temporary break. Her partner, Stu, would share the childcare, he'd probably be better at it than her, it was all sorted, but they weren't anticipating twins. And they weren't anticipating Cam's complex and challenging needs. If Naz could cope with all that, how could I say no to anything?

Shona took the decision out of our hands. 'There's no point in you adopting a child with a physical disability.' She put a firm cross in the box. 'You're both physically fit and active,' she explained. 'Play to your strengths. You can offer an excellent home to a child with a lot of surplus energy who requires physical challenges. Besides, you have a house on three floors with too many stairs.'

And so it went on. I hesitated over the possibility of Down's Syndrome. She shook her head. 'But at my age, if I got pregnant I might well have a child with Down's and I'd be fine with that.'

She nodded. 'In that situation, you would have no choice, and I've no doubt you'd embrace that child and provide them with the love and care they needed. However, you do have a choice and you must ask yourself if this is the best use of your skills and talents. You could do it, Eve, but do you want to? Really? If you were going to be a stay-at-home mum, then I'd say, yes, but that isn't the case. You told me yourself, you want to go back to work. You have a degree, a job, have a career you love, it's important to you and that's fine. You must be honest with yourself about *your* needs. If you try to be something you're not then this adoption will break down and we don't want that to happen.'

I called Naz. It was weak of me. I knew her answer, but I had to hear it from her. I had to be given permission. She didn't hesitate. 'Say no. Say no to anything that will restrict your life unnecessarily. You aren't doing this for charity. And anyway, you'd be crap. You're too much of a control freak.'

'Ouch.'

'OK. Unfair. You like things to be nice. To run smoothly. Nothing is nice and nothing runs smoothly when you've got a child with a disability. I can do this. I'm pretty good at it. I wish I didn't have to do it, but shit happens. You wouldn't last five minutes.'

Dear Naz, setting me free in her usual sledgehammer style. I took Shona's advice and, as we made our way through that list the following week, I began to feel better about my decision. Our decision. Neil was happy to be steered by Shona, relieved. When it came to questions about the child's psychological history I was on firmer ground. Were we prepared to take a child that was born as a result of rape? Incest? I was surprised to find that I was OK with this, though Neil was quite resistant at first. Shona pushed me, asking if we'd be able to find a way to discuss such a tricky subject with the child as it became appropriate, and I can understand why some people might baulk at this, but I think I could find a language, a story to share that was honest and kind. I could work with Neil and enable that discussion and make it safe. He wasn't comfortable at all with this scenario but I talked it through with him and, in the end, he agreed, as long as I was happy to take responsibility for it. Having a child with a traumatic history requires a different sort of courage. I believe I have that courage and those ticks in those boxes made me feel better about all the crosses that had preceded them.

Dawn kneels on the rug and tips out the contents of the bag: dolls and furniture in bold, primary colours. 'This used to belong to my girls. I have two little girls, just like you.'

Not so little. Dawn's daughters are teenagers. Glossy, thoroughbred girls with long, lean limbs. I wonder how Dawn would have dealt with a child with a disability?

Everything in her world is so perfect. I could imagine she would have unravelled, but who knows? Maybe she would have risen to the challenge. A dependent child, that could never leave, might have suited Dawn. The dolls she's brought are a little family with a mother, a father, a girl and a boy. All white, of course, and there's no wheelchair, but there is a rubbery dog. Milly's eyes widen with anticipation. I'm going to have to give in to a dog eventually.

Dawn opens the front of the doll's house and starts to put things inside. I think she's more excited than Milly is. I was never a fan of dolls when I was a child and I didn't have a doll's house myself. Should we have bought one for Milly? I watch her inching forward. Dawn holds out the girl doll. She has two wiry orange plaits and a pinafore. Dawn smiles then turns back to the doll's house, giving Milly time to make up her mind.

There is no incest or rape in Milly's story, at least as far as we know. Milly's mother's drug problem is a familiar scenario with many young children and babies given up, or taken away, for adoption. Claire has remained stubbornly silent on the subject of Milly's father. We suspect she doesn't know who it was. She's tried, but has been unable to stay clean and even her parents have decided adoption is the best way forward. It's a sad enough story to tell a young child, but it's no secret. Milly has been coping with her mother's weaknesses all her life. She's been lucky to have two loving, stable grandparents to care for her. Her foster mother, Ruth, and Helen, her social worker, made a life-story book with her that we look at regularly and keep on the shelf in her bedroom so she can reach it whenever she wants. There are photographs of her mother and grandparents and the world she came from, as well as the foster family, who are now a significant part of Milly's history. Her life-story book is less popular than the one we created for her about us, but Shona tells me that's normal and healthy. She's investing in this life, but she'll come back to the old one when she's ready, and when she does, there will be no burden to disclose. It's our responsibility to keep that book to hand, to be there to talk, to leave the door open so Milly can walk in any time she needs to. We can do that.

If we get that far. What if Claire does manage to turn it around at the eleventh hour?

Slowly, gathering courage, Milly creeps over and kneels on the rug. Dawn hands her the doll. 'Shall we sit her on a chair? Where do you think she'd be? In the living room? Or maybe she's sitting on her bed?' Dawn is kind. The high-pitched voice is irritating, but she likes children. I feel I should kneel with them and play with the doll's house too, but it's not really my thing and there's something about the way Dawn and Milly are interacting that doesn't invite me in. If I'm honest, playing with Milly bores me. Does that make me a terrible mother? Dawn is so good at this. She clearly loves it. Should I love it? Maybe I'm too old. I've lost the ability to play. I don't mind board games, but creating imaginary worlds, playing with dolls, doesn't work for me. I like being with Milly, I like doing things with her, but I don't want to play. I'm not like Dawn; she was a full-time mum and I could never be that. Would Claire play with Milly? Would she be there, full time? Could she be a better mother than me?

Milly's mesmerised. Dawn is in her element. I ask her if she'd like a tea or coffee, eager to escape before they see my distress. 'Coffee would be lovely,' she replies, taking the opportunity to get up, brushing her knees. I try not to think it's a comment on the state of my floor. She follows me to the door. Glancing back at Milly and lowering her voice, she asks, 'How is your mum?' There's something about her tone. Concern and something else, something creeping, cloying. She steps closer, lowering her voice a little more. 'She seemed quite upset.'

'When?' Dawn has never said more than a sentence to me at any one time before today: a comment on the weather, a welcome drink at her parties before she drifts off to more important guests. Why would Mum talk to Dawn? What has she said?

'After the search.' Of course. Dawn will have seen the police cars, the helicopter. 'She felt awful. Not that you can blame Neil for being angry. It must have been terrifying for the two of you.' She's looking for gossip. Her face is hungry for it. I feel a wave of nausea and swallow it down. 'She said he wasn't in the house when she knocked?'

I need to escape before Dawn sees the effect she's had. 'Milk and sugar?' I stretch my mouth into a smile, but the rest of my face refuses to follow. She hesitates. I don't want her to think there's a problem here. 'It was a misunderstanding. Mum's fine.' And I walk out of the room quickly.

In the kitchen, I lean against the work surface, trying to steady the tremor rippling through me. How could Mum be so indiscreet? Why would she talk to Dawn about Neil?

The phone rings. I grab it, relieved to have something to distract me. 'Evangeline?' Before I can confront her, my mother's voice breaks into a sob.

# Chapter 12

We're in Hitchin, my home town. I'm in the house I grew up in with my mother downstairs in her usual spot, sunk into the armchair under the window, watching a black and white film on the old TV.

I told her I was tired and after putting Milly to bed I'd probably get an early night myself. She's not happy but I don't have the patience to sit with her this evening and I can't take any more food. My mother is always trying to force food down me. There was a beef casserole waiting for us when we arrived last night, which I felt obliged to eat, though I had told her not to get dinner ready because I'd be stopping at services to break the journey for Milly and she would need to eat earlier. Tonight, she presented us with a huge tray of lasagne which would have fed six people. I've had to undo the zip on my jeans I'm so bloated. And then she produced tiramisu. One spoonful and I had to admit defeat. She was so offended by this you'd have thought she made the damned thing herself.

I'm furious with her right now. I drove for six hours in heavy traffic yesterday, in a state of anxiety, with a young child, believing my mother to be seriously injured, only to find her greeting us at the door with a smile, as if nothing was wrong. To be fair, she was limping, and she's clearly in pain from the fall, but it was hardly the emergency she made it out to be. It was all a ruse to get me down here and I fell for it. Neil's right, I am a bloody fool.

I'm in my old bed, in a room that hasn't been decorated since I was fifteen. Floor-to-ceiling wallpaper with pink roses. It's always given me a headache to look at it, but I can't tell her that. She stripped, repapered and painted it all herself, with curtains she ran up on the old Singer sewing machine that stands under the window in the box room off her bedroom. That's where she's made up a bed for Milly. More roses. More pink. How could I say that I didn't like pink? That the roses were too much? That I'd have preferred to choose and, if I'd been able to choose, I would have chosen plain white walls? Calm. Order. I'd have happily done it myself. Stripped the awful Disney scenes she'd chosen when I was five, enjoyed ripping each piece back to expose the bare wall beneath. There'd have been something empowering about that process. A rite of passage. Instead I had her surprise, delivered in vibrant pink with added roses. I've never liked pink. Why doesn't she know that?

I want to be with Milly. She could have slept with me but Mum had already made up the little fold-out bed, 'All nice and cosy for you!' off her bedroom. Milly wasn't convinced and asked me to stay with her until she fell asleep. I should have brought her in here, but I didn't want to start a row, and when I went through Mum's room to check, Milly was sleeping quite soundly, one arm flung out above her head, mouth open. I'm constantly surprised by how tired she gets. Processing all these new experiences drains her as much as any physical exertion. She was meant to attend her introductory sessions at school this week. I was looking forward to connecting with other mums in the playground, starting to build the network that we'll need, but that will have to wait. The school have gone to a lot of trouble to rearrange the timetable to accommodate Milly's absence, arranging additional sessions next week, I can't mess them about any more. We're here now. Neil is coming down at the weekend and we're going to visit his parents in Stevenage. There is no point in driving another six hours all the way back north now only to travel back down again and we can't let Betty and Mike down. They've invited Neil's sisters and Milly's new cousins are looking forward to meeting her. I'll have to make the best of it. Maybe here, in her world, Mum might win Milly over. We can share some memories of my childhood, Mum will love that and it might be fun for me and Milly.

I call Neil. He's not in a great mood. The first weeks of term after the long summer break, with the new intake, are always tiring and he'll be missing us. My question is automatic – 'What's up?' – but as I deliver it I feel a sudden anxiety, as if I've stepped off a path and taken a route that was more precarious than I anticipated. When he tells me we've had a letter from social services about Milly's mum, I can taste the bile at the back of my throat. I don't want to discuss this over the phone. I want to be at home, face to face, dealing with it together.

'She wants regular supervised contact with Milly.'

So, Claire is not simply going to accept what's happening. I'm almost relieved. I realise now I've been quietly waiting for this, shrinking at the possibility but unable to tackle it. Now it's in the open it's easier to confront. They warned us. Shona tried to play it down, 'Sometimes it's simply that they want to be seen to be doing the right thing,' but in Claire's case I believe it's more complicated and raw than that. She's losing her mother and that will pull her closer to her daughter. I can't deny a mother access to her child. I feel enormously privileged to be adopting Milly. 'This could be good news. It means she's accepting the adoption is going ahead. She isn't planning to contest it.'

But Neil is less positive. 'She had four years to prove herself and failed. This isn't good for Milly.' I wish I could see his face. There's fear behind what he's saying. His own experience with his birth mother will be on his mind. As far as he's concerned Betty and Mike are his parents. 'It's not about blood,' he's said, more than once. 'It's about being there.'

But sometimes there can be love, even if someone can't physically be there. Is it right to deny that?

We end the call, frosty with one another. He's too harsh, his judgement coloured by his own experience, and I'm too weak, always worrying about everyone else. But it's more than that, I want to do the right thing. I want Milly to know I did the right thing. Her mother wants contact; who am I to deny that?

Too wired to go to sleep, I head downstairs. Mum is still in the wing-backed chair half watching a soap she's recorded, a fresh glass of sherry on the side table in front of her. 'Do you have any more of that?'

She looks at me over her glasses, clocks my mood and nods to the drinks cabinet. 'Help yourself.'

I'm not a sherry drinker, but right now anything will do. The room is warm and cosy. I remember sitting here when I was a teenager, watching the weekly episode of *Inspector Morse*, a family sized bar of Cadbury's Fruit and Nut on the coffee table between us, broken into squares. Me and Mum in our own little world. I was safe here. I was loved and I took that love for granted. Milly hasn't had that from Claire, but she had her grandparents to provide stability. How important is Claire in Milly's life? Neil's right, I must put Milly's needs first, but if she is with us, if she's in a stable environment, with support, then a supervised visit once a year might work. It would be unsettling, but cutting off all contact might be worse and would leave Milly with a dilemma at eighteen. More vulnerable to an experience like Neil's. Far more unsettling to visit a stranger at eighteen and try to make sense of that relationship.

'What's worrying you, Evangeline?'

I hesitate. I'm not sure it's right to discuss this with Mum. I know Neil wouldn't want me to, but I need to talk to someone. 'Claire, Milly's mum, has been in touch.'

She raises an eyebrow. 'What's going on?'

'She'd like contact with Milly.'

My mother snorts. 'You've got to be joking!'

'Supervised. And probably only once a year.'

'What on earth for?'

'She is her birth mother.'

'So? What has she done for that child since she's given birth to her?'

The moment is shattered. I shouldn't have talked to her about this in so much detail. This is Milly's story. Mum is unlikely to be respectful of Milly's privacy. If she talked to Dawn, who else might she talk to? What if she says something next time she's visiting Tarnside? She might mention Millie's 'druggie mum' in town, and Milly will have to grow up with that shadow over her. Someone like Dawn wouldn't hesitate to spread that information across her network, like an itchy rash. Mums. Kids. Neighbours. Milly has the right to create her own story. Her past is something she should be able to choose to share, or not.

'Mum, do you think you could try and be a bit more discreet? This is confidential information.'

'Not between us.'

'It's a sensitive issue.'

'I understand that.'

'So, if you could avoid terms like "druggie"?'

'Well, pardon me for not being PC. I won't say another word.' She sips her sherry. 'What does Neil think about this contact thing? Does he believe it's a good idea for the child to carry on seeing her mother?'

I sigh. 'No, he doesn't. He thinks we need to put Milly first. She's had enough disruption in her life. What she needs now is stability, a clear routine and I can see his point, but this is her mother.'

'*You're* her mother!' Mum is on her feet, her face pink with indignation. 'For God's sake, Evangeline! Where's your gumption? Where's your self-respect? This is a wonderful and generous thing you're doing and I'm so terribly proud of you, but you must remember that you have rights too. And you have feelings. You have to put yourself first.'

'You're proud of me?' Everything else she's said falls away, leaving that one word upright and gleaming. She is proud of me, for adopting Milly, for creating a family.

'Of course, I'm proud of you!' Her eyes fill with tears. She sniffs them back. 'I've always been proud of you! Haven't I told you that, over and over, all your life?'

I stand up, put my arms around her, sink into the familiar folds, a relieved child. My mother is proud of me. She loves me. 'I thought you didn't approve?'

She pulls away to reach for a tissue, wiping her eyes, blowing her nose. 'I'm sorry if I gave you that impression. It wasn't my intention. I...' she hesitates, 'I was simply giving you some space. Isn't that how Neil puts it? It was clear that, for whatever reason, you preferred to pursue your life without me.'

'That's not true!'

She holds her palm up to stop me. 'My mistake. He...' She hesitates.

'He what?'

'Anyway, I understand now.' She frowns to herself, as if she's working something out.

'Did Neil say something to you?'

She shakes her head, dismissively. 'It doesn't matter.'

'Did he tell you not to contact us?' I thought she was sulking. I thought she was punishing me for not visiting. Did Neil warn her off?

She squeezes me tight. 'I love you. I'll always support you in everything you do.' Her voice is choked with emotion.

'What did Neil say?'

But she won't be drawn on this. It's unlike her not to take the opportunity to put him in the wrong. This makes it worse. He must have said something to her. I can imagine him losing his temper, telling her to leave me, us, in peace, but why would she pay attention to that? My mum's a fighter, she wouldn't give up that easily. Why did she listen to him? What did he say? I remember venting to him about her, how she suffocates me, how I struggle to get free of her, but these were emotional rants, not something I'd ever want her to hear. Did he repeat any of this? My guts clench at the thought of her hearing that I find her suffocating. How deeply that would have hurt her. Did he tell her?

He let me think she was ignoring me. He let me believe that my mother didn't want to speak to me. He saw how much that hurt me, and said nothing?

She sniffs again and blinks, tears brimming. 'I hoped that you'd have a child of your own, of course, what mother wouldn't? A babe in arms.' She sighs. 'A five-year-old... But it is what it is. She's your daughter now. You need to think about yourself. Why should you be driving all that way, putting yourself out, to meet a girl who couldn't be bothered to look after her own child? She probably won't even turn up.'

She has a point there. We tried to meet Claire once before. Neil and I took a day off work and drove up to Carlisle. We waited, with her social worker, in the family centre, for an hour, but she never came, and, with hindsight, we decided this was for the best and made the decision to play safe and remain anonymous. I imagine sitting in that bland room on the royal blue chairs with Milly, at some point in the future, watching the clock eating away at the time, making excuses, trying to distract her. I want to protect her from that. But what if Claire turns it around? What if she does manage to take control of her life and Milly, when she's eighteen, finds out I denied contact? How will she feel about that?

Mum says, 'Tell them to go hang. The whole damned family.'

'I can't do that.'

'You can. They're lucky to have you, Evangeline. You do it on your terms.'

'It's not about me, it's about Milly. She has a good relationship with her grandparents. They're kind people and they love her. She'd be devastated if she couldn't see them again and she'd never forgive us.'

'She'll forget soon enough.'

'It's not an option, Mum. We've agreed she will have contact with her grandparents.'

'But not her. Neil doesn't want contact with the mother.'

'Neil thinks that this is an opportunity to make a clean break from Claire and we should grab it, for Milly's sake.'

'For *your* sake! For once, I'm in agreement with him.'

'I'll talk to Shona.'

My mother groans. 'Why do you have to make life so difficult for yourself?'


Back upstairs, I feel adrift. As if I've lost my compass. What did Neil say to Mum to stop her calling? Was it deliberate, or did she misinterpret him? I pick up the phone. His voice is heavy with sleep. My old alarm clock with its splayed feet and bells on either side tells me it's gone midnight. 'Sorry! Sorry.'

'What's wrong?'

'Nothing.' He waits. 'Did you say anything to Mum, after we moved? Did you warn her off?'

He's quiet for a moment. 'What's she said?'

'She didn't. I just... It sounded like she was keeping a distance because she thought that's what you, what I, wanted.'

'She told you I said that?'

'No, no.'

'What exactly did she say, Eve?'

'I can't remember. It wasn't what she said, it was just… look, forget it.' Why did I open my big mouth? Now I've created more friction between them. Memories of that hotel room. The New York skyline. What it must have cost, all the planning that went into it, the Christmas surprise of a lifetime, but all I could do was fret about her. Why is it always so difficult? Why did she have to choose that same weekend to throw a party? Neil said it was deliberate, that he'd told her about New York, but she denied it. 'He said he wanted to take you somewhere special. I thought he meant a meal somewhere, maybe a night away. And then he went ahead and booked flights without saying a word to me!' I did think about postponing, but Naz soon put me straight. 'If you don't get on that bloody flight, I will!' she said, refusing to attend Mum's stupid party even if it did go ahead.

'I'm sorry.' I sigh, trying to articulate what I'm feeling. 'I miss you. Milly's asleep in the box room and Mum's getting ready for bed so I can't get to her, and you're all the way up there and I feel, I don't know, sort of lost.'

He's silent. 'What do you want me to say, Eve?' His tone is weary. We've been here before, so many times. I'd hoped, with Milly, it would be easier, but it isn't; if anything it's more difficult. He gives a long sigh and all that love vibrates down the line. I wish I could reach him now. I need those arms around me.

'I feel that we were this unit and now we're all separated.'

He's quiet for a long time and I'm wondering if he's fallen back asleep when, finally, he says, 'That's what she does, Eve.'

# Chapter 13

I wake late the next morning, my head thick and throbbing. My mother has the heating on full blast and sealed windows. I search for a key along the window sill, but can't find one. Downstairs I can hear her moving around in the kitchen, talking, and Milly's voice, answering questions. When I get to the kitchen Milly's standing on a stool, wearing a little apron and brandishing a sieve. The battered Kenwood Chef is on the kitchen counter along with the rusty kitchen scales and Mum's ancient *Reader's Digest* recipe book.

'We're making a cake!' says Milly, brightly. Mum's face is flushed and she's wiping a dusting of flour from the kitchen surface with the corner of her apron. She's never been a baker. She's a competent cook, generally. The portions are excessive and the dishes she favours are a bit stodgy for me, though perfectly tasty. She can make a cake for an occasion if she must, but it's no pleasure for her. I suspect this activity was Milly's suggestion. This is a good sign.

'That sounds delicious.' Maybe this wasn't a wasted trip after all. Maybe it will prove to be a bonding opportunity for Mum and Milly. On her own patch, Mum might be a little more amenable.

She doesn't sound amenable. 'What a mess you've made! Do you think you could try and get some of it in the bowl?'

I offer to help but Mum waves me away with a wooden spoon. 'No, no! You get your breakfast and leave us to it.'

'It's fine. I don't need any breakfast—'

'Nonsense. Most important meal of the day. There's a bowl of that muesli stuff you like on the dining room table, I got it in that fancy new deli they've opened, and fresh fruit and yoghurt in the fridge.'

I look at Milly but she's frowning at the recipe book, pretending to read the small print, while my mother hovers, anxiously awaiting the next spillage. I'm not needed nor wanted here, so I take a couple of headache tablets and do as I'm told. It was thoughtful of Mum to get me muesli. When I was growing up, breakfast was thick porridge with whole milk and golden syrup. The very thought of it makes my stomach churn.

There's an insulated jug of weak coffee on the table in the dining room. I fill a mug, drink it black, swallowing the pills, and pour a small helping of muesli, but I can't eat it. The lasagne from last night is still working its way through my system. The window in here is also locked, but I find a key beside the plant pot and shove it open, thrusting my face out into the cool air and breathing deep. If I had my trainers I'd go for a run but, in the hurry to leave, I forgot them. I sit back down in the silent room alone, listening to Milly's continual chatter next door, feeling childishly excluded. Why am I in here on my own? I thought this would be a time for the three of us to be together. I want Milly to bond with Mum but I want to be part of that too. Is that selfish? I take my bowl and empty the contents into a plant pot, spreading the soil over the top with my fingertips to hide the evidence.

Mum keeps a selection of board games in the sideboard. We used to play on Sunday afternoons when we'd cleared the table and washed the pots from the weekly roast. She would put on a story tape in the background, *Anne of Green Gables*, or *Little Women*, and we'd play quietly, breaking the silence with the occasional protest as a counter was sent back to base. Happy times. Maybe we can recreate that with Milly now.

The sideboard is wide and low, in a sixties design which I always thought was old-fashioned and ugly but now looks quite stylish. It has a door on each side and four drawers in the centre. I open the door on the left and retrieve a battered box of Ludo, but the dice are missing. Mum keeps loose change, paperclips and other random bits and pieces in the top drawer of the sideboard, but there are no dice in there either. The second drawer down has envelopes of various sizes and stamps. The drawer below has passports, Mum's most recent and a stack of old ones with the corners cut off. I spend a few moments looking at my old photographs, my crooked front teeth before the brace, the heavy fringe. When I pull out the final drawer I discover letters. Crumpled airmail envelopes with foreign stamps from around the world. My scrawled handwriting an exotic reminder of another time. I pull one out and unfold the translucent sheet. Neil's name sings out from the page again and again. Memories flood back: the weight of my pack digging into my shoulders, lifting it away from my back as I walked, to dry the sweat.

Bare feet in heavy-duty sandals, grinning brown faces with sparkling eyes and white, white teeth, temples and beaches and shacks serving food, starry nights spent stretched out on the sand.

There are about a dozen letters in this pile. A similar pile for the Australian adventure, a few from the year we spent teaching in Greece, but by then we were able to maintain regular telephone contact. One letter a month. How she must have waited for these, pored over every word, drinking it up. How distant I must have seemed. I try and imagine myself, waiting for news of Milly, unable to contact her, utterly powerless. No wonder she was frantic. No wonder she sobbed down the line whenever she accepted my calls from far-flung telegraph offices. I was so irritated by her need of me, but now, I can imagine how she felt.

As I go to replace the letters I notice a scrap of paper, crumpled where it's got trapped towards the back of the drawer. I smooth it out. It's not airmail thin, but a thicker piece, torn from the back of an envelope, the triangular fold and strip of glue still visible. The writing is unfamiliar, but the name at the top stops my breath: William Leonard.

My father.

My hands are trembling. I can hear Mum grumbling in the kitchen, Milly approaching. I shove the address in my pocket, sliding the drawer shut.


We find the dice in the Snakes and Ladders box. Milly is eager, never having played Ludo before. Mum's reluctant at first, but we manage to persuade her to join us while the cake is in the oven. Milly unfolds the board and I help her set out the counters. 'Which colour do you want to be, Milly?'

'I'll be red,' says Mum. She was always red when we played together.

Mum told me she didn't know where my father was. He left when I was not much more than a baby and she never heard from him again. I have no memories. There are no photographs. She told me she burned them all after he'd gone.

Milly frowns. 'Me be red. Pleeeeease.'

I try and persuade Milly to take another colour. 'You can be green, yellow or blue. Why don't you take blue? That's a lovely colour.' I can feel my chest tighten.

Why does she have his address?

'Want red!'

Mum snaps back, 'Well, I've chosen red.'

Neither of them is going to budge and I don't know what to do. All I can think about is the letter. Did he write to her? Was he asking after me? Milly shakes her head, her mouth set in a stubborn line. 'I choosed red. I want red.'

'I want doesn't get.'

I try and laugh this off. 'Come on, Mum.'

'Fine.' Mum pushes the board around so the red counters are in front of Milly. Why didn't she tell me she had his address?

A memory: I'm thirteen years old, sitting at this same table. She is sitting opposite with my maths homework open in front of her. I want to be at Naz's. It's her birthday and there's a party. I wanted to get there early to help set up, so I rushed the homework, but she insists on checking it before I can go. 'I'm disappointed in you, Evangeline.' She shakes her head. A long silence for me to register this sufficiently. 'Just like him.' I know she's talking about my father. She doesn't do this often, but when she does it's like she shines a torch on something inside me. 'Always looking for a shortcut, hoping for someone else to bail him out.' I don't want to be like him, but what he's planted is deep and festering. 'Well, I'm here to teach you there are no shortcuts in this life. If you want something you have to work for it.' She is here to help me be a better person. She loves me, despite the rot inside. She is my ally. I don't seek details from her because she is protecting me from the rancid truth.

I shudder. I don't want to be here now. It's like playing Ludo with two children, Milly smugly triumphant, Mum seething with resentment, and I'm stuck in the middle, trying to keep the peace, and so the game continues and it's not a bonding experience but an excruciating ordeal and my mind is elsewhere, trying to make sense of it, trying to understand why he wrote, why she kept the address.

Mum lightens up as soon as she starts winning and there's something rather ugly about this. When she gleefully snatches the last of Milly's counters and sends it back to base, Milly's eyes brim with fat, wobbling tears. I snap, 'Mum!'

'What?'

'This is a game. It's meant to be fun! Milly's never played before.'

She looks at Milly. 'You took my counter. Fair's fair.'

The tension around the table is sour in my mouth and I've no doubt Milly can taste it too. I stroke her head. 'Do you want to stop, darling?'

She nods. Mum gives a loud tut. 'Nobody likes a poor loser, young lady.'

'That's enough.' I take Milly's hand and lead her out of the room without looking up. I'm not in the mood to see my mother's injured face right now.

*

There's nowhere to go but my bedroom. It's raining outside and this house is so small. I can feel the walls creeping in, the ceiling lowering towards our heads. There's no escape. I want to get away. I want to get Milly away. Where did Mum get that address? When? Has she been in contact with him? Spoken to him? Seen him?

I find my old Ladybird books and pull out a copy of *Little Red Riding Hood*. This edition was published in 1974, three years before I was born. On the cover is a painted image of a rosy-cheeked girl, in a red hooded cape, and a small deer, which reminds me of Bambi. We curl up together on my bed with the book. Milly can't read, but the pictures fascinate her. While she examines each page in detail, I take out the scrap of paper.

Milly glances up. 'What's that?'

'Nothing important. You look at your book.'

Is it important? Maybe she contacted him, but he wrote back to say he didn't want to know. Maybe she didn't tell me because she didn't want me to feel rejected again.

Milly pokes at the page in front of her. 'Grandma!'

I look down. She's right. The picture does look like my mother: apple cheeks and a kindly smile. But looks can be deceptive. My mother is no gentle granny, she's made of steel. A proud woman. If she did get in touch with him, it will have been for my sake. There was a time, when I was fourteen, fifteen and she was struggling, that she might have gone to him for help. And I did ask about him then, seeking an alternative, more liberal parent who might allow me the freedom I craved. What was her response? *'Forget about him, Evangeline. He doesn't want us. Good riddance to bad rubbish.'*

Outside the bedroom window, the birds sheltering among the branches of the old apple tree vie for attention. We can't see them, and I don't know which birds make which sound, but Milly decides to give them names and I half listen, smiling and encouraging, suggesting Trish for the bird that trills, while Milly insists on Monty for the one that croaks and there's Wendy the warbler and Letitia who titters, but my thoughts are tugged back to this father who left and never came back.

Eventually, Mum calls us and we head dutifully back downstairs. The Ludo has been cleared away. I can't look Mum in the eye, but she doesn't seem to notice. 'Do you think you could pop to the shop?' she asks. 'There's a few bits I need.'

I grab the opportunity to escape the house and am about to suggest we stop at the swing park when Mum gives Milly a little push towards the living room. 'There's a DVD on the table. Do you know how to put it on?'

Milly doesn't need to be asked twice. The film is *Bedknobs and Broomsticks*. Memories of damp winter afternoons snuggled up next to Mum on the sofa. I clap my hands in delight, 'I *love* this film!' Has she remembered this? Is she trying to make amends for the Ludo fiasco?

She looks tired. Elderly. Red Riding Hood's grandma. No one will ever love me like she does. She should have talked to me about my father. I should be angry, but it's difficult to be angry with someone who is acting out of love. She will have been protecting me. Right now, we're making progress. Milly is the focus. 'Shall we watch the film together when we get back from town?'

'Let her watch it while you get the shopping and then you and I can have a little catch-up when you get back. I've barely seen you.' She presses the list into my hand. 'You can get everything in Sainsbury's.' Milly is examining the DVD cover. Mum takes it from her. 'We'll put it in the machine.' As Milly settles herself down on the sofa, perfectly happy, I feel flat and a bit tearful, which is silly. Milly would clearly prefer to watch a film and I need to get out of this house and get some air.

I walk past Sainsbury's and turn off the main road towards the residential streets. The shopping can wait. Something is stirring inside me, that I hadn't realised was dozing, and it isn't comfortable. I left Hitchin for university at nineteen and I have been leaving it ever since and yet here I am again. It's like a loop I can't escape. My first attempt was university, but I was back every few weekends and for much of the holidays. Then Neil and I spent a year travelling. Mum was frantic. It was something we'd been planning since we first got together and I knew it wasn't going to be easy, but we worked up to it slowly. Every summer through the university years we went on mini expeditions for weeks at a time. Europe first, then South-East Asia and India. A week after I graduated, Neil took me to Trailfinders in London to book a round-the-world ticket. He'd been working for a year, saving for the trip, and was desperate to get away as soon as possible. All the staff were young travellers, fresh from their own adventures, full of enthusiasm and I wanted a taste of what they had. Neil was so determined to prevent Mum scuppering our plans, he lent me the money for my flight. There was no going back.

We had to come back, of course, but it was always temporary, always with another trip in the planning. Australia, then the year teaching in Greece. Neil was good at that, creating little oases of hope until we finally packed up entirely and headed north.

I move into narrower streets with two-storey houses. On the corner, where there used to be a butcher's shop, a girl stands reading a message on her phone. We went travelling before either of us had a mobile, so I was uncontactable for weeks at a time and I remember how delicious that felt. A rope had been severed and I was floating free. Weeks on end where I didn't have to think about anyone but myself. I didn't give Hitchin, or, to my shame, Mum, a second thought. We became almost telepathic, Neil and I, a flow to and fro between us, a rhythm. It's held us together ever since. We could never have that freedom now with phones to connect us at any moment. That ease, being utterly selfish, without responsibilities, came at a price, of course, as everything does. As we approached any major city with a telephone exchange I'd become increasingly anxious, dreading the call home, my mother's tears, the guilt that would creep like a shadow into the pool of sunlight we'd created between us.

I try and imagine how it must have been for her when I started to spread my wings. She'd been abandoned by William. She'd had to cope alone, to build a life for the two of us, with no help. She'd kept me on track, a firm grip, but I was going to leave her eventually. University. Neil. Travelling. She was losing me. Was that when she contacted him?

His address is in London. Is he still there? What took him there? He lived in this town once. He will have walked along this street. Did he come back, like I have, and feel the same disconnection? The same person but different, in this familiar place that's not so familiar any more. There are patterns imprinted in my bones that nudge me in certain directions. This was the route I took for my swimming lessons in the outdoor pool, holding Mum's hand – I must have been about six or seven – then through my teens, with

Naz, flip-flops, silly sunglasses and beach towels, whatever the weather. I can still remember the excitement of the new indoor pool that was built beside the outdoor one. A few years later, I would walk this way to meet Neil from work when he finished his shift as a lifeguard, and then with Naz and her boys, taking my turn pushing the double buggy on a Sunday morning. I'm a child, a teenager, a grown woman. Daughter, best friend, girlfriend and now mother. Local girl and a visitor from some other place. My multiple identities scuff and rub against one another.

And William Leonard has known none of them. My father. A stranger.

But he was here once, with me. There may be another version of me that walked this street with her daddy, a version I have lost.

She chose not to keep the letter, just the address from the back of the envelope. Maybe he didn't write to her. Maybe he wrote to me.

If I'd received a letter back then I would have wanted to know more. I would have been afraid, but I might have contacted him. A letter, not a phone call. Safer, more distance, no need to interact, but an opportunity to find out some details. But if he had written to me, she would have seen the letter before I did. She always collected the post in the morning. She could have chosen to hide it but I don't think she would have done that. She wouldn't have needed to. She would have stood over me while I read it. She would have been involved. And I wouldn't have been able to hurt her. If she'd shown me a letter back then I'd have thrown it away. I would have had to.

I try and imagine him now. An elderly man. If he's still alive. All those years. Did he meet someone else? I may have half siblings. I have his address. I could contact him without Mum knowing now. I could do it without hurting her.

I'll talk to Neil. I could write to William. I can't call him Dad. Dad is a foreign word on my tongue. He'll never be Dad to me. I realise that, until now, he'd been as good as dead in my mind. I had no memories, Mum never talked about him except as an unpleasant episode in her life to be forgotten; he simply didn't exist any more. But now he does. He's been in the world all this time, moving through it, forming relationships with other people, friends, family. He exists. He is no longer so easy to dismiss. I will write. I'll find out more, but I won't tell Mum anything about it for now. I may never need to tell her. There may be nothing to tell.

I turn the corner and stop outside the little terraced property that was my first independent home. This was Mum's gift. She has been generous to me, to us. Without her help, Neil and I would not have the house we live in today, with its space and light, the views over the tarn. Milly would not have that additional garden with her trampoline. My mother has never had much money, but she is canny. She put down the deposit and got in tenants to cover the mortgage until we were ready to move in. I remember holding Neil's hand, wandering through the empty rooms, thinking, this is the beginning of the rest of my life. The house is double glazed, thanks to her generosity. Neil preferred the original windows, but she insisted. 'It's important to be warm, Evangeline.' The front door, which we painted olive green, is now a deep cinnamon. It looks classy. The small front garden with the privet hedge dividing it from the street has been thoroughly weeded and trimmed back. I try to imagine us in this house now. Me, Neil and Milly. Our car parked on the street outside. I like the cinnamon front door. It's a much smaller house than the one we have in Tarnside, but if we lived here it's probably as much as we would be able to afford. Neil might still be working at his old school or any one of a number of secondary schools within driving distance. I might be travelling a bit further afield, possibly into London. I wouldn't have a flexible job on my doorstep the way I do in Tarnside and I'd probably have to work full time. Mum would be a constant in our lives, which Neil wouldn't like, but that might be easier than her coming to stay and being under the same roof with us day in day out. This was the future she imagined when she bought me this house.

This is what she did for me. William was not part of that. He has no claim on me.

I turn away and head back to the town centre. It was a good start for us, but I don't want to live in Hitchin. I don't regret the move north. Neil was right. It was an opportunity for both of us. The park job, the head of sixth form. But more than that. I'd miss Tarnside now. I like the life we're building there.

# Chapter 14

I'm about to head back via Sainsbury's when Mum phones.
'We're in the café on Sun Street. I've ordered a large pot
of tea and scones. Would you like cream with your scone?'

'I don't want a scone.'

'Don't be silly. I'll see you in a moment.' She hangs up.

The café is quiet when I enter. A low-ceilinged Tudor
building with middle-aged waitresses in white aprons serving
traditional afternoon tea. Mum is sitting at a table with
Milly and a pale, twitchy woman I don't recognise. White
hair, papery skin.

'Why are we meeting in a café when you've made a cake
at home?'

'Oh,' she waves her hand dismissively, 'it didn't rise. I want
you to meet my friend. Ann, this is my daughter, Evangeline.
Evangeline, this is Ann.'

Ann shifts in her seat, fiddling with her cuff. All the colour
seems to have been sucked out of her, even her clothes. She
looks desperate to escape, hovering just above her seat,

neither sitting nor quite standing, clearly unsure what to do. I walk over, 'Please, don't get up,' and hold out my hand to shake. 'It's nice to meet you.'

She nods her head, a nervous smile fixed to her face. She's about my mother's age, knee-length skirt, sensible shoes.

'How do you and Mum know each other?'

'Oh, we only met last week. I volunteer in the charity shop.'

'Mum in a charity shop?' I look at my mother. She nods, as if this is completely in character. The woman who insisted on soaking my charity shop purchases in disinfectant, wrinkling her nose in disgust at the thought of 'other people's sweat'? She once shrank a beautiful cashmere cardigan by putting it on a hot wash. I have never seen her set foot inside a charity shop.

Ann says nervously, 'She was looking for a DVD. I think it was for your daughter.' She looks down at Milly and her face changes dramatically, all the anxiety dissolving into something warm and longing. She pulls at the edge of a handkerchief tucked inside the sleeve of her cardigan. 'Did you like the film?'

Milly glares at my mother. 'Grandma stopped it.'

Mum ignores her. 'Ann has a daughter, a couple of years younger than you. Tina. Tina Lord?'

Milly points at a photograph on the menu. 'Can I have tea with rose petals?'

I have no idea who Mum's talking about. 'I'm afraid I didn't know Tina.'

Mum adds, 'But Neil knew her.'

I shrug. 'Before my time.' Ann plucks at her handkerchief and glances towards the window. I feel I should say something, so, out of courtesy I ask Ann, 'How is Tina?'

Another glance at the window, those fingers tearing at her

sleeve. 'Tina's doing well. Thank you.' She glances at Milly and blinks.

Mum says, 'She lives in the north now, like you,' clearly prompting Ann to elaborate, but Ann is looking back towards the window.

Milly tugs at my sleeve. 'Mummy? Can I have I rose tea?'

Mum cuts in, 'Don't be silly. Children don't drink fancy tea.'

Ann scrambles to her feet, nudging the table. Her handbag strap is tangled in the chair. 'I should be going.'

Mum places a hand on her shoulder and literally pushes her back down. 'I've ordered tea.'

I intervene, 'Mum, leave the poor woman alone.'

Ann manages to disentangle her bag and wriggle free. 'I'm sorry. I can't stay. My husband.' She gestures to the window. A black car has pulled up outside. 'You have a lovely family.' Glancing anxiously at me, she hurries to the door.

Mum gives a sharp tut. Whatever her plan was here, it's been thwarted.

The waitress brings a large pot of tea. Milly has a glass of milk. She's unimpressed. 'I want rose tea. And a cup and saucer.' I tell her to ask the waitress politely. Mum makes it clear she thinks I'm being overindulgent, but I ignore her. There's something else going on here I need to get to the bottom of.

'What are you up to?'

Mum gives a little shrug. 'I wanted to introduce you to my friend.'

My mother doesn't have friends. She appropriates acquaintances for as long as they're useful and then drops them abruptly when they start to irritate. They tend to be nervous, gentle characters who are no match for her. She conducts her life solo and always has. *If you don't rely on anyone they can't let you down.*

'Why was she so nervous?'

'She wanted to meet Milly.'

'She didn't,' says Milly, looking up from her book with a frown. 'She didn't know I was going to be here.'

'I wanted to show off my granddaughter.' Mum raises her shoulders. 'So, shoot me.'

Milly turns back to her book. Another from the Ladybird collection. The image on the page is of a tall brick tower surrounded by forest. I lean across. 'What story are you reading?' She closes the book to show me the cover. I read the tricky word out loud for her, '*Rapunzel.*'

'An ugly witch tooked her from her Mummy and shut her in a tower!'

Mum tuts loudly. '*Took.* There's no such word as tooked.'

Milly looks at me and I give her a wink. I think tooked is great. She'll grow out of these little verbal anomalies all too soon; I'd like to hang onto them for as long as possible.

Milly's tea arrives and there's a lot of fuss about the accoutrements and how to navigate them. Milly's delighted. Mum watches us, rolling her eyes. Her presence is like a heavy weight bearing down on me. I have to get away from her. 'I should give Naz a call and take Milly round to meet her boys.' Naz will give me a bit of perspective. I can already hear her hooting with laughter over the Ludo game. '*You should have cheated, Eve. Nicked one of her counters while she wasn't looking!*' Why didn't I think of that at the time? Why haven't I called Naz? My best friend is within walking distance and I haven't been round to see her or even let her know I'm here. There's something about being back at Mum's, back in that house, that saps my energy. I lose something of myself. I forget I have options.

Mum pulls a face. 'Are you sure you want to take Milly round there?'

'Why not?'

That irritating little wriggle of her shoulders, as if she doesn't want to own what she's about to say. I should stop her, but I can't. 'Won't he frighten her?'

We look at one another across the table. There are so many things I'd like to say right now, but I don't know where to start. Cam's a child, not Frankenstein's monster, but what's the point? My mother's attitude to disability is so outdated and inappropriate it doesn't bear thinking about. There's no point in getting into an argument about this again. I decide it's best to say nothing at all.

'I don't know why you waste your time with that girl.'

I close my eyes. I've heard this so many times over the years. 'She's not a girl any more, Mum, she's a forty-year-old woman.'

'You'll always be girls to me.'

Mum hurries past Sainsbury's, insisting the shopping, that had been so urgent, can now wait until tomorrow. 'I've got a shepherd's pie in the freezer that I made last week. We can defrost that for tea.' I notice she seems to be keeping up a pace, with no evidence of her knee injury.

In the kitchen, on a wire cooling rack, are two perfect sponge cakes side by side. 'I thought you said it didn't rise?'

'I couldn't persuade Ann to come back to the house.'

This was all a set-up. The phone call, the trip down here, the tea-room. My mother knows something about Tina Lord, but, whatever it is, I don't want to hear it. She's scratching around for gossip to cause trouble and I'm not going to let her do it.

We watch the rest of *Bedknobs and Broomsticks*. The three of us, but not all snuggled up on the sofa, because Mum prefers the straight-backed armchair. Milly wriggles up close to me. Three generations together, watching a family film, wasn't this what I wanted?

When the film has finished, I run Milly a bath and tell her she can eat tea in her pyjamas. Once she's settled amid the bubbles with my old rubber duck for entertainment, I head back downstairs to Mum. She's preparing the vegetables for tea. I take a tea towel and dry the bits and pieces on the draining board, bracing myself.

'How *is* Neil?'

'He's fine.'

'He just seemed a little uptight.'

'Really? I can't think why.'

'Now, Evangeline, there's no need to be like that.'

I sigh. 'You wind him up, Mum. You know you do.'

'I'm just worried about you.'

'Well, you don't need to be.'

She looks at me, steeling herself. 'Have you ever thought that might be the reason you can't have a child together?'

'We have a child!' I throw the tea towel onto the work surface. 'She's sitting in the bath right now. Your granddaughter!'

'You know what I mean.'

I thought she was behind me. I thought she understood. 'We always planned to adopt, whether or not we had our own kids. You know this.'

'I know that Neil always planned it, I'm not sure—'

'Don't!'

'They do say that when a couple aren't compatible—'

'We are com—'

'—and they've not managed to find any medical issue. I'm just saying, that with someone else you might—'

'Enough.'

'You deserve a baby.'

'Stop!'

But she keeps going. 'A five-year-old is a huge responsibility and she will always be someone else's child. You wanted a baby, Evangeline. Ever since you were tiny, you assumed, like every girl does, that you would have a baby of your own. Why shouldn't you have that? I want you to have that.'

Deep breaths. 'Milly is everything I could wish for.'

'But she's not a baby.'

'I said STOP!' My mother shrinks back against the hob. 'I don't want you to bring this subject up again!'

She glances at the door nervously. 'Sssshhh. You don't want the child to hear you.'

'MILLY! Her name is MILLY!'


Milly is sitting rigid in the bath with her legs crossed, frowning. When I ask her what's the matter, she tells me, 'I want to go home.'

Did she hear me shouting? Probably. This house is small and the doors were open. I kneel beside the bath, taking the flabby pink sponge and dribbling soapy water down her back.

'Can we go home?' It's a reasonable question. We could leave. We could run away from all this, drive back tomorrow. 'I want Daddy.'

I sigh. 'Me too. But he's driving down on Friday to be with us.'

'Want to go home now!' She bangs her heels against the bottom of the bath, splashing soapy waves up over the side. I know the best thing for Milly right now would be to go back to Tarnside, there's nothing I'd like more than to go home, but we've made a commitment to Neil's family this weekend and we can't let them down. Neil's looking forward to that too. Mum has met Milly and spent time with her, it's only fair that Betty and Mike have the same opportunity. Neil will be here late Friday night, after he's finished for the day. It's a long drive. It will be way past Milly's bedtime by the time he arrives. We'd planned to stay here and go over to his parents on Saturday morning, but I think bedtime is a secondary issue now.

'We'll go with Daddy to Nana Bet and Grandpa Mike's on Friday.'

'What day is it today?'

'Wednesday.' Milly frowns. 'But tomorrow I'll call my friend Naz and we'll spend the day with her and her two boys, how about that?' She doesn't look too sure. 'I'll tell you what. Why don't I phone Daddy? My phone's in my room.'

She pouts. 'Not your room.' At first I don't understand. 'Your room is the blue room with the big bed.' She's talking about mine and Neil's bedroom in Tarnside.

'Yes, you're right. This was my room when I was a little girl, but it isn't my room any more.'

'I want to talk to Daddy!'

'I'll bring you the phone and you can talk to him from the bath, how's that?'

*

I call Neil from the bedroom and vent down the phone, repeating every word Mum said, about our compatibility, about a baby, though I know it'll only make things worse between them, but I need his reassurance, a counterbalance at least. I stop abruptly, spent. I don't mention meeting Ann Lord. I don't mention William. These are things to discuss face to face.

Neil sighs. 'What do you want me to say, Eve?'

I don't know. I sit listening to the silence filling the miles between us. 'I wish I was there, with you.'

Eventually he says, 'Yeah, me too,' but the accusation in those words echoes across the miles that separate us. I shouldn't be here. He told me not to come and he was right, I should have put Milly first. I thought I was doing what any reasonable daughter would do, my mum needed me, but Mum's fine and Milly's miserable and with hindsight I can see it was a bad call.


Milly tells Neil about *Bedknobs and Broomsticks*. I can hear his voice, affectionate, light, on the other end of the line, and feel a pang of jealousy.

Downstairs, Mum has burnt the top of the shepherd's pie. She wasn't expecting us to take so long. I struggle to scrape off the burnt bits for Milly, without looking like I'm making a point, but fail. Mum gives impatient sniffs and stabs at her food, making her feelings abundantly clear. Milly refuses to eat more than three mouthfuls. I shovel food into my mouth, barely pausing for breath and don't stop until my plate's empty, as if this will somehow compensate. Milly asks for cake. Mum makes a barbed comment about dessert only being available to children who have cleared their plate, so

I cut myself a large slice, wrap it in kitchen paper and take Milly up to bed.

Mum calls after me, 'Do you want to watch a film with me when you're done?'

I pretend I haven't heard.

I let Milly eat the cake sitting cross-legged on the matted pink rug in my bedroom. She delights in the subterfuge. I'm not sure what I'm teaching her right now, but it feels good. She brushes her teeth and gets into bed happily enough. Squeezed in alongside my mother's sewing table in the narrow box room, she offers me a minty kiss before I turn out the light.

I can't go back downstairs.

Here I am again, standing in my teenage bedroom, pink roses crowding in on me, my fists clenched at my sides. Powerless. Trapped. My husband is hundreds of miles away missing me and my mother will be waiting for an apology. Torn between the two of them. Who needs me most? What am I supposed to do? What have I achieved by coming here? They're both angry, resentful, feeling let down, and Milly is unhappy.

I feel hot and bloated. I walk slowly into the bathroom and pull the latch across the door. Time expands like a balloon, and I'm trapped inside it, an adult and, simultaneously, that teenage girl again, and all those feelings are back and I'm struggling to breathe, leaning over the sink, my fingers down my throat and I'm heaving and it feels disgusting but satisfying to be taking control, to disgorge that shepherd's pie, the heavy mashed potato and greasy mince, to rid myself of the stodge. And it's bitter and burning, but it's purging and cleansing and I am, momentarily, back in control. I throw back my head and gasp for air.

# Chapter 15

Naz screamed with delight when I called this morning. 'You're here? In Hitchin?'

'I have to get out of this house, Naz. Can I come to you?'

'Oh my God! Eve! I can't believe it! Have you got Milly with you? This is so bloody brilliant! I was going to take the boys to the outdoor pool. It will take me for ever to get my shit together, but I can be there in about an hour, if I shout enough.'

We set off early, despite Mum's best efforts to put me off. 'The outdoor pool? Are you sure it's open?'

'May to October, Mum, every year.'

'I thought it was derelict.'

'No, Mum. I had a look when I passed it yesterday and it was buzzing with people.'

'The sun was out then, it's freezing today. You don't want Milly catching a cold.'

And so it went on, until we were out of the house and

closed the door behind us. I knew Naz would be at least another hour, but I couldn't listen to any more.

Though it's still cool when we arrive, I strip down to my costume. Milly needs no encouragement to do the same, it's all I can do to get her armbands on before she throws herself in. After the chill of Coniston, it feels positively luxurious. I hold her around the waist and tip my head back, the water lapping gently around my ears, stroking my skull. It comes back to me then, last night's dream. It's a dream that haunted my teenage years. In it I'm swimming in the open sea. It's windy, the water choppy, and I'm just about managing to keep my nose above the surface, my legs working hard beneath to tread water. I'm struggling, not with the conditions, but against an increasing pressure determined to push me under, and my legs ache from keeping me afloat. I'm straining my entire body upwards, against this weight. I woke, in the early hours of the morning, that familiar choking, straining to scream, that same low moan issuing from my mouth.

'Are you crying?' Milly wipes her finger along my cheekbone, her face a question.

I shake my head and smile back at her. 'Just a splash from the pool.'

She frowns, watching me carefully, then drops a damp kiss on my lips, like a gift, and it's all I can do not to sob. Forcing a grin, I hoist her high above my head and threaten to throw her back into the water. She screams with delight and begs me, 'Do it! Do it!' landing with an almighty splash, which results in a scolding from the lifeguard and fit of giggles from the pair of us.

*

Naz turns up forty minutes later, trailing towels and bulky bags, gripping Cam firmly by the hand, half dragging him along the poolside, looking back over her shoulder to holler at Max, who's lingering behind, distracted by the shouts of a family playing ball. Naz's twins have milk chocolate skin and Naz's blue-black hair, but Max's hair falls in sleek loose curls to the nape of his neck while Cam's hair is frizzy and cropped short. Max is long and slender, Cam more solid and clumsy with an elastic dribble of saliva that bounces at the corner of his mouth. When he wipes it and then wipes his hand against my arm I struggle not to shudder. I try and persuade myself it's because I have a thing about saliva, but I'm not sure that's true. There's something about a ten-year-old boy not being in control of his bodily functions that disturbs me. How does Naz deal with this? Shona was right when she went through the tick boxes, I would not have coped, and in recognising this I burn with shame.

Naz laughs and hands me a wet wipe. 'Gross! Sorry. He does that.' She gives Cam a playful slap. 'Stop it!' He honks, grins and dribbles some more. She scoops it up with a wipe, grimacing, but there's something more to that gesture, a gentleness, a hint, and then I see it, as she leans her head towards him and peers right into his eyes, a moment between them, and I know that for all her harsh words, all the frustration and anger, she'd fight to the death for this boy. There's something that continues to tether him to her as tightly as if that umbilical cord had never been cut, and Naz accepts this, whilst railing against the injustice of it. I lean across and place my palm against her shoulder blade, sliding it down her back. She stills, not turning, but the gesture's been accepted and I don't need to explain.

Beside us Cam honks and dribbles again. Milly picks up the wet wipe this time and cleans the spittle from his mouth, handing the wipe back to Naz when she's finished, as if this is something she's been doing for years. Cam is simply another new experience in the continuing adventure of her daily life and she's taken him in her stride.

'Mummy?' That word. Her voice saying that, to me, will I ever get used to it? I hope not. I want it always to fill me up, warm and syrupy as it does now. 'Can we go in the water again?'

'Of course.'

She's wearing her new swimming costume (navy blue, plain) which I was smart enough to pack while I was throwing things together. We couldn't come to Hitchin and not go to the outdoor pool.

'Your mummy met your daddy at this pool,' Naz tells her, balancing precariously on one leg, resting a hand on Cam's shoulder for support as she wriggles out of her pumps.

Milly frowns at me. 'Tell me.' It's a command she issues regularly, wanting to know our history, making it part of hers.

'I was seventeen.' I look around the pool and point to a group of girls about that age, sitting in a circle, painting one another's toenails. 'Like those girls over there.'

'We were never like those girls over there!'

Naz is right. The girls I've pointed to are the right age, but they're far more polished and glamorous than Naz and I ever were.

Naz says, 'We were cool.'

'We were not cool!'

She looks offended. 'I was cool. You were cool by proxy.'

I have to concede. Naz always had style. A flair with vintage clothing. 'Fancy dresses from the time your nana and grandma were girls,' I explain to Milly. 'And hats.' I grin at Naz, remembering the trilby and the little flowerpot hat that sat close to her skull, accentuating her cheekbones, and the great floppy seventies number with the silk scarf trailing behind it. 'You wore great hats.'

Naz nods, pleased, then looks down at herself and pulls a face. A faded pair of jeans and a white collarless shirt, but even this has been lifted by a silk scarf loosely draped around her neck, a flash of electric blue. She's filled out and toned things down a little, but she's still got style and when I tell her, she lights up, delighted.

Milly interrupts us. 'Tell me the story!'

I'm suddenly shy. I've never told this story before. When people ask how Neil and I met, I simply tell them he was a lifeguard at the pool. It's a fact, not a story. Milly is watching me, waiting.

Naz says, 'Your daddy was sitting up on that giant chair.' She points to the lifeguard looking down at us and gives him a wave. He doesn't wave back, probably still a little grumpy about our earlier misdemeanour. Milly is impressed. The lifeguard is clearly an important person. Naz looks at me, weighing things up. She's waiting for permission. I'm interested to hear how she's going to present this story. I give a nod. She grins. 'Your mummy was sunbathing by the side of the pool, looking beautiful and glamorous.' I snort with laughter, but Milly is drinking it up. Was I beautiful? I didn't feel it. I remember, too clearly, being horribly conscious of my wobbly white thighs, holding in my belly, envying Naz's taut dark flesh, the way she delighted in her environment with no thought for how she looked. Diving into the water, slicing her way up and down the pool, hoisting herself out, shaking her hair over my goosepimpled, dimpled flesh, honking with laughter, drawing the attention of everyone around us, while I squealed and hid myself beneath a towel. Naz was lean and solid; I was curved and soft. Naz was confident and challenging; I was achingly shy and prone to extreme blushing.

'What happened?' Milly prods.

Naz hesitates. I wait. 'Your mummy didn't want to go in the water.' It was cold. I remember I'd recently permed my hair, at home, very badly. I struggled with my hair as a teenager. Neither curly nor straight, I've learned, over the years, that I can pretty much leave it to its own devices, but I didn't have the experience or the confidence back then to allow it to do that. My hair was caked in gel and I was terrified the pool water would either turn it into rock-hard ringlets or an unmanageable frizz. 'I dragged her in. She was kicking and screaming and clinging to her towel, making a terrible fuss.'

I took the towel in with me. I remember falling sideways, my leg hitting the pool edge, an almighty splash as my ungainly lump broke the surface, water shooting up my nose, struggling to right myself, the sodden towel wrapped around my arm. Flailing, furious. A hand reaching down into the water. Long, lean fingers wrapped around my wrist. The force of that grip. Kicking, shaking the towel loose, feeling his strength pulling me up, my face breaking the surface, gasping for air. Blinking, clearing my eyes to see him staring down at me, the wrinkled concern opening out into a smile. Rusty hair and freckles. He stopped pulling, but didn't let go of my wrist, just stayed absolutely still, waiting for me to catch my breath, smiling patiently.

'Your daddy,' Naz continues, 'jumped down from his throne and rushed to rescue the drowning girl.'

'Did he dive in?'

Naz snorts. 'Oh no. He didn't have to dive in. She wasn't really drowning, just making a lot of fuss to get his attention.'

'That's not true!'

Naz ignores me. 'He reached down and pulled her out.'

He tried, but I was too heavy for him. I had to swim to the steps and climb out, once I'd retrieved my towel from the bottom of the pool, but I don't want to spoil the story.

Milly beams at me, delighted. Naz watches the two of us. I can see she's itching to carry on and tell Milly how Neil turned on her. How he reprimanded her like a schoolteacher, humiliating her in front of everyone at the poolside, threatening to have her banned if she ever did anything as stupid and reckless as that again. But she stops, generous enough to give Milly the edited story, knowing that she doesn't need to tell me how embarrassed and furious she felt in that moment and how it's coloured her opinion of Neil ever since.

She watches me, waiting for the memory to pass between us. I give her a sympathetic smile, let her know I'm grateful for the editing and change the subject. 'Do you remember Tina Lord?'

Naz shakes her head. 'Why?'

I glance at Milly. Naz gets the message. 'Max, take Milly down to the shallow end and show her your handstand.' Milly runs straight off, but I call her back to put on her armbands. She pouts and points to Max.

'He isn't wearing armbands.'

'Max can swim. We'll organise lessons as soon as we get home, I promise.'

'So,' Naz leans forward as soon as Milly's gone, eyebrows raised, 'who is Tina Lord?'

I tell her about Mum's set-up with Ann Lord in the café. Naz frowns. 'Neil's never mentioned her?' I shake my head. She shrugs. 'Ask him.' I chew my lip. She watches me. 'Why can't you ask him?' Too sharp. She knows it's not as simple as that, but she gets impatient when I talk about Neil. To be fair, I did, pretty much, abandon her when he came on the scene. Before Neil, Naz and I were a team, and suddenly I had someone else. She didn't have a boyfriend, said she preferred it that way, though I think some of that was bravado. Naz is full-on and she was a bit much for a lot of boys our age. She raises a fuzzy eyebrow sceptically and says, in an Inspector Poirot voice, 'You think he's hiding something?'

'Stop it!'

She leans back, as if I've pushed her away, resting on her hands, reading me.

I've overreacted. She isn't suggesting anything sinister. There's always been friction between her and Neil. He follows the rules she flouts. He's a suit and tie man; she's a dance naked down the street woman. But there's more to it than that. Neil thinks Naz is a bully. Not intentionally, but she's a strong personality and used to getting her own way. I was shy and pliable. She was the one in control until Neil stepped in.

Things eased up once she got together with Stu. He's nearly ten years older than us, calm, easy in his own skin. He sees through all the colour and noise that Naz hides behind, to the loving, loyal woman inside. To do that requires a degree of tolerance that Neil just doesn't have. He couldn't see that Naz's attitude to him was defensive, a need to show she didn't care, when really, at heart, she was hurt. I let her down. I still feel guilty about that, but I fell in love with Neil, and he was good for me. I felt safe with him in a way I'd never really felt safe before. I know Naz loves me, but she could be impatient and, albeit unintentionally, cruel at times. Neil was always kind. And he offered me an escape from Mum. The travelling, the freedom, the possibility of living a different life. I know Naz understands all this, but she will never forgive Neil for taking me away. She was the one who was meant to escape this small town and claim the world, not me.

'You should come to Tarnside,' I say, meaning it, though I can't picture how it could happen. 'Bring Stu and the kids. We can make it work.'

'Maybe.' But she won't.

'Come on your own. Let Stu have the kids for a couple of days.'

'So we can paint your little market town red?' Tarnside? Where would we start? Tequila slammers at the Crown's quiz night? A burlesque number during the interval at the Roxy? She tilts her head to one side. 'Why have you come down without Neil?'

'Mum had a fall. Couldn't walk apparently.'

Naz snorts and I feel a little guilty. Mum was clearly in a lot of pain when I left today, sitting with her foot up, having overdone it yesterday. It's all right when I'm critical of her, but when Naz or Neil start, I always feel the need to defend her.

She's thoughtful for a moment. 'Are you worried about Tina Lord?'

I shake my head. She frowns, watching me, as if she's waiting for something, but I'm not sure what she's driving at. 'Be careful, Eve.' She hesitates. That cold drip-drip-drip. Goosebumps on my flesh. Her dark eyes are intense. 'You have a family now. You need to protect that.' I'm not sure what she means, but I'm too frightened to ask.

# Chapter 16

Naz is distracted by Cam who's manoeuvred his way towards the pool edge some distance from us to watch the other children playing. She grabs his buoyancy aid and follows him. Milly leaps, bringing her knees up to her chest, and bombs into the water with an almighty splash. Her skinny arms slice the air as she comes back up, her face stretched to the sky, gasping. With a bit of help she'll be swimming like a fish.

Naz throws herself back down onto her towel. 'Look out. Lesley Butler has spotted you. I give it three minutes and she'll be over here, getting the gossip. If it was just me and the boys she'd pretend she didn't recognise me, but you, my darling, are too much to resist.'

Lesley was a classically cool girl at school. The right hair, the right clothes. The girl my mother would have preferred me to choose for a best friend. She was frighteningly sorted in a way that Naz and I never were, always one step ahead, been there, done that, prepared. Not adventures, but calculated steps. Everything was always controlled with Lesley; she passed her driving test, got a job, bought a car, bagged an attractive, if boring, boyfriend with career prospects, got engaged and invited us all to the party. A proper party that was almost a wedding itself, in a hotel with waiters and canapés. She got a mortgage for a pretty little terraced house, had the wedding. Naz and I weren't invited to that (I think we failed to be sufficiently appreciative of the engagement party). She's clearly had the babies too. Girls. One in her early teens looking a little sullen and aloof, the other two or three years younger, licking an ice cream and pulling faces at her sister. Lesley looks much the same. Her hair is shorter, straighter, blonder, but she's still slim and elegant and a little snooty. She's getting to her feet.

'Told you,' says Naz, as Lesley picks her way between the towels and camping chairs.

'Hello? Is it Eve? Eve Leonard? Oh my God! Eve Leonard!' She claps her hands together and does a little jump like a grown-up Shirley Temple. 'I don't believe it!'

'You'd better believe it,' says Naz, tartly.

Lesley ignores her. Milly is climbing out of the pool, heading towards us, dripping. 'Is this your daughter?' I feel stupidly delighted to be able to say yes to this question. Yes, Lesley Butler, I am a mother; I've joined the golden club at last. 'Oh, my God!' She claps again and bends down, from the waist, not crouching the way Dawn from next door did, but bending at the middle, with her legs straight, looking down. 'What's your name, darling?'

'Milly.'

Lesley beams at me. 'She's adorable!'

I think Milly is adorable. But would she be to anyone else? All she did was say her name and yet I'm delighted by this praise. I'm inexplicably proud that Milly has impressed Lesley Butler.

'I didn't know you had a daughter?'

So this is it. Lesley will have heard on the Hitchin grapevine, she saw me in Hitchin, while I was still living here, without any children. Lesley wants the story and though it's a story I should be happy to tell, a story I'm usually eager to tell, I don't want to tell it to Lesley. I don't want to see her clap her hands and say how perfectly lovely all this is. It's Milly who says, 'I'm adopted.'

Lesley's face creases with concern. 'Oh, darling. You poor little mite!' and before I can react to this, looking at me, 'Couldn't you have your own children then?'

'Milly *is* my child.'

'Of course. Of course, she is.' She smiles a plastic smile.

I want to carry on. I want to say that she is not a 'poor little mite', but I don't want to draw any more attention to this crass statement in front of Milly. 'How old are your two?' I ask as I imagine yanking her head back with a handful of that glossy hair. The violence of this image startles me. I'm not that person, I've never been violent, yet something deep inside me has begun to stir; a low growl rumbles through my veins.

Lesley glances back, as if to check they're still the perfect-looking specimens she left behind. 'Iris is thirteen and Violet is almost eight.' Iris chooses that moment to reach across and casually yank the beach towel from under her sister, sending her toppling onto the concrete with a yelp of indignation. Lesley laughs a little stiffly. 'Sisters! Mine was the same. Always teasing. She loves Violet really.'

Naz yawns and says sleepily, 'I was going to call Max Nasturtium if he was a girl. Wild. Bold. Into everything.'

Lesley frowns, unsure if Naz is serious or not. I keep my eyes fixed on Iris and Violet. Naz, always one to take it that step further, continues, 'And Cam over there, he'd have been a dandelion. Pain in the arse weeds. Can never get rid of them.'

Lesley draws back. She just about manages to hang onto her smile. 'I'm sure you don't mean that.'

'I do,' says Naz, that blade in her voice right at the surface now. 'You try changing a nappy a ten-year-old's shat in and you might feel the same.' Lesley's smile crashes to the ground. And though Naz has scored, it's an own goal and she knows it. I watch her glance over to Cam, her face a silent apology.

Lesley swallows and turns to me. 'Well, it's been nice seeing you, Eve.' She resurrects the smile for Milly. 'And you, Milly. You are a lucky little girl.'

I hug Milly to me and say, 'We're the lucky ones,' but what I want to say is that it has nothing to do with luck. That Milly deserves to be loved and nurtured just like any other child. Why should she consider herself lucky?

Lesley nods, 'I do admire you,' and the growl rolls out inside me and I want to roar into her smug little face, but I don't. I turn on my professional voice and wrestle control. 'There's nothing to admire. We wanted a family. Adopting Milly has given us a family. It was entirely selfish.'

Naz says, 'Do you admire me?'

Lesley hesitates. She glances at Cam and quickly away again. 'Of course.' But she doesn't. Here is Naz, playing the brutal card that life's dealt her. Brave. Patient. Self-sacrificing. But Lesley doesn't see that as admirable. It's as if Naz is somehow to blame for the situation she's in. Unlucky. Tarnished. Whereas I'm to be admired. Where's the justice in that? I feel I should say something in Naz's defence.

Something sharp and witty that drives the point home, as Naz would do for me, but I lack her skill.

Lesley says, 'Well, it was lovely seeing you. Have you moved back from wherever it was you went, or are you just visiting?'

I run my hand down Milly's warm back. 'Visiting.'

She nods. 'Well, see you next time.' With a little wave, she swings back to her girls.

Naz says, 'She always was a bitch.' She looks at Milly. 'Sorry. You didn't hear that.'

'I did,' says Milly, matter-of-factly, adding, 'I've heard worse.'

We laugh. I assume this is her nana's phrase. I don't like to think what Milly's heard in her life that she should not have heard, or seen. No doubt we'll discover it over time. Her grandparents were pretty good at protecting her. She's a well-balanced, confident little girl. It could have been so much more difficult. Apart from the odd showdown over clothes and chicken that isn't coated in orange breadcrumbs, Milly has been happy with us. I grab hold of her and squeeze her to me, losing my balance, so the two of us roll onto our backs, laughing up to the sky. She is so delicious. So bright and funny and spilling over with love. Why can't my mother appreciate that? Why can't she share in my joy over this child?

Tears prick my eyes and I sit up, blinking them back furiously, but Milly's seen. Her forehead puckers. 'You're crying again!'

Naz's head snaps round. I turn away. 'No, I'm not. I just laughed a bit too much.'

Max is at the far end of the pool, preparing to dive. Three little girls with bouncy ponytails wait, their skinny legs dangling over the side, toes skimming the water. I sniff, shake myself and try to laugh it off. Naz digs around in the enormous bag she's brought and pulls out her purse. 'Milly, go and prise Max away from his fan club and tell him to get us all an ice cream.'

Eyes huge, Milly snatches the note from Naz's hand and dashes off before she can change her mind.

Naz doesn't ask me what's wrong, she doesn't have to. We've been friends for thirty years. Not all language is spoken. 'I don't know what's the matter with me,' I say, swallowing more tears, struggling to contain this sudden typhoon of emotion. 'Why can't I just be happy? I'm so quick to judge Mum, but she was struggling to manage alone, working full time. She did her best.' Naz waits. I'm not making sense. 'She's so... indifferent. I thought she'd love Milly. How can she not love Milly?'

'Because she's jealous.'

'Jealous?' Of me? It's possible. Mum was a single parent. I have Neil to support me, to talk to, to lean on, and on a practical level, to bring in some of the money and to do stuff that I don't understand or want to understand, like fiddling with the boiler to make it work or changing the wheel on the car if we get a puncture. Typical boy stuff, of course, which makes me wince. I'm such a cliché! I remember Mum having to go out, in her dressing gown, in the middle of the night, to knock on our neighbour's door because she'd discovered a leak in the hot water tank and was worried it might flood the house before she could get a plumber out in the morning. The humiliation of having to ask for help from a man she detested, who made a ritual of griping about the birds she fed because they made a mess on his patio. I can remember the pinched fury of her body as she mopped up after he'd left.

That woman would never have contacted my father. No matter how difficult things were. She would never, never have asked for his help. She didn't write to him. He wrote. And she will have told him where to go. I can picture her tearing the letter into shreds. Furious. *'How dare he!'*

My mother is bitter and lonely. I have Neil. I have a job I love, a beautiful home in the Lake District and now a daughter of my own. I don't have to ask hostile neighbours for help. I don't have to prove day after day that I can manage alone. 'I have the life she never had, I guess.'

'I didn't mean you.' Naz gives me a poke. 'She's jealous of Milly.'

I snort. 'Don't be daft! How could she be jealous of a five-year-old child?' But then I remember the abandoned game of Ludo.

'Eve! Wake up! Your mum always needs to be the centre of your attention. She wants you all to herself. That's why she hates Neil. Why she's always hated me.' I shake my head, but she grins back. 'Oh, come on! I know she slags me off. I don't care! It's you I care about, Eve. I don't give a monkey's what your mum thinks of me, and nor should you.' She wrinkles her nose in sympathy. 'Your mum wants you all to herself. She's your baby; there's no room for Milly.'

Max, Milly and Cam settle with their ice creams a little distance from us. Max has the wipes and regularly cleans his brother's chin, taking his cone to lick the drips. Milly observes them both, her face giving nothing away, storing the details. Is Mum jealous of her? I remember the Play in the Park, Mum insisting she needed a chair, not being able to sit with Milly, waiting for Mum to release me, to say that I should go and put my daughter first. She would never say that, I realise now. Those words would never come from her mouth.

When I look back at Naz, she's frowning at her boys, deep in thought. I'm about to say something about the address I found in the drawer, about William, though I'm not sure what it is I want to say, but she speaks first, without looking at me. 'I sometimes think, if they were both drowning, which one would I save?'

'Jesus, Naz!'

'Don't.'

'What?' She frowns, shaking her head, but still looking towards the pool. 'Don't shut me down like that. If I can't talk to you, who can I talk to?'

'There's no answer to that. How could any parent answer that question?'

'I have to answer it. On some level, every day. Who needs me more?' She watches Max get up, wiping the last of the ice cream from his mouth with the back of his hand. He grins at a group of girls and runs past them, hurling himself into the pool so the water rises like a magnificent sea creature and crashes over them, sending them squealing and dripping in all directions. Naz's eyes do not leave her beautiful boy. 'He needs me too.'

Cam bum-shuffles across the grass towards us, sensing something. Naz sniffs. 'Always liked dandelions. Popping up in the middle of those pristine lawns, burning bright; a miniature sun.' She rubs Cam's hair and wrinkles her nose towards his. 'Cheeky little buggers.' She blows a raspberry into his chest as he giggles and wriggles.

Naz has given herself up to her boys. She had no choice. Her father, rather brutally, suggested she let Cam die and focus on the healthy twin, but Naz wasn't going to do that. She'll never be Kate Adie now, but she'll be something else. She campaigns on behalf of children with disabilities. She's had features on the radio and been interviewed by Jenni Murray on *Woman's Hour*. She may not report back on war-torn countries and international injustices but she'll move things forward closer to home. Perhaps that's what motherhood does? It makes us step back and put someone else first. We take an alternative path and channel our energies differently; we've had our turn, now it's about them. As if she's reading my thoughts, Naz asks, 'If Neil and Milly were both drowning, which one would you save?'

'Naz!'

'Humour me.'

'Milly, of course.'

'And if it was your mum – her or Milly?'

I hesitate. 'This is horrible. Why are you asking this?'

'Why can't you answer it?'

'I can answer it! The answer's the same – Milly!'

'But?'

'No but!' I can feel my face burning. Why is she doing this?

'You hesitated. You didn't hesitate with Neil.'

'Neil's a strong swimmer. Neil can look after himself.'

'And your mum can't?'

'Not as well as him.'

'Maybe.' She pauses, waiting. Not wanting to encourage her, I turn away, but she carries on. Her voice is softer, but the words are just as brutal. 'If Milly was drowning, Neil wouldn't expect you to save him.'

She stops. She doesn't need to spell it out. If I was the one drowning, there's no doubt, Mum would dive straight in and save me. I am her world. No one else comes close.

Mum would let Neil drown.

I refuse to go any further. I cannot think about Milly.

# Chapter 17

We land back at Mum's tired, damp and chirpy.

'Did you have a nice time with Naseema?' Mum always uses Naz's full name. She's trying not to be racist. She tries so hard it has the opposite effect. The first time Naz stayed for tea at our house, Mum asked me, 'What does she eat?'

'Food?'

'I haven't got any curry.'

Seriously. She had no idea. I told Naz and the next time she came around she put on a heavy Indian accent and asked Mum if she could have, 'Some of the special potatoes you are roasting,' and Mum was delighted to oblige, unaware that she was the subject of a joke.

'How is that boy of hers?'

'The disabled one or the normal one?' I ask, channelling Naz.

Mum pulls a face. 'There's no need to be like that.'

'They're both good, in their individual ways, Mum. What

do you want me to say? He got better suddenly? It's all going to be all right?'

'Of course not. Why are you being like this? I was only asking.' She looks hurt.

I take a deep breath. 'Sorry.'

She turns, with an air of purpose, to face Milly. 'You need to hang out those swimming things, young lady.'

'I don't know how to do that.'

'Well, it's time you learned.' Milly looks at me and wrinkles her nose. I offer to do it for her but Mum stops me. 'Milly can take the wet things upstairs to the bathroom and spread them out in the bath for the time being.' She's adopted her schoolteacher voice. Milly gives a low growl. 'Stop that, this instant.'

Milly stamps her foot. 'No!'

Mum looks at me, one eyebrow raised.

'I'll come with you, Milly.'

'For God's sake, Evangeline!'

Milly lowers her head and, looking through her fringe, growls, 'What big teeth you have.'

'I beg your pardon?'

Milly gives a short bark, and then again, 'What. Big. Teeth. You. Have.'

I take her hand. 'Milly, stop. Come on. We'll hang out the things together.'

'You're making a rod for your own back there.'

Milly snatches her hand away and turns on Mum. 'I hate you. I HATE YOU!' and then she pinches her eyes shut and howls.

Mum's face is flushed deep red. 'Stop that! Stop that at once. Do you hear me? I will not tolerate that sort of behaviour in my house.'

'HATE YOU! HATE YOU! HATE YOU!'

'You, young lady, need to be taught some respect!' And before I know what's happening, Mum has grabbed Milly by the arm, raising her off the ground, and slapped her across the back of her bare thigh.

There is a brief second where everything stops.

And then Milly shrieks. One wild, guttural sound projecting a riot of emotions: shock, pain, indignation. I gather her up in my arms and hug her to me. 'Mum!'

'You are ruining that child, Evangeline!'

'How could you?' Milly curls into me sobbing. I check her leg. The pink outline of my mother's hand has appeared like a brand. I can feel the sting on my own flesh, a memory, sharp and hot. Something steams and billows inside me. Something uncontainable. I look at my mother, facing us, still rigid, eyes hard. 'How dare you?'

A flicker of hurt crosses her face before it sets in a belligerent line. 'That child—'

'That child is my daughter!'

'She's controlling you.'

'She's five years old!'

My mother's face is pink with indignation, the hair around her face is damp with sweat. 'She needs to know who the adult is here, Evangeline.'

'Well, it clearly isn't you!'

Shoving her aside, I carry my daughter upstairs.


Milly curls up on my bed with Gerry, her thumb in her mouth. She hasn't sucked her thumb for weeks and seeing her like this is a fist in my gut. I slide down alongside her and she snuggles into my arms reassuringly, allowing me

to smooth her hair back from her sweaty forehead. I wait
for her breathing to steady. Her body slowly softens against
mine. She doesn't want to go back down to Mum and I'm
not about to make her, so I offer cheese on toast in bed and
leave her tucked up with the door closed.

Downstairs, Mum hovers, weighing up the situation,
working out her next move, but I have no time for her
machinations. Naz is right, she's a jealous toddler and she's
crossed the line. If social services find out about this – if
Shona had seen – I feel sick to the stomach. Milly is a 'looked
after' child, at risk. She is meant to be safe with us. We are
meant to protect her. This could jeopardise everything.
I've been naive, thinking that Milly would create a bridge
for us, shifting our relationship to a more equal footing.
That's never going to happen. My mother is stubborn.
She's used to getting what she wants and she doesn't
want Milly.

'It was a little smack. Anyone would think I'd given the
child a severe beating.'

'It's unacceptable. I'm pretty sure it's illegal!'

'Don't be ridiculous. Sometimes, when a child gets themselves into a state like that, a short, sharp smack is what they
need. It never did you any harm.'

There is so much I could say to this. Memories whipping
through me. Humiliation. Fury. Shame. The back of my legs,
a swipe across my shoulders from behind, a cold slap against
my cheek. Flinching, ducking, running up the stairs to be
dragged down by my foot, my chin banging against the stair
edge. 'Milly did not get herself into a state; you upset her.
You didn't get your own way so you resorted to violence.
She's five years old. She's vulnerable and we have a duty to
keep her safe!'

Mum gives a little snort. 'There's nothing vulnerable about her, believe me. She knows exactly what she's doing.'

'And what is it that you think she's doing?'

'This. Creating divisions between you and me. She's jealous. She wants you all to herself and she needs to learn that she can't have that, Evangeline.'

'She's a child. She's been removed from her home. She's struggling with an enormous change in her life. Everything she believed to be stable has gone. It's our responsibility to make her feel safe and loved. We promised to do that!'

'You don't have to spoil her.'

'I'm not spoiling her, I'm being kind. I'm building a relationship.'

'On her terms. She needs to respect you.'

'She needs to trust me.'

Mum shakes her head, as if she knows better, but she doesn't. She would not be a good mother for Milly. She would not have been approved by social services, not with this attitude. We may not be approved if they ever get wind of this. I look at my mum. She has no idea how vulnerable we are right now. I feel so tired. How do I make her understand? Will she ever understand? Maybe Neil's right. The last two years have been so much easier without her around.

'Why is it, Mum, that when we're on our own, when you're not there, everything is fine, but as soon as you're involved—'

'Because she has you to herself then! That's what she wants.'

'Is it? Is it what she wants, Mum? Or is it what *you* want?'

This winds her. Her face hardens. 'How dare you!'

'Are you going to slap me now too?'

A moment. She would like to, but things are different now. Something has changed. She's not used to me fighting back. I can protest, I get grumpy sometimes, but I don't fight like I am now. This is new. Something has been woken in me that I never realised was there. I'm the lioness fighting for my cub. Milly may not be my flesh and blood, she may not have been with us long, but it's there, that instinct. I am a mother. I can do this.

She changes gear. 'Evangeline, sit down. I want to talk to you.'

The words project from my mouth like vomit. 'Why didn't you tell me you had his address?'

She stares at me, uncomprehending.

'William. My dad. You've got his address, torn from the back of an envelope.'

'You've been snooping?'

'No, not snooping. I don't snoop, because I thought there was no reason to snoop. I didn't realise you were lying to me.'

She sighs. 'I haven't lied.'

'You told me you didn't know where he was!'

'The truth is, Evangeline, he didn't want to know.'

'He wrote to me!'

She frowns. 'When?'

'The letter. The letter you destroyed!'

A beat. She's watching me. 'Did you see a letter?'

I hesitate. 'You know I didn't.'

She nods. 'You'd better sit down.'

'I don't want to sit down! Milly needs to eat.'

She takes the bread knife from my trembling hand. I have to keep moving. I fetch the cheese from the fridge, the pickle from the cupboard. It's a different pickle to the one Milly likes, but it will have to do. She probably won't notice given the state she's in.

'He sent a card for your eighteenth birthday. No letter, just a card. And I was angry, yes, on your behalf. How dare he? How dare he send a card, as if that's all it takes, as if he can just step back into your life as soon as the work is done.'

'He wanted to see me!'

'Where was he when we needed him, Evangeline?'

'You should have told me!'

'He had no right!'

'He's my father!'

'He didn't deserve you!'

'That was not for you to decide.'

'Yes it was! How dare he presume he can waltz back into our lives and enjoy the fruits of my hard labour! You are *mine*! I raised you! I did it all! He has no part of this!'

'I had a right to know.'

'You think it was a coincidence he got in touch as soon as his financial responsibility came to an end?'

So it comes down to money. He no longer needed to hide because he no longer had a legal obligation to pay. Something inside me collapses.

'I didn't want to ruin your birthday. And then you were going to university and things were beginning to happen for you and I wasn't going to let him to spoil that.'

I slice the cheese. Milly is upstairs, a red welt on her leg. Why are we talking about this now? I'm being selfish. This isn't about me, now, it's about Milly. We are supposed to be taking care of her. What would Shona say if she saw what Mum did? Helen? I picture the reviewing officer scribbling a report. How would she describe it? Violence? Abuse? Will

Milly say something? 'If social services find out about you smacking—'

She slams the knife down on the bread board. 'To hell with social services! Right now, they are the least of your problems. Do you have any idea what you're getting yourself into? Adopting a child with that man?'

We are back to Neil. The demon Neil. Here we go. I brace myself. Somehow, she is going to twist this around to make it his fault. Well, good luck with that. She has my undivided attention. I can't wait to hear just how she's going to manage this.

'Neil has a child.' She is looking at me, her eyes steady, giving nothing away. 'When Neil met you, Tina Lord was pregnant with his child.'

Pregnant.

That word. It hits the floor between us, exploding into tiny particles that echo through the air.

Pregnant. The blue line that never appeared.

'Neil has a son. He abandoned his child just like that feckless father of yours. Don't make the same mistake I made, Evangeline. There's still time for you to get out of this.'

I shake my head, as if I can shake this information out of it, but I cannot shake her away. She is still there, the expression on her face triumphant. I want to run, but my feet are pinned to the ground.

'There's more.' She swallows. The triumph has gone. Now she is a mother, concerned for her daughter. I want to slam my hand over her mouth. 'He raped her.'

Rape.

This word doesn't explode. It hovers in the air, waiting. The world stills around it.

# Chapter 18

Naz put our bag in Max's room, relegating him to the pull-out mattress in Cam's bedroom. Max was not enthusiastic about sharing with his brother. 'He snorts and he stinks!'

But Naz was having none of it. 'So do you,' she said, shooing him into the bathroom to brush his teeth, while he objected most robustly.

Naz doesn't know what's going on. I asked if we could stay and she didn't hesitate. She has been efficient and kind, asking no questions. Milly is tucked up in the top bunk. I'll sleep in Max's bed below, under a *Star Wars* duvet. Her obvious relief when I went up to tell her we were leaving Mum's tore at my chest. I failed to protect her. What sort of mother am I? I'm supposed to be keeping her safe, providing her with a nurturing, loving environment. I shouldn't even be in Hitchin with her now, but back in Tarnside, allowing her to settle gently into her new life.

With Neil.

With Neil?

Pregnant. Son. Rape. Words that have no place in my world. Circling around me, trying to find a way in.

If I hadn't come back to Hitchin, I wouldn't know. If I hadn't sent that bloody photograph, none of this would be happening.

But we are here now, sitting in Naz's messy kitchen with an empty bottle of wine and Mum's grenade on the table between us. Neil has a child. He is a father. He raped Tina Lord? Neil. My Neil. It's unimaginable. My Neil is kind. He is patient. He would never, never…

It isn't real. It can't be real. As long as I don't pull the pin, the grenade can stay where it is.

Neil is picking us up tomorrow night. We will spend the weekend with his parents. I told him we're having a sleepover at Naz's for a bit of fun, but he could tell. I could barely speak. His voice. 'What is it Eve? What has she said?' Too much. The concern. The fear.

'*I know about you.*' This is what she knew. '*What are you afraid of?*'

'*You.*'

I made the excuse that Milly was too tired to chat. If he finds out about the smack, all hell will be let loose.

All hell has let loose.

'*What has she said?*' not *what has she done?* '*What are you afraid of?*'

What do I do now?

Naz fed us curry from the freezer. 'Mum makes me two a week and we can never get through them.' This is what normal mothers do for their adult daughters. They cook meals to store in the freezer, they embrace their grandchildren. But these mothers have sons-in-law they can trust. Milly hesitated and procrastinated, stirring the curry around her plate while watching Max gulp spoonful after spoonful, but not actually eating any herself. I said nothing. There were naan breads she could eat, if all else failed, or plain rice, but there was no need to worry. It was Max who shoved the bowl of yoghurt towards her, saying, 'If you stir that in, it's not so spicy.' She gave him a shy smile and then, wanting to impress, did exactly as he suggested. I watched this, aware that I should be delighted, but more relieved that Milly seemed largely untouched by the upheaval. I watched as she took the first mouthful and gave a little grimace as she swallowed. I listened to Naz laugh and encourage her. I saw Max give her the thumbs up, but I was not there with them. While Milly's life continued, while she polished off her first curry, my life hung, suspended. Now Max is reading her a bedtime story on her insistence.

Neil. My Neil.

'*What are you afraid of?*'

Naz is sitting across the table from me, waiting. I have to say the words, but if I say them out loud I give them substance.

Naz, incisive as ever, asks, 'What has she said?'

What has she said. Not, what is the truth, but, what has she *said*. It may not be true. Cling to that. 'She said Tina Lord had a child, a son. Neil's son.' I can't tell her the rest.

Naz frowns. She takes her time, digesting the information. She doesn't reject it. She doesn't snort and dismiss it, she takes it in. Eventually, she says, 'Does Neil know?'

Does he? Maybe he doesn't. Maybe it isn't true. Maybe it's someone else's child. Gossip. Something twisted out of shape?

'He can't. How could he?' All those tests? Waiting to find out if... he would have said. He would have told me.

'Where did your mum get this information?'

I don't know. I stare at Naz dumbly. Why didn't I ask? Did I ask? I don't remember. I don't remember anything except grabbing Milly, packing our bag and running away. I ran away.

'You met Ann Lord in the café? Did she say anything about Tina?'

I shake my head. I can't speak. There are no words. I struggle to remember. She said Tina was fine. She didn't mention a child. She didn't mention rape. She wouldn't sit in a café with me if my husband had raped her daughter.

But she didn't sit in the café. She left. Tugging at her cuff. Glancing to the window, looking for the car. She couldn't get out of there fast enough.

'We need to talk to Tina.' Naz is matter-of-fact. The journalist she was meant to be is kicking in. She isn't afraid of the truth. But I haven't told her everything. I have to tell her.

'There's more.'

Naz frowns. She waits. I can hear the dishwasher whirring, the hum of the fridge. Stu is in the living room, giving us a bit of space. I stare at my hands. The wedding ring Neil slid onto my finger. Neil. My Neil. Vomit it up. 'Rape.' The word is out. That ugly word. 'She said he raped her.' I stay focused on my hands, afraid to see Naz's horror.

A moment. Then, '*Who* said? Tina?'

No. I shake my head. Not Tina. A glimmer of light. I look up. 'Mum.'

I want to see relief on Naz's face. I want her shoulders to lower, her frown to slide, but she stays as she is, thinking. She believes it's possible.

She reaches across the table to take my hand but I snatch it away. I don't want her pity. I don't want this to be true!

The still of the kitchen. The whir. The hum. This moment stretching out. This can't be happening. I need to take control. I'm up on my feet. 'I think I'm going to be sick.' I run for the stairs, up to the bathroom, sliding the bolt across. I take a deep breath. I lean over the sink. I retch and my body convulses. I taste bile in my throat, but this is not enough. I slide my fingers along my tongue, further, further, until I gag, once, twice, and then it comes. Yellow, curry goo, filling the sink. Grains of rice. Saliva and slippery digestive juices. Up it comes.

When I'm done, I splash my face with cold water, tilt my head and hold my mouth under the running tap, rinsing away the sour taste. Rinsing it all away. Then I sit down on the toilet seat, spent, trembling.

Naz is waiting for me when I return to the kitchen. 'You OK?' I nod and sit back down at the table facing her. My hands are trembling. The world, my world, is trembling. She says, 'I've been thinking. What proof does your mum have? I mean, was there an accusation made at the time? If there was, then there'd be a record, wouldn't there? This isn't something you can hide. He's a teacher. They'll have done a full DBS check on him. They'll have done the checks for the adoption. I mean, they found out about the bloody weed when they checked me out, and I was just a referee, surely they'd have found a rape charge?'

She's right. We were both checked. Any criminal history would have come up. How does Mum know Neil raped Tina? Did Ann tell her? Why wasn't it reported? 'I should have asked. Why didn't I ask?'

'Because you couldn't think straight! Because it's the most hideous, spiteful accusation anyone could make? Because this is your husband, the man you've loved for over twenty years and you're in shock?'

I start to cry. Big, fat, childish tears. I sniff and wipe my nose with the back of my hand. 'Why did I listen to her? I should have defended him!'

'You need to find out the truth.' I don't. I need to hide. I need to pretend this never happened, I never heard, I don't know anything about this, but Naz is determined. 'Tina was probably at school with Neil, so she must have been from Stevenage.' She's thinking, taking control. 'Did Ann mention where she lived?' I shake my head. 'Come on, Eve. You need to help me here.'

'I'm scared.'

She nods. 'I get that. But you can't stop being scared by pretending you don't know.'

'Do you think…?' I can't bring myself to say it.

She does it for me. 'Do I think he did it? Do I think Neil raped a girl?' She shakes her head. 'Of course not.' Her eyes nail me. 'I'd never have let you marry him if I thought he was capable of that. But I don't *know*.' It could be true. She believes it could be true. 'You need to *know*, Eve. You can't run away from this. Now think. The only person who will know the truth is Tina. We need to talk to Tina. What did Ann say? Anything that might help us find her.'

'She said she met Mum in the charity shop. She works in a charity shop.'

'And she met you in Hitchin?' I nod. 'It will be a charity shop in Hitchin; I can't see your mum going to a charity shop in Stevenage. Did she say which charity?'

'No.'

'So we'll start with a bit of bargain shopping tomorrow morning.' She tops up my wine. 'Now drink. This could all be a pile of crap. You know what your mum's like. Anything to bad-mouth Neil.'

She's right. There's no reason to suspect that this child is anything to do with Neil. He would have told me. If he knew he already had a child he would have said. All those tests. All that anxiety and doubt on his part. He thought he might be infertile. He couldn't fake that. All those months, struggling to conceive. Sitting with the GP. Racing to Furness General, the plastic container of sperm wedged between his legs, to keep it at the right temperature for as long as possible, hooting at the tractor to pull over and let us pass. Did he know then?

Does he know?

Is he the man I thought he was?

The next morning, Naz drops both boys at their respective schools and comes back to have a late breakfast with me and Milly. There's no point in heading into town until ten o'clock, as most of the charity shops won't open until then.

Mum has been digging for dirt on Neil for years, but if this were true, someone would have said something before now. Why wasn't it reported? Why has Tina never said anything? It can't be true.

Milly is chirpy, a guinea pig nestled in her lap as she eats her cereal. Naz has scored points over me in the mothering stakes because she lets her boys eat sugar-coated cereals whereas I've been insisting on cornflakes. 'Choose your battles.' The domestic banter and jostling comforts me. Rape does not belong in this world of children and domesticity. Naz will not allow it in. I will not allow it in.

We start in Scope on the market square. The young girl behind the counter doesn't know Ann but can't be sure she doesn't work on a different day. At Animal Rescue they have no Anns working for them. Age Concern also can't help, but they do have an abundance of soft toys that delight Milly and I'm unable to leave without purchasing a hideous glittering unicorn. Naz groans as I take it to the counter to pay. 'Sucker.'

'*Choose your battles.*' Keep it light. Keep it safe. Sidestep the drip-drip-drip.

Outside the Oxfam shop, there's a familiar black car with the engine running, blocking the entrance. We walk round the back of it and squeeze through a small gap to get through the shop door. Naz, swearing under her breath, strides in while Milly and I follow. As I pass, I glance through the passenger window. A small, balding man in his seventies grips the wheel with stubby hands, refusing to look in my direction.

Ann is at the back of the shop, dressed in a beige raincoat, talking urgently to another woman who's kneeling in front of the bookshelves, arranging the paperbacks. They both glance towards us as we enter. At first, Ann doesn't recognise me. As I step forward, she looks down at Milly, making the connection, and her instinctive smile is abruptly sliced with panic. She stumbles forward, knocking against the precarious stack of books, sending them toppling across the floor around her feet. She tries to step over them but in her haste misjudges and stumbles again, flailing. Hurrying forward, I grab her arm to steady her before she falls.

'No! No!'

'Ann, please.'

'No, he mustn't see you. I'm sorry.' She turns her face away from me, cringing into her shoulder.

'I need to talk to you.'

She's terrified. And now, close to, I can see beneath the crudely applied make-up the traces of a fresh bruise, flowering purple-red from her cheekbone up to her eye. 'I can't.'

Naz hangs back with Milly, out of earshot. 'Is it true?' I can't say the words, but I don't need to. I can see from Ann's face that she knows what I'm talking about. 'Tina?' I lower my voice. 'Was she... pregnant?' She bites her lip, her eyes darting over my shoulder to the door. The man in the car. I know before she nods that the answer will be yes. Tina was pregnant. This isn't some fantasy of my mother's, an idle piece of gossip. I clutch a thin thread of hope, 'Was it Neil?'

Her face folds into creases of pity and she nods. I feel sick. She glances back at her colleague, lowers her voice to a whisper, 'I'm sorry,' and shrinks past Naz and Milly, out of the shop, straight into the black car. The driver pulls away before she's had time to close the door.

The woman sorting the paperbacks gets to her feet, rubbing her knees. 'Oh dear.' She looks perplexed. 'Do you know Ann?' It takes a moment for me to realise she's waiting for an answer, but I can't speak. 'She hasn't been with us long, but she was a good sort. Says she can't work here any more.'

Naz asks, 'Why not?'

'Says her husband needs her at home.'


Outside, Naz hisses into my ear, 'What the...?'

'It's true.'

'She was terrified. That was a nasty bruise.'

We stand staring at one another while the reality settles around us. I can see my own conclusions settling on Naz's face. Tina had a child. Neil's child. Neil may not know about his son, but he must know what happened between him and Tina. If he has nothing to hide, why hasn't he told me about her?

There are bruises in Neil's past. Places I avoid. Questions that make him flinch. I thought they were to do with his birth mother. Not Tina. Not rape.

Neil. My Neil? It's impossible.

But if it isn't true, why hide it from me?

I stand in the street with the truth reverberating around me, like the pause after the clash of symbols.

Milly is unwrapping a chocolate mouse from its foil. As she raises it to her mouth, Naz asks, 'Where did you get that?'

Milly hesitates. She looks from Naz to me and then to her unicorn. 'I finded it.'

Naz crouches down and takes the chocolate from Milly's hand. 'Found it?'

Milly looks at me.

Neil is already a father.

Did he rape Tina Lord?

However it happened, he has a son. Tina was pregnant. I'm the one who is the problem. I am infertile.

Naz continues to probe, 'Did you take that chocolate, Milly?'

Neil was eighteen. I was seventeen. I do the maths. Twenty-six years.

Milly is holding up her unicorn. 'He tooked it.'

This son will be a grown man. Not a child any more, but a man.

'You know that taking something from a shop without paying for it is stealing, don't you, Milly?'

'Naughty unicorn!'

I stare at Naz. She grabs my hand. 'Eve, listen to me. What you need to focus on now is Milly. You and Milly. You are so close. Just a few more weeks. That's all you need to do, get through those weeks, get that final review out of the way, the adoption approved, the court hearing, and Milly is yours. What happens after that is your business. Do you hear me? You can't rock the boat now.'

She's right. If I want to keep Milly, I have to hold onto Neil, at least until the adoption is approved. As a single parent, I'd have to be reassessed and I'm unlikely to be able to adopt Milly on my own. There are so many couples who could offer more. And they'll make me wait, while I get over this. They insist on grieving time if you've miscarried; how much grieving time will they insist on for a rape accusation? Milly can't wait. She needs a family now. I'd lose Milly.

Naz is waiting for me to catch up. 'Do you see? You have to present a united front. You have to do this, Eve. Focus on Milly, on getting Milly. All this with Neil, you can deal with that later, once Milly's yours.'

Naz takes Milly's hand. 'Shall we go back inside and pay the lady for the chocolate? We can tell her we made a mistake.'

But Milly doesn't want to go in and face the music. Instead, she lifts the unicorn in the air and gives it an almighty smack.

# Chapter 19

'Mike! Get the bread out!' The timer on the oven is beeping, but Betty's busy ladling soup into the children's bowls as they push and shove one another around the table, their parents milling behind them, drinks in hand, filling the kitchen with their chatter. It's the usual broth made from tomatoes and stock and whatever else she's got to hand. I can see some sort of beans, peppers, green beans. It smells delicious. I glance nervously at Milly, but she's sitting up straight, taking her lead from the other children, spoon ready in her hand.

This house is a world away from my mother's. There's food encrusted on the hob and splattered over the surfaces. The patio doors are open and dogs, four of them, run in and out. The floor is covered in mud and clumps of dog hair but no one cares. Two of the dogs, what looks like a hairy greyhound and something similar but smaller, belong to Mike and Betty. The chocolate Labrador hoovering up the bits of vegetable that have fallen from the kitchen counter belongs to Neil's eldest sister, Julie. The yappy little cockapoo pup is a new addition to the extended family, arriving a few moments ago with Neil's youngest sister Laura and proving a huge hit with all the children, Milly particularly. I watch Neil stoop to stroke its head as it rubs up against Milly's legs. He and Milly exchange a look, no doubt preparing for a charm offensive on the way home.

Neil could not have raped Tina Lord. This man, this easy, loving father, my friend, my attentive, gentle lover, could not, would not, rape a girl. I will not believe it.

But he has a child. Ann confirmed it. There is no escaping that fact. I reject the rape, but I have to deal with the facts.

How did my mother manage to get this information?

Neil picked us up from Naz's late last night. I told him about the smack. I had to say something to explain the state I was in. Betty's spoken to him, calmed him down. She agrees with Naz that it was unfortunate, but not the end of the world. 'There was a time when a smack was a perfectly acceptable way to reprimand a child,' though I doubt she ever resorted to this herself. Neil was not placated by this. He said he'd never let Mum anywhere near Milly again, but that's the least of my problems right now.

If I tell him what I know, Mum has got what she wanted. Our family, our little unit, is threatened. If I tell Neil about his son, we'll have to tell social services, we'll need to be reassessed. Certainly, it will need to be documented. This is a sibling for Milly; there could be implications. We know nothing about Tina's son. He could be a criminal, an unstable influence. He could be more of a threat to Milly's well-being than her birth mother.

Milly. Our Milly. She is our Milly now, there's no going back. She's part of our lives and we're part of hers. We have the beginning of a shared history. I thought it would be the big things that make the memories: the excursions into the Lakes for family activities, the cruise we took along Coniston in the summer drizzle on the steam gondola, that first trip to Brockhole adventure playground on Windermere, or the bike ride through Grizedale Forest, with Milly's bike attached to Neil's on the tailgator, me bringing up the rear, twisting and turning and pushing over muddy roots and hidden stones, but I was wrong. It's not about those photograph moments. It's about the incidental experiences and repeated day-to-day activities: the way Milly slips out of her bed every morning as soon as she hears Neil heading into the shower and is waiting for him at the kitchen table when he comes down, the little conversations the two of them have before I'm up, how she stands in front of the hall mirror, her face set in a look of concentration as I brush her hair, the last minute 'Where are my shoes!' panic when her trainers are not on the shelf where they should be, but wherever she kicked them off when she came in the day before.

As adopters we have the added delight of the transitional rituals that Milly has carried from one world into the other, like the way she prepares the teapot in the morning, with a little warm water from the tap, and puts the kettle on to boil. We've had to buy a tea cosy and I postpone my morning coffee to allow her to continue with this. It's important; a thread from one world to the other, a gift, from her to us. Watching her carefully measuring the milk into each cup I think of her grandparents and how they must be missing her. Shona tells me not to worry, they're confident that she's well cared for and loved, but still, I'd like for them to see her in our world. It's as much for me as for them. I need their blessing.

Would they give their blessing if they knew what I know now?

Naz thinks it's better not to talk to Neil until after the review. She's worried I won't be able to keep a secret like this, but she's wrong. I couldn't before, but I can now. I can do this for Milly. I will do this to keep Milly.

What has Mum done? The smack was shocking, but this is worse. To accuse him of rape. To take the fact of a child, a child we didn't know about, is shocking enough, but to embellish it with this additional horror is beyond cruel. The smack was a moment of poor judgement, but this is calculated and devastating. She has been talking to people, gathering information to incriminate Neil, to break my family apart. Who has she spoken to? Who else knows this awful secret?

I am not going to let her get away with it. Nothing has changed. Neil wouldn't have known about the pregnancy. He still doesn't know. He never needs to know. My mother wants me back. She's prepared to go to any lengths to achieve that, but I don't have to let her. I've managed without her before and I can do it again. If she wants a relationship with me it will be on my terms from now on.

Neil is never going to find out about this. We're going to carry on as normal.

The level of noise is deafening. They're all talking but no one is really listening to anyone else. It's like a competition in this family, with everyone vying for attention, whoever can shout loudest wins, but it's done with good humour. No one expects to be heard, they're just delighted to be back with one another. This is Neil's family, here in this room.

This is the family I want for Milly. This is the world I hope to create. I'll never be Betty, I've left it too late to have so many children and, in truth, I wouldn't cope with this level of chaos, but something on a smaller scale. Something as warm and embracing and healthy as this. If we do our job well, Neil and I, if we're the parents we envisaged and explored during those assessment meetings, if we achieve that, then Milly will have her own version of this, a family home to return to, where she's allowed to be the adult she's become. Love without strings attached.

This is our family. Tina Lord has hers. She has made that work. Ann said Tina was fine. She lives somewhere in the north of England now. This is history. Tina must have made the decision not to tell Neil. She has not asked to be part of his life. She and her son do not belong here. That's been their choice. I am respecting that choice.

Betty called Mum and invited her over today, but she wouldn't come. Of course she wouldn't. Here, where Neil is loved and supported, she'd be outnumbered and insignificant. She prefers to sit at home and sulk. Good luck to her.

Tina brought up her child alone. She's coped. She's built a life. What business do we have interfering in that? Or she may have married. Tina's son may believe that man to be his natural father. If Tina wanted Neil to be involved, she would have told him. He'll want to meet his son, but is that necessarily for the best if that son believes his natural father is someone else? Why cause so many people so much unnecessary pain?

This is our family. Here. Now. Me, Neil and Milly. This house. These uncles and aunts and cousins and dogs. This is Neil's world and now it will be part of Milly's. She belongs here. It's Milly we need to focus on. Milly is five years old. She is still a child. Neil's son is an adult man. He doesn't need us.

Neil comes over, relaxed in a way I haven't seen since Milly first arrived with us. This is my Neil, this jovial, jostling man, so loved by his family and at ease with himself. He's still that boy with the wide smile who reached down into the water to help me. I was dripping wet, my costume twisted, exposing part of my breast, but he wasn't looking at that, he was looking into my eyes, and I knew then it would be him. His strong arm pulling me up, that firm grip around my wrist.

He was eighteen then. When did the Tina thing happen? Months before? Weeks? I picture that boy with the khaki freckles and gentle smile. Not a rapist. Not my Neil.

He hands me a bottle of beer and holds his own up in a salute. 'Happy?' I nod, determined, shoving all that ugly doubt out of my mind.

Betty has decorated this house in her usual bohemian style: bold yellow walls in the kitchen-diner leading onto broad decking and a vast lawn with an apple tree at the far end. We're sleeping in the spare bedroom, all three of us together. Milly has a little mattress on the floor, but she crawled in with us this morning and I lay there with Neil beside me, our daughter between us, feeling the beginning of something resembling peace.

Laura waddles over, face flushed, her distended pregnant belly protruding in front of her. She rolls her ice-filled glass across her forehead. 'You aren't missing anything by avoiding this, Eve! What I would give now to have a child delivered to me, clean, dressed and sleeping through the night!'

'Broken in with table manners and all,' says Neil, grinning across at Milly who is tearing at the hot soda bread with the other children.

Laura is saying something about parenting sabbaticals. 'When it all gets a bit much we could just send them to a temporary family for a bit of respite and they come back sorted.'

Betty calls over from the hob, 'I think they do that already. It's called fostering.'

'For people who genuinely need it,' Neil adds, giving his sister a playful punch. 'Not lazy arses like you!'

It's such a relief to be able to laugh about our situation, rather than tiptoeing around it. People with no experience of adopting can sometimes make me feel like we've got a disease of some kind. They mean well, trying to spare our feelings, but in doing that they are as good as blowing a whistle and saying, 'Watch out!' Laura has no such reservations. In this family being adopted offers you no special privileges and there are no apologies. We are normal.

Laura's husband Joe, a large, cuddly man with a lopsided smile, is surreptitiously buttering a piece of soda bread and throws a guilty glance in her direction. He gives an apologetic shrug and grins. 'He's supposed to be on a diet,' she tells me, shaking her head. 'But my man loves his food.'

*My man.* Neil is my man. More than twenty years. I know him. I know the truth. The truth is not words, it's what we know on a different level. It's what we *feel* to be true.

The children slip away from the table, bowls wiped clean by bread, and the dogs and adults follow them into the garden leaving me in the kitchen with Betty.

'Are you all right, Eve?' she asks. 'You seem a bit preoccupied.'

'I'm fine.' She isn't convinced. There's nothing I'd like more than to talk to Betty, to lay this whole thing out on the table in front of her and let her tell me what to do, but I can't. How can I tell Betty she has a grandson she's never met? But if I could tell her, she would dismiss the notion of rape. I would have an ally in this. Betty knows her son as well as I do, better, perhaps.

'Eve?' Betty leans towards me. 'You can talk to me. Is everything OK with you and Neil?'

'Of course! Why do you ask that?'

She sighs. 'Your mum...'

'What has she said?'

'Nothing. Nothing, really.'

'Tell me.'

She hesitates. 'She popped in, after she'd been up to see you. To show us some photographs.' To show off. To rub it in that she'd seen Milly first. 'And she was asking, we got talking.' She bites her lip and glances out to the garden, to Neil.

'What did she ask?'

Betty looks down at her hands. 'We got talking, about teenagers, I don't know how... She's good, your mum, at getting people to talk.' I wait. Betty glances back out at Neil. 'He's told you, about Tina?'

I hold my breath. Shake my head. Does Betty know?

She pulls at her lower lip with her tooth. 'I shouldn't have said anything. It's not important. I shouldn't... We got talking about teenagers and those first, difficult relationships and...' So this is where she started her search. With Betty, with Neil's own mother.

'Tell me.'

She shrugs. 'It's nothing. Really.'

Nothing really. She doesn't know. She can't know.

'She wasn't – just a girl he met at a party. Just the once – before he met you. He tried calling, but her dad wouldn't let him speak to her. It upset him. More than – I don't know. It wasn't a good time. I shouldn't have mentioned it. I'm sorry. I don't know why...'

We both look out at Neil. She's worried at betraying him. He's standing under the apple tree with Milly on his shoulders and she's stretching up to reach the branches. My mother, with her clever questioning. Twisting, not just the truth, but people. Betty, Ann. Who else has she manipulated? 'It's all right.' My voice is steady. 'I won't say anything.'

It upset him, not being able to talk to Tina. More than it should have done and Betty doesn't know why. But I do.

She pats my hand. 'This whole adoption thing. It's so much more complicated than it was in our day. Are you sure you're all right, the two of you?'

Dear Betty. She knows Mum's stirring. How can I tell her? I have become a keeper of secrets, but I'm not a liar. 'You know my mum, Betty. She worries about me.' This is our code. Betty knows it's far darker and more destructive than that. 'We're good, Neil and I, there's nothing she can do to shake that.' Betty smiles, reassured, while I do my best to swallow the hot bile rising in my throat.

# Chapter 20

The spare room at Betty's is an adult room, all vestige of Neil's teenage years stripped away and painted over. In this house, children grow up, time moves on.

As we get ready for bed, I tell Neil about my dad. There are only so many secrets I can keep, and sharing this one eases my conscience temporarily. 'She says it was a birthday card, but I'm not so sure. There might have been a letter.'

Neil pulls back the duvet and climbs into bed. 'What difference does it make?' He removes his watch, placing it on the side table, oblivious, then looks up. 'What?'

It takes me a moment to respond. 'Is that all you've got to say?'

'What do you want me to say?'

'This is my dad we're talking about.'

It's as if we're speaking a different language. He tilts his head a little. 'But he wasn't, was he? Not in any real sense.' His words are like little pinches. I can feel my face stinging and it must be visible because he softens his tone and adds,

'I'm sorry, but it's not like you missed him. You've never talked about him.'

Is this how he sees it? Out of sight, out of mind? Is this how he's justified it to himself? Did he know Tina was pregnant, but chose to forget? Did he pretend it never happened? I look at him, this man I thought I knew, and see a stranger.

He frowns. 'What is it?' I can't speak.

All those tests when all the time he knew it was me who couldn't conceive, not him? Who is this man? Do I really know him at all?

'Eve?' He's worried now. 'I'm sorry. What is it? What have I said?' I shake my head. 'You always said he wasn't important.'

'I thought he didn't want to know me.' My voice cracks.

He moves over to make space, waiting to envelop me, but I can't move. I climb into bed beside him because I don't know where else to go. He slides his arm around me and I let him pull me against his chest. I can hear the steady beat of his heart. Not racing. Not panicked or scared. He is calm. He has no idea. Resting his chin on my head, he strokes my hair. His voice rumbles through me. 'Do you want to see him?' The question is gentle, compassionate. This is the Neil that I know. This is the Neil I want to cling to.

'I don't know.'

'What good would it do now, do you think?'

Maybe he's right. What's the point? He wrote over twenty years ago. He'll be an old man now, if he's alive at all.

'You don't need him.'

Neil drops a kiss on the top of my head.

A father is the man who's there while you're growing up. Taking care of you, guiding you, witnessing the milestones in your life. My father was not there for that. Neil was not there for his son. What's done can't be undone. It's too late.

But it isn't as simple as that. It's like an itch I need to scratch, returning later, snagging me from sleep. I slip out of the bed. Neil's snoring softly, Milly's on her mattress on the floor, face buried in the pillow, her hair a sweaty tangle. She fell into bed before I could brush it tonight. It was all I could do to get her clothes off her and brush her teeth, she was that exhausted from all the excitement with her new cousins and the dogs. She's happy here. Neil's world. Already she belongs. I had no siblings or cousins growing up. There was none of this bustle and energy. I'm glad we're able to provide it for Milly.

I kneel beside her and stroke her hair gently. She stirs. This little girl. My daughter. I can no longer imagine a life without her. She belongs. We belong. Brushing the matted hair from her face, I touch my lips to her cheek. She gives a little groan of contentment and rolls away from me.

I straighten up and check my watch in the moonlight that seeps around the curtain. I'm not surprised to see it's ten to four. I often wake at this time, but usually manage to drift back off. If I don't, I know it'll be at least an hour before my brain settles again. Grabbing the jumper Neil tossed onto the chair, I pull it over my pyjamas, slip out of the room and creep downstairs.

In the darkness of the kitchen I can see I'm not the only night owl. Laura is sitting outside on a garden chair, her feet raised onto the table, head back, looking at the stars. Her hands rest on her belly and her profile is outlined in silver, as if the moon has dissolved over her face. She looks up and smiles as I open the door. 'Ah! Someone else who can't sleep.'

I pull up a chair next to her and she explains the various constellations. Neil's talked me through this before; Mike taught all the kids how to recognise the stars on family camping trips. Neil introduced me to them on our first proper date, taking a detour as he walked me home one night, lying back in the grass on Windmill Hill, his hands drawing the shapes in the air. I remember when we first moved to Cumbria, how delighted he was to see the night sky, the diamonds burning so much brighter away from the urban light pollution. 'As if they're telling us we've done the right thing by coming here,' he whispered, still searching for reasons to justify the huge upheaval. I forget that he had to leave his family behind too, that he must miss them as much as I miss Mum. He gave this up for us.

'So,' says Laura, getting straight to the point. 'What's keeping you awake?'

'Is it that obvious?'

She laughs. 'Spill the beans.'

I realise that Laura will be the same age as Tina. They were both Stevenage girls. 'Did you know Tina Lord?'

'Tina? Yeah. She was in my year. Didn't Neil...?' She trails off and waits and I'm glad of the night and our inability to see into one another's eyes. How much does she know? A pregnant school girl would have been major gossip. A beat and then, 'She was months before. He didn't two-time you, Eve. Neil wouldn't do that.'

She doesn't know about the pregnancy. How could she not know? If a girl in her year had had a baby, that cautionary tale would have been repeated at every opportunity. Jenifer Martin had a baby at fifteen. A little girl. She was two years ahead of me at school and I remember every detail. She carried on at school. Her mother took care of the baby. If Tina Lord had a baby, why didn't Laura know about it?

She says, 'Why are you worrying about this now?' I shrug, give a dismissive grunt, trying to make light of it. 'I used to be the same. Wanted to know every detail. And there were a lot of details with Joe, you know what I mean? He wasn't always a pudgy, middle-aged man!'

'Did he hide anything from you?'

She pauses, peering at me in the silvery light. 'Neil isn't hiding anything, Eve. He's just private. You know that. He'll be protecting you.'

'From what?'

'From something that doesn't matter. She got to him, not because she was special, but she was trapped and he couldn't help her and there was all that stuff going on with his mum.' She leans closer, searches my face. 'He didn't tell you.'

'No, he didn't tell me. What else hasn't he told me?'

Laura leans in. 'Eve, listen to me. He never speaks about it. He's never spoken to me about it and you know he tells me pretty much everything. I only know because Mum told me. She told us all, because he was being... It upset him and he didn't handle it well.'

'What happened?'

'He wrote to his birth mother. When he turned eighteen. He got the files and he wrote and arranged to go and see her and... I don't know. I don't know the details. This isn't my story to tell, Eve, but she was in a bad way and he couldn't help. She didn't want help. She didn't want him. And then Tina. It was bad timing, the two things. He was worried about Tina, possibly more so than he would have been normally, but Neil is honourable, he needs to do the right thing, and when he tried to see Tina, after the party—'

'What party?'

She shrugs. 'A house party. Someone's eighteenth? I think he would have seen her again, but her mad dad wouldn't let him. She told Neil she'd climbed out of the bedroom window to get out that night.' I picture the man gripping the steering wheel. The bruise on Ann's neck. What sort of life did Tina have with a father like that? 'If Tina was important I'd have known, Neil would have told me.'

But he didn't. He didn't tell her.

She leans forward and places a hand on my arm. '*You* are important. You were from the moment he met you. Nobody that came before could hold a torch to you.' She stands up, rubbing the small of her back and wincing, but her eyes remain fixed on me. 'He met you that day at the pool and that was it, he never stopped talking about you: Eve this and Eve that. "Do you think Eve will like this T-shirt?" "Do you think Eve will want to see this film?" He was desperate to impress you.'

'Seriously?' This isn't the way I remember it. The Neil I remember was confident and in control, but what do I know?

'What you have to understand about my brother is that he has no sense of entitlement. Everything he has is hard earned. Mum says it's as if he's never got over being grateful for being adopted, though they've done all they can not to make him feel he should be grateful.'

I know this is true. They're good people, Neil's parents. Hard-working, which is probably where he gets it from, decent. Their love for him is unconditional and no less than they feel for the girls who were born naturally after Neil. Betty's admitted to me, after too many beers during a summer barbecue in this very garden, that, if anything, she loves him more. 'He was my first and I wanted him so much, and he released something in me, Eve. In some way,

I believe he brought me the other two. Without him there would be none of this,' and she waved her arm to encompass the grandchildren, and Julie and Neil fighting like two kids over the ketchup as Mike distributed the burgers.

There is always a goal with Neil. He's a man with ambition. Driven, not for wealth or power, but a certain life. He wanted a family. He wanted to adopt a child, as his parents had adopted him. He wanted to teach as his mother had taught, and open doors for those less fortunate than himself. He wanted a house and a garden and a solid career and he's achieved all those things. But why did he want all that? Why was he so dogged in the pursuit of that? Was it because he nearly lost it before he began? If Tina told him she was pregnant, if he accepted responsibility for that, he would have had to go to work. He would have had to support her. The travelling, the teaching abroad, the freedom and adventure he craved and achieved, wouldn't have been available to him. Is that why it was so important? Maybe this has been driving him all these years.

Laura is still talking. 'He wanted you, Eve, but he never assumed you'd want him. He had to earn you, the way he's had to earn everything in his life. He's the same in sport. If he swims, he must be fast, achieve a certain number of lengths. If he plays cricket he has to do his best to win. He's not a bad sport, he can cope with losing if it's a fair game, as long as he's satisfied he's done his best.'

Tina falling pregnant was not fair. It scuppered his plans. I know how frustrated he gets when things aren't going his way.

But Neil is patient. He follows the rules. He gets frustrated, but he's honourable. He tried to get in touch with Tina but her dad wouldn't let him talk to her. If Tina had told Neil she was pregnant he wouldn't have walked away. He would have taken responsibility. He would have talked to Betty and Mike. They would have supported him.

If it happened. If Tina Lord was telling the truth.

Why didn't she tell Neil? All these years. Would she keep a secret like that for so long? How did she keep it a secret? No one knew all this time. Did she move away? Did her parents send her away? Maybe Neil isn't the father of her child, and that's simply a convenient lie. Neil was what every reasonable mother would regard as 'a nice young man'. But if Tina Lord broke out of the house to get to a party once, maybe she'd done it before. Maybe Neil wasn't the first. There may have been someone else, someone who wasn't 'a nice young man.' Someone who raped her. She might not tell her mother. She might not admit it, even to herself.

'My brother gets frustrated when things impede him,' says Laura. 'But he's a good man and he loves you.' I allow myself to be comforted by this. Laura knows her brother. Tina is history. Unimportant history.

The door creaks as I go back into the bedroom and Neil stirs. He rubs his eyes, squinting at me in the half light from the hall. 'What time is it?'

'Go back to sleep.'

He sits up, stretches, yawns. So relaxed. While I carry the burden of everything. I can't help myself; the words are out before I can stop them. 'Why didn't you tell me about Tina Lord?'

He is absolutely still but I can feel the tremor of fear as he waits, silent, weighing up what I know. He shakes his head. 'Why do you let her do this, Eve?'

'Don't turn this on Mum. I asked you a question!' Milly shifts and rolls over. I lower my voice. 'Why can't you answer the question?'

'Why are you talking to me like this?' He's defensive. Why is he defensive?

'Why can't you answer the question?'

'I can answer it, I'm just not sure I want to right now. Why are you interrogating me? What has she said?'

'No. No, you don't get to do that. You don't get to check what I know before you tell me the truth.'

'For God's sake!' He sighs, dragging his fingers through his hair so it stands up in tufts. 'Look, it was a horrible time, OK? I told you. I don't like to think about it. I met Tina once, at a party. I didn't see her again.'

'Why not?'

He shrugs. 'I don't know. You'll have to ask her. She wasn't interested.'

'What happened between you?'

'Nothing. Nothing happened. We were two teenagers. We got a bit hot and sweaty. That was it.'

'How hot and sweaty?'

He squirms. 'Eve. Why is this important?' He's embarrassed. 'What is it your mum thinks she knows?' He had sex with her. He doesn't want to come out and say it, but I know and he knows I know.

I examine his face. He's embarrassed, but he's not ashamed. There is no evidence of shame. If he'd raped her he would be ashamed.

I have to stop. I have to stop this now. Naz is right. We can't let this come between us. We have to think about Milly.

'I'm sorry.' I sit down on the bed.

He strokes my back. 'I felt bad about her. I felt bad about that whole time. Talking about it won't change anything. You don't tell me everything.'

'I've told you about all my boyfriends.'

'All two of them.'

I hadn't slept with either of them. The first time Neil and I made love is a watermark in my memory. We spent the night in a hotel, in Rome. We were inter-railing and had slept on trains for three nights to save the money to pay for the room. He'd been out and bought candles, selected the music. He knew it was my first time and he was tender, cautious, 'Are you OK with this? Are you sure this is OK?' Never pushy, never anything other than respectful and gentle. Was he like that with Tina? Or was it more urgent? Something frantic and hungry and more difficult to gauge? Maybe. Maybe it was eager and faster, but Neil would never be disrespectful, never forceful, not Neil, not my Neil.

He's entitled to his secrets. I may have told him about my boyfriends, they weren't serious, I wasn't giving anything away. He knows nothing of the episodes in the bathroom. Fingers down my throat. Heaving over the sink. I have not shared that shame with him.


Home. I feel it beckoning to me as we turn off the M6 and head west across the top of the peninsulas. Morecambe Bay is all silver puddles and hammered pewter under gunmetal sky. We're heading home and I can feel the tension loosening as Neil navigates the winding road. Milly is fast asleep in the back, her mouth wide open. We stayed for Betty's Sunday nut roast which is always planned for three o'clock but never ready before five. It's now almost midnight and we'll all be shattered in the morning, but I'm blissfully drifting. I don't need to worry about Tina. She was not important. Her baby has nothing to do with Neil.

I glance back over my shoulder. Milly's head has dropped onto her chest and she's snoring gently. She will start school this week and I'll be back at work full time, making it up to Lizzie for last week. Kath will take care of Milly at the park in the afternoons and I'll be in the office if anything crops up. This has all been agreed in advance with social services; I'm not taking any risks. Poor Kath had to attend an interview and complete a Disclosure and Barring Service check to make sure she had no convictions. I felt terrible asking so much of her, but she was very generous and upbeat about it all over the phone, and India has reassured me that with her own younger grandchildren miles away, and having retired from teaching, it's as good for Kath as it is for us.

We pull up outside the house and Neil switches off the engine. Neither of us moves for a moment. He takes a long, deep breath and turns to me. 'Home,' he says firmly and I plant a kiss on his soft mouth.

# Chapter 21

It's the last day of September and our probationary period with Milly is almost complete. We've been back in Tarnside for two weeks and life has returned to a comfortable rhythm. Neil and I are back at work, Milly is settled into school and there is a pattern to our days. This is our safe place. This is home.

We're almost there. On Monday we'll have the final review and if all goes according to plan we'll be given the green light to apply for our adoption order. It really is happening. I've done it. I've shoved all that horrid business aside. Here, in Tarnside, far away from Hitchin and Mum and that whole ugly episode, I can do this. We're a family and soon it will be signed and sealed and this fear that's been puddling at my feet, this sense that at any moment it could all be snatched from us, is beginning to drain away. Life is good.

I haven't spoken to my mother. There's nothing to say.

Today is the Tarnside Lantern Festival. Neil and Milly are in the garden, putting the finishing touches to her first lantern. Betty and Mike are on their way. They were planning to stop at a B&B in the Forest of Bowland last night. I did offer for them to come straight here, but Betty insisted they would prefer to break the journey. I know she was thinking of us. Neil finishes work late on a Friday and I was in the park until nearly midnight last night, helping the lantern team rig the lights. We're lucky with the weather. The forecast is for it to cloud over later, but hopefully the rain will hold off. The procession and finale in the park are an annual event that's been taking place in Tarnside for over thirty years. It's my job to manage it but, in truth, it's the local community who make it happen.

Milly holds out a soggy square of gluey tissue paper between her fingertips. Neil takes it carefully and presses it into place against the withy frame.

I shout, 'Let Milly do some!' He's so fixed on it looking perfect the poor child won't get a look in. The theme for the procession this year is Once Upon A Time, an excuse to revisit our favourite fairy tales. Milly has chosen *Little Red Riding Hood* and we've used my Ladybird edition, which I brought back from Hitchin, for inspiration. I thought, for her first year, she should make the standard pyramid from withies and tissue paper, but Milly wanted a full Red Riding Hood, which even Neil baulked at, so we persuaded her that she could be Red Riding Hood and the lantern would be the basket she was carrying to her grandmother's house. She was a little disappointed, until Betty sent a photograph of a red duffel coat she'd found in a charity shop. I'd assumed the basket would be basket size, not the giant structure I can see on the lawn in front of me, but Neil's competitive streak has kicked in.

He's a wonderful father. He's the right father for Milly.

Whatever happened that night with Tina Lord was innocent. Two teenagers. Hot and sweaty. Not ugly or violent. He is not a predator. He is a good and honourable man. He's head of sixth form at the high school, for God's sake. The kids love him. Kids know. Milly knows. She has a sensor. She sussed Mum. She adores Neil.

This is Milly's first lantern procession. We'll remember this one for the rest of our lives. The procession is led, every year, by a giant lantern, commissioned from a team of artists-in-residence during the week running up to the event. Milly's basket is almost as big as Milly herself and will require the two of them to carry it, but it's no match for the giant wolf I saw being assembled in the park this morning. It looked spectacular, even in the daylight, spanning the length of two cars with vast, moving jaws and alarming jagged teeth. The bulk of it will be carried on three custom-made packs strapped to the back of the artists, with two more people managing its lower jaw, and it will be lit by LEDs rather than the standard candles. I can't wait to see Milly's face when she sees it.

Milly's basket is simple in design, as the withies naturally lend themselves to circular shapes. Neil sensibly soaked the long, skinny twigs in advance. He insists it's all in the preparation. There are squares of tissue paper cut neatly and piled on the garden table with a stone to stop them fluttering off in the breeze and the glue is in a shallow jar, diluted with just the right amount of water. Milly's pressing the tissue paper into place, under Neil's supervision. I can see him itching to straighten it. At the end of the day no one is going to be looking at the detail, they just need to get it covered before seven thirty tonight.

I'm in the kitchen when the doorbell rings, Neil is in the garden with Milly, but I call him to greet his parents while I flick the kettle on. Milly remains on task with her lantern. I'm expecting hearty welcomes and cheerful banter as I take four mugs down from the shelf, but instead there's an awkward hush. I instinctively move into the hall. Betty is ushering Neil away from the front door, her hand on his arm, whispering urgently. His face is dark. Behind him I can see Mike and, leaning heavily on his arm, my mother.

The space around me stills. Why is she here? Cold fingers inching up my spine. A chill puddle at my feet. Drip-drip.

Betty is manoeuvring Neil towards me. She throws me an apologetic smile and mouths a quick 'Sorry', but the full force of her attention is concerned with calming Neil. 'This isn't about you. Whatever you think of the woman, she is Milly's grandmother and she's sorry and you have to put this behind you.' She looks to me for support. 'She really regrets the smack, Eve. She wants to make amends.'

Mum gives me a pathetic smile. 'Darling!' and holds out her free arm. I step forward automatically and give her an awkward hug. 'Will it be all right for me to stay? I can book into a B&B if it's not convenient?'

'Don't be ridiculous.' She knows we have room. I've made up the bed for Betty and Mike in the spare bedroom next to Milly's, but Mum will need to go in there if her knee is as bad as it appears to be. She won't be able to manage a flight of stairs to get to the toilet in the night. Betty and Mike will have to sleep on the sofa bed in the study next to us on the top floor.

Fortunately, Milly remains in the garden, more concerned with her lantern than the visitors. Mike and Betty go out to greet her and are immediately presented with a glue brush and enlisted to help. Neil hovers for a moment but I send him out to join them. 'Let me and Mum have a chat.'

I close the door after him and turn to face her. 'What are you doing here?'

She looks wounded. 'Is that any way to treat your mother?'

'What do you want?'

'To see you.' A look of concern settles on her face and I have to turn away. 'Have you spoken to him?'

I shake my head, try to swallow. My heart is galloping. I grip the table. In the garden Milly is laughing at something Mike has said. Betty's focus is on Neil, who is standing stiff as a rod, a little distance from them, looking back into the kitchen, at us. My family out there. My mother, here in my home, waiting to pull the pin on her grenade.

'What are you going to do?'

She's all innocence. 'What do you mean?'

I slam my fist against the table. She jumps back, shocked. 'Evangeline! What on earth do you think I'm going to do? I'm here for *you*. To support *you*.'

'I don't need your support!'

'Well,' her voice trembles, 'maybe I need yours.'

I say nothing. Milly is distributing tissue squares to her grandparents. Her kind, loving, normal grandparents who have no agenda, no ammunition. Neil mouths 'OK?', ready to come in and rescue me. Or is he worried about what Mum's going to say? Does he know what she knows?

I shove the thought from my mind. I am not going to let her do this to me again. She's watching me, waiting. 'You say nothing!' I hiss. 'Do you hear me? You keep your poisonous little lies to yourself.'

She gives a slow blink and nods. She nods. Poisonous little lies. She nods. I am back on firm ground. I can do this.

*

Work on the lantern resumes after lunch, with Betty and Mike to assist, while I tidy away and load the dishwasher. Apparently, it was Betty's idea to give my mother a lift, though I'm sure Mum engineered the invitation. She paid the entire bill at the B&B before they checked out. Betty is embarrassed and wants to pay her back but Mum refuses to take any money from her. A typically extravagant, apparently generous gesture on the part of my mother, but there is always an agenda. She needed Neil's mother on side. How else was she going to arrive, uninvited, at our house and be allowed to stay? Betty feels doubly beholden, because she knows Mum didn't want to make the overnight stop herself. Mum would have preferred to press on and get here as quickly as possible, but Betty was concerned for us and the additional stress that would cause the night before a big event. She's brought a huge vegetarian pie with her so we don't have to prepare lunch. Mum's not a fan of vegetarian food, but she manages to keep her mouth shut and eat a small portion without drawing attention to herself. She's being overly apologetic and a little pathetic, which is her way of letting me know she's making an effort not to upset anyone. It's quite irritating, but better than the sulking or poking. Neil is cautious around her, suspicious. 'What's she up to?'

'She's trying to be nice.'

He doesn't buy it. I'm not sure I do, either, but I have an event to manage and other things to think about. She accepted 'poisonous little lies'. She has agreed to keep quiet. There's nothing more I can do. If I send her packing she will pull that pin and our life will explode.

The latest drama is her wheelchair. She isn't confined to it but has brought it with her, 'Just in case.' I can't believe her knee is so bad she needs a wheelchair, she seems sprightly enough when she needs to be, but what do I know? It could be a bid for attention, as Neil seems to think, but it's not a crime to be pathetic and I'm not going to let it spoil the weekend.

I look at my watch. It's already three o'clock. Mum has gone into town. I had hoped we'd get away with burgers from the van that will be at the event, but she's keen to cook dinner after Betty's contribution. I've made it clear that we need to be out of the house by half past seven, the latest. I now wish I'd said seven. She wanted me to drive her into town, but it'll be impossible to park today, so I've told her to phone when she's got everything and I'll nip out and pick her up. She's been gone a while. There are probably queues at the greengrocer. The lantern festival attracts thousands of visitors to the town. What started out as a one-off event, with thirty Brownies, has grown into a major tourist attraction, with five processions setting off from different meeting points to make their way to the park for the finale. Maybe her knee is playing up. I glance guiltily at the wheelchair, folded in the corner by the back door.

I'm about to try her phone, to see where she's got to, when I receive an incoming call. It's Lizzie, breathless, urgent. 'Eve! Can you come quickly? We've got a bit of an emergency.'

Raf, one of the artists, has cut himself with a Stanley knife. It needs stitches, which means a trip to A&E. Lizzie's car is piled high with materials for the finale and there's no room for a passenger. I drive straight to the park, pick him up and head to Furness General, about twenty minutes' drive away. He's hugely apologetic. His own stupid fault; he wasn't paying attention. He's young, in his twenties, with dreadlocks and a beard. The wolf is his design and he's agitated because he was planning something extra for the finale that might not be possible now.

'Maybe we can help. What was it?'

'A raft. I thought it would be kind of neat if the three little pigs chased the wolf through the crowd to the tarn and onto a raft and then we could set fire to him? If we push the raft out into the middle of the tarn we could watch it burn. It would look pretty cool.'

It would. It's tempting. It's also very last minute. The simplest thing to do would be to dismiss the idea at this late stage, but Raf is an experienced artist. He's worked on some amazing projects. I trust him. It's a bit gruesome, but no more so than the original story and the kids love that sort of thing. We've never used the tarn before, but have floated mini rafts with tea lights for events in the past and it's been magical. I like the idea. It's clever too, because it allows us to burn a giant lantern safely, with everyone able to get a good look. 'How far have you got with it?' I ask, overtaking a lorry and navigating a particularly vicious bend in the road.

'The raft isn't quite finished. There's still a bit of work to be done.'

I throw him my phone. 'Find Neil's number on there.'


Neil rises to the challenge, even though it means letting go of the basket lantern. He hands over to Betty and Milly and enlists the help of Mike to head up to the park and complete the raft. I can rest a little easier knowing he and Mum are going to be nowhere near each other for a while. I'm feeling rather pleased with myself, sitting waiting for Raf in the A&E reception area, when my phone rings. It's Mum. She freaks when I tell her I'm at the hospital.

'It's all right. One of the artists needed some stitches. You'll have to walk back, I'm afraid.' It's five minutes on foot from the town centre to our house.

'You said you'd pick me up!'

'I'm in Barrow, Mum. What do you want me to do?'

'Can't Neil get me?'

'I have the car. And he's at the park.'

'Can Betty come and meet me?'

'Betty's finishing Milly's lantern with her and if she's in the garden, she won't be able to hear the phone.' I'm losing patience now. She went out to buy some vegetables. How heavy can it be? 'Look, I'll see if there's anyone at the park who can help.'

'No, no. Don't worry. You're obviously busy.' She falters, 'I'll get a taxi.'

That won't work. I once called a taxi to pick me up from the train station when I arrived back from Hitchin, laden down with a suitcase of my old records that needed rescuing from Mum's damp attic. The woman who answered the phone barked, 'Now?' as if such a request was unheard of, and told me her husband was busy feeding his pigeons before slamming the phone down. Maybe Mike will be able to pop out and get her. 'I'll call you back.'

Mike is, literally, knee-deep in the tarn with Neil, and can't help. I ask Lizzie. I know this isn't fair. I know everyone has better things to do, but if I don't sort this out mum will play the injured victim or worse. She might decide to cause a scene. I can't afford to let that happen. I need to keep her on side. I don't have to explain to Lizzie; she's heard enough about my mother to get the picture. 'I'll sort it. Don't worry.'

It takes another hour for Raf to appear, his hand neatly

bandaged. My mother phones three more times while I'm waiting for him.

'Where do you keep your garlic salt?'

'I don't have garlic salt. There's garlic in the ceramic pot by the chopping board.'

'I need garlic salt.'

'Well, I'm sorry. You'll have to manage without it. I'm sure no one will notice.'

Ten minutes later, 'Do you have any onions?'

'I thought you bought vegetables?'

In the silence that follows, my irritation echoes back to me. It's not her fault I'm under pressure. 'Check the salad drawer in the fridge, there might be half a red onion in there.'

'Has Milly had anything to eat since lunch? She's been out there fiddling with that lantern thingy all day. She didn't eat much of that pie.'

I slap the steering wheel. 'I don't know, Mum. Why don't you ask her if she's hungry?'

A pause, and then she says quietly, 'I'll get her something.' Again, I'm left feeling ashamed at having snapped. She's doing her best.

I drop Raf with Neil and Mike, who have created an awesome raft and are delighted to be able to show it off. It's all coming together. The mood in the park is buoyant. I drive home and skip up to the house.

Mum greets me, face flushed. 'Oh! Thank God, you're here. I can't work this damned oven!' The kitchen looks as if something's exploded. There's flour everywhere. 'The bag had a hole in it.' Vegetable peelings litter the table, covering paperwork that has not been cleared; bank statements, letters and bills that need filing.

'Mum! Couldn't you have tidied up a bit and made some space first?'

'Oh! Oh, I'm sorry. I wasn't sure where it all went.'

I start collecting things, shaking them clean. There's a pile of raw chicken breasts on the chopping board. 'Betty and Mike don't eat meat!'

'It's chicken!'

'Chicken is still meat!"

She starts to flap and says, desperately, 'They can just leave the bits of meat to one side.'

'It doesn't work like that!' I glance at the clock. 'There's no way this is going to cook in time.'

'Don't worry, I'll do it. I'll leave the chicken for you for another time. I couldn't work out this oven of yours and I've only just got in because I had to wait for that girl to arrive and then she had to move all the bags of electrical cables and boxes off the back seat.'

I literally chew my tongue. There's a strong smell of burning from the hob. As I lurch for the frying pan the smoke alarm starts to screech. Grabbing the entire pan, I carry it out into the garden. Betty and Milly look up. Red Riding Hood's basket is complete. Milly is grinning from ear to ear. I dump the frying pan on the patio and ignore the piercing alarm, my mother's voice, and walk away from it all, towards Milly and her lantern.

'Everything all right?' Betty asks, glancing towards the chaos in the kitchen.

'She thinks chicken is a vegetarian option!'

Betty smiles. 'Don't worry. There's plenty of pie left over. It will be fine.'

*

It isn't fine. My mother insists on continuing with her plan, minus the chicken, but insisting that chicken is just the same as fish and most vegetarians eat fish. I ignore her. Neil and Mike come home to get showered and changed while I dash to the park to check how it's all going. They've completed the rigging for the finale. The raft is in place and Lizzie and Jonty are stringing fairy lights around the stage at the far end, by the woodland trail, where the pigs will confront the wolf before they chase him to the tarn. Three dancers with pig-shaped lantern bodies lit by tiny LEDs will perform for the crowd. They're practising on the grass now, in black leotards and leggings, their hair tied back from their faces in ponytails that pull their cheeks taut. Lizzie assures me everything is under control. I'm so grateful to her. Never again will I allow my mother to visit when I'm managing an event. She has no concept of the responsibilities I carry. She's unable to see anything from anyone else's point of view. It's like dealing with a toddler. Milly is less demanding.

I check my watch. It's almost seven o'clock. As I walk home I pass a father and son pushing a shopping trolley on top of which they've built a lantern gingerbread house. They grin proudly as I admire it. The town is hushed. The police have closed the roads into the town centre and the stewards are gathering in their high-visibility bibs with their portable fire extinguishers. People have set out chairs on the street in front of their houses preparing to watch the parade. Tarnside trembles with anticipation.

At the house, Mum's laying the table. Betty has put the pie out and pours me a glass of red wine. 'Drink that.'

I do as I'm told. Milly's skipping around the kitchen and getting under everyone's feet. She's still wearing her glue-splattered leggings and T-shirt. I send her upstairs to get changed. 'Where's Neil?'

Betty nods to the garden. 'We forgot to make a window in the lantern, to light the candle.' He's painstakingly cutting into the tissue paper with the Stanley knife. I should find this funny, but I can't. All I'm aware of is the clock above the dresser, counting down the minutes. It's seven fifteen. We should be getting ready to leave. Milly isn't dressed yet and we haven't eaten. I'm a piece of elastic being stretched tighter and tighter.

Seven thirty-three. Mum dishes up the rice. It looks like mashed potato. I don't even want this meal. She huffs and puffs as if it's all too much, but no one asked her to do this. She pulls the casserole or stew, or whatever the hell it is she's cooked, out of the oven and places the hot dish on the table. It will burn a mark that will remind me of this day for ever, but I say nothing. My mouth is squeezed shut.

Seven thirty-six. Betty calls the men to the table and volunteers to gee Milly along.

Seven forty-two. We're all sitting down in the kitchen, while in the street people are gathering outside the churchyard with their lanterns.

Seven forty-five. I can hear their voices, greetings, exclamation, the hum of expectation.

Seven forty-eight. The stewards will be moving through the crowd with their lighters, lighting the candles, flame by flame, bringing each lantern trembling to life.

Seven forty-nine. The procession is assembling. As our meeting point is closest to the park, the giant wolf lantern will lead us to the market square where the four tributaries will flow into one long river behind us for the final route back for the finale. I wanted Milly to be there, at the front, with us. This is the time, just before the procession begins, when it's all still to come and there's something so special about Tarnside in that moment, so proud. I wanted Milly to feel the magic building, to be part of it, but instead we're here, summoned to the table by my grumpy, flush-faced mother, eating a meal that no one really wants.

Seven-fifty. The elastic snaps.

I'm on my feet. I'm shouting. I'm stamping my foot like a child. I know I look ridiculous, I'm being rude, I'm behaving badly, but I can't stop. I grab Milly by the hand and I run.

# Chapter 22

Neil shouts after me from the top of the street. He's struggling to carry the giant basket on his own. Milly squeals with delight and we run back up the street to help.

'It's all right,' he says, squeezing my hand as we make our way back to the crowd gathered at the end of the street, lanterns dangle from bamboo poles in the twilight that drapes down over our little town. 'The procession hasn't set off.'

'But I wanted to be there for the lighting up. I wanted Milly to see.'

'She'll have plenty more chances to see.'

'My Red Riding Hood coat!' Milly shouts.

Neil turns to run back up the street. I put my hand on his arm, 'Next year it will be just us.'

'Promise?'

'I promise.'

While he's gone, I lift Milly onto a low garden wall and climb up after her. I behaved like a stroppy child. I should have handled this better. What if Mum retaliates? What if she says something about Tina?

I don't want to think about that. Here. Now. This moment. With Milly. This memory. From here, we're looking down onto the crowd and have a good view of the lanterns.

There's a quivering hush, people meet up, exclaim over one another's creations, but their voices are lowered, just a little, in deference to the occasion.

'Look!' Milly beckons to Neil as he hurries back, red duffel coat draped over one arm. 'A witch's hat!' She points to a modest, triangular lantern carried by a child about her age.

'Perhaps more sensible?' I ask, smiling at Neil as he threads Milly's hands into her coat.

'Who wants to be sensible?'

Milly shouts, 'There's Roisin!' jumping up and down and waving frantically at her new friend from the reception class. Roisin's mum, her hands full, gives us a nod, her lantern bouncing against the bamboo pole attached to her son's buggy. Their lantern looks like a vegetable of some sort. Neil hazards a guess, 'The magic turnip?' There are wands, moons and cauldrons, but also more adventurous designs. It always amazes me how creative people can be. There's a castle, a cat, a fir tree, a wishing well, a frog and several very evil-looking goblins and trolls. One family have splashed on green paint and created their own Shrek, much to the delight of the crowd. Two young people carry a large, flat, oval-shaped lantern which baffles us until they turn, face on, and we see the silhouette of an evil queen on the surface. 'Mirror, mirror, on the wall!' Milly shouts, apoplectic with excitement.

There's movement among the gathered figures. The lanterns have wobbled into place and are forming a thread the length of the street. We hurry down to join them as the giant lantern wolf gracefully navigates the corner, undulating his way towards the front, to a gasp of admiration from the crowd. Raf animates the terrible jaw with a bamboo stick, making the children squeal, and gives us the thumbs up as we slip in behind him. From his pocket, Neil produces the lighter we keep in the kitchen drawer. Milly gently prises open the little tissue window and Neil reaches in and lights the candle, transforming our lantern into ghostly, quivering life. Neil has attached two bamboo sticks to the interior to balance the bulk and together he and Milly raise the basket above our heads, where it glows gold against the darkening sky.

And it's as if this final light breathes life into the procession. We're blown forward. A community moving together in wonder. I catch sight of Guy and India in the crowd, with their son, who is now taller than his father, and Kath and her husband. I take Milly's free hand. 'Was I awful?' I ask Neil, over her head. 'Were your mum and dad horrified?'

He grins. 'I think they understand.'

'What about Mum?'

His face hardens. 'Don't worry about her.'

I hesitate. 'Did she say anything?' He shakes his head. I watch his face for clues but can see nothing beyond the normal level of irritation she causes him. 'Are they coming?'

'I told them to head straight to the Market Square and meet us there.'

'But how will they find us in the crowd?'

He glances up at the lantern. Of course. He winks. He wouldn't be winking at me if Mum had said anything about Tina. I feel calmer now we're here, the three of us, together.

Lizzie, dressed in her hi-vis vest, falls in beside me. 'Hello, Milly. Awesome lantern.'

'Me and Daddy maked it!' says Milly, proudly. 'And Nanny Bet. Nanny Bet is my daddy's mummy,' she explains. Listing the family members is her latest thing. Names and titles, keeping a log.

I ask, 'Is Pearl here?'

Lizzie points over the heads of the crowd. Pearl is sitting high on someone's shoulders, but it won't be her dad; Jonty is stewarding for us in the park tonight. Lizzie sees me frowning and mouths, 'Sam.' Of course, Jonty's son. Pearl's eighteen-year-old half-brother. I watch as she grabs a handful of his dark hair in her little fist and pulls. He yelps in pain and reaches up to disentangle her fingers.

'You OK?' Lizzie asks.

I groan. 'My mum.'

Lizzie laughs. I wish I could laugh at this situation. I've never met Lizzie's mother, but I've heard about her. Lizzie has her own problems. She makes the occasional duty visit to London, but their relationship isn't close. She seems to suffer none of the guilt and angst that I battle with. Or maybe she's just better at dealing with it. What would Lizzie have done in my shoes this evening? She would have insisted that tonight was not the night for an elaborate meal. She would have been firm and reasonable and things would never have reached that exhausting, emotional climax. Why can't I be like that?

Sam lifts Pearl off his shoulders and turns her to face him, shaking his hair at her as she squeals in giggly delight.

We hear Betty shout over the crowd as we reach the Market Square, where four more processions join us to head together towards the park. We're effectively looping back on ourselves, but it's wonderful to navigate these streets, lined with people cheering us on. Some sit on chairs, outside their front doors, with cups of coffee or tea, while in the town centre a more raucous crowd gather outside the pubs and shops clutching glasses and bottles of beer. The crowd is thick here and bodies press up against us. Neil calls out and rises on tiptoe, craning his neck to see over the mass of heads. Above the shops people hang out of the windows of their flats exclaiming and pointing at the more adventurous lanterns as we pass. The shopping trolley gingerbread house gathers lots of laughs. Someone shouts, 'Look! Red Riding Hood with her basket!' and Milly beams up at me proudly.

I see Betty's grey bun, held together with jewelled pins, strands of hair spiralling free. She shoulders her way through the bodies, apologising politely, determinedly insistent, clearing a path until she reaches us. Behind her, Mike is struggling to navigate the wheelchair, with my mother sitting like an overgrown toddler, grimacing at every jerk and bump.

'Nanny Bet,' Milly announces to Lizzie.

'Well, hello, Nanny Bet,' Lizzie replies with a little bow.

Milly doesn't introduce Mum, who sits huddled in her chair, shivering. 'They really need to manage this better.'

'*They*? I'm *they*, Mum! I'm the one managing this.'

'I meant the council. The police.'

I shake my head. 'The council and the police are here. The stewards are prepared and keeping an eye on things. Everyone else seems to be enjoying themselves.' I can hear the petulance in my voice and hate myself for it.

Mum throws me an injured look and suddenly her face is transformed with a smile that disarms me. It's her proud mother smile. 'You work so hard, Evangeline. It's extraordinary.' I'm immediately ashamed of the resentment

I've been feeling towards her. She turns to Lizzie. 'Isn't my daughter amazing?'

I interrupt, quickly. 'Lizzie's had as much to do with all this as I have, probably more.'

'Really?' Mum sounds unconvinced but Lizzie laughs, taking it with good grace. I search the crowd for Sam and Pearl. They're with India and Guy's son. He and Sam will have been at school together. Different years, but they're both into their music and I seem to remember were in a band together, briefly. Pearl is back on Sam's shoulders, drumming a rhythm on the top of his head. He reaches up to take her hands in his. She wriggles and squirms. I watch the two of them for a moment, mesmerised. All that affection. What they have is unique; beautiful and valuable in its own right.

Tina's son will be twenty-six. A young man. He may be troubled and difficult and better kept a secret. But he may be someone like Sam. Someone Milly might love. Someone who might love her.

I glance at Mum. She's watching me, her face concerned. I don't want her reading my thoughts. I don't want this knowledge that exists between us. 'That's Pearl,' I explain. 'Pearl is Lizzie's daughter. And Sam's her brother, Lizzie's stepson.'

Mum beckons me to her. Her face is full of pity for me. I shake my head and turn away. Neil is introducing his parents to India and Guy. Milly is gazing up at her lantern, head tipped back towards the sky.

'Evangeline.'

She starts to struggle out of the wheelchair. Betty says, 'Are you all right there, Joan?'

'I need the toilet. Evangeline?' She reaches for me to support her.

Betty offers to help. 'Let me take you, Joan.'

But Mum bats her away. 'No, no. You go ahead. Evangeline will take care of me.'

Neil, seeing Mum on her feet, asks, 'What's going on?'

'Mum needs the loo.'

He folds the wheelchair. 'We'll come with you.' But I don't want Milly to miss the procession. I tell him to go ahead and promise to catch up and take the wheelchair in one arm while Mum leans heavily on the other. Clumsily, we nudge our way through the surrounding bodies.

Inside, the pub is empty, everyone having spilled out onto the street with pints in hand, to watch the gathering procession. Mum sits down heavily on a bar stool with a sigh.

'I thought you needed the toilet?'

'Evangeline, I have to talk to you.'

'Now? You want to have a conversation *now*?'

Her fingers are interlaced, thumbs circling. 'You can't keep this up.'

A twitch in my peripheral vision. Chill breath on my neck. The barman is loading the dishwasher with dirty glasses. Two men that might be father and son walk in looking for refills. I take a lungful of air, straightening up to full height. I am not going to discuss Neil's past in here. 'Mum, I've warned you.'

She shakes her head. 'All this – it's too much for one person to cope with alone.'

Something inside me is unravelling. I swallow, lean in close, whisper, 'That baby is not Neil's. If it was, Tina would have told him. This is the truth. Do you hear me?'

She's silent, watching me. Unpicking me. 'I'm worried about you.'

'I'm fine.'

'Darling, you are not fine. This is not fine. You can't do this.'

No, no, no. Tensing, holding it in, tight, tight. 'I have to. For Milly. Do you understand? If you say anything, I could lose Milly!' She watches me, processing this. And then she nods and I relax the tension a little. Breathe. 'The review is on Monday. We just have to get through that so we can get the adoption approved and ratified in court.'

'I understand.' Her voice is firm. She is capable, strong. She has recognised the challenge ahead of me and she is on my side.

'This is about Milly, now. My daughter. We have to think about her.'

'You're sure you can convince them?'

'I have to.'

She frowns, watching me. She isn't sure, and again, I can feel everything loosening. I clench my teeth and look away. As she takes my hand in hers and squeezes, I count the upturned bottles that feed the optics, blinking back tears.

'Don't worry, Evangeline. We can do this.'

We.

# Chapter 23

The sky is completely black by the time the crowd gathers in the park and the scaffold tower has been draped in black cloth, so all we can see is the twinkling outline of three fat pigs wearing illuminated masks. The community police officer estimated about ten thousand people, but it's eerily quiet beyond the haunting, lilting music that conjures the dance. Milly sits on Neil's shoulders, mouth open, transfixed.

Mum believes Neil has a son, but Ann Lord may be wrong, Tina may have been lying. What's important now is Milly and making sure the adoption goes ahead as planned and, whatever she thinks of Neil, whatever she believes, Mum understands this. No one else knows. No one can know. I have to keep this secret, but I'm scared. I'm not sure I can carry this responsibility on my own.

*I understand.*

Mum is on my side. She is here, for me. I can feel her strength. I need to draw on that strength. For Milly's sake, I have to pull this off.

The wolf breaks the hush, running from the pigs with a panicked roar, across the lawn, towards the tarn, not through the crowd as Raf had planned, but to one side to avoid any accidents. There's a trickle of enthusiastic applause swelling into a flood of hoots and whistles of delight as the pigs pretend to do battle with their predator at the shore. A sudden gasp and hush. One of the pigs has stumbled. A young woman in black, wound in tiny lights, falls on the ground. Her fellow pigs haven't noticed, they're too busy helping Raf and his colleagues divest themselves of their harnesses and balance the wolf lantern on the raft. The wounded pig struggles to her feet and gives the crowd a reassuring wave, limping towards the tarn.

I knew I was never going to conceive. Not because of any scientific evidence, not in any way I could prove, I just knew, as if it had been scratched into my bones before I was born. I'm not a person who expects things to go well. It's not that I'm a pessimist, I like to think I'm a hopeful person. I'm not negative or downbeat, I'm just a realist. Never presume. Things will be what they will be. I've always been aware there's a limit to how much I can control, but this doesn't mean I need to be powerless. *Be prepared.* I'm always prepared. This is why I'm good at my job. *Expect the unexpected. Life throws you lemons, make lemonade.* I know all the lines. I've never expected anything to be easy. It hasn't stopped me moving forward or having dreams, like everyone else, I just make sure they're modest. I don't ask too much. And I don't expect to get what I want first time around; it doesn't work like that for me. Patience. Persistence. Flexibility. The trick is to always have a Plan B.

My mother taught me: you want something, you must work for it. And she supported me in that. She gave me courage. She believed in me. Everything that matters to me I've fought for. She was always proud of me. Until Neil.

Did I ask for too much? I found Neil, his wonderful family. I found foreign adventures, new experiences and this place, this town, this job, this community. Was it too much to ask for family of my own?

Maybe Mum's right. There was a reason I didn't conceive – a bigger reason. Maybe I wasn't meant to be with Neil. We were not meant to be parents. I'm not cut out to be a mother. Maybe the writing is on the wall. Maybe Claire will sort herself out and take her daughter back. A happy ever after. Just not mine.

I try to focus on what's happening in front of me, to be here, right now, in this moment. The wounded pig grabs the torch and with a quick flick of flame at the glue-stiffened tissue, the wolf begins to burn and floats out across the water. The crowd roars and the pigs raise their arms triumphantly in the air as they take their lap of honour, one, a step or two behind, dragging a little on one leg. I slip back, putting some distance between myself and the crowd. Lizzie is busy taking photographs from the top of the slide in the playground. She gives me the thumbs up. We've done it. She shouts, 'I think this might be the best one yet!'

Tina was pregnant, but that doesn't mean she gave birth. She may have terminated the pregnancy. That would explain why no one knew about the pregnancy. She may have miscarried. There may be no child. But I'm clutching at straws. Ann Lord would have told me. She knows. Neil has a child. She told Mum, Tina had a son.

Betty makes her way over to join me, the woollen shawl she bought in the local boutique earlier today wrapped tightly across her shoulders and under her chin. She has befriended the girl who knits these shawls, after meeting her in the shop last year, and has made a point of returning to buy one in a different colour this time. She'll have recommended the website to friends, because she's generous like that, a community-minded woman, who sits on the board of the local arts trust and fundraises and lobbies for all sorts of interesting, creative projects. She's the one who understood that teaching wasn't for me. It's thanks to Betty that I got involved in community arts and discovered an alternative, more creative career. She appreciates what I do in a way my mother can't. For my mum work is all about money and status. She was a teacher, like Betty, but it was a means to earn a living, not a vocation. I was my mother's vocation.

Tina was pregnant. Tina has a son. Neil is the father.

How was that child conceived? What happened between Neil and Tina? Why did no one know about the pregnancy?

We were asked if we would adopt a child born of rape. I said yes. Neil resisted. The idea appalled him. I said yes to a child born of rape. Did I invite this into my life?

Neil is standing with Milly on his shoulders, talking to Sam, oblivious. Has he forgotten? Has he justified it in his mind? How could he live with himself? Is he the man I believed him to be, or have I been blind? Drip-drip-drip.

Betty snuggles up beside me with a shiver that could be delight or simply the chill, and wraps the shawl around us. I am bone cold. I long to confide in her, to ease this burden, but she doesn't have the strength to keep a secret like this. I remember her biting her lip, admitting how she'd betrayed Neil to my mother. That was such a trivial indiscretion. How would she cope with something of this magnitude? Only my mother knows and she is holding her tongue. The breeze is picking up. Betty says, 'We've been lucky with the weather tonight.'

Last year, the wind and driving rain whipped the lanterns into soggy submission, but rain never deters the crowd. Families invest too much to give in. They'll always line the streets or walk the route, carrying their lanterns proudly, whatever obstacles they face. This festival matters to them. 'What's a bit of weather?' they say. Tonight we've been blessed. I must hang on to that. Milly is here. Neil is happy. Mum understands what I need to do and she is a far stronger woman than Betty. She will help me through this. I must put everything else out of my mind.

We stand quietly and watch as the giant wolf blazes against the inky sky. There's something frenzied about it. I wriggle a little further into Betty's shawl. 'It's lovely,' she says with a little sigh, as we watch a group of children trying to snag the raft with their bamboo poles. Some have lowered their lanterns onto the water to see if they'll float. One resourceful father has found a plastic lid and balanced the lantern on top. Betty says, 'This, you and Neil, Milly...' but the words get clogged and she can't say any more and a dark, lonely part of me thinks that's just as well.

# Chapter 24

The next day, I'm awake at dawn, unable to sleep, while Neil snores softly beside me without a care in the world.

Tina's son is an adult man. A baby that was born while I was still at school. A child that was Milly's age when Neil and I were at university and travelling in South-East Asia, free as birds. A little boy that grew up without a parent, that has never known his father. A child that was never claimed.

Ann Lord told me it was Neil. She may be wrong, but if Tina did lie, initially, because she was afraid, why, in all those years, once she'd established an independent life, would she continue to lie?

This is not my secret to tell.

Neil and I have always been honest with one another. It's the basis of everything. If he knew and I didn't, I would expect him to tell me. Unless the truth was too terrible to speak.

This is not my secret to keep.

I wait until Neil is awake and let him go downstairs. I can hear Milly with Mum. She's laughing. Mum is making an effort. She's on my side. She's strong. I can do this. Can I do this?

I don't go down until I hear Betty and Mike in the kitchen. Neil has made a start on breakfast and Mum is showing Milly how to lay the table. She glances up as I come in, emanating concern. She hasn't said anything to Neil. She's respecting my choice.

Neil asks if I'm OK. I tell him I'm just tired from yesterday, but Betty and Mike sense something. Mum remains quiet, shooting me reassuring glances. Neil keeps everyone distracted, talking about the different lanterns and the finale, determinedly upbeat.

Neil has a son. When they've all gone, when we're on our own, I will have to keep this secret alone. I will have to navigate that review meeting tomorrow. I don't know if I can do that. I have to do it, but my fear is pooling around my feet. What if I panic, fail to convince, or cry? What if I mess it up?

After breakfast, Milly goes to help Mike sweep out the car with a dustpan and brush while Neil carries the suitcases downstairs. I'm filling three water bottles at the sink when Mum comes into the kitchen. She pulls her cardigan tightly across her chest and moves alongside me as I screw the lids on the bottles. 'I'm worried about you.'

'I'm fine.'

'I wish I could believe that, but I know you, Evangeline, and you are far from fine.'

'Mum, this isn't helping.'

'I can help. You need me. You need my support. You can't do this alone, and you don't have to, my love. Why don't I stay? If I'm here you'll have someone to lean on, someone to talk to if you have a wobble.' Her voice is gentle, but strong, the voice that comforted me through fevers and playground traumas. 'Tomorrow is a big day. There's a lot at stake. You can't afford to mishandle this.'

I grip the sink. I could mess it up. The reviewing officer with her piercing stare. She reads between the lines. She will sniff out my fear.

'If I'm here, you will have an ally.'

She understands. Whatever the truth is about Neil, what matters most to me, right now, is keeping Milly and Mum has accepted this. She will do what is necessary to make that happen for me. We are a team again. I breath in long and deep, letting relief fill me up. We can do this. Together we can do this.

'I feel we're starting to make progress, me and Milly. After what happened...' She gives a little smile. My mother, who loves me, who has stood by me, whose life has only ever been about me and helping me realise my potential. I feel her reassuring squeeze on my arm. 'I can help with Milly. I can cook some proper meals for you. Take some of the pressure off? It's not easy being a working Mum. I can help. It's not like I have anything to rush back for.' Finally, she's recognised that I am an adult, a mother in my own right. She is a strong woman, my mother, she has endured, and she is a solid parent. I need to be that strong for Milly. With Mum's support, I can be.

Neil swings into the kitchen. 'All set, Joan?'

She hesitates, waiting for me to speak. I close my eyes and let her take responsibility. 'I'm going to stay for a few more days,' she says brightly.

The silence pulses through the kitchen. 'Eve?'

I turn to face him. He wants her gone, but she's on my side and she knows what's at stake. She is the only person that knows the secret I'm keeping and I need her. I can't risk making a mess of this. I can't do it without her.

'I'd like Mum to stay.'


As soon as we've waved Betty and Mike off, Neil tries to take me aside, but I grab my jacket and bag, telling him I have to meet Lizzie back at the park.

Lizzie can sense my mood immediately. 'Everything OK?'

'Just tired, that's all.' We are circling the tarn with two bin-liners. I'm collecting rubbish while Lizzie picks up the plastic bottles and recyclables.

'How long is your mum staying?' The question is loaded. Lizzie and I have talked about the difficult relationship we both have with our mothers. Not in any detail. I sometimes left off steam, encouraged by Lizzie's candour, but it makes me itch with guilt. I regret confiding in her now. My mother loves me and complaining about her is an ugly betrayal.

'She's going to stay a few more days,' I explain brightly, making it clear that I'm happy with the situation.

She gives a small laugh and says, 'I don't let mine come up here if I can help it.' I envy her this lightness. Her ability to find a difficult relationship so amusing. Is it a front? If it is, she maintains it well. 'The last time my mum was here, the barman from the Crown had to phone me to go and collect her because she was too pissed to remember where I lived and didn't have enough money to settle her tab.'

Lizzie has confided to me the traumas of her childhood, but the brutality of this makes me shrink from her, I can't help myself. There is something raw and painful behind these words that I don't want to feel. This is Lizzie's story, not mine. My mother is difficult, but she isn't a drunk, I wasn't abused. I should be grateful. Lizzie's mum is an alcoholic who neglected her children. There is no comparison. My mum has never neglected me. She has always been there and she's here for me now. I'm the centre of her world.

# Chapter 25

First thing Monday morning the team arrive for our final review. This is it. The day they decide whether we can go ahead. I've been longing for this day for months, but now it's here I'm sick with nerves, because I know something they don't and I cannot tell.

Neil has a son. I'm the one who's infertile. I can't have children.

What was it Mum said, back in Hitchin? There is a reason we couldn't conceive. There is a reason I couldn't have a baby with Neil.

I was not meant not be a mother.

Shona, Helen and the reviewing officer gather in the living room. Milly isn't at school this morning, so I've arranged for Mum to take her to the park until we're ready for her. Mum was efficient and cheery and Milly, for once, was compliant. She knows that today's a special day. She's eager to present herself to the panel and tell them we are her Forever Family.

We discuss the suggested contact issues and agree to visits with Nana and Gramps twice a year, as was always the plan. In addition to this we need to agree what sort of contact, if any, will be appropriate with Claire, but before we can start, I hear Mum approaching the doorstep with Milly. I apologise and go to meet her in the hall.

'What are you doing here? I said I'd call you when we were ready.'

'Milly wanted to come home. I think she'd rather be here. Maybe if she waits upstairs?'

Milly shakes her head.

I crouch down. 'Darling, Shona and Helen are here and they'd like to talk to you in a moment, but we're not quite ready yet. Would you go into the kitchen with Grandma for a bit?' But Milly is glued to the floor. 'Milly, please? For me? There's some cake in the tin; Grandma will cut you a slice.'

Milly narrows her eyes at my mother. 'Two slices.'

'Let's see you eat one, first.' Mum turns to me. 'You OK?'

Her concern, that irritated me before, is now an anchor. 'I'm fine.' I drop a kiss on Milly's forehead and return to the living room, closing the door behind me.

We've just settled back into a discussion of Claire's request for contact, when Mum makes a big fuss of bringing in a tray of tea and biscuits that nobody really wants. We wait for her to distribute cups and entreat everyone to take a biscuit, but when that's done she doesn't leave. Instead, she pulls up a chair and makes herself comfortable. Shona isn't happy and Neil is bristling. The reviewing officer and Helen exchange a look. After a few awkward moments, the reviewing officer asks Mum to leave.

Mum shakes her head. 'I'm family. I'm involved.'

I apologise to everyone. 'Mum, please. It's not appropriate

for you to be here. We need to discuss contact issues. There's no need for you to be involved in that.'

'What contact issues?' Mum asks, not budging from her chair. I know she's trying to show her support, but she's misreading the situation.

I try and catch her eye, but she's focused on the reviewing officer, who says firmly, 'I'm afraid that's confidential information.'

Mum looks her up and down through narrowed eyes. 'My daughter has rights too, you know.'

'This isn't about rights, Mrs Leonard, it's about what's best for Milly.'

'What about Evangeline? How is she supposed to mother this child if she's constantly being undermined by you and whoever else it is you think should be parenting this—'

'Mum!'

Neil stands up. He's shaking. 'Get out, Joan. You've been asked nicely and that clearly hasn't worked now so I'm telling you. Get out before I throw you out.'

No, no, no! Burning. Crimson fear, the colour of blood seeping from scalded flesh. I grab Neil's arm and try and pull him back into his seat but he shakes me off.

'Mum, please. You're not helping.'

Absolutely still. She glares at Neil. All the knowledge she has is in that look. I can feel him falter. She's scared him.

This is enough for her. She gives a little nod and turns to Shona. 'I was simply trying to support my daughter.'

'I don't need you here, Mum. Please. Just wait in the kitchen and look after Milly.' I'm begging her. 'Please.'

That pinched look. This was a mistake. She can't hide her hostility to Neil, to anyone who she sees as a threat to me. She gets up with an exaggerated wince and rubs her knee.

We wait for her to straighten up. She takes her time. No one speaks, we all seem to be holding our breath until she closes the door behind her.

I look at the reviewing officer. 'I'm sorry. She didn't mean to be rude, she can get a bit defensive on my behalf. She means well.'

Shona picks up her paperwork, looks around at us with a smile and says, 'So, contact. Claire. Where were we?' We can move on.

Shona reads a letter from Claire outlining her request. She would like supervised contact once a month. My heart sinks. I feel Neil's hand reach for mine, his fingers stroking my palm. Once a month is a big commitment; regular disruption for Milly and a regular opportunity for disappointment, but before we can say anything, Shona is explaining, 'I've spoken with Claire's parents. As Milly's primary carers for the last four years, they are best placed to advise us on what they feel would be best for Milly. Whilst they appreciate that Claire's intentions are good, and they love their daughter very much and hope she will, eventually, overcome her difficulties, they're not confident in her ability to do so, at this point in time. There is, apparently, a boyfriend on the scene, who is proving a negative influence. It was a difficult decision for them to give Milly up for adoption, but they remain convinced that this is what's best for her. A clean break. An opportunity to have a stable life. They've been there and seen, first-hand, the consequences when Claire lets Milly down. They strongly recommend that there is no direct contact until Milly is an adult and can choose for herself.'

Neil squeezes my hand. I feel terrible for Claire but if her own parents recommend this, then that gives me confidence. It's Milly we need to focus on, her needs. Everyone in the room agrees. I'm the one who suggests letter-box contact, via social services. I know I'm making life difficult for myself but I need to do this. I'm not able to have children of my own. I wasn't one of the chosen, for whatever reason. Claire is a mother, she's losing her daughter. Her tragedy is my gain and I need to do something in return. 'I could write. Once a year. Just to let her know how Milly is. Nothing too personal, but checking in. I could send a photo.'

Shona's shaking her head. 'No photos. Too loaded. And Cumbria's a small county, Eve. We need to protect your anonymity. Milly's safety is an issue here, given her mum's life choices.'

'OK, no photo. But some news. Just letting her know she's OK. That she's loved.' I can feel tears pricking at my eyes and my voice is catching. I swallow, steady myself. 'I would like Claire to know how grateful we are.'

It's no use. They think I'm pathetic and I feel pathetic, tears streaming down my face. But it's true. I am so grateful and my heart is breaking for Claire, who's made such a mess of things, but isn't much more than a girl herself and will suffer so much. Neil slides his arm around me and rocks me gently until I've got a grip of myself. He suggests a compromise. We'll write, if Claire writes. She can request information once a year and we'll provide it. If she doesn't contact us we won't communicate. He looks at me. 'I don't want to raise Milly's expectations if Claire isn't interested.'

I agree to this, because I cannot imagine a mother not asking for information about her child. Neil thinks Claire won't bother, he's cynical, but his mother gave him up and severed all contact until he was eighteen. And then, when he did meet her, what happened? I try to imagine how she might have felt, how difficult it would have been to meet

Neil, afraid that he wouldn't like her, wouldn't be able to forgive. Laura said he tried to help her, but she didn't want his help. Did she feel judged? Did she realise that she wasn't the mother he wanted her to be? How devastating that must have been for her. And for him. He has never spoken to me about this. Private places. Bruised places.

Is this how it was with my father? Did he keep a distance because she told him to? Did he have to overcome his fear to make that initial move? Does he think I received his card and didn't want to respond?

But these are our stories, Neil's and mine, not Milly's. Milly will make her own choice one day. And so must I. The address is tucked into the pocket of my diary. Waiting.

Shona fetches Milly. I hold my breath while the panel ask about her trip to Hitchin and she tells them all about the outdoor pool and Max and the dogs at Nana Bet's. She says nothing about Mum or the smack, or the arguments she's overheard. They ask about school and she talks about Roisin and a boy called Barney who does smelly farts and thinks it's funny. She also announces that we're to get a dog next week, which is news to me and, thankfully, to Neil too. There are a few careful questions about food and Milly rolls her eyes. 'I eat ham, cucumber, pasta and fish fingers and Mummy says that's enough.'

I add, 'And Nanny Bet's soup.'

Milly gives a solemn nod. 'And Naz's curry and rose-petal tea.' Everyone laughs. They're delighted with her progress.

Shona is smiling at me. She glances at the reviewing officer. 'Well, I think we're good to go?'

The reviewing officer nods, gathering up her papers. 'Yes, I think so. I suggest you submit your application to the court promptly.'

I hear Neil exhale slowly beside me. He reaches for my hand.

Shona nods. 'Good. Hopefully it won't take too long.' She looks at Milly and back at us. 'The sooner we get all the paperwork signed and sealed the better it will be for all of you.' She hesitates, clears her throat. 'Neil, your mother-in-law has something she'd like to discuss with us privately, and has suggested that you take Milly out while we talk.' Neil stiffens. He shakes his head. 'I've agreed to hear her out.'

'When?' My voice is a croak. Cold, cold. An icy drip. 'When did Mum talk to you?'

'She called me first thing this morning.'

Drip. Drip. I try to swallow. 'She has your number?'

'The call came through the main switchboard.'

She called social services? This morning?

Neil's voice is low, firm. 'Whatever she's got to say, she can say it in front of me.'

Shona continues in a steady voice. 'Why don't we let her say her piece to me in private, and then, when that's done, I'll ask her to leave? I'll tell her that you need bonding time with Milly and that she must give you that time. How does that sound?'

'What does she want to talk about?'

'I've no idea.'

But I do. I get up and run to the kitchen. Neil follows me out.

Mum is sitting ramrod straight at the table, poised, ready. 'Mum, please! Don't do this!' Her face is set firm. I know that look. She's on a course and nothing's going to stop her. Stupid! Stupid! I thought she was staying to defend me. I thought she was on my side. 'Please!'

Neil looks at me, his face panicked. 'What's going on?'

Mum says, 'I'll explain when we're in there.'

'Mum, please! Please! You promised!'

'I did not promise, Evangeline. I said I understood. I'm doing this for your own good.'

'No!'

Neil's voice cracks the air. 'What's going on?'

'There's a lot riding on today. They're about to give us permission to apply for the adoption order. If you say anything now it could ruin everything!'

'If I don't speak, it will be worse.'

'Eve?' He looks bewildered. What have I done? I should have talked to him.

And then he turns to face Mum. He's trembling, his fists clenched at his sides. 'Do it!' he spits. 'Go on, you poisonous bitch! Do it!'

He takes a deep breath, pulling himself in and looks at me, his face cold. 'I'll take Milly to the park. Call me when she's done.'

The three social workers are waiting in the living room. Mum marches in, ignoring my pleas to stop, to let me explain, as if anything I say could possibly make any difference to the bombshell she's about to deliver. She unfolds a page of A4 paper, like someone preparing to deliver a speech. Has she made notes? One side is covered in typed text. She smooths it out and I think she's going to start reading, but instead she looks up. 'I'm afraid to tell you that my son-in-law is a sex offender and, as such, poses a sexual threat to Milly. You need to protect her from him. I have proof. A statement from the father of a child he raped.'

# Chapter 26

I grip the mantelpiece for support. My mother pushes the page towards me. There's a look of triumph on her face that makes me feel physically sick. This is her moment. 'Read it.' She gives the page a little shake. 'You have to read it.'

I look at Shona. There's a stone in my throat and I can't swallow. My arms hang by my sides. I can't lift my hand. I can't touch this.

Shona reaches out. 'Shall I read it?' Mum frowns, considering. After a moment, she hands the sheet of paper to Shona. I watch as Shona pushes her reading glasses back up her nose and scans the page. Helen and the reviewing officer sit either side of her, watching, waiting. A film of my life is unfolding before me. A horrible parallel that has split away from the life I thought I was living, and whirls into an abyss. The colour seeps from Shona's face. This is bad.

Shona reads, 'This is my formal record of the serious sexual assault that took place against my daughter by Neil Wright in the spring of 1991 and the subsequent consequences.'

My knees are trembling. I feel my mother's arm around my waist. She steers me to the armchair. I let my legs fold and slide down as she guides me into the seat.

'My daughter was fifteen years old.'

Fifteen! She was just fifteen!

'She attended a party with a friend who subsequently left her there. She was plied with alcohol, which she was not used to, and Neil Wright, who was eighteen, and therefore an adult at the time, took advantage of the situation and raped her.'

Not Neil. Not my Neil. He couldn't do this. Could he? Why hasn't he told me about Tina? If he has nothing to hide, why has he kept this a secret from me?

Shona gives a small cough to clear her throat before she continues. The paper is trembling in her hand. Does she believe this? 'My daughter was too ashamed to report the assault at the time. We felt it best to protect her reputation. However, as a result of this episode, Tina's behaviour changed. She became unpredictable, volatile, wilful. Some weeks later she revealed she was pregnant.'

Shona pauses. The room spins. The walls are shifting, moving closer. My head is too heavy for my neck. There's saliva building in my mouth, a metallic taste, my stomach flips and I heave. My mother shouts, 'She's going to be sick!' and she's on her feet, grabbing the waste-paper basket from beside the door and all I can think, as she thrusts it towards my face, is that this is no good, that the vomit will seep through the wicker, but that thought is overwhelmed by the heaving and I no longer care about the basket, the carpet, I just want this to be gone, to vomit it up and be rid of it.

Shona's paperwork slid from her lap to the floor as she

jumped up. The file has fallen open and there are sheets of paper all around it. My mother bends down and retrieves the statement. I close my eyes.

Shona fetches me a glass of water. I'm aware of the other two women moving about. Someone wipes my forehead and chin with a damp cloth. I'm incapable of doing anything for myself.

When I've stopped shaking I ask to see the rest of the statement. She has proof. I cannot hide from this now. Written proof. Mum passes it to me, silently. She rests her hand on my shoulder. I swallow. The sour taste of vomit lingers in my throat. I try to clear it. I take a sip of water from the glass Shona has left on the coffee table beside me. She's sat back down and arranged her papers in a neat pile on the sofa beside her. Her hands are trembling. I start to read, 'We did our best to support Tina, of course, but her character had been changed by the incident and she refused to communicate with us about it.' I imagine Tina, a girl of fifteen. 'I believe she was deeply ashamed.'

Shame.

This is what I feel now. The reviewing officer's eyes are on me. Helen. Shona. Hot, burning shame.

'In late July 1991, some months after the incident, Tina left home. She contacted us to let us know she was safe, but wanted no further communication with us. We have not heard from her since. Neil Wright...' I stare at the word in front of me. Five letters. Individually harmless, together they scream from the page. I read the word but my voice won't work. I take a breath, try again. My voice cracks but I force myself on, '... raped my teenage daughter and destroyed our family. This is my true and accurate account of what happened. Vincent Lord.' At the bottom, beneath the type, is a heavy signature scratched into the page.

The room is silent. Mum is stroking my back.

Neil. My Neil. Eighteen years old. Reaching down into the pool to pull me up. Those eyes looking right into mine, as if he could see inside me, as if nothing outside that moment, that connection, mattered. His shy smile. He wouldn't. He couldn't.

Rape.

Tina Lord fell pregnant. Fell. Such a soft word. An accident. Involuntary. But there's nothing soft, nothing accidental, nor involuntary about rape. Rape is brutal, determined, ugly.

A child. Neil is the father of a child. A child born of rape? Somewhere out there is his son. An adult now. Does he know? Or has Tina kept her secret all these years? I shudder.

Shona is watching me. She holds out her hand for the statement. She has to lean right over to reach it. I wait while she scans the text. Is she checking that I've read it all? Is there anything I could have missed? Isn't it damning enough?

She looks up at me over her glasses. 'We have to take this seriously.' The reviewing officer is nodding her head.

Mum's voice is prim, sharp. 'Of course you do.'

Helen's gaping. It must be like some awful soap opera unfolding in front of her eyes. She'll go home and talk about this. *That couple, you know, the teacher and the one who works at the park, with the nice house – you'll never guess!*

Shona glances at her watch. 'Do you know how long Neil will be?'

Mum shrugs. 'You think he's going to be able to defend himself against this?'

'He has a right to hear any allegation made against him. It's only fair.'

'Fair? What's fair got to do with it? You think this is fair?' She squeezes my shoulder. 'My daughter lied to, trapped in this nightmare?'

Shona's voice is low, deliberate. 'He's with Milly.'

Milly. Neil and Milly in the garden building the lantern. Milly on Neil's shoulders watching the dancing pigs. Neil leaning over the bath, gently squeezing the sponge, dribbling warm soapy water down Milly's naked back, his chin resting on her head, eyes closed, breathing her in. I say, 'She's safe,' and I know this is true. Whatever else has happened I know. 'He wouldn't. He couldn't. He isn't that man.'

My mother grunts. But she doesn't know him. Black and white and nothing grey between.

Shona nods, but her lip is caught beneath her tooth and she's frowning. She glances at the reviewing officer and Helen, then her watch. She's worried. I say, 'I'll call him.'

Mum snaps, 'Don't bring him back here.'

'This is his home.'

'After what he's done?'

Shona takes my hand. No reassuring squeeze, no suggestion that she can make this right, but something is communicated, a thin thread of something that I refuse to define, because I need it to be hope. Shona's voice is serious, professional. 'This is now a child protection issue. I'm sorry, Eve. We need to refer it immediately. There are strict procedures we must follow.'

'What does that mean?'

'I have to phone the Safeguarding Hub now. Do you mind if I use the kitchen to make the call?'

Mum answers, 'You can make the call right here.'

'I'd rather do it privately, if you don't mind.'

I nod. 'You can use the kitchen.'

'Thank you. And if you could call Neil?' I feel for my phone. 'And if you could just ask him to come home. Don't mention...' She glances at Mum and then back at me. 'We just need him to come back with Milly as soon as possible.'

She wants me to keep this from him. She wants me to speak to him but not tell him our world has exploded. Whatever it is that happened all those years ago has landed in the centre of our lives and erupted and my head is ringing, the debris still flying through the air, and I have to pretend none of that's happening, because I need to lure him back. I must get Milly back. Because Shona's afraid that Milly isn't safe with Neil. That Neil might... I squeeze my eyes shut, as if this will somehow stop these thoughts.

The world has slipped off its axis and everything's falling. I've nothing to grip hold of. I lean back and stare at the ceiling, follow the fine cracks in the plaster, paths that lead nowhere. How do I navigate my way out of this? Who do I follow? I can feel myself lurching in one direction and pull myself back, only to fall the other way. I close my eyes, trying to steady myself. I'm Little Red Riding Hood, lost in the forest. My stomach is in my throat. Everything that was familiar is now unfamiliar. Which path to safety? What was it Mum used to say? If you're lost, stay still and wait. Stay still and wait. Stay still and wait.

I lose all sense of time. I hear Mum saying we need to phone Neil, but I can't open my eyes. I hear her take my phone. I hear her tell him in that tight little voice that he needs to come back with Milly, immediately. He'll be worried. He'll think something's happened to me. Something has happened to me.

When Shona comes back into the room, Mum is sitting in the armchair. The reviewing officer and Helen are going through their paperwork. All that was settled has been unsettled. The life we were about to embark on is drifting away from me, becoming blurred as the distance increases. I'm still on the sofa, pressed back into the cushions, my body taut. Shona has sheets of notes, scribbled in her loose, curling script. She sits down beside me. I feel her hand on my knee and look into her eyes. Brown eyes. Dark lashes. I try to picture her before her hair turned white. Did she wear it long when she was younger? Did she dye it when it first began to lose its colour? My mind is leaping from this to that. She's watching me, concerned. This is serious. This is really serious now. She gives a little nod, which is a question. She's asking if I can go on. I don't know the answer to that, but I do know that I have no choice.

She looks down at the notes and clears her throat. 'I need to talk you through what's happening.'

My mother responds curtly, 'Please do.'

Shona pauses. She gives Mum a cold stare. 'I have to say, Mrs Leonard, that given the nature of this allegation, allowing Neil to leave with Milly does seem rather odd. You felt no need to stop him leaving the house, unsupervised, with your granddaughter?'

She wasn't thinking about Milly, she was thinking about me. This is nothing to do with Milly. Mum knows that. I know that. Neil would never do anything to harm Milly.

Shona turns back to me. 'The matter has now been referred to the Safeguarding Hub.' She gives the reviewing officer a nod and looks at Mum. 'You have the right to remain anonymous—'

'I have nothing to hide.'

'The Hub—'

Mum interrupts, 'What is this "hub"?'

'The Hub is multi-agency; a group of identified professionals who are able to check all the relevant agencies – health, education, to see if the family are known—'

'Which family? Not our family,' Mum sniffs. 'Our family has never had cause to be investigated for any misconduct.'

'Nevertheless, we have a duty, to Milly, to investigate this thoroughly.'

'You'll be wasting your time.'

Shona looks down at her notes. She breathes deep. I can almost hear her counting. She swallows and looks up. 'We'll talk to the police, see if there are any previous involvements with any agencies and check to see if there is a police record of this incident.'

'It wasn't reported at the time. I've told you that.'

Shona shifts her body around in her seat to look directly at me. Her voice is gentle, kind. She's trying to reassure me. 'We know Neil, as a teacher, has been DBS checked and nothing came up in our adoption checks.' It's small comfort, but it is something. Shona doesn't want this to be true. Shona's our friend. She knows us. She knows Neil. 'The Hub will make a decision as to whether to take this further. If there is no evidence of a sexual offence—'

'I have given you evidence!' Mum snaps.

'An accusation is not evidence.'

'It's a signed statement by the father of the girl who was assaulted.'

'Nevertheless, it is simply his word.'

'That's outrageous!'

Shona takes a breath as if she's about to respond, but stops. She looks steadily at Mum and sighs, looks back down at her notes. The reviewing officer and Helen sit silent, either side of her. 'You will be informed, in writing, that a referral has been made and the matter will be investigated immediately.' She pauses, shifts a little closer to me. 'If no further action needs to be taken it could be a week from referral to closing. They work quickly.'

Mum's voice slices the air between us. 'And what about him? What happens to him now? He can't stay here. He's a threat to that child. Isn't *she* the one you're concerned about? He can't be allowed to stay here with her.'

'We will need to talk to Neil.'

That's not enough for Mum. 'What about the police?'

Shona nods. 'We will consult the police.'

'And he'll have to leave now, won't he?'

I can't look at Shona. The air has been punched out of my lungs. I'm falling off the edge of the world. No one can help me.

Shona says, 'I'll have to ask Neil to leave the house.' She looks at her watch again.

I don't know how to deal with this. How do I face him? Why did he lie to me? Did he lie? Why didn't I talk to him? My head is pounding and the room is shifting again. I struggle up. 'I need to lie down.'

Mum says, 'Good idea. You leave us to deal with this.'

I hear them return as I lie on our bed. Milly runs through the door chattering about something that's amused her while they were out. I hear Neil ask, 'What's she said now?' and Shona's low voice ushering him into the living room. Mum brings Milly upstairs.

'Here's Mummy.'

Milly hovers in the doorway. 'Are you poorly?' I force a smile and shake my head, holding my arm out to her. 'Just a headache. Come and give me a cuddle.'

She climbs onto the bed. Mum closes to the door behind her, but she doesn't go down. I listen for Neil to shout. For him to deny it. I wait for him to come thundering up the stairs, but all I hear is an ominous silence.

# Chapter 27

Mum brings me some pills and suggests I try and have a nap. I think I'll never be able to sleep, but I'm wrong. When I stir the room's dark and Milly's gone. I try to get up but my head's too heavy. My limbs are sunk into the mattress. I must speak to Neil. I roll over to the side of the bed, lower myself to the floor and crawl out onto the landing. Downstairs, I can hear someone moving around and for a moment I think it's all been a horrible nightmare and it'll be Neil, making Milly something to eat. I pull myself up against the banister and look down. The stairs plunge alarmingly. 'Neil!'

Mum appears in the hall and calls up the stairs. 'You go back to bed.'

'Where's Neil?'

'He's gone. It's all under control. You don't have to worry.'

'I want to talk to him,' but she's shaking her head and I'm spinning. 'Where's Milly?' A surge of cold panic shoots through me. Have they taken Milly? 'Where's Milly?'

I feel like I'm tipping backwards. I grip the banister. Mum is at the top of the stairs. She's holding me. 'Hush, darling. Sssshhhh. Milly's fine. She's downstairs eating her tea. Now you don't want her to see you like this, do you? Get some rest. I've told her you've got a bit of a chill.' A great black wave is engulfing me and I feel my way back to the bedroom, crawling the length of the bed and allowing my head to sink down, down.

I sleep and sleep. Day merges into night. I'm aware of the bedroom door opening and closing, Mum's cool hand on my forehead, stroking my hair. 'There, there. Mummy's here.' Is that her or is that me? Milly crawling in beside me, her little body warm against mine. The light from the hall falling in a shaft across my face. Mum easing Milly's body away from mine, her sleepy protests, or are they mine? Sounds from downstairs. Mum moving about in the kitchen. My phone ringing. The low murmur of Mum's voice. The doorbell and voices on the step. I can't move. Mum eases me into a sitting position and feeds me soup with a spoon. I'm a child again. 'Come along, Evangeline. Eat up!'

Where's Neil? Why isn't he here? Why isn't he protesting his innocence?

*Who* is he?

Could it be true?

We were always honest. No secrets; we talked about that. He had his bruises and I have mine, but there should be no secrets. Love is being brave enough to share it all. Nothing to hide. But he didn't tell me what happened when he met his birth mother. He didn't tell me about Tina. He hasn't talked to me about that time. I thought we were a team, in this together; we signed up to that: a contract, but the contract has been broken. Neil is not the man I thought he was.

Eventually, I gather enough strength to get up. Where is Milly? I pull on a dressing gown and drag my weary body down the stairs. My mother's sitting in the armchair beside the reading light with a needle and thread, glasses perched on the end of her nose, mending a hole in the sleeve of Milly's hoodie. I look at the clock on the mantelpiece. It's after nine. Outside it's dark.

'Evangeline! What are you doing down here? Get yourself back up to bed, darling.'

'Milly?'

'She's sound asleep.'

'Is she OK? What has she said?'

'She has no idea what's going on. You know what children are like at that age. I told her Daddy's gone away with work and you're a bit under the weather. She's perfectly happy.'

She is so calm, in the midst of this madness. Taking care of me, taking care of my child. She can do this. She can do this so much better than me.

I was never meant to be a mother.

'Has Neil phoned?' She shakes her head.

'What did he say, when Shona told him about the statement?'

She keeps her eyes focused on her task. 'Nothing. He was very quiet. I think he knows the game is up.'

'It's not a game.'

'A turn of phrase, Evangeline.' In out, in out with the needle. 'It's not my intention to trivialise this.'

'Did he ask to speak to me?' She stops stitching and looks at me, her face pitying. I turn away. 'Does he know? That I knew...?'

She's silent. I can feel her looking at me. He knows. He knows that I knew, about the pregnancy, his son. I knew and I didn't tell him.

Why didn't I tell him? If I'd told him he might have told me the truth.

I didn't tell him because I was afraid of the truth. Well, here it is. Here is the truth. No hiding from it now.

How do I do this? Neil has been there for the whole of my adult life. I've shared every waking moment with him for over twenty years. When we're apart, we're only ever a phone call away. I don't think there's been a day where we haven't communicated with one another since we first met. It's not possible to live with someone, to love them, to know them the way I know Neil and to get it so wrong. If it wasn't for Neil I'd still be in Hitchin, Mummy's little girl. I would never have travelled, had the adventures. The bike rides through the forest, running up the fell, this job; Neil made all this possible. Neil encouraged and enabled. Neil set me free.

But I have betrayed him. I should have told him about his son. He will never forgive me for this. We are no longer a team.

'Where's my phone?' She nods towards the mantelpiece. I pick it up, check incoming calls and messages. Nothing.

I go upstairs to the bathroom, slide the bolt across, lean over the sink and slide my fingers along my tongue. Purge myself. Bring it all up.

I cannot look at my reflection in the mirror. I'm well aware of my seventeen-year-old self who would be staring back at me. I'm back there, as if none of this ever happened. No Neil.

No Milly. They will take Milly away. They should take Milly away. I'm not a mother, I'm a pathetic, vomiting wreck, a child who's never grown up. I went from Mum to Neil. I have never been independent. I can't manage on my own. I am nothing. This is why I didn't conceive. Milly will be better off with someone else. I don't deserve her.

I slip into Milly's room. It feels warm and safe. A little pink haven. I kneel on the floor beside her bed and breathe in the warm, cinnamon smell of her skin, her apple shampoo, resting my head on the pillow beside her, comforted by the steady rise and fall of her breath. A soft whistle every time she breathes in, an almost moan as she breathes out. They will take her away. Ruth will comfort her. She will be safe there until another family is found. A better family with a proper mother. I lift the duvet and climb in beside her, feeling like an imposter. She smacks her lips as she shuffles over to accommodate me, unaware of my inadequacy. I curl around her, though I have no right, I press against her back, feel the steady beat of her heart in my own chest. And I fall into a guilty sleep.


I wake in the bed alone. Milly has climbed over me and started her day.

I must speak to Neil. I need to find out what's going on. Descending the stairs is difficult, my legs are weak and I feel light-headed. My phone's not on the mantelpiece. Mum's in the kitchen. She's pulled a chair up to the kitchen counter and is kneeling on it to reach the shelves above. She doesn't seem to be in any pain, in fact, she seems rejuvenated. She's taken the plates and bowls down and is wiping the shelves with a damp cloth. Does she think a bit of bleach will clean up this mess?

'I need my phone.'

'I don't think that's a good idea.'

'Why?'

She hesitates. 'You don't want to know.'

'What's that supposed to mean?'

'Gossip. It's better you keep your distance from all that.'

'What are they saying?'

'Not about you.'

'Neil. They're talking about Neil? What do they know?'

She gives a little shrug. 'It isn't important. You focus on yourself right now.'

I walk through to the living room in search of Milly, but she's outside in the front garden, playing with next door's cat. She has a ball of string and is creating jumps, like a miniature gymkhana across the lawn. As I watch I see Dawn turn into our gate and make her way up the path. She pauses and chats to Milly for a moment, discussing the cat, the plan Milly has. She's good with Milly. She engages with her. She plays with her. Dawn is a proper mother, that's why she had babies and I didn't. She can do this; I can't.

She will be coming to see how we are. News will have got out. Neil will be suspended from work pending the investigation. I know the language from the television dramas we watch on a Sunday evening. My life has become that drama. I go to answer the front door.


Dawn sits in the kitchen with her cup of tea. I'm glad Mum's here. If she wasn't here I don't know what I'd do. Mum can handle Dawn. She was right behind me in the hall as soon as she heard the knock on the door. I hesitated, but Mum produced a welcoming smile and bustled Dawn in. Mum isn't one to hide, she'll meet this head on.

'Please, please, make yourself comfortable,' pulling out a chair, standing over her, making Dawn feel as uncomfortable as possible.

An immaculate white tooth catches her glossed lip. 'Really, I don't want to...'

'Intrude?' Mum bites. 'Not at all. Not at all.' Mum almost shoves her into the chair. 'It's nice for someone to show a little concern. My daughter has had a terrible shock. Terrible.'

I hover beside the table, staring at Dawn. Her neck is flushed, her cheeks hot. She was expecting us to be evasive, on the back foot, but not Mum. 'How do you like your tea?' All smiles. She looks a bit manic, to tell the truth, but I'm almost enjoying this.

'However it comes.'

'It comes any way you like it. It's so kind of you to drop in. Isn't it, Evangeline? So kind.'

'It's really no – I was just...'

'Milk?'

'Please. No sugar. Thank you.'

I'm in the clothes I was wearing the day of the review. I have no idea how long ago that was. My T-shirt is crumpled and I can smell my stale sweat. My hair is matted against my head. I must look like a mad woman.

I slide into a chair opposite Dawn where less of me will be visible. Her face wrinkles with concern. 'I'm so sorry.'

'What are you sorry for?' Mum barks. 'You haven't done anything wrong.'

My voice is a mouse peeping out of its hole. 'Does everyone know?'

'Neil hasn't been at school. Something to do with the adoption...?' She waits. Her younger daughter is one of Neil's sixth formers.

'They're doing a final check,' I say, lamely. 'Just to be sure.' She nods. She knows more. Dawn has come to gather the facts. To put the record straight. She is the gatherer of information. She is the source of truth. But what is the truth? What can I tell her?

Mum says, 'They're investigating an incident in my son-in-law's past.'

'An accusation,' I interrupt, before she can say any more. We have to continue living in this community. Neil's job. So much at stake. 'It's a procedure. It should all be over in a few days.' I stretch a smile across my mouth.

'Well, if there's anything I can do, just let me know, won't you?'

What can Dawn do? Spread the word. A rape accusation. *Who would have thought? And him a teacher. A head of year. It just goes to show...*

'Thank you. That's very kind, but I've got Mum here.'

Dawn smiles, relieved. 'Of course. Every girl needs her mum. Lucky you.'


The next day, while I watch Milly sitting on the front lawn, chastising Gerry for some imagined misdemeanour, Dawn's words come back to me: *'Every girl needs her mum.'* I have barely seen Milly. When she's awake, I'm asleep, when I'm asleep she's awake. I don't have the energy or the will to leave the house. Lizzie will be holding the fort at work. She knows. Everyone knows. Mum seems to have it all under control. Right now, all I want to do is crawl into bed and pull the duvet over my head and hope this all goes away, but I drag myself out of my stupor and head into the kitchen where Mum is sitting at the table doing the crossword. My kitchen looks different. Less cluttered. All the condiments and oils, the tea and coffee and cooking utensils have been put away. The surfaces are bare and gleaming.

'Shouldn't Milly be at school?'

Mum gives a little shake of her head. 'I thought it best she stay home for a while. Under the circumstances.'

'What does Shona say? Has she talked to Helen?'

'What do they know!'

'Helen is responsible for Milly's well-being!'

'Does Helen live here? Does she have any idea of the impact of this? You want Milly in the playground with those children and their parents gossiping? Have you heard what they're saying?'

'What are they saying?'

'I'm not going to repeat it. Suffice to say, Milly doesn't need to hear it. The sooner we get back home the better.'

'This is my home.'

'For God's sake! Your home is Hitchin and always will be. You can't stay here after what's happened!'

'There will be an explanation. He was just a boy.'

'An adult.'

'No one is an adult at eighteen. He was only a couple of years older than her.'

'Three years.'

'They could have been boyfriend and girlfriend.'

'But they weren't.'

'Do you know that?'

Mum shakes her head, wearily. 'He raped her, Evangeline.'

The word is brutal as a hammer blow. 'Face it. She told her father. He wrote a statement.'

'*Did* she tell him? If she was raped why didn't she report it? Why didn't her parents talk to Betty and Mike? They're good people. They would have taken it seriously.' But they wouldn't have believed it. They would not think Neil capable of this. He's *not* capable of this. My fingers rake through my greasy hair, scratch at my scalp. 'This can't be happening. Not to us.'

'To him. Not to you.' She puts her arms around me and pulls me close. My brain is gloopy, my nose full of the sickly smell of rose oil. 'You're safe with me. It's all going to be all right. I know this is awful and I know you're in a lot of pain right now and if I could take that away from you, I would.' She steps back to look me in the eye, her hands gripping my shoulders. 'I wish I could go through this for you, but I can't, my love.' Her eyes pool with tears. 'But I'm here with you. You're not alone. And you don't need him. His past is catching up with him, but you're safe.'

'Mummy?' Milly's voice is a fine thread, lacing through the air between us. She's standing in the doorway, her face crinkled with concern. This is not how it should be. She shouldn't be worrying about me.

'I want Daddy to come home.'

I look at Mum. 'He's away with work,' she says briskly.

'He'll be home soon.' Will he? How can I say that? 'Listen, darling, why don't you get those lovely crayons Lizzie bought you and draw me a picture?'

'Will you come with me?'

'Yes, of course.'

'Can we go to the café?'

Mum snaps back, 'Don't be silly! Can't you see your mummy's ill?' Milly glares at my mother and growls. 'What have I told you about making ugly noises? Now stop this, you're upsetting your mummy.'

'I am not! You are!'

'How dare you!'

Milly looks at me. She holds out her hand. She is a lifeline.

'Let me get washed and dressed. I won't be long.'

'Evangeline, no!'

'Get your shoes.'


It's a mild day. I have worn too many layers and have to loosen my scarf and unzip my jacket as we walk. I move slowly. The town centre, usually not much more than a five minute walk, seems miles away. Milly holds tightly to my hand, guiding me, as if I am an invalid. The park café would be closer, but I don't want to go to the park; I can't face Lizzie right now. And I've promised Milly a bag of pick and mix.

The lady in the sweet shop is patient as Milly debates the merits of a humbug over a jelly snake. The snake wins on the grounds of size. She skips out, clutching her paper bag in her fingers. I notice Dawn further up the street and give a weak wave. She hesitates, offers a quick nod and heads off in the opposite direction. She's clearly had enough of our mad family for one day. I slip into the greengrocer's to pick up some late raspberries that are on offer. I know the young girl who is serving by sight, if not by name, and we usually share a bit of meaningless banter. I don't know if it's me or her, but we're not in the mood for a giggle today. It's only when I glance up from putting my purse away and catch the look that passes between her and the woman replenishing the chiller display that I realise they know something. It's the look of concern they throw towards Milly that undoes me. What exactly do they know? How do they know? I usher Milly out on to the street before she can clock what's going on.

'Can we go to the café now?'

The tea rooms are at the end of the high street, but at least it's downhill. Inside, Kath is sitting at the table by the fire. When the bell over the door rings she sees us and leaps to her feet. 'Eve! I've been so worried about you!' She hesitates. Milly is watching, head cocked to one side, that puzzled little frown between her brows. 'I heard you weren't so good.'

I collapse onto a chair. 'Who from?'

She hesitates. 'Your mum came in to the office to explain.'

I tell Milly to sit down and take her crayons from my bag with trembling hands. 'I've forgotten your drawing pad.'

Kath intervenes, 'Milly, why don't you go and ask the waitress if she has some paper?'

What has Mum explained? This is a small town. Kath isn't a gossip, but she will have talked to her husband, to India. Guy teaches at the high school; he'll know that Neil's off but does he know why? How much privacy are we entitled to in a situation like this? The kids at school will know something's going on. Every family in Tarnside will know that there's been some sort of accusation. Our family. Neil's career. Our home.

Mum's right. I may not have an option. I may have to go back to Hitchin.

Milly returns with the waitress, who has found several sheets of printer paper. I sink back into my chair while Kath talks to Milly about her lantern and the red duffel coat. It's difficult to hold my head up. What will happen to Milly now? How will I live without her? How will I ever get over this? Kath suggests Milly draw a picture of the finale. The waitress takes our order. I have no idea if she asks me what I'd like or if I answer her, but when she returns she deposits a cup of steaming fruit tea in front of me and Kath places a hand briefly on my shoulder.

I knew about the pregnancy and I said nothing. If I'd spoken to Neil we would have talked it through, he would have explained. I would know.

Milly draws crowds of lanterns gathered in the park, the glittering pigs dancing in the air, the burning wolf on the tarn. She concentrates as she draws, pressing hard with the crayons, the tip of her tongue between her teeth. What will happen now? Will they let her stay? Will I be allowed to keep her if I'm alone? Will I manage? Right now, taking care of Milly alone seems beyond me. Will Neil be allowed to see her?

When she's finished, Milly smooths the picture on the table in front of me and points out a group in the foreground, naming each one. 'Nanny Bet. Grandpa Mike. Mummy, Daddy and Milly.'

'You've forgotten Grandma.'

She points to a squat figure standing some distance from everyone else, under a tree. Her face is drawn in red. Her mouth is an angry black line.

'Why have you drawn her all the way over there?'

'I putted her away.'

I glance up at the door, as if Mum might be there, watching us. Kath looks down at her cup, stirring her tea. I say, 'Milly, that's unkind. Your Grandma loves you.'

'I hate her.'

'That's naughty. You mustn't say things like that.'

'*You* don't like her.'

'That's not true.'

Milly looks at me, unconvinced. 'She maked you sick.'
I hold my breath. The room is stuffy. Kath is listening.
'I heared you.' She has heard me in the bathroom. I put
my hand on hers. 'Are you sick?' The anxious little lines
across that perfect forehead; I am responsible for these
lines.

She's waiting for an answer. 'No,' I say, as firmly as I can
manage. 'I was upset and very tired, but I'm not sick. Not
any more.'

'I want Daddy.'


Exhausted, and unable to face any more pitying looks, afraid
that there may be worse – disgust, suspicion – I say goodbye
to Kath, who hugs me to her, and take Milly back home,
walking hurriedly, head down.

As we enter the kitchen I catch the tail end of a message
being left on the landline. Shona's voice. A click as she hangs
up. Mum is standing at the kitchen counter. Milly goes
straight to the living room. I hear canned laughter from the
television. 'Was that Shona?'

'I don't know, I wasn't paying attention.'

I lean against the kitchen table for support. 'Why didn't
you pick up the phone?'

'I had my hands full.' She's preparing another beef
casserole. The pink meat makes my stomach heave. I press
Play on the answer machine. It takes me three attempts to hit
the right button with my finger.

'Hello, Eve. This is Shona. I'm just calling to give you an
update.' Her tone is brisk. I can picture her standing at her
desk, tall, competent. Shona, our ally, our friend. What does

she think of us now? 'Neil is cooperating with everything, which is helpful. You'll appreciate that this changes things.' A chill breath at my neck. They are going to take Milly away. This family of mine is finished. We have failed the test. Neil has gone. Milly will go and I will be alone. 'We have a duty to investigate. The adoption order can't go ahead until we've had another review meeting to decide what action should be taken.'

Mum gives a loud cluck. 'These people and their meetings!'

'Shush! I need to listen to this!'

'... won't involve Milly. This will be to discuss issues around you, the adopters. The sooner we can organise this the sooner we can get back on track.'

I ignore the snort from Mum. Back on track. Shona hasn't given up on us. She still thinks it's possible.

But what if Neil has gone for good? What if he cannot forgive me? Will things go ahead then, or have I lost Milly too?

A pause. A different tone. Softer. Urgent. 'Eve, Helen needs to check on Milly. We need to arrange a visit. I'm concerned about you both.' Mum mutters something beneath her breath. 'Could you give me a call to arrange a convenient time as soon as possible?'

Mum throws the meat into the hot fat. The pan sizzles and spits. 'I don't think so!'

I stand by the telephone, unable to do anything. I should phone Shona back, but I don't want to have that conversation with Mum listening.

'Milly wants to see Neil.'

Mum gives a little grunt. 'Well, she can't.'

'I'll talk to Shona.'

'She's not going to let him anywhere near her!'

'What do you think he's going to do, Mum? She's five years old! She's his daughter.'

'She's not, though, is she?'

'Mum, however much you dislike him—'

'I don't dislike him.'

'Mum!'

'I don't. I have nothing against the man. Well, I didn't, until that statement, but before that I simply didn't believe he was right for you. He controls you, Evangeline. He's used to getting his own way. You don't see it, but I do. You used to be so independent, so ambitious. You wanted to live in the city, live abroad, take part in all the exciting international projects. Do you remember that exchange you had lined up in Berlin? But he stopped you going.'

'He didn't stop me. How many times?' I lean heavily against the table, facing her. 'I didn't want to go to Berlin and stay in some stranger's house. I wanted to travel. Explore. I wanted to be free. Neil understood that. Neil listened to me.' She grimaces, and in that moment she looks small and mean. 'He doesn't control me,' I continue, emboldened. 'You did. And he stopped that. And that's why you hate him.'

'I don't hate him.'

'He let me do what *I* wanted to do, not what *you* thought was best for me. I didn't miss out on anything. It was better! We went travelling, together. We worked abroad, for God's sake! It was better than your plan for me.' Her eyes narrow. 'But that's it, isn't it? That's what needles you. He loves me. You say you love me, but it has to be on your terms. You love *Evangeline*. You love the version of me that fits your plan. You don't love Eve. You don't love the adult I've become,' and I'm right. The look on her face says it all. She is repulsed by this attack. 'You can't love Eve. He does. That's what you can't stand: he loves me better than you do.'

Her expression is stone now. 'You think so.' She nods, slowly. 'What can I say? After all I've done for you. To have it thrown back in my face. Well, you can see it that way if you prefer, but I know you, Evangeline. You used to dream big. You wanted it all. You believed you could have it all and he robbed you of that. He's a small-town boy. Oh, he works hard, I'll grant you, but there's nothing special about him. He's a plodder and he's dragged you up here to this backwater and stamped out your spark. I've watched it happen. It's broken my heart, but it's going to be all right. You've got me, and I'll see you through this, I promise.'

'Neil's not a danger to Milly.'

'Let the professionals decide about that.'

'He'd never do anything to hurt her. He loves Milly. He wouldn't!'

'You think that.'

'I believe it!'

'You believed he was honest with you. You believed he had no other children. He raped that girl.'

'It's not true! I refuse to believe that.' I am crying now. 'Neil would never do that.'

I am no match for her. She lowers her voice. Slow. Calm. 'What you need to consider, Evangeline, is that it *could* be true. I know it's difficult. I know it's awful, abhorrent, it doesn't bear thinking about and you don't want to believe it, of course you don't, but...' She pauses, glances at Milly's abandoned hoodie on the back of the chair, and then at me, her eyes two lasers burning into mine. 'Could you ever forgive yourself if you were wrong?'

# Chapter 28

I am spent. My outrage has taken every last drop of energy and what did it achieve? I haven't heard from Neil and all I can do is wait in limbo to see what the decision will be about Milly. I refuse the pills Mum brings to my bedside. I sleep and sleep. Later, when she offers a bowl of stew, I tell her to leave me to eat it and flush it down the toilet when she's gone. I lose track of time. The doorbell pierces the fog. I force myself up, mouth like tracing paper. Mum answers it. Shona's voice. I get to the top of the stairs and see Mum blocking the door. Shona is speaking. 'I really must insist that you let us in, Mrs Leonard.'

'My daughter is not up to visitors.'

'This is not a social call. We're here to conduct an emergency review meeting. We must see Eve and Milly. If you don't let us in I'll have to alert the police.'

'Don't be ridiculous!'

'Mum!' She spins round, and in that moment, Shona steps into the hall with Helen behind her. 'Eve! Thank God! I've been worried sick about you!'

'She's perfectly fine,' Mum insists tartly. 'I'm taking care of her.'

I don't feel perfectly fine, I feel like a shadow person, I have no substance and all I want to do is crawl back under the duvet, but my head is a little clearer than it has been. I grip the banister for support and descend into the hall like an elderly woman. 'Let's sit down in the living room. Mum, could you make us some tea?'

She throws me a look of such fury it nearly knocks me over, but I hold onto the newel post and concentrate on Shona and the strength that's emanating from her. She is sassy and confident. Beside her, Helen looks like a schoolgirl in her skinny jeans and denim jacket.

Milly's in the living room, staring listlessly at the television. It's a cookery programme, but I don't think she's registering what's on the screen. She turns her head slowly as we enter the room and perks up a little on seeing Shona and Helen, but she's not the bright, exuberant little girl that came to live with us. She's troubled. We've troubled her. I sit down and scoop her up onto my lap and she clings to me for a moment, but soon wriggles free. 'Too hot?' I ask, and she nods, but she remains close, thigh to thigh, and I hold her hand.

Mum brings in the tea. Four cups. Milly says, 'Where's my tea?'

'Don't be silly. Little girls don't drink tea.'

'I want tea!'

'What have I told you about, I want?'

'Tea!'

Mum glares at Milly and holds out her hand. 'You can come with me, young lady!'

Shona intervenes before I can. 'I don't think that will be necessary.'

'Well, I'm afraid I do.'

'We'd prefer Milly to stay here, with us, Mrs Leonard. The purpose of our visit is to check on Milly.'

'You can be assured she's absolutely fine. I'm taking care of her.'

Helen says, 'But you haven't been approved as a suitable carer for Milly.'

My mother's entire body is rigid. She does not take kindly to be spoken down to by a woman young enough to be her granddaughter. 'I beg your pardon?'

Helen flushes pink. Shona steps in. 'Milly is still a "looked after" child and the responsibility of Cumbria County Council Children's Services. Neil and Eve have been carefully vetted and approved by us to take care of Milly until the adoption order is granted. If they're unable to take care of her, for whatever reason, we must be alerted and we'll make alternative arrangements. The most suitable arrangement for Milly would be for her to return to her foster family.'

'I'm her grandmother!'

Helen says, 'Not yet, you're not.'


Helen conducts the review meeting. Mum refuses to leave the room. 'I'm here to support my daughter.'

Milly's anxious about Neil. 'Where is he? When can I see him?' She whispers to Shona that she wants Mum to leave. 'Don't like her.' Mum blushes scarlet. Helen writes all this down. They'll take Milly away if I am not seen to be competent. I need to pull myself together.

'I haven't been feeling too good,' I explain, trying to sound in control. 'It was a shock.'

Helen nods. 'It's a dreadful situation for you.'

'Mum has been a huge support. I'm so grateful to her, but I'm OK now. I can cope. You don't need to worry. Can you tell me what's happening with Neil?'

Shona says, 'You haven't spoken to him?' I shake my head. She frowns.

'Has he said anything?'

'He's been very cooperative. He wants to resolve this matter as quickly as possible.' Mum snorts. Shona ignores her. 'I do think it would be a good idea to talk to him.'

Mum interrupts. 'I can't imagine what he can say that would redeem him. My daughter will decide for herself if she ever wishes to speak to him again.'

I look at Milly. She's glaring at Mum. She begins to growl, softly at first, but increasing in volume and then she barks. Mum shakes her head, sternly.

'Mrs Leonard,' Shona's voice is firm, 'could you leave us alone for a moment?'

'Absolutely not.'

'I'd like to talk to Milly and her mother on their own.'

'I am staying with my daughter.'

Milly starts to growl again. Shona looks at me. 'Mum, please, could you give us a minute?'

'I'm not leaving you.'

Another bark, and then a long, wretched howl. 'Milly, stop that, please!' I turn back to Mum. 'I'm fine.'

'I'll be the judge of that.'

'No, *I* will be.'

Milly stops howling abruptly and looks up at me. Her eyes flare, geeing me on. She needs me to be strong. I have to prove that I can stand up to my mother or they'll take Milly away. 'You're not helping, Mum. Please go.'

'Well, that's charming! Is this the way to treat your mother? Is this what you're teaching your daughter?' She glares at Shona. 'Is this the sort of behaviour you condone?'

Shona says, 'I think Eve's made her feelings clear.'

Momentarily beaten, Mum turns on her heel and retreats, leaving the door open behind her. Shona gets up and closes it.

There's a moment of silence as we wait for the room to settle around us. I lower myself into the armchair, my knees trembling. Milly climbs onto my lap and asks, 'Who is your mummy?'

For a moment I think she must be talking to Shona, but she twists round to look me in the eyes. 'My mummy?' She nods. 'It's Grandma, darling. You know that.'

She shakes her head. 'Not that mummy. Your proper mummy.'

'She is my proper mummy.'

Milly shakes her head as if this is unacceptable to her.

Helen leans in. 'Milly, why do you think Grandma isn't Mummy's proper mummy?'

Milly shrugs and stares at her feet. 'She maked her sick.'

Helen looks at me, thoughtful for a moment, and then turns to Milly. 'Where's Gerry Giraffe?'

'Hiding.'

'Who from?'

'Grandma.' I wince, but Helen and Shona remain focused on Milly.

Shona says, 'Do you want to go and see if he's all right? He might want a cuddle.' As soon as Milly's run out of the room, Shona turns to me. 'Eve, I think you have to tell your mother to leave. For the sake of your family.'

'What are they saying? Do they think Neil did it?'

She watches me for a long moment and I wish I hadn't asked. I don't want to hear the answer. 'Eve, all I can say is that there's no police evidence, but they are making enquiries.'

'Has he denied it?'

She hesitates and in that moment everything disintegrates around me. 'Phone him, Eve. Talk to him.'

'He doesn't want to talk to me.'

She glances at Helen. They exchange a frown. 'He told me he's called you, repeatedly. And texted.'

'I haven't heard from him.'

'He told us you sent a text telling him not to communicate with you.'

We look at one another. While the thought is still forming in my mind Shona asks, 'Where's your phone?'

# Chapter 29

Mum's adamant she did nothing wrong. 'I was only doing what any mother would do! I was protecting my daughter!'

She sounds so reasonable. She always does.

Shona offered to stay and I was tempted to accept the offer, to lean on someone normal with a grip on things who could sort this out for me, but I can't do that any more. I'm a mother now. I have family and that family is under threat.

I try and speak like Neil; a teacher, firm, rational. 'You lied to me.'

'I didn't lie. I just didn't see the need to upset you unnecessarily. I wanted you to have some peace.'

'I've been worried sick!' Too emotional. Keep it down. Don't let her do this.

'Because of what *he did*. You don't need to listen to his excuses. He'll only manipulate you and twist things and you won't know what to believe.'

She sounds so plausible. My head's spinning. I don't know what to think any more. I need to speak to Neil. 'Give me my phone.'

'I think the battery's dead.'

'Give it to me!'

She rummages in her bag. 'There really is no need to get hysterical. You're starting to frighten me, Evangeline.'

Deep breaths. Counting. Don't lose it. 'My phone.'

She lets go before I've managed to grasp it and the phone clatters to the floor, the back coming away, sim card sliding free. I bend down and collect up the pieces. It shouldn't be a problem. One of the reasons I keep this old phone is because it's robust. I place the sim card inside and slide the back into place. The screensaver photograph I took of Neil and Milly has disappeared leaving a black nothingness against which the white digits spell out an incorrect time and date. I select menu and the yellow envelope to check my messages, but there are none.

'Where are my messages?'

Mum shrugs. 'Don't ask me!'

The battery's almost dead. 'The charger?' She looks at me blankly. 'Where's my charger?'

'I don't know. Maybe Neil took it.'

It's possible that in dropping the phone I've somehow lost my message history. The screensaver always disappears, but the photographs are still stored and can be re-established. My messages usually reappear automatically. Not this time.

My mother's watching me, alert, trying to read what I'm going to do next. I need to phone Neil, but I'm not going to do that with her listening. Her eyes are like pins holding me in place. My chest is tight. I struggle to breathe. 'I'm going to take Milly out and get some fresh air.'

'But it's late. She needs to eat and get ready for bed. It's getting dark outside.'

I don't have the energy to argue. Sliding the phone into my pocket, I ask, 'What's for tea?'

She brightens at this. 'Fish pie. I got a lovely bit of salmon at the fishmonger's today.'

'I'll get Milly bathed and into her pjs and she can eat with us.'

She smiles.

I call Neil from the bathroom, while the bath's running. He picks up the phone but doesn't speak. 'Neil?' I can hear him breathing, but no words. I don't have long; the battery icon is red. 'Neil? I'm so sorry. I didn't know you'd been trying to call me. She took my phone. And I've been completely out of it. I didn't...' What can I say? How can he ever forgive me? 'I lost my mind for a bit. I lost... Neil, I am so... Please, please don't let her win.'

He sighs. And that sigh is an opening. I hold my breath and wait. But when his voice comes it isn't the weary, we've-been-here-before tone I'm hoping for, but something else. Something shattered. Sharp shards. 'What if it's true?'

'What do you mean?'

'What if I did do it?'

'Of course you didn't! You're not a rapist!'

'I don't know, Eve. I can't remember. I was drunk. I thought – but maybe... She wouldn't talk to me. I called her. I went round there, but her dad... and then she disappeared. And I've always wondered if it was me. If it was something I'd done.'

'You wouldn't do that. You couldn't.'

'I was eighteen and drunk. What if I misread – if she... How can I be sure?'

'*I'm* sure.'

He's quiet.

My phone dies.

I stare at the blank screen. I didn't tell him I love him.

The bath is full. I turn off the taps. My mother calls me from downstairs.

All our life together Neil's intervened and protected me. I haven't recognised it as that, but I've appreciated the benefits. I have this life here in Tarnside, I have this family, because he rescued me. Now he needs me.

I tell Mum I'm bathing Milly and will be down shortly. While Milly plays in the bath, I pack a small backpack: underwear and a change of clothes for me and Milly, toothbrushes and toothpaste, anything else we can buy. Slipping out of the front door, I take the bag down to the bottom garden where I throw it over the wall into the rhododendron bush on the other side. The tarn winks in the evening sun. I take it as a sign of support.

Mum's in the kitchen when Milly and I creep out. I tell Milly it's a game, but I think she understands that it's more serious than that. She tiptoes downstairs, holding her breath until we get outside, and then she grips my hand tightly as we hurry down the garden towards the park. I expect a shout at any moment, my mother to be watching from the window, 'Evangeline!' and I'm half laughing at myself and half appalled that at forty years of age I'm so frightened of my mother, I'm having to run away.

I lift Milly over the wall, my heart bouncing against my ribs.

# Chapter 30

I call Lizzie from the office and tell her, briefly, what I need to do. She's surprisingly alert to the situation, agreeing to drive over to the park and drop us at the station and asking no questions. But then she knows everything. She was there when Mum decided to air our dirty laundry in front of everyone I work with. She will have been appalled. She will have read between the lines. This is a small town and Neil and I have not been here long. We will always be off-comers, but we have earned respect in this community. We have friends. Lizzie knows who we are. Lizzie is loyal.

The trains out of Tarnside are, more or less, every hour. We're lucky, there's one leaving in twenty minutes. Lizzie arrives with a small holdall which, she tells me, has some bits and pieces for the journey, stops at the cashpoint so I can draw out some money, and parks up to walk us to the platform. She's focused on Milly, chatting non-stop, but keeping a careful eye on me. Still no questions and though I'm surprised, I'm also relieved. Maybe she's spoken to Neil.

I want to ask her, but as the train pulls in, a single rickety carriage, she wraps her arms around me and pulls me close. 'He's a good man,' she whispers into my ear. 'Find out the truth.'

Her faith in Neil, in us, is a shot of hope and as I step onto the train I shake off any remaining doubts.

At Carnforth, we get off to wait for a connection to Leeds. I take Milly's hand. Her small, plump hand in mine. I can feel that connection, something merging between our palms and I never want to let her go. She is the reason for everything now.

The retro café that's based on the tea room in the film *Brief Encounter* is closed and we have a long, cold wait for our connecting train. We press our noses to the glass and peek in. I imagine a black and white Celia Johnson and Trevor Howard leaning in close over one of the little tables and explain to Milly how the production company had to use this rural station to avoid the bombs in London. Milly yawns. I look at my watch. It's almost eight o'clock. She'll be exhausted by the time we get to Leeds. 'Why don't we stop here tonight?'

'In the station?'

'No, silly. Come with me.'

We cross the street to the Railway Hotel, an imposing Victorian building with dark woodwork and deep red carpets. They have a double room for a reasonable price. I pretend it's all a great adventure. 'We're investigators,' I explain to Milly. 'Solving the mystery. Daddy's hiding and we have to find him.' For a few seconds I can almost believe this is all a bit of fun. Something to entertain Milly. The idea that Neil's waiting to be reunited with us soothes a wound inside me. He's been trying to reach me. Lizzie believes he's a good man. There's a truth to be found that will exonerate him and I must find it. I owe him that.

I let Milly bounce up and down on the bed for a while, pretending it's a trampoline, and open the holdall Lizzie gave us. Inside are two cheese scones, a packet of biscuits and two apples. 'Look! Lizzie made us a picnic!' Milly throws herself at the food. She's brightened since we left the house. Since we left Mum. There's a washbag in the holdall with two toothbrushes, a container of very fancy bubble bath and some moisturiser. I hurry into the bathroom and start running a bath before Milly can see my tears.

When we've eaten, we strip off, giggling, as we slide into the bubbles together. Milly wriggles her soapy body up and down my limbs and eventually settles with her back to me, resting between my legs, her head on my chest, and it's the most comfortable and wonderful feeling in the world.

I help her brush her teeth and settle her into the wide bed. My phone's still dead. There's no phone in the room; everyone carries a mobile now.

It takes a few moments for Milly to start snoring softly. I slip out to reception and ask the young barmaid if I can use their landline. She directs me to a pay phone in the hall, under the stairs. I can't phone Shona, I don't know her number without my mobile. It's the last thing I want to do, but I dial my home number and wait for Mum to pick up.

'Evangeline! Thank God! Where are you?'

'We're fine.'

'What's happened? Has he abducted you?'

'Of course not.'

'I've phoned the police!'

My stomach twists. 'Why?'

'Because I was worried. You'd both disappeared. I thought—'

'For God's sake, Mum! Phone them now and tell them it's a false alarm.'

She's quiet. When she speaks her voice is low, authoritative, 'Come back, Evangeline. We can sort all this out.'

'I can't. Not yet.'

A pause. 'You're not yourself.'

Now I'm afraid. Red-hot fear. The dragon with its flaming breath. My rational mind tells me this is my mother, an elderly woman with a mobility problem, what possible harm can she do to me? But my body is alert, hairs on end, like an animal picking up the scent of a predator. 'I'm fine.'

'You're not fine, Evangeline. Your behaviour – this is troubling.'

'There's nothing to worry about.'

'Shona is concerned for Milly.'

The silence gathers between us as I try to swallow. 'What have you said to her?'

'She says Milly should be returned here immediately.'

'What did you tell her?'

'I told her I was worried about you. About your mental health. You don't know what you're doing any more. He's a liar. He's a manipulator and he's got you so confused you don't know who to trust. You no longer know your own mind, Evangeline.'


Back in the room, I sit on the bed, Milly curled into the foetal position beside me. My heart is leaping hurdles, my brain trying to keep up. I was planning to go to Betty and Mike's, but I can't do that. Neil will be there and I need to be careful. Until the inquiry is completed he can't be anywhere near Milly. I must follow the rules. That's what Neil's been doing, that's why he left immediately. It wasn't guilt. He's doing what's necessary to achieve what he needs. He's proving himself worthy, protecting me and Milly, our family, whatever it takes. Betty and Mike's is the first place Shona, or the police, will look for us. Will the police be looking for me? Seriously? I can't imagine they'll listen to my mother. I'm a grown woman; I can leave home if I want to. But Milly's not yet my child. I have broken the rules. This could jeopardise the adoption. They could they take Milly away.

Think. I try to imagine Shona, her cool, steady voice. What would she tell me to do?

Shona would want Milly to be with someone known to social services, someone they trust, but all those people are in Cumbria and we're heading south. Our contacts, our established network, are in Hitchin. And as I think this, I remember saying something along these lines to Shona during the adoption process. I was frustrated by the number of referees we had to identify. It's not easy to find people to vouch for you as potential parents when you've only been living in a community for two years. We needed three referees, and only one of these could be a family member. Neil's mum, as an adopter herself, was an obvious choice, but after that it was more difficult. It was Shona who decided to make the case for someone further afield. 'What about a friend from Hitchin or Stevenage?'

I phone Naz's mum. Her landline number is imprinted on my brain from childhood. She'll give me Naz's mobile number and Naz will give me Shona's.

*

'Jesus, Eve! You've had me worried witless!' I've never heard Shona so emotional. She is always professional and controlled. Her panic sends my heart sprinting faster.

'I'm so sorry. I didn't expect her to phone you. I was going to call and explain, but my phone—'

'Never mind that now. Where are you?' I hesitate. Is she going to take Milly away? Have I ruined everything? 'Eve, Milly's safety is paramount right now. Don't do anything stupid.'

'I had to get her out of there.' I try to sound like an adult, like someone who can be trusted. 'I can't go back. I know that sounds pathetic, but if I go back she'll mess with my head and I won't be able to think straight.'

Shona sighs. I start to cry. She's quiet on the end of the phone and waits for me to pull it together. She believes me. She doesn't look at my mother and see a harmless little old woman and she doesn't see an ungrateful, hysterical daughter in me. She knows how complicated this is. 'I'm scared.'

'Eve, you have to do exactly as I say. At the moment this is a low-level inquiry and Neil is playing it by the book and I'm doing all I can to help, but you have to be very careful and this...' She stops, choosing her words.

I've messed it up. I should have called her. I should have talked to her before I ran. There's a faint crackling down the line. I stand with the receiver in my hand, my eyes squeezed shut, begging the universe to give me another chance.

Eventually Shona speaks. 'Listen, I've been in touch with the foster family. Ruth says they can take her while you do whatever it is you need to do. I'll say you need some respite, the stress of the allegation. It's perfectly understandable, but if you take Milly away now, without prior consent, you could be jeopardising everything.'

I don't want to let Milly go. I may never get her back. I want to cling to her, but she needs security. Routine. She is the priority. She liked the foster family. They have two dogs. We'll say it's a treat. 'Could she see her grandparents while she's there? Could you organise something? Would that be possible?'

'I'll see what I can do. Where are you? I'll come and get her.'

'Carnforth.'

'Carnforth! Bloody hell, Eve! You don't make things easy, do you?'

'Can you come?'

'It'll take me an hour. Talk to Milly. Get her ready.'

# Chapter 31

Naz was waiting for me at the station. She asked no questions and I said nothing until we got back to the house. Then she exploded. 'That fucking woman!' Her rage was entirely directed towards my mother. She had no time for Vincent Lord's statement, not even when I told her Neil's own doubts. 'She fucks with your head, Eve! And now she's fucking with his! You saw Tina's dad! You saw what he did to his wife, how scared she was of him. He's a nasty piece of work. Why would you believe a word that odious little bully says?'

I need to speak to Neil, but it isn't easy finding a charger for my old Nokia among the small independent shops of Hitchin. Naz has nipped to Cam's school with a bargain-shop tray-bake, for a fundraiser she forgot about, and is going to phone me when she's done. Without a car, I can't get to the bigger electrical shops. I'm about to give up, when I see an elderly gentleman in the churchyard, checking messages on a phone identical to mine. I explain my predicament.

It turns out he lives a ten-minute walk from where we're standing and he's happy to take me back with him to charge my phone.

Ted is a retired schoolteacher. Catkin-fluff hair and liver-spotted hands. There's something comforting about falling in alongside him as he keeps a slow but steady pace along Bancroft. He tells me that his wife died last year. I can almost feel her hovering close, looking out for him. I wonder if he feels her too. I'd like to tell Ted everything, hand the whole ugly mess over to this kindly gentleman and wait for him to fix it, but it would be too much for a man like this. My mother's accusation has sullied us all.

The sense of that other, benign, presence gathers substance as we reach Ted's house. I can almost picture her, standing beneath the last of the wisteria, sweeping the dried flower-heads from the stone step. Inside the dark hall there's a round oak table at the foot of the stairs, a vase of dried hydrangeas at the centre, along with an abandoned clothes brush and a pile of post and free papers. Umbrellas and wellington boots are lined up in the corner. It's a grand house, but not showy. Dusty, welcoming. A family home with its own unique history. There are photographs of children and grandchildren hanging everywhere. Ted offers me a cup of tea and a scone while we wait for the phone to charge. The scone is excellent. 'Joyce used to make them for the WI and I've kept up the ritual.' He offers me home-made jam and clotted cream. Damson jam. The words are written in a shivery script. I can picture her at this table, the labels laid out in front of her, pen in hand. What would it be like to have a father like this, a kindly, gentle man, happy to have me pop in? How different my life might have been with a second parent, someone to temper her need and take some of the pressure off. Why did my father leave?

Did he abandon me without a second thought, or was it more complicated than that? I think of Neil trying to contact me, Mum wiping the messages, sending him the text to say I didn't want to talk to him. What was it she said in her defence? She was trying to protect me?

What lengths will my mother go to, to protect me?

Did my father try to keep in touch? Did he write or phone over the years? Did she decide, on my behalf, that he wasn't to be trusted and I was better off without him? What if he is a man like Ted? Gentle. Maybe a little weak. Someone who prefers to keep the peace and avoid an emotional confrontation. Someone a little like me.

Is he alive? Is he somewhere close right now? Would I know him if I passed him in the street? Does he know me?

I find myself telling Ted about Milly, about the adoption, and he isn't patronising, he doesn't tell me I'm noble or that Milly is lucky, he simply says, 'Well, that's a wonderful thing.'

Naz calls just as I'm unplugging my phone. I tell her I'm on my way. I try to call Neil, but his phone is switched off.

# Chapter 32

'So, I've done a bit of investigating.' Naz pulls the spiral-bound notepad out of her pocket. I'm folding a huge pile of laundry, mostly bedding and boys' T-shirts, that have been screwed up in a plastic basket so long they've stiffened into crumpled lumps. Naz is clearly never going to iron this stuff, and I need to feel I'm doing something, so I shake out each item and smooth it into folds. 'I went back to the Oxfam shop. The woman there said she thought Ann lived in Shephalbury, on Wood Drive. My aunty lives on Rowan Lane which is in that area. Aunty Rupinder knows everyone and everything that's going on in her patch. She's the coordinator for her local Neighbourhood Watch scheme.'

She pauses for dramatic effect, clearly enjoying herself. I shake out a dark blue sweatshirt with a school logo stitched to the front. The cuffs are unravelling. 'Go on.'

'So, I gave her a call. She has this snazzy little folder she keeps in the top drawer of the sideboard. Max found it when we were there a while back and pulled it out. She went bananas when she saw him; apparently, all that stuff is confidential. Anyway, I remembered that at the back of the folder was a little map with all the houses in her area. The ones who'd signed up to the scheme were highlighted and the names of the residents listed next to them. I asked her to check for me.'

Her chirpiness is beginning to get to me. Has she forgotten what this is all about? I shove the basket towards her. 'Make yourself useful.'

'I told her I'd got a Body Shop order to deliver to Ann Lord, after one of my parties, but I'd written down the wrong address.'

'They were on her list?'

'They were! Jump two spaces and collect £200 for passing Go, Detective Parker!'

'Seriously?'

'They live at number seven.'

She gives a yelp of delight, holding her hand up for a high five.

But I can't match her celebratory mood. I slip to my knees, a crumpled sheet settling around me. If that bruise of Ann's is anything to go by, Vincent Lord is a violent man. Naz tries to comfort me but I shove her off. 'Naz! For fuck's sake! This isn't some stupid prank! This is my life. My *family*!'

Her face is serious now. Her eyes remain fixed on mine as she waits for me to get a grip. 'I'm sorry. Sorry. I know.' She sits down on the floor facing me. 'I can't do this for you. I wish I could. I'll do what I can to help, but you're the one. You have to fight, Eve. You have to protect them.'

I remember the day at the outdoor pool. Lesley Butler and her patronising, hurtful comments. The indignation that welled up inside me on Milly's behalf. Something stirring, a growing power, and I remember the moment it erupted, after the smack, exploding at my mother in defence of my child. I know now what mothers mean when they say they would kill anyone who tried to hurt their children.

But this is not life and death. Milly's not in immediate danger. This is a quieter menace, though just as dangerous in its own way, precisely for that reason. Angry retaliation will achieve nothing here and, judging by Ann's bruise, will only make the situation worse. This isn't just about Milly, or Neil, or me; there are other people at risk. We need a different approach. And in the absence of anything else I have to consider the resources we have available.

I wait at the far end of the street watching Ann Lord's front door as Naz talks to someone inside. At one point she glances over her shoulder and gives me the thumbs up. Then Vincent Lord appears, pulling on a tweed jacket. His movements are jerky, irritated, his face creased into a frown. He follows Naz up the street away from me. I'm relieved to see that he's quite slow and struggling to keep up with her, though he's a sturdy block of a man. Small, but compact. His face is stern. He's not someone to mess with. I'm beginning to regret this, but there's no going back now. Naz's Aunty Rupinder is waiting for them. Some fake paperwork for Neighbourhood Watch volunteers that Naz has put together. I haven't got long. The form will take five minutes or so, but Aunty Rupinder has been tasked to keep Vincent Lord plied with tea and goodies for as long as possible.

Ann trembles in the doorway. She whispers, 'What are you doing here?' searching over my shoulder as if he might return at any moment.

'I need to talk. Please? It's all right; he's gone, but we haven't got long. I need to ask you about Tina.'

Her face is stricken. She looks anxiously up and down the street once more to be sure, and ushers me inside, closing the door behind us. Hesitating on the threshold of the living room, she changes her mind and leads me through a small galley kitchen and out the back. She has to press her shoulder against the door to shove it open, 'It's swollen after the rain,' and leads me down the garden, to the end of the lawn where there are several mature fruit trees, beyond which is a wooden gate. We stand in the shade of the trees. It's chilly out of the sun, but her eyes flit to the kitchen window and back and I feel safer here. I'm aware that Vincent might return at any moment. Naz will call me as soon as he leaves her aunt's house, but that will only give me three or four minutes' warning. I'm as frightened by the possibility of him returning as Ann is. For her sake, more than mine.

I cut to the chase. 'You know about the statement?'

She nods.

'My husband's being investigated. We could lose Milly. I don't know what my mother told you, but we're in the process of adopting her. Still in the trial period. He's... Please! He's a good man. He had no idea. I know it's awful, unforgiveable, but he was a boy and he didn't – I can't believe...'

'He didn't.' Her voice is firm. More solid than I've heard before. 'Vince lied.'

I close my eyes and feel the world spin around me. I knew. Of course I knew, but I still needed to hear it.

'Tina told me what happened. Vince lied and he lied about her age. She was sixteen. She turned sixteen a few weeks before, but they wanted to make it sound worse.' They. Not just him, but my mother. She knew he was lying. She knew.

'It wasn't assault. It wasn't anything nasty. She's a good girl, my Tina. She wouldn't...'

They lied. If they lied about that, what else did they lie about? Maybe Tina's son wasn't Neil's after all. 'Why didn't she tell Neil she was pregnant? Why didn't you?'

Ann chews her lip. 'She liked your boy, but he wasn't the one for her and she knew he had plans. She didn't want to spoil that for him. She wanted the baby – I think she wanted something for herself – Vince never let her...' Her face contorts. 'He's a cruel man.'

'Neil doesn't remember. He's worried sick.'

The lines in her face deepen. 'Your mother came to see us. She's good with words.' Her eyes search me for clues. She hesitates. 'She tried with me first, but I wouldn't do it. But Vince, he's still angry, well, he's looking for someone else to blame, and she sniffed that out.' She pauses again, and I think she's going to carry on but she doesn't. Instead, she reaches into her handbag and takes out her purse. There are several pockets inside it for credit and store cards and she flicks through these to the back and pulls out, from behind a library card and a book of stamps, a tatty strip of photographs from a photo booth. Her hands are trembling. Glancing over my shoulder, terrified he might appear at any moment, she unfolds the strip, to reveal four images. The colours have aged into blues and oranges. A young woman, blonde, with a wide smile and a gap between her front teeth, and on her lap a little boy with rusty hair and freckles. And Neil's eyes.

# Chapter 33

My phone rings. It's Naz. She whispers urgently, 'Eve? It's Cam.' She's hurrying. I hear her unlock the car. 'He's had a fit. I have to go.'

'Go. Go.'

She's starting the engine. 'He's still with Aunty Rupe, but I don't think you've got long. She's struggling—'

'Don't worry about that.'

'Be careful.'

'He didn't do it, Naz.'

'Of course he didn't.'

I hang up and tell Ann, 'We need to hurry. He could be back any moment.'

But she is strangely calm. 'Tina writes, once a week,' she says, smiling, loosening in front of me as she speaks. 'She lives in Leeds. Went there to stay with a cousin on my sister's side, until she got on her feet.' Her voice ripples with the love she's had to keep suppressed. 'My sister got in touch. We decided it was better not to tell Vince.' Her eyes dart back to the kitchen window, but her body does not tighten as it did before. 'He would have gone up there and got her.' She looks at me, as if there's something more binding us in this moment. I don't like the way this makes me feel. 'He loves her, you know. That's what makes it so difficult. In his own way, he does love her. But that isn't good for her.' She watches me, looking for clues again. I focus on the photographs, aware of the quiet, her waiting. Eventually she says, 'Tina sends her letters to the post office now, and I collect them from there. I have to burn them in case he finds them.'

She doesn't hold out her hand, but I can feel her need for me to return the strip of photos. How many years has she carried it with her? Has anyone else been allowed to touch it? Did my mother see it? How did she gather her evidence? I imagine her confiding to this new friend how much she was missing her own grandchild, weeping, manipulating Ann into revealing her secret.

'I get to see them.' She folds the strip gently and slides it back into her purse. 'They come down on the train. I tell Vince I have a hospital appointment.' She smiles, sniffs, takes the tissue from her cuff and blows her nose. 'He didn't know, your husband. I don't know if that was right, but...' She waits for me to say something but I don't know what to say. Neil has a son he's never seen. A man now. That childhood has gone. The relationship they might have had can never happen now.

'He came. Yesterday. Your husband.'

'Here?'

She nods. 'Vince answered the door. He didn't recognise him. I did, of course, he's the image of... but when your husband introduced himself...' She hesitates, twisting the tissue around in her hands. 'I'm so sorry. All this upset.'

Neil. Here. I can almost feel him. 'How was he? Was he angry?' She shakes her head and looks at me with troubled eyes. 'Did you tell him it wasn't true?'

Her eyes brim. 'I'm sorry. Vince slammed the door in his face and he...' She reaches up, instinctively to her chest. I take her hand. She sniffs, gathering herself. 'Tell him she's fine. Tina. She's done well for herself. Hairdresser, has her own salons, two now. Weddings and stuff. Quite a businesswoman. Always was a bright girl. Got Steven into a good school. University. It doesn't come cheap, that, but he's doing ever so well. Vince would be proud.' She twists the tissue. 'If things... if he...'

Steven.

She's calm, unhurried. Her voice is lower. 'Sometimes, if you love them, you have to let them go. It's for the best.' She chews her lip. 'I'm so sorry about Vince. The trouble he's caused you.'

'Do you think I could have Tina's number? Do you think she'd speak to me?'

But she isn't listening. It's as if I haven't spoken. 'He was always too much of the disciplinarian. Close when she was little, but as she got older, teenager, it was a battle of wills. He was afraid for her, but she didn't understand that. What happened with the boy, your husband, it wasn't like Vince said.'

'Please?'

I see him before she does. A dark shape across the window, then the thump of his shoulder against the back door. She gives a little gasp, as if reality has kicked back in, and shoves me towards the gate. 'Quick!'

'Tina's contact details?' but she's gone, hurrying up the garden as he barks, 'ANN!' and I slip into the lane.

I hesitate.

She yelps.

I push my way back through the gate. Vincent Lord has his wife by the hair. I run across the lawn. He's dragging her into the house. The back door is still hanging open. A whimper. This frail woman, tossed like a doll. Something inside me explodes and I run in, roaring like someone primeval, 'NO!'

He's momentarily paralysed and I charge at him, knocking him back against the kitchen dresser. A plate slips to the floor and shatters. He gives a low 'Oof' and tips back, his knees buckling. Ann is screaming. I push her away. 'Get out! Get out into the street! Quick!'

She doesn't move. She looks from me to him and back to me, her eyes wild, but she doesn't move. He's regaining his balance, straightening up. 'Go!'

But she can't. And he's back on his feet now and he's ready for me. His hands reach for my throat. I kick at him and thrust my knee up towards his groin, but he's strong. A block of muscle. He has his fingers around my neck and he's squeezing so tight and I think how stupid I've been, how long it will take for Naz and the police to arrive, how I should have grabbed something, anything, but it's too late and the pain, the pain...

And then suddenly there's a thud and the pressure is released and Vincent Lord is sliding down the dresser, his eyes huge and round, blood trickling down the side of his face and Ann's there, trembling, a bloodied bread board in her hand, a look of victory on her face.

Ann says, 'I've been waiting for years to do that.' We stand, looking down at her husband, unconscious on the floor.

'We should call an ambulance. The police.'

She turns away and places the bread board in the sink. Her movements are slow and deliberate, as if someone else has entered her body and is trying it out for size. 'There's time enough for that. He's strong as an ox, Vince. A head wound isn't going to cause him any long-term harm. Might knock some sense into him.'

He looks so much smaller on the floor. That tight barrel of a man who moments earlier oozed with violent rage, reduced to a shell. Ann opens the cupboard under the sink and takes out a length of pink washing line. 'Just to be on the safe side.' She kneels beside him and ties his hands and feet.

She fills the kettle.

She's making tea. Her husband just tried to kill me. She has knocked him out cold and he's bleeding onto the kitchen floor, and we are going to sit down and drink tea. I stare at her. She flashes a smile. 'It will be all blue lights and questions once they get here. Let's just make the most of the quiet for a bit.'

I start to laugh. I'm shaking. My throat is beginning to throb where his fingers dug into my flesh. She says, 'Sit down. You've had a nasty shock.'

I do as I'm told. This new Ann speaks quietly, but she commands attention.

She makes the tea and puts a steaming cup in front of me. It's sweet and stings as it trickles down my throat. She watches me grimace and flinches in sympathy. 'Your little girl. Milly?' I nod. 'Where is she?' I explain about the foster family. Another nod. 'You're a good mum.'

I shake my head. 'I'm not.'

'She's safe. You've kept her safe.' She frowns, looks at the body on the floor. 'I didn't keep Tina safe.'

'You were afraid. And who could blame you? He's a nasty bully.'

'Bullies come in all shapes and sizes. Some are loud and violent, like Vince here, exploding when things don't go their way. She looks at me. 'Others are quieter, less visible.' A moment. 'You're braver than me.'

'You knocked him out!'

'Too late for Tina. I should have stopped him years ago.' She frowns, painful memories leaving shadows across her features. 'A good mother fights for her child.'

'My mother has always fought for me. Continues to fight for me.'

'But you are no longer a child.' Her gaze makes me itch. She says, 'The quiet ones are the ones you need to watch.' I take a sip of tea, focus on the cup, the table in front of me. 'Your mother is a strong character.'

We sit in silence. I know I should say something, but I can't. I hesitate on the threshold.

'Vince is all shouting and fists, but underneath that he's a coward. Truth is, he needs me more than I need him. I've always known that. Should have used it to my advantage.'

I look up. She gives me a small smile. Pity. I squirm.

She says, 'The dangerous ones sneak up on you. They talk about love, but they don't understand it. What they want is control and they'll stop at nothing to get it.' She gives me a final nudge. 'You know what I'm talking about, don't you?'

There's a low groan from the floor. Ann sighs and takes a last gulp of tea. 'Be brave,' she says, placing both hands on the table and pushing herself up to standing. 'If not for yourself, then for your daughter.'

There's a growl as Vincent Lord realises his hands and feet are bound. 'What the...?'

Ann nods to me. 'Best call the police. Time's up.'


Naz arrives as I complete my statement. Vincent Lord has been removed by the paramedics and a representative from the local women's refuge is taking care of Ann. We sit on the garden wall in the evening sunshine.

'So that's the charming Mr Lord banged to rights, now what about your Neil?'

'He didn't rape her.' I'm spent. No room for anything but relief.

Naz is quiet for a moment. I don't want her to ask; I can't go there yet. That photograph. A boy with Neil's eyes. She pulls me close. Some things don't need to be said out loud. She squeezes me tight. 'It will be all right.'

I want to see Neil. I want to tell him in person.


Betty's eyes widen as she opens the door. 'Eve? What are you doing here?' Her hair hangs loose across her shoulders. I have never seen Betty with her hair down. She's become an echo of the girl she once was, but she looks so tired. She takes a step forward and looks over my shoulder. 'Where's Milly?'

'I didn't bring her. It's all right, she's safe. She's with her foster family.'

She's ushering me in, following me down the hall. 'The kitchen. We'll sit down in there.'

I glance up the stairs, wondering if Neil's heard us. I have no idea how much Betty knows. I assume Neil's explained everything. She seems agitated. Diminished.

'Where's Neil?'

Her eyes well up. She plucks at the collar of her blouse. 'I don't know. I was hoping...'

'I thought he was staying here with you?' I'd assumed he'd come here. That he was with family, that he had support. 'Have you spoken to him? Do you know what's been going on?'

She nods. 'Yes. He was here. But he's gone.'

'When?'

'This morning. He set off before we got up.' She picks up a folded sheet of notepaper from the table and passes it to me. Neil's tight script.

*Need to sort this out. For Eve and Milly at least. N.*

'Have you tried calling him?' I'm selecting his number as I speak.

'His phone's switched off. I left a message but he hasn't got back to me. I don't think he's checking his phone.'

His phone is still off. I read the note again. 'What does he mean, sort it out?' For me and Milly 'at least'?

'He doesn't remember what happened.'

'He didn't do it!'

'I know that. He wouldn't. He couldn't. But it's got into his head and he can't—'

'He *didn't* do it. I *know*. I've spoken to Ann Lord. She said her husband made it up. It isn't true.'

Betty closes her eyes. She's usually so robust. Nothing daunts Betty. She's been there, done that, seen it all. To see her so fragile, so diminished, is alarming. I steer her to a seat. The old Betty would have clucked around me and produced cake and biscuits and dropped a hand to my shoulder as she passed. But this Betty allows herself to be led. Blind-sided.

'This is all my fault!' she sobs. 'Me and my big mouth. Why did I have to go and mention Tina? She was only asking about the adoption.'

She's talking about mum.

'I had that chest infection. She brought some cuttings from her garden. She can be very kind.' When she wants something. 'She was asking about Neil, you know, that time. How it was for us, when he contacted his birth mum.' Digging for dirt. She knew that period of Neil's life was delicate. She knew there was a secret in there somewhere.

'This is not your fault, Betty. My mum...' I dry up. What can I say?

'She was worried for you, knowing you were planning to adopt. What you were getting into. She loves you.'

I shake my head. 'It's not as simple as that.' It's not as simple or generous or healthy as that, but Betty is kind, she believes in the good in people. Betty remembers my mum buying us the house, paying for the double glazing, doing things Betty and Mike couldn't afford to do, while all the time seeking ammunition to use against their son. Betty will never understand my mother.

I ask her where Mike is, assuming he's tinkering in the garage and will join us, help cajole her a little, but she shakes her head in that sorry way and says, 'Looking for him.'

Mike's out driving the streets looking for his son. I want to ask how Neil was when they last saw him but I don't need to ask, I can see in Betty's face how bad this is.

I focus on making tea, because this simple domestic task makes everything ordinary. Ann made tea while her husband bled on the kitchen floor. Nothing bad can happen while you're making a cup of tea. Betty talks while I move around the kitchen, filling the kettle, fetching the cups. 'She was never Neil's girlfriend, you know. He met her that once, at the party and then nothing. It got to him. He was having a hard time, what with his mum and all that.' I wait, a hundred questions circling my head, unable to voice a single one. Neil chose not to share this with me. 'We tried to manage his expectations, but it's difficult. He was so hopeful. We didn't want to undermine anything, we just... but he got all defensive, the way teenagers do, and we just had to let him get on with it.'

'Laura said his mother was in a pretty bad way?'

'It shocked him, of course it did. Nothing anyone said would prepare him for the reality, because he had this scene in his head. He thought he could help her. But she didn't want his help. She didn't want him.'

This is why he's so hard on Claire, why he doesn't want Milly to be disappointed, because he's been there himself and he's felt that rejection. Not all mothers want to be reunited with their children. Sometimes that's just too painful. Sometimes it's easier to keep your past at a distance. My dad might have found it easier to let go and accept that chapter of his life was over.

'He came back from that visit broken. He's a rescuer, Neil. He has a good heart. He was eighteen and at the start of his adult life and he went there full of hope, convinced he could put everything right, but he couldn't. He was in a dark mood. Frustrated. Angry. I was worried about him, but I thought it was probably better he went out with his mates that night and let off a bit of steam. Afterwards, he was worried that he might have done something to offend her. Not that. He's devastated by... He wouldn't. Not our

Neil.' She falls silent. I pause, place my hand on her shoulder as I pass on my way from the dishwasher to the kettle. 'He went to see her, but her dad saw him off.' She takes a tissue from the box on the table and blows her nose loudly. 'He was a kid. He was drunk and unhappy. It was his first time. And now he's doubting himself. Maybe she wasn't as keen as he'd thought. Maybe he misunderstood. He's been torturing himself with it.'

I place the tea on the table. 'We have to find him. Where would he go?'

'He feels responsible. He's worried about you and Milly. About you losing Milly.'

'Neil plays by the rules. He left the house as soon as Shona told him to. He didn't argue. He'll do anything to ensure this adoption goes through.'

Betty nods. 'What do you think? How were they, the social workers? Do they think…?'

'Shona said she doesn't believe Milly to be at risk of significant harm. Whatever happened between Neil and Tina that night, there's nothing to suggest that Neil is a threat to children.'

She closes her eyes, drops her chin to her chest.

Neil is afraid of what he might have done that night. He's afraid that Vincent Lord's accusation will stick. He's afraid he might be guilty. He doesn't know he's innocent. He's worried that the adoption won't go through because of this. Because of him.

He'll try to fix it.

But as far as he's concerned, the accusation remains. He sees he's the problem. The only way he can solve the problem is to take himself out of the picture. I look at Betty. She can't raise her head.

This fear slithers up from behind. Cold, slimy, creeping the length of my spine and over my shoulders. I shudder, but it holds fast.

I need to find Neil.

# Chapter 34

I get the train back to Cumbria. Four trains. Hitchin to Stevenage, Stevenage to Leeds and then the bone-rattler with its vinyl-covered benches careering across the width of the country to Carnforth where I pick up a connection to Tarnside. There's a more direct route with just one change at Lancaster, straight into Euston, but I'd taken the cross-country route on the way down with Milly, to avoid being stopped, and it didn't occur to me to simply buy another ticket until I was on the Leeds train, by which time it was too late. I've tried calling Shona but she's in a meeting and hasn't got back to me. I left a message telling her as much as I know. They'll need to talk to Ann and possibly Tina, of course, but this will take some of the pressure off Neil.

Mike returned having failed to find him. I didn't ask where he'd been looking. He and Betty were talking about notifying the police but I'm not sure what the police can do. Neil's an adult. He hasn't been missing long. We might be worried about his state of mind, but I suspect the police have more urgent matters to attend to.

Where would Neil go? Who would he talk to? We don't know anyone up here well enough to be able to confide the horrors of this situation. There's Lizzie, but Neil isn't close to Lizzie. Our life in Tarnside has been about creating a good impression, impressing our employers and gaining the respect of our staff, making gentle inroads into an established community, presenting a positive front to social services, persuading the adoption panel that we are suitable parents. We are only just beginning to forge friendships. I have Naz, back in Hitchin, but Neil doesn't even have that. Neil has his sisters, his family. He never had a best friend. He was sociable, popular, but always self-possessed. He never needed anyone else.

Neil has most likely driven home. I cling to this possibility and do my best to ignore the darker scenarios unfolding in my head. I tell myself that Neil's angry about what's happened, not defeated. I remember his fists clenched the day my mother went off with Milly. I picture him raging at the injustice of what's happened to him, to his life, to his family. He will have gone to confront the person who is responsible: my mother.

I ignore the memory of his voice on the phone the last time I spoke to him. How broken he sounded. I ignore the fear I saw in Betty's eyes before she closed them and shut out the awful possibilities parading in front of her.

I could call my mother, but I don't. I tell myself that this is because I don't want to warn her. Let her face his rage. But the truth is I'm afraid to phone because I want to hang on to the belief that he'll be there and I don't want her to tell me otherwise. I've tried calling him repeatedly but his phone is still switched off. I have left a message reassuring him that Ann has declared him innocent, but he isn't checking his phone. I picture him in my mind, talk to him silently across the miles, as if by conjuring him I can protect him. I will him not to give up.

At Carnforth, I climb onto the local train which carries me over the sands of Morecambe Bay. Pools of water encircle banks of white gold and grassy mounds where sheep graze, blissfully unaware of anything beyond their own immediate hunger. I realise I'm chanting the same phrase over and over in my mind, to the rhythm of the train: Please be safe. Please be safe. Please be safe.

Home. Tarnside, not Hitchin. Cobbled streets, dark ginnels and pretty shopfronts. Houses fanning out from the park and the tarn, sparkling in the weak evening sunlight that filters through the bulbous clouds. This Cumbrian market town. This community. This is where we dropped our anchor and came to rest. Tarnside, Neil and Milly. I will find him and I will bring my family home.

As I come up the path, India's front door opens and Kath steps out. I give them both a quick wave. I have no time for idle chat now, but India intercepts me. 'Eve?' She steps out in her slippers, pulling her cardigan tight around her chest. 'Is everything all right?' They're both watching me. Not searching for gossip, but genuinely concerned. India continues, 'It's just, I saw Neil earlier and he seemed… in a bit of a state.'

'Neil was here?'

Before she can say any more, Mum opens our front door. She will have heard our voices outside the living room window. 'Evangeline!' She breaks into a smile, as if this is her house and she's welcoming me in. Only her dishevelled hair and the fact that she's wearing the same clothes she had on when I left give any clue to the devastation she's caused. She throws Kath and India a wide smile, 'Oh, hello!' and turns back to me. 'I've been so worried about you. Come on, let me take that bag.'

'Is Neil here?'

Her face drops. 'No, darling.' She throws a pained look in Kath's direction. 'Come in. You'll catch a chill hanging about out there.'

I look back at India. 'You saw him?'

India hesitates. She glances at Kath and then back at me. 'He came up the path earlier.' She looks at Mum. 'He must have lost his key, because he was banging on the door.'

Mum's face is pink. She drops her eyes and shakes her head. Her voice trembles. 'I didn't know what to do! The things he was saying! That temper.'

I look at India. The fine line between her eyebrows deepens. She will know all about the Child Protection investigation from Guy. There is nothing to hide here. 'I'm sorry, India. Could you do me a favour?'

She nods. 'Of course.'

'Guy has Neil's number, doesn't he? Could you ask him to try calling Neil for me, please?'

My mother snaps, 'Evangeline!' but I ignore her.

'He isn't answering my calls and I'm worried about him.'

'Worried about him?' Mum spits, forgetting herself, and then, immediately, the timid old woman is back. 'Darling, you need to stop worrying about him. He can look after himself. It's you we need to worry about.'

I look at Kath. She is competent and resourceful. She will help. 'We need to find him.'

She nods and that nod acknowledges the urgency in my voice. I give them both a weak smile, turn and step inside the hall, pulling the door closed behind me.

As soon as the door is closed, the frail old lady routine is dumped. Mum is torrential, 'You need to stay away from him, Evangeline! He's dangerous! He was like a wild animal. Out of control. Banging on the door with his fists, and then the window.'

'Why couldn't he get in?'

'I put the bolt across. He isn't allowed to come here!'

'He isn't allowed to be near Milly right now, but she isn't here. What did he want?'

'You. He was demanding to see you. As if that was his right. As if you belong to him. Well, I gave him what for.' She gives a satisfied sigh. 'He won't be bothering you again.'

I take a deep breath. I don't want to scream and shout. I need to stay calm. I need to remain in control if I'm to have any power here. 'You said he threatened you?'

She nods, her lip trembling. Oh, she's good. Now I see through her it's so obvious. I've been blind for so long. I've been blind for the same reason that everyone around me is blind. Mothers are good. Mothers are self-sacrificing. Mothers only want what's best for their child. The alternative is sickening and too awful to contemplate.

I close my eyes, to contain the rage that is coursing through me right now. Neil was here. He needed me. He's devastated and vulnerable and she drove him away.

Mum shifts gear, switching from trembling victim to loving mother in an instant. 'Are you hungry? You must be shattered. Come and sit down.' It's as if none of this has happened. I could be returning from college, or a school trip and she's waiting to greet me. I don't move. 'What is it? What's wrong?'

I stare at her. This woman. My mother. This apparently harmless, doting, lonely mother who loves me so much. Loves me so much she'll stop at nothing to keep me. She'll slander my husband, wreck his reputation, his career, our marriage, our life, to be rid of him. And Milly? I've been such a fool. I thought she would love Milly like we do, that this would be the start of something new and wonderful, but Milly's just debris to my mother. She's of no consequence. A distraction. Her needs, her security, her mental well-being, don't matter; all that matters is me. And not really me, not Eve, the adult woman with a life of her own, but Evangeline, *her* Evangeline, the daughter, the child she still sees when she looks at me. I'm her possession that she feels Neil has stolen from her. I'm Rapunzel trapped in the tower. Another Ladybird book from my collection. The princess with the long, golden plait, locked up by the wicked hag, jealous of the prince who came to Rapunzel's rescue. This is my story.

I belong to her. She will never let me go. Neil took me away, so Neil must be destroyed. She really will stop at nothing. And that's frightening, but this, this cool denial, this pretence that everything here is normal, this is more dangerous than any physical attack, because it's so easy to accept her reality; it looks so plausible. Here she is, a concerned mother, and all she wants is what's best for her daughter. She's simply protecting me. In her reality, she is my rescuer.

I think of the relationships in my life she's curtailed. I begin with my father. I only have her version of events. Who was he really? Did he betray her? If he did, did that make him a monster? How do I know that he abandoned us? That's what she told me, but now I wonder if that was also a lie. Maybe he loved me. Maybe he did want to keep in touch but she wouldn't allow it. Friends of mine she didn't like, who presented a challenge, she'd chip away, insinuating, undermining. 'I don't think you can trust her, Evangeline. She's the sort that would be nice to you one minute and then bitch about you the moment your back is turned.' She told me Daisy Prior stole her watch and sold it, that she heard her bragging about it in the playground. She said Patrick, from next door, who used to knock for me, was laughing about my greasy hair to his friends. She tried to do the same with Naz, but Naz never gave up. If I ever had a wobble with Naz over something Mum had said, Naz would challenge it straight away: 'What's the old bat said about me now?' And Neil. It took Mum a long time to undermine my faith in Neil, but she did, eventually. She made me doubt him and I'll never forgive myself for that.

She hasn't asked where Milly is. She's forgotten all about Milly, because Milly doesn't matter to her and that rage that stirred in me when Lesley Butler failed to respect my daughter expands, filling me out to the tips of my fingers, the ends of my toes, pressing against the top of my skull, hot behind my eyes. 'What have you done?' My voice is so much smaller, so much quieter than I expected it to be, but it slices through the silence. She gives a little moue of distaste, but I'm done with this. 'Go and pack. I want you to leave.'

Her face hardens. She pulls back her head in that injured gesture, but there's steel there. I've crossed a line, but I'm not afraid of her any more. 'Get out. You're not welcome in our home.' I can feel myself growing taller, straighter, bolder. A weight that's been bearing down on me for years has taken flight. I drop my shoulder blades, shake my head, lengthen my neck.

The words she wants to spit at me tremble inside her lips but she holds them back. She can smell the power in me. Turning on her heel, quite nimbly, I notice, she marches towards the staircase, but remembers suddenly, and feigns a stumble, gripping the newel post and reaching for her stick, which is propped against the shoe cabinet. I'm wise to her now. I don't rush to help. I don't ask if she's all right as she leans heavily against the banister and laboriously makes her way up. I turn away.

And as I turn I see it: a flash of yellow poking out from under the shoe cabinet. I bend over and tug it free. Milly's Gerry.

Milly? I shout, 'Milly!' Why is Milly here? Mum turns on the half landing outside the bathroom and looks down. She's slow to respond, her face unreadable. 'Where is she?' Mum's eyes are on me, silently accusing. 'Milly!'

'She's not your child, Evangeline. She will never be your child.'

'Where is she? Did Shona bring her back?'

Her words rain down, cold. 'You and I, we're blood. That bond. That sacrifice. Does that stand for nothing?'

'What have you done with her? Tell me!'

She watches me, eyes narrowed. 'That child you've known for five minutes, that *stranger*, is more important to you than *me*?'

'She *needs* me. I'm her mother. She comes first now! Get used to it! SHE COMES FIRST!'

A slow, half smile settling on her lips. A slight shake of her head, as if she can't quite believe what she's hearing.

'Where *is* she? What have you done?'

Low, cool. 'You don't need to worry about her.'

A cold fist unfurling inside my gut, clawing up to my throat. 'Milly!' I spring up the stairs, two, three at a time. Mum backs against the wall and I'm almost at the top when I see her raise the stick, stretching herself to full height. She swings it down with a sharp crack. The blow sends me tipping back. My shoulder hits the wall and I grab for the banister but she's raised the stick again, her face red with fury. It comes down across my chest, catching my chin, and I'm crashing backwards down the stairs.

## Chapter 35

There's a cry and my mother hurries down after me. I'm lying awkwardly, my cheek resting against an oiled floorboard, left hip pressed against the stair-rise, my legs behind me, one foot trapped between the spindles of the banister. An insistent, siren pain emanates from my ankle. 'Evangeline! Oh my God! My darling! Are you all right?'

There are balls of hair and dust coiled beneath the hall cabinet, a hair grip, a dry leaf that will have blown in through the front door. I groan and try to release my foot, but the pain explodes, sending an alert to every cell in my body. 'Don't move.' My mother's hands are on my foot. Gentle hands, stroking along my shin, manipulating my calf and coaxing my foot free. Did I imagine what happened back there? My legs and hip slide down to the floor and I lie, face down, aware that as soon as I raise my head I'll have to look her in the eye. I need to wrestle control and I have no idea how I'm going to do that. Already what happened is blurred. Did I stumble? Did I imagine that stick arcing through the air?

Focus. This is about Milly. Milly is upstairs. Milly's in this house. I don't know how or why. Shona would never have allowed this. But my mother is a resourceful woman. Milly was with the foster family. Their details are in the hanging file I keep in the study. My mother's seen me take papers from that file, check Milly's NHS number, details of vaccinations. She'll have contacted Ruth. Ruth's not stupid, she's been trained, she'll have been cautious, following the rules, but that won't have stopped my mother. She'll have found a way. She'll have lied. She's a good liar, my mother. That kindly, rather pathetic little old lady routine works well. No one would expect a doting grandmother to lie. No one would believe that this woman could be dangerous.

Milly is upstairs. Why hasn't she come out of the bedroom or responded to the noise? What's my mother done to her? An absurd image leaps into my mind of Milly bound and gagged and thumping her heels against the floorboards, but there's no sound from upstairs and my mother's too subtle for that. Milly will be sleeping, drugged with whatever it was Mum fed me after Neil left.

'Let's get you up.' She slides her hands beneath my ribs and tries to turn me onto my side. She's determined, however hard I press down against her. Surprisingly strong. I'll have to give in. My ankle is too painful to stand on. I won't be able to shake her off or get up the stairs. Physically, I'm no match for her now. This is no accident; she has me where she wants me. I didn't imagine what happened at the top of the stairs. I must hang on to that truth: her arm rising, that stick cracking down. She meant to do this. She didn't help me right myself; she hit me again.

I let her manoeuvre me into position with my back against the wall, keeping my eyes on my legs as she straightens them out in front of me. My right foot rests at an awkward angle and the pain pulses through me leaving a sickening feeling in the pit of my stomach. She unties the laces on my shoe and slips off my sock. My ankle is already beginning to swell. 'This will need ice.' She's kneeling on the floor beside me. I can feel her looking at me. I raise my eyes. She's all worry and loving concern. 'Those stairs!' she says, shaking her head. 'It's that carpet. It's slippery. I've nearly taken a tumble down there myself.' So, this is how it's going to be: an accident. I slipped. Already she's rewriting the story to absolve herself and I can see it gathering substance, this gossamer-thin image becoming a faint piece of footage. I can see the definition improving with each telling, the colour being added, until it's as strong as a memory. Stronger. This is how it's been. All my life. Her story, formed inside her head and related to me as a truth. Did my father even know I existed? Did he send me a birthday card, or was she lying about that too? I have no memories of him. She told me she burned every photograph. But what if there were no photographs? What if he, like Neil, never knew I was born?

Milly's upstairs. I need to get to her. 'Could you get me some ice? Please? It's in the top drawer of the freezer in a blue tray.'

'Yes, yes.' She grabs the newel post and pulls herself to her feet. I glance up the stairs. How long will it take to drag myself up there? There's a landline in the spare room. If I could reach that I could call someone: Shona, the police. But as I glance back, my mother's looking down at me. Her face hardens and I flinch, pulling my injured foot towards me instinctively, bracing myself, but in an instant the look has disappeared. A flick and she's back to her part: anxious, maternal. Could she do that? I can imagine it. I've glimpsed what I'm up against. There'll be no negotiating with her. I don't have the physical ability to overpower her. I can't get up the stairs.

I can't hear Milly. She must be sleeping. Drugged, but safe. Please, please let her be safe. I need to find another way to reach her.

'Let's get you into the kitchen.' She slips one arm behind me as if she's going to cradle me to her and slides me away from the wall, placing her other hand beneath my armpit, proceeding backwards along the hall towards the kitchen, dragging me. It's amazing what strength she can find when she needs to. I protest, but she's not going to take any risks. Propping me against the kitchen units, she crosses the room to the back door, where her wheelchair is folded into the corner. 'Just the thing!' she says, flashing me a triumphant grin as she opens it out. The wheelchair will, at least, get me off the floor and give me a little mobility. I allow her to help me in. 'There's a good girl.' She relaxes as I succumb. If I do as I'm told she's happy. This is my role in her reality: dutiful daughter, the victim she's rescued. I must be grateful. I need her help. I can play that role, if it gets me what I want. I can do that.

A memory. Naz in my bedroom, singing. *Never smile at a crocodile.* I remember frustration. Tears. Neil had asked me to meet him at a party in Stevenage but Mum wouldn't let me go. I'd known she wasn't keen on Neil, barbed comments and that pinched face whenever I mentioned him, so I'd been keeping things to myself. Then, one day, she'd asked me about him, all smiles, acting like she was genuinely pleased for me, encouraging me to confide, and, relieved to be able to talk at last, buoyed up by the joy of this new relationship, I'd told her he was the one.

*Don't be taken in by his welcome grin.*

She'd turned then. Panicked. Set about making it as difficult as possible for me to see him. My mother has razor teeth, I can see that now. Back then, I put it down to her being overprotective. I assumed she was afraid that I'd throw away my opportunities and make the same mistakes she'd made, but it's more menacing than that. My mother is dangerous, but she's utterly predictable. This is my only weapon.

As she bustles about, fetching the icepack, wrapping it in a towel, strapping it against my ankle, boiling the kettle for tea, 'A strong cup of tea with a spoonful of sugar, for the shock,' I play the part. I'm defeated, grateful, apologetic. I persuade myself that Milly's safe upstairs, as long as Mum's downstairs, fussing around me. She isn't interested in Milly. Milly's an inconvenience; I'm the one she wants. I need to keep her here.

'I'm sorry, Mum.' My voice wobbles. 'I've made such a mess of things.'

She hurries over and strokes my hair. I tense my jaw in order not to recoil. 'Evangeline, my baby.'

'I should have listened to you.' Memories of my teenage years. How many times have I said this to her? How many times have I been cornered without realising it?

As she pets, cajoles and fusses, I manoeuvre the chair so that I am at the opposite side of the table, closer to the door, where I can see into the hall. If Milly wakes up and comes downstairs I will see her first. I don't know what good this will do but it gives me a degree of control. Mum places a cup of tea on the table in front of me and refills the kettle. She's fretting, worried; I'm not the only one trying to work out what to do here.

There's a knock at the door. Mum freezes. I look down the hall and see a small figure, the outline of India's wiry mane on the doorstep. Bracing myself, I propel the wheelchair forward. I hear Mum lurch after me, but the wheels move smoothly across the wooden boards and I have the advantage. I bellow to India, 'Call the police! Quickly. She has Milly!'

I am almost at the door when Mum grabs my hair and yanks me back. I shriek with the sudden pain. She blocks the door, grips my arms, her nails sinking into my flesh, but her voice is sweet as syrup. 'Evangeline darling, please. Don't do this to yourself,' and before I can say anything else she's shoving the damp dishcloth into my mouth. I gasp for air, but she packs it in. 'Calm down. You need your pills. What are people going to think?' and back to India, 'It's all right. I've got it all under control, thank you. If you could just leave me to sort this out.'

I'm kicking, writhing and moaning like a beast caught in a trap, but Mum's stronger than she looks and the dishcloth has hit the back of my throat, making me gag.

India calls through the door. 'Eve? Eve? What's going on?' I hear the flap of the letter box lift as Mum wheels me out of sight.


Mum sits down at the kitchen table. She's trembling, the muscles in her face twitching as she thinks of her next move. I yank the dishcloth from my mouth, but I can't speak. There are no words. We've entered some other place now. I'm trapped in a different reality with a woman who will not be beaten. What will she do? Milly is upstairs and I can't reach her. But India heard, India will call the police.

Mum looks at me. I try and read her face. A disappointed mother reprimanding an errant child. 'What have you done, Evangeline? The *police*? What do you think is going on here?'

'Where's Milly?'

Her face is innocent, her voice soft. 'I have no idea.'

'She's upstairs.'

'Upstairs?' A frown. 'Is that what you think?'

The room shifts around me. There is nothing to grasp hold of. She shakes her head, 'Oh dear, this is worse than I thought,' reaching over, patting my thigh. This fear is frozen shards, sliding down my gullet, compacting in my gut. Solid and so cold. 'Don't worry, darling. No one can blame you. All this stress. I'll explain when they get here.' Her hand lands on mine, heavy, thick fingers coiling around my palm. 'We'll work it out, Evangeline. You're not alone. We're in this together. Don't forget that.'

The sound of a key in the lock. 'Eve?' It's India. She's hurrying down the hall. She has a spare key. It was Neil's idea. *'Always good to have a neighbour with a key.'*

Mum freezes. I shout, 'Did you call the police?'

India appears at the threshold of the kitchen. 'They're on their way. What's going on? Where's Milly?'

'Upstairs.'

India turns and runs back down the hall to the bottom of the staircase. I hear her feet on the treads as she makes her way up. Mum is watching me, that pitying look resumed. I know before India reaches the top of the stairs that Milly won't be there. 'Where is she?'

Mum shrugs. 'I haven't seen Milly since you ran off with her.'

India returns to the kitchen. 'She's not there. I checked all the bedrooms.' She's looking at me, hesitating, wondering what she's caught up in. Mum sits calmly, wearing an expression of maternal concern. I'm trapped in her reality. She is rational while I'm hysterical. Milly is not here. Milly was never here. My mother is innocent and I am unhinged.

The roar of an engine as the police car turns into the street. The screech of brakes as it pulls up outside. Here we go again.

# Chapter 36

Mum does the talking. I have no words. I am a mad woman. Paranoid. I no longer know my own mind.

PC McAdam gives nothing away. She nods, makes notes. We're sitting in the living room. A paramedic has looked at my foot and is waiting outside to take me to the hospital for an x-ray. The police are trying to track down Neil. Helen, Milly's social worker, has confirmed that Milly's safe, with Ruth and her foster family. She must have dropped Gerry in our hurry to leave. She will have realised at bedtime, but by then she was at Ruth's and I was on my way to Hitchin.

PC McAdam is accompanied by a male officer in plain clothes. She asks the questions while he listens, watching me and Mum carefully, trying to read between the lines. What does he see? An elderly woman who is doing her best to take care of her paranoid daughter. She sounds so convincing. If I hadn't seen her raise that stick at the top of the stairs, if I hadn't felt her yank my hair and ram that dishcloth into my mouth, I would believe that she has my best interests at heart, that in some warped, inappropriate way, she was simply doing what any mother would do to protect her child. If I try to explain, now, what happened I'll struggle. I'll get emotional, I'll sound ridiculous. This is her power. She appears reasonable. She's the one in control, while I flounder. All her lies are rooted in truth. I'm not hysterical, as she's claimed, but I'm pretty mangled right now. It's believable.

She tells the police, 'She hasn't been right since she found out – you do know? About the rape charge?'

The male officer's face remains impassive as he corrects her, 'At this stage it is still an allegation.'

Mum gives an irritated cluck. 'The evidence is there.'

My voice emerges like something newly hatched. 'He didn't do it.' My throat aches, the inside of my mouth is sore. Everyone's eyes are on me. 'I spoke to Ann Lord. Her husband lied. Tina Lord will provide a statement. She'll confirm that it wasn't rape.'

It isn't easy to expose your mother to the police. Even at my age, even after what she's done, I'm scared. There's still a part of me that's expecting not to be believed. I could tell them that my mother has set out to destroy my family: that she manipulated Vincent Lord into writing that statement, that she wants Neil out of my life and will use any means available to her to achieve that, with no concern for the consequences and how many people she hurts along the way. I could tell them she pushed me down the stairs and rammed the dishcloth in my mouth, but I'd sound hysterical, which only proves her claim. It's my word against hers and I don't want to go there. She's my mother. She's my problem. I'm an adult and I have to deal with this myself.

Mum shakes her head and gives me a disappointed look. 'Evangeline, darling. Ann Lord is a timid woman. You saw how nervous she was. Tina will be the same. If they're disputing the story it will be because Neil's got to them. If his temper when he came here is anything to go by—'

'Enough!'

Her nostrils flare. 'Evangeline—'

'You have to go.' She twitches, momentarily startled, but regains her composure quickly. Her eyes narrow. She goes to speak, but I stop her. 'Go and pack your case. Now.'

I wonder what PC McAdam's thinking. I'm doing my best not to get emotional, but the only way to achieve this is to remain detached, matter-of-fact. If I think too much, if I allow myself to engage, I'll lose my resolve.

My mother loves me. That love is twisted and toxic, but to her it is simply love. I'm betraying her, that's how she'll see it, that's what this is: the ultimate betrayal. A daughter rejecting her mother. She's dedicated her life to me and I'm telling her to leave, in front of the police. If it was me in trouble, if I'd made a mistake, she'd stop at nothing to protect me, but I'm not going to do that for her.

'I'm not going anywhere! You need me. That man... I am not going to let him come back here – he's a bully! Can't you see that? You need me.'

'I don't. I don't need you.' I can feel her pain, imagine the tears she will shed, the bewilderment. I can hear the great hiccupping sobs she'll produce when all else fails, but this time I must be strong, for Milly, for Neil, for us.

'I'm your mother!'

I turn to the plain-clothed officer. 'Can you escort my mother off the premises, please?' His face is calm. He is an intelligent man who has learned to assume nothing. 'Could you do that for me?' He gives a small nod.

'Evangeline!'

'My name is Eve.'

I hear the car pull up outside as I sign the statement. A door slams. I drop my pen and limp into the hall to throw open the door as Neil comes up the path.

Neil follows the ambulance to the hospital. It takes us a while to work through it all. Mum wouldn't let him into the house. He didn't want to do anything that might create problems with social services, so he phoned Shona. She agreed to meet him at her office in Barrow. By the time he got to her, she'd received my message and was able to reassure him of his innocence and update him on my meeting with Ann Lord.

The x-ray reveals a fracture and I'm given a splint and some painkillers.

Shona calls as we're driving home. Neil switches to speaker and her voice rings out from the phone, rescuing us from the grim puddle of Mum's spite. 'Good news. Tina Lord has been in touch. She's sending us a signed statement refuting her father's accusation.'

Neil blinks. A solitary tear escapes and tracks its way down the grooves of his face to his chin. I reach across and wipe it away. I will never forgive my mother for what she's done to him. I've tried so hard to maintain a relationship with her, to make it work, but she's left me no option. I must choose. I should have done it years ago; I could have spared him this pain, but I wasn't strong enough. It took Milly, it took becoming a mother myself, to provide me with the courage to face up to my own.

Shona says, 'They've decided this is clearly a case of malicious intent and can be set aside.'

Malicious intent. I picture the words typed on a screen, printed out on headed paper, placed on an anonymous desk, copied, circulated to people who make decisions, who hold the power. My mother's intention was malice. Not my words, not something that can be put down to hysteria or misunderstanding, but the conclusion of an official investigation. My mother is not loving and reasonable and misunderstood, she is dangerous.

'Have you seen Milly? Is she all right?'

'She's fine. Missing you both.'

'Can we see her?'

'I'm collecting her today.'

Neil asks, 'What about the adoption hearing? What needs to happen now? Can we go ahead?'

'The team are happy to continue. We'll need to schedule another review, and discuss the ongoing relationship with your mother, Eve, but I don't envisage any problems. I'll try and sort it this week or next, to keep things moving. And as soon as that's done you can submit your application to the court.'

When we get home, we sit in silence, Neil and I, looking out of the bay window, across the tarn. This world. This life we've built. Milly is coming home. We'll find a way to tell her what's happened. I'm already framing it in my mind. Grandma is ill, confused. I don't suppose Milly will care too much. She's always seen through my mother. She has Nana and Gramps. She has Betty and Mike and Neil's extended family. She doesn't need my mother.

I don't need my mother.

And there's Steven. Milly has an older brother. Neil has a son to get to know. We sit, side by side, holding hands, in a strange sort of limbo, between chapters.

Malicious intent.

# Epilogue

The final review took place a week later and we were given the green light. I was worried that we might have to press charges against Mum, get a restraining order, prove our intent, but there was none of that. All it needed was for me to say that I would not allow Mum anywhere near Milly. So simple. They have confidence in me and that confidence empowers me. I'm not the girl my mother bullied and controlled any more. I am Eve Wright. I'm the woman who runs over the fell, pounding the earth with her steady rhythm. I am strong. I am in control. I am Milly's mother.

Neil had the application form ready, completed it and got it in the post that day and our hearing was scheduled for two months later. We were at the magistrates' court this morning, with Shona, Helen, Betty and Mike. Milly is officially recognised as our daughter: Milly Wright. Betty has baked a cake. There are tears and laughter and everything rolls forward easily. I'm not anxious or torn, but free to enjoy and focus entirely on my husband and child. There's no more drip-drip-drip of fear.

I've no idea where my mother is while we celebrate. She knows nothing about it.


Like fear, joy can come in many colours. I've always pictured it a deep, warm orange, tinged at the edges with something more citrusy. This joy is different. The orange bleeds into crimson. Nothing sharp here, simply warm warm warm. Back at the house, Betty feels her way around my kitchen, enlisting Milly's support, producing lunch and treats for the extended family who've gathered with us to celebrate. Neil's sisters, brother-in-law, nephew and niece and, much to Milly's delight, the dogs are all here. Ruth and the foster family have come down from Carlisle, though, thankfully, they've left their dogs behind on the farm. And Lizzie and Pearl, Kath, India and Guy have joined us. We're having our own Thanksgiving. It's like one of those sentimental Christmas adverts. The music isn't quite as effective, drowned out by the raucous Wright banter as they bellow to one another across the room, and the dogs are making a terrible mess, but this will do.

Pinned to the noticeboard on the wall is my father's address. Not hidden in a drawer or tucked out of sight, but there, in plain view. I will write to him soon, when the celebrations are over and things have settled back into a routine. I have no idea where this will take me, but I have a family to support me. It will be what it will be.

I have no contact with my mother but Betty drops by every now and then to check on her. I haven't asked her to do this but I'm grateful that she does. She understands. She is a mother. She is a daughter. That connection can never be entirely broken. I would like to make peace. I would like things to be different but that's impossible. This is my bruise.


There's a knock at the door and Neil goes to answer it. I glance at Betty, who's as nervous as I am. Mike takes her hand. Laura, baby Jonah resting in his papoose, moves beside me. We wait, all eyes on the door. It was my suggestion to do this today, with bustle and distraction and other people around. I thought it might lessen the intensity but now I realise how intimidating this must seem, such a huge crowd. Maybe something quieter would have been better. I want to press the pause button, rewind. I'm not ready for this. Will we ever be ready for this?

Neil comes back in, followed by two women, and for a moment I don't recognise her. It is Ann Lord but she looks so much more present in the world, coloured-in and animated. And the younger woman, with glossy hair and bright, intelligent eyes, must be Tina, a little older than the photograph, but still as vivacious. Mother and daughter are holding hands, taking cautious steps into the crowded room, shy smiles, and that's when he steps over the threshold, looking just like someone I knew in a previous life.

Rusty hair, freckles and that kind smile. A hand reaching down to pull me from the pool.

That same hand reaches out now to take mine.

Milly skips from the kitchen. 'Who are you?'

He crouches to look her in the eyes. 'I'm Steven. I think you might be my sister.'

# Acknowledgements

Thank you to my wonderful editor, Madeleine O'Shea, for her ability to see the light through the trees. Her incisive, generous feedback, delivered with a cheerful smile, made the writing of this novel a pleasure. To Lauren Atherton, assistant editor, for her patient attention to detail and calm communication as the deadline loomed. To Anna Green for the beautiful cover, to Liz Hatherell for copy-editing and valuable feedback, and to the Marketing, Publicity and Sales teams who work so hard to get this book read.

I have been fortunate to have great early readers: Judy Rouse, Caroline Gilfillan, Jan Heffernan and Karon Nougher, who have read drafts, often at very short notice, and given thoughtful and honest notes. My brother, and fellow creative, Ian Culbard, has been a patient, compassionate ear throughout the writing of this book and appreciates, as no-one else can, how important it was to me. Thank you.

Thanks to my lovely agent, Diana Beaumont, for sound advice, solid support and a great choice of cafes!

For providing me with shelter when I need to navigate meetings far from home and escape to write, I'd like to thank the Veacock family, Wendy Bowker, Aga Lesiewicz and Ola Walsh.

Thanks again to James Bailey, neighbour and police officer, for advice about procedure in the case of a missing child.

Tarnside Community Park is inspired by Ford Park in Ulverston, South Lakeland, which provides the people of our town, and our visitors, with a beautiful open space to enjoy. A proper grass roots initiative that shows just what can be done when a community work together for the benefit of all.